THE DRAGON CALAMITY

JAMES WHEELER

ISBN: 979-8-9912790-5-5

Published by The Rogue Planets LLC

therogueplanets.com

First edition 2025

Content Warning: This book contains depictions of fantasy violence, blood, kidnapping/enslavement, homelessness, and death.

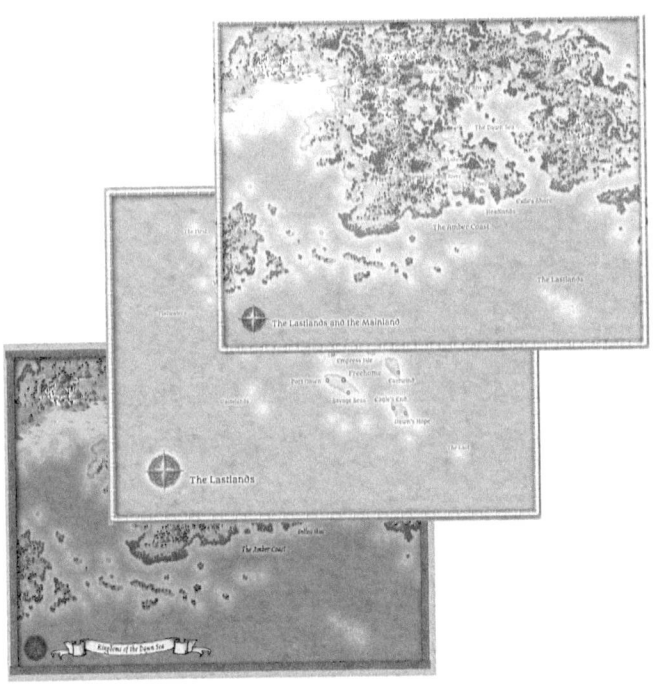

Check out large, full-color maps at
therogueplanets.com/books

CONTENTS

CHAPTER ONE

DARK HEART

T he world has a way of warning you when the waters are rising.

The old woman remembered this piece of her lost ancestors' wisdom, and so she stood, staring out the window at the front of her small shop, studying the feeling of foreboding that seemed so out of place on this lovely summer morning. It was peaceful and misty outside, with a pulse of early insect songs accompanying the murmuring noise of the awakening harbor. This was one of her favorite times of year, rich with the promise of a warm, busy day, where people would be out doing things. She usually did brisk business on a day like this.

But today, the morning's song had a dissonance to it that bothered her. Nothing emerged to provide her with any answers, though, so after a moment, she frowned and turned back to her work.

She bent over, grunting, and reached stiffly down to sweep the remaining dust into a small copper pan. She straightened and leaned around the corner into the back room and dumped it all into a bucket she kept there. Then she tucked her misshapen old broom and the pan into the corner behind, and slowly stood, sighing.

That was the worst of the work finished, at least. She turned around and stepped out from behind the counter to her shop floor, taking a last glance around to make sure she hadn't missed anything before customers started arriving for the day. Bundles of herbs hung from the rafters to keep the insects outside, and she took a long sniff of their spicy smell. It mingled with the ever present notes of the bakers' ovens down the block, the dirty potatoes and onions in their bins, and the fresh hint of the cucumbers that were in that corner of the shop. No hints of rot marred the usual inventory of aromas, at least that she could detect.

She nodded. Everything was ready.

She was slipping back behind the counter when the front door opened with a tinkle of tiny bells.

A customer already! Excellent. The last several days had been slow, so it would be a relief to have the coffer start filling up a little more quickly today.

She peered into the morning light angling in through the windows, eyes narrowed, and started to greet the three figures entering her shop. But the words collided with one another and refused to emerge from lips gone slack with surprise…and dismay.

"Do…uh…do you boys need something today?" she managed, silently cursing the tremor in her voice.

"Don't you know?" The first of them, the big, stupid, lumbering one that always did the talking, sneered at her. "It's Contribution day, gran." The other two, his usual hangers-on, snickered.

She frowned. "I paid my coin to the Depths two days ago. You know that, as you were with them when they collected it."

"So what?" the big one said. "You can Contribute some extra today, can't you?" His brutish expression pinched in around his nose even further. "Or maybe we'll just take it for ourselves, would you like that better?"

She lowered her head as the three young men, no longer smiling, loomed at her counter, staring down at her.

She nodded and bent to retrieve her coffer.

The door opened with another tinkling of bells.

"She's closed," the big one spat over his shoulder.

The old woman looked up around him, and saw that someone in a dark gray cloak, with the hood up over his head, had stepped into the shop and closed the door behind him.

"Interesting, that's just what I was about to say," the figure replied, his voice calm and even. He turned around and flipped the sign in the window. Then he locked the door with a pronounced *click.*

The big, dumb one slowly turned, staring at the new arrival. The other two, upon getting their first look at the cloaked stranger, were starting to back toward her counter, stepping behind their stronger comrade.

She looked at the stranger, and could just make out his eyes under the hood, meeting hers. "Please stay behind the counter, madam, for your safety," he said quietly. He stepped forward into the shop and dropped into a slight crouch, his hands open, held up before him.

The big stupid one saw the fighting stance and guffawed, a single loud bark of laughter. He lurched forward.

The old woman groaned. So much for all the extra work she'd done over the last several days, getting her shop so nicely cleaned. It was about to be plunged right back into a nightmarish mess.

The big, stupid one threw a big, stupid punch at the stranger.

What happened next confused her, but it was surreal and beautiful to watch, and the old woman's mouth dropped open in amazement. The stranger didn't leap back, or duck, or defend himself. Instead, he seemed quite ready for the attack, and threw a punch too.

The stranger's punch was very well-aimed. It met the big fist in mid-air between them, and a thudding *crunch* resounded in the small shop. All went silent and still for a second. Then the oaf screamed, a roaring bellow that sounded like a sheep being slaughtered. He bent forward over his hand, cradling it, and the stranger hammered him on the back of the head with his clenched fist. The big, stupid one collapsed forward onto his face in the aisle of her shop, the bellowing cutting off with a *smack.*

After a long, shocked moment, the other two hissed and drew their daggers, then came at him more slowly. The old woman gulped and drew back, peeking over the top of her counter to watch as first one, then the other, lunged forward to stab at the cloaked stranger. He handled each one the same, grabbing the blades of their daggers with one bare hand, then leveling each flat to the floor with a single hard punch to the face.

It was all over in a matter of seconds.

She stood slowly upright, mouth still hanging open, and glanced around in amazement.

Not a single piece of merchandise was disturbed. Other than the fact that three large wastes of food and mothering were presently cluttering up the floor in the front of her shop, everything was just as it had been a few minutes before.

The cloaked stranger watched the three motionless lumps for another moment before slowly relaxing from his fighting stance and standing up. He looked down at the two daggers he was still holding by their blades. She expected to see blood flowing from his hands onto her floor, but somehow, there was nothing. He peered closely at the daggers, looking for all the world like a potential customer examining a coppersmith's wares. But right away he wrinkled his nose distastefully at the quality of the work before bending and tucking them back into the unconscious thugs' belts. Then he turned toward her finally, lowering his hood to reveal a handsome, kind face and long, wavy hair. He smiled as he stepped over to her.

"Are you well madam? I'm sorry about the excitement, here. But we'd been following these three lads for some time, and when I heard them say what they were about, well...I hope you don't mind my intervening."

She slid her coffer back into its place down on the shelf below, grinning. "Oh no, thank you, dear," she said, still panting a bit. "The Depths already came and took their 'contribution' for the week. These three were just robbing me."

"The Depths," he repeated, his smile vanishing. "That's what we'd assumed."

Something about his suddenly grim demeanor cut through her initial relief at not being robbed after all. Yes, these dimwits had been shaking her down, and probably on their own initiative, too. But they were, like it or not, *hired* dimwits. The ones in charge, the ones who looked *actually* dangerous, called themselves the Depths, and had been bringing these and others around to make sure that all their shopkeepers' extra "contributions" to them were paid on time. It had been going on for half a year at this point. People that had tried to report them to the Council Magistrate suffered break-ins and worse, so most just did the best they could to keep up.

But now she began to wonder whether there might be consequences for something happening to some of their affiliated goons in her shop.

The stranger didn't see the look of concern come over her face. He was on his way to the front door, unlocking it and stepping out, peering down the street. She heard him say, "Oh good, they've caught up."

He waved to someone down the block, and after a moment, a pretty young woman wearing braids at her temples and a similar gray cloak appeared, along with half a dozen men and women whose garb and dark gray tabards shouted "sailor" to the old woman. The stranger waved them in and the sailors immediately bent to dragging the unconscious thugs out the front door by their boots.

"Wow," the young woman said, staring around and grinning. "You did an excellent job in here! It doesn't look like anything at all got damaged, this time."

The young man met the old woman's eyes and grinned. "Thankfully. They went down pretty quick. Madam, again, we're sorry for the inconvenience. These three," he said, gesturing over his shoulder with a thumb, "are headed to the Council Magistrate, and hopefully won't trouble you again." And with that, he and the pretty young woman turned and left her shop, closing the door behind them with a wave and one last tinkling of bells.

She peered around, quite taken aback by all that had just occurred. Everything was still pristine, like none of it had even happened. Finally, shaking her head, she collapsed onto her chair in the corner.

She stared at the front windows for a while, wondering for the hundredth time over the last few months whether any of this was still worth it. Ever since the Depths had appeared six months earlier and begun "protecting" the shops here in New Brightwall, her business had gotten harder and harder to keep above water. Now, there was rarely anything at all left in her coffer once she resupplied the shop and paid her own expenses.

Her neighbor kept telling her that she ought to just sell the place, try her luck somewhere else. He said that New Brightwall was falling apart. But the old woman wasn't so sure that was the extent of it. She'd heard from friends in other holdings that things were hard everywhere, these days. And the archipelago was so small, really. What difference would any change make? Where else could any of them really go?

She leaned back against the wall, closing her eyes. Maybe a dragon would finally find them there in the Lastlands, the huddled survivors, still trying to cling to civilization after two centuries, and none of it would matter anyway.

Aether and Lyrrek walked through the streets of one of New Brightwall's fancier districts, admiring the polished stone and wood of the buildings here. The gravel lanes had recently been raked flat, and the dusty smell of them mingled with that of the briny sea breeze.

He offered to take Lyrrek's cloak and laid hers with his over his arm. The day was warming now that morning was thoroughly established, and the cloudless blue sky promised a hot summer afternoon. The bangs and thuds of activity throughout the nearby city had an urgency to them, as people tried to get their work in before the day became uncomfortable.

"Thanks," Lyrrek said, smiling at him. "I'm not looking forward to the heat today."

"We ought to be back on *Horizon* and bound for Vigil by then, I hope," he said. "Plenty of sea spray to cool off in."

She sighed, nodded, and took his arm.

Aether would be relieved to be back on the sea too, but before they could depart, they had a report to make. The gray spires of Castle Brightwall rose up over the buildings ahead, but they turned aside to a large apartment building on a low hill several blocks away from the gate. Lyrrek led the way up the staircase at the corner to the second level, then down the long balcony to the door of an apartment with windows that offered a rather good view of the castle's main entrance. That view meant that rent here was abnormally high. But the Wizards' Guild, though less than two years old and far from an official organization, had already produced some decent flows of silver for them to work with. And this apartment, a sort of guild refuge here in the city, had proven its investment in the leads they had just successfully followed, in some threats to the people of New Brightwall taken off the street.

Still, Aether thought to himself, it would be nice if they were making more progress toward some of his grander ambitions for them. Figuring out how Origin's new wizards were going to fit into the society of the Lastlands was proving to be a more expensive proposition than he might have expected a year ago. Their land-dragon hunts were keeping them going. But that going always felt slow.

Aether knocked on the apartment door, and after a moment, it opened to reveal a young woman, a bit shorter than Lyrrek, who smiled excitedly at them both. "Masters," she said, bowing slightly and drawing aside to let them enter.

"Thank you, Jyhnda," Lyrrek said, returning the apprentice's wide smile. Aether followed them into the small, minimally-appointed apartment, pulling the door shut behind them.

Lyrrek held her arms out wide, ready to engulf her friend Amrelyn in a hug, as the other master came out of a back chamber to join them, pulling her hair back into its usual ponytail before returning Lyrrek's embrace.

"Well, how did it turn out?" Amrelyn asked, smiling at Aether over Lyrrek's shoulder in response to his wave of greeting.

"They tried to shake down a shopkeep, that little produce shop on the south side, the one near the Bakers' Guild," he said.

"Oh, I've been in there," Jyhnda said, dismayed. "She's so nice!"

"She's fine," Lyrrek said. "Aether caught them in the act and stopped them."

"Oh good," Amrelyn said, relieved. "That ought to do, then, in terms of getting the Magistrate to involve himself. Maybe we'll finally find out where his loyalties lie."

"We turned them over to his officers," Aether said. "They seemed to take the accusations seriously, and bound them and all, but...I don't know. I still think something felt a little off to me about how they acted."

Lyrrek nodded. "Hard to say if they were just weird about us doing their job for them, or if there was something more to it."

"They haven't been the most responsive to anything we've brought them, so far," Amrelyn said. She shrugged. "I guess we'll find out what they do." She looked at Aether, and put her hands on her hips, grinning. "Next time, though, we get to have some fun too."

Aether laughed. "I must admit, it was an entertaining one. I promise. We'll be *your* backup next time."

Amrelyn nodded grandly, mollified, and they all chuckled.

The door opened behind them, and Aether turned to see a young man entering. "Hello, Neres," he said pleasantly, stepping aside to make room for him.

Neres's eyes widened. "Master Aether, Master Lyrrek," he said, bowing to each of them. He wasn't much younger than they. But he had only worn his apprentice bracers for a few months, and he still seemed rather impressed by the full wizards among his guildmates.

Neres held up a bound Couriers' Guild parchment to Aether. "There was a missive for you, Master," he said, a bit breathlessly. "It's marked urgent."

Aether's smile faded, and he took the parchment, breaking the seal and opening it to read. He was silent a moment, then gasped.

"What is it?" Lyrrek asked, and all of them drew a bit closer, concerned.

"It's from Pemana," he said. He looked up at Lyrrek. "Something's wrong. She doesn't go into detail, but says she thinks she might be in trouble, and wonders if we would be able to meet her in Port Omen." He looked back down at the parchment, taking in the noted date and time. "By today…this afternoon."

Lyrrek swallowed. "That will be tight." She turned to Amrelyn. "Well, it was good seeing you for a moment."

Amrelyn nodded. "I hope Pemana's all right," she said. "Tell her we're thinking of her."

"We will," Aether said. "Thank you, Neres, and good seeing you all." Then he followed Lyrrek back out and down to the street below.

"There was more," Aether said to Lyrrek quietly as they turned onto the lane that led to the harbor. "A warning."

Lyrrek looked at him quizzically.

"She doesn't say why, but she said not to bring *Horizon* into harbor at Port Omen. She said we should anchor a few coves over and sail a tender the rest of the way. And…there's one other thing." He looked at her out of the corner of his eye. "She said that you, specifically, should probably stay with the ship…just in case you have to get *Horizon*…and yourself…out of there on short notice."

"What in the world?" Lyrrek exclaimed, and they both increased their pace. "What's going on?"

"I have no idea."

Lyrrek kept walking for a while, staring straight ahead. Finally, she spoke, her voice quiet.

"We're sailing into a problem here, aren't we?"

Deldrum scratched at the rough discomfort of the black tabard at the back of his neck and tried not to look miserable. Those last few ales the night before had been a mistake.

The wide, echoing, formal hall of the Swordfish's subterranean palace was almost crowded with the usual complement of guards and servants, their black robes and tabards soaking up nearly as much of the abundant candlelight as the dark, polished stone of the carved walls. A hushed murmur of voices originated most of the echoes, for at the moment, the Swordfish's black throne on its raised dais was still empty.

Deldrum looked back and forth quickly. He was posted by the main door opposite the throne. The Swordfish would be staring right at him once he arrived and sat down. Deldrum knew he couldn't risk being out of place when that happened. That had been made clear to him on his very first day here. But still, he wished he had time to make it to the garderobe.

This job was pretty terrible so far, he thought, resisting the urge to spit. The pay was good, of course, as he'd been led to believe it would be. But in the week since he'd arrived, all he'd done was stand around, trying not to make it too obvious how hard he was leaning on his spear.

To be fair, there were upsides, too. There was always plenty of food for the guards back in the barracks, even if it was a far cry from the luxurious feasts that were laid out every day for the Swordfish and his inner circle to enjoy. And the work, while painfully boring and hard on his feet, was also both predictable and easy, not nearly as hard to pull off as the thieving he'd been struggling to get away with back in Freehome. And it certainly beat the Deep out of hauling fishing nets, there was no question. He resisted the urge to spit again, vowing to himself, as he always did, that he would never go back.

A rustle of activity at one of the side doors into the hall caught his eye, and he cursed silently to himself as the Swordfish entered, followed by a few servants and several of his personal guards. Deldrum quickly drew himself upright, trying to make sure he looked like part of the furnishings.

The Swordfish wore a fancy embroidered black robe and cloak, trimmed with golden threads and buckles. He was saying something quiet to a few of his closest attendants, some in the black robes worn by his servants, some in the knee-length half-robes and tall boots favored by Lastlands nobility lately. They all laughed, heartily and too loud, at whatever it was the Swordfish said.

Deldrum watched as the Swordfish climbed the dais steps and seated himself on the polished black throne. He saw the man's dark eyes, peering out at him from between symmetrical waves of black hair, and felt them slide across him. Deldrum tried hard not to squirm, and thankfully, the Swordfish's gaze didn't linger on him.

A servant in black robes hastened in his direction, eyes down, and opened the double doors which Deldrum guard-ed, opposite another uncomfortable-looking young man in a black tabard whose name he hadn't bothered learning. Through the doorway, a shocking blaze of golden-yellow robe appeared, hanging from the thin frame of a balding man who carried a black-sheathed sword and dagger before him, laid across his open palms. Two more black-tabarded guards followed the man, who was, Deldrum had heard, an emissary from one of the holdings. He and his escorts made their way forward to the space before the dais.

"Your Majesty," the emissary said. "The Lady Fehndala sends you her gratitude, as well as this gift, as promised." He knelt, holding the sword and dagger up toward the throne.

The Swordfish stared down at him for a moment, then rose and gathered his robes around him before slowly pac-ing down the stairs toward the kneeling emissary. Deldrum silently urged him to hurry up, trying to ignore the discomfort in his bladder.

The emissary adjusted his grip on the weapons so that he held them by the scabbards, their hilts upright. The Swordfish reached out and took the sword's longer hilt in his hand, drawing it forth with a pronounced metallic *shing* that rang out in the hall.

Sparkles of pure, golden candlelight blazed across the chamber and into Deldrum's eyes.

Staring in disbelief, he watched the Swordfish hold the gleaming sword aloft, and hushed whispers trickled along the walls of the hall where servants and guards were gathered. Deldrum couldn't silence his own sharp intake of breath, either.

He had never seen steel before. But he knew what he was looking at. It was a clean, pure, silver color, entirely free from the morning-piss yellow of polished bronze that Deldrum hated so much. Its blade reflected everything around the chamber in rippling bands of color and blackness.

Desire erupted in him that was beyond any lust he had known.

And then the Swordfish reached forward with his free hand, and pulled the dagger from its black sheath, holding it up. Its blade, too, was gorgeous steel, perfectly framed by its black hilt and guard. The rippling gasp through the hall was louder this time, and accompanied by actual murmurs.

Deldrum almost fell over. The Swordfish held a perfect, beautiful, *matched* sword and dagger set of steel, ancient weapons from before the time of the dragons. The Lastlanders had lost the art of steelsmithing in the Great Flight. No one that knew the secrets had survived.

Deldrum had never dreamed such a treasure existed in all the world.

The Swordfish looked on the blades for a moment, then suddenly flipped them both forward, crouching back into a combat stance, the dagger held forward in his offhand, the sword's hilt back by his ear. Both blades pointed forward at the yellow-robed emissary, who trembled noticeably. Deep silence fell across the hall.

But the Swordfish only relaxed forward from his stance and stabbed the blades skillfully back into the sheaths where the emissary still held them. Then he turned and made his way back up toward the throne.

Deldrum felt the tension drain back out from the chamber.

"Tell the Lady we are pleased," the Swordfish said in his warm, carefully charming voice. He flicked his fingers toward the emissary, and black-robed servants hustled forward to take the still-uplifted weapons from him and help him to his feet.

"Thank you, Your Majesty," the emissary said, allowing the servants to lead him away.

Deldrum didn't see him walk back through the hall toward him. His gaze was welded to the sword and dagger as the servants carried them reverently toward the side door through which the Swordfish had originally entered.

He had known the Swordfish's wealth was astonishing. Just look around at this unbelievable palace he was having built for himself, carved out of the rock of this remote island by dozens of unfortunate souls who, even now, continued their backbreaking work in the deeper bowels of it.

But *this* was like nothing he had imagined.

His usual daydream came to his thoughts, featuring himself as the dashing captain of a lean, dangerous pirate ship, surrounded by his hard but honorable group of rogues, whose deadly skill he had employed to make himself the richest pirate lord in all of the Lastlands. Only now, in his mind's eye, he wore those black stalkerhide scabbards at his belt, and drew forth the gleaming steel blades to point his men at some pathetic noble lord's fat merchant ship, and its cargo hold full of undeserved wealth.

Deldrum sighed softly.

Then he realized a hush had fallen over the chamber again. He snapped his attention back to the dais, and saw that a handful of people were walking quietly across the hall, having entered from a different side door. The Swordfish had leaned forward on his throne, and was staring at the group with interest, watching them approach.

They wore practical gear, not dissimilar to the leather armor that Deldrum and the other guards wore, but obviously much finer. None wore tabards.

Deldrum had seen a few people like this visit a couple days earlier, and later one of the others had quietly told him they were some of the Swordfish's field agents, and warned him to stay the Deep away from them if he possibly could.

The agents strode forward. But unlike the last group of them he'd seen, who had breezed in with laughing confidence and made their report, matching the Swordfish's forced charm with their own, these five all clustered together and walked in grim, nervous silence to stand before the throne and bow low.

"Well?" the Swordfish said. The usual, fake-sounding charm was gone. In its absence, the Swordfish's voice was cold…dangerous.

Deldrum swallowed.

The man at the forefront of the group stepped forward a little further, and bowed again.

"Forgive us Your Majesty," he said, his voice admirably solid under the circumstances. "But I must report that we have been unable to reacquire the ship *Horizon* since she and her crew gave us the slip in the harbor at Merit that night." He turned to look at the others arrayed next to him, then looked back up. "We have come to believe that they know, or at least suspect, that they are being watched. We don't know how they would know that."

The Swordfish said nothing. Deldrum saw the head of black hair tilt slightly to one side, the eyes narrowing. The agent saw it too and went quickly on.

"I have doubled our watches at Vigil's harbor, and at Merit as well, just in case they should return there, Your Majesty. All have orders to pursue, and specifically to report on the activities of the Lady Lyrrek once the vessel is located."

Deldrum's eyes opened wide at that. This Lady Lyrrek was a young noblewoman of House Silversea, the family that ruled Vigil Isle. She had become suddenly famous last year when, according to some truly ridiculous tales, she and her crew had supposedly snuck all the way across to the far north of the distant, dragon-infested mainland and recovered the Crown of the Empress, a relic of Empress Isle's ruling house.

She had traded this priceless crown for one of the few other steel swords that Deldrum had ever heard of, a lost artifact of her own house that had been in Empress Isle's possession for some reason.

Ever since hearing of her, Deldrum had dreamed of meeting her. She sounded like she was probably one of the most skilled con artists in the Lastlands, to have pulled such an incredible heist from one of the wealthier noble families.

The crown was a fake, of course. It had to be. No one could survive the dragon-infested mainland, except occasionally the Hunters' Guild. And they only tiptoed onto the edges of the continent, hunting a bit, before fleeing back to the safety of the Lastlands. Sometimes, their expeditions didn't come back at all.

But by the tale, Lady Lyrrek and her crew had sailed for days further north through the seas and rivers that bisected the mainland, under skies filled with dragons, and survived to return. It was nonsense.

She was supposed to be quite pretty, was the Lady Lyrrek. Deldrum had never seen her, but sometimes he added her to the deck of his imagined pirate ship anyway, a nebulously beautiful young woman with a steel sword at her side. Only now, he had a steel sword as well, and a matching dagger. And together, they'd terrorize these worthless lords and ladies...ones just like the rest of her family, which was, admittedly, awkward.

But she was obviously different. She had to be.

Deldrum snapped his attention back as the Swordfish moved. His frown had deepened, and he leaned forward and placed his elbows on the arms of his throne, slapping a black-gloved hand over the other fist.

The agent's eyes widened, and he coughed and cleared his throat. Then he went quickly on.

"I do also bring good news, Your Majesty, regarding the guard captain, Pemana. The vessel *Champion* was reported as returning to harbor at Port Omen. So your plans in this matter seem to have been executed. The agents on watch in Port Omen are under orders to report in as soon as the public notices are posted."

The Swordfish leaned back, letting his fist relax, and stared down at the agent for a long moment. Finally he spoke, his voice charming again.

"Very well. You are fortunate that I'm in a good mood today."

The agent squirmed.

"That will be a good start, I suppose," the Swordfish went on. "You will report the Silversea girl's activities to me within the turning of the moon."

Deldrum watched the agents bow and scrape, withdrawing as quickly as they could.

He wondered what that had all been about, and decided he'd try to ask about it back in the barracks later, if he could manage it quietly.

Aether sat calmly in one of *Horizon's* tenders as a member of his crew, Beras, steered them skillfully around other sailboats and ships in Port Omen's busy harbor. The shouts of sailors, the call of sea birds, and the clanging of copper bells all surrounded them as they bobbed across the choppy water toward the docks at one of the public marinas. It had, indeed, gotten pretty warm by that afternoon. And with the heat, the usual fondness he felt for the charming city of Port Omen was replaced with a strange sense of oppressiveness.

"I hope we'll be in time." Beras said quietly. Aether turned and looked at him, and saw that while steering the boat with one hand on the tiller, his other hand was absently playing with one of his Wizards' Guild apprentice bracers under the long sleeve of his loose shirt. Aether coughed, and Beras saw his eyes, and pulled his other hand away, chuckling. "I'll get used to 'em eventually, I'm sure," he said sheepishly. "Something about this whole thing just feels…off, I suppose. Making me a bit nervous, I think."

"Yeah," Aether replied, sighing and turning back to watch their course. "Believe me, I know exactly what you mean. We've faced dragons together before, and for some reason, something about this feels similar."

"Well, I've learned to trust your intuition, Captain," Beras said with a grim look on his face.

At last, they bumped up against the end of an empty slip. Aether tried to gauge the late afternoon shadows as he helped Beras tie the boat off to cleats on the edge of the weathered wooden dock. Pemana's message had said only to look for *Champion*, so they started up the harbor's crowded shoreline of stone piers, headed for the northward section from where the Port Omen Guard's docks blossomed out to occupy a significant portion of the harbor.

It was tricky to pick *Champion* out amongst the many other ships clad in Port Omen's blue and silver. They walked along the pier, craning their necks and shading their eyes with a hand, trying to spot her. The guards stationed nearby took notice of them and began to watch them closely.

Then, Beras spoke. "Ah. I see Batthius," he said, stopping and pointing, then waving. "Yeah, there's *Champion*."

Aether stopped with him. A couple of nearby guards were starting to head their direction, spears in hand. But Beras's waving caught Batthius's eye several docks out, and when the guards looked and saw an officer from one of the ships wave and start their direction, they turned back to their posts, disappointed.

Batthius made his way to them quickly, the lines in his weathered face deeper than ever. He didn't smile in greeting, the first time Aether could remember that being the case.

"Come with me," he said quietly, and didn't slow as he passed them. Aether and Beras blinked and jumped to keep up with him as he started up the road that led toward Omen Castle.

"What's happened?" Aether asked as they caught up with Batthius.

"I was just promoted to captain of *Champion*. Cap…well, Pemana…is being stripped of her command and rank. There's a hearing underway at the castle as we speak."

"What?" Aether gasped, jogging to get into step with the older man's long stride. "Why? On what grounds?"

"We didn't know until we docked, but once she reported in for the hearing, one of the top guard commanders came out to speak with me about the promotion. He would only say that it had to do with problems regarding her reporting on an incident that occurred last year. But you'll be familiar with which incident he meant, I think."

Aether sighed again.

"Well," he said finally, "before I forget in all of this, despite what's happening to Pemana, I will still say congratulations, Batthius. You'll be a great captain."

Batthius made a rude noise with his lips, but nodded at Aether as they turned up the last corner toward the castle. "Hmph," he said, shaking his head and staring out ahead of them. "What a strange couple years it's been. Feels like not that long ago, I only knew you as the shipwright's lad in Vigil. And now, here you are, a captain with more experience than me, congratulating *me* on finally becoming a captain myself." He turned his head toward Aether and met his eyes, then reached over to shake his hand. "With everything you lot have managed lately? That actually means a great deal to me, thank you."

Aether could only smile and nod as he returned Batthius's handshake, his pleasure at the compliment fading quickly as they neared the main gate of Castle Omen.

The guards saluted Batthius and nodded them through. They crossed the open courtyard inside the gates and jogged quickly up the few steps that led to an entrance into the castle's main hall.

It was very quiet inside, and they all three made an instinctive effort to silence their bootsteps as they slipped through the doors. Batthius led them only a short way into the broad chamber where Lord Moredon held court. Though the hall was crowded, there weren't a lot of courtiers present.

The gathered audience seemed to be mostly naval officers of the Port Omen Guard, a congregation of milling blue tabards trimmed in silver.

He saw Pemana right away, at the front of the hall. She still wore her tabard, at least, so perhaps that was a good sign. But she did stand before the dais, alone, facing away from them toward the lord's seat above. Aether swallowed. From the way she occasionally shifted from one booted foot back to the other, it looked like she had probably been standing there for some time.

Lord Moredon was not sitting in his chair on the dais above. He was down, standing next to a table at the foot of the steps with a few servants and guards, staring down at a parchment in his hands. He was the youngest of the lords and ladies on the Ruling Council, but nonetheless looked rather exhausted, even a bit diminished. His shoulders slumped as he flipped the parchment over and scanned the back side quickly. Then, stony-faced, he bent and picked up a quill off the table, dipped it, and signed the document.

He handed it carefully to one of the servants and turned back toward the dais, not meeting Pemana's eyes as he passed, climbing back up to resume his chair.

A servant in embroidered blue and silver robes that marked him as a senior official stepped forward, took the parchment, and held it up, clearing his throat.

"Pemana of Port Omen," the gray-haired servant said, his voice ringing and formal. "Judgment has been rendered for the failures documented in this hearing. Your rank of captain in the Guard of the House of Omen is hereby nullified. All rights associated with your command of the vessel *Champion* are revoked, and your assignment to her is canceled. You will receive your orders regarding your new posting in due course. These matters are hereby registered under the signatures of Lord Eglamon of New Brightwall for the Ruling Council of the Lastlands, and Lord Moredon of Port Omen." The servant took a breath, then spoke in a louder voice, his tone even more formal. "Present your sword for confiscation."

A silence fell for a long few seconds across the still, warm air of the hall, and no one moved. Aether noticed that Pemana's knuckles, visible on the hand gripping the hilt of the sword sheathed at her side, were very white against the rest of her flesh. Then she spoke, her voice steady, and firmer than Aether remembered ever hearing it.

"This sword was my grandfather's, a reward for his honorable service to *your* grandfather, my lord," she said. She raised her head, and Aether could tell from the uncomfortable look on Moredon's face that she had met his eyes. "This sword was not issued to me by the Guard. You will not take it from me while I stand."

The last notes of her voice echoed in the chamber until the silence was, once again, complete.

Aether met Beras's eyes. This assemblage of Port Omen's military might probably did not have the power to take Pemana's sword from her against her will, though they wouldn't have known it. In the past year and a half, she had become a rather skilled wizard, and she was the best of the Wizards' Guild with a blade. Aether doubted very much it would come to a fight, but he wondered what *he* would have to do if one broke out here, right in front of them.

After a moment of blinking silence, though, Lord Moredon simply nodded. "Of course. It's an oversight," he said quietly, his words barely carrying to where Aether and the others watched. "She can keep her sword," he said, louder, and the servant bowed up to the dais and bent to the table to make a notation.

For a long moment, Aether watched her continue to stare up at Lord Moredon. Then, slowly, she raised her fist to her heart in salute. She turned sharply on her heel and marched back through the hall toward the courtyard doors. If she noticed Aether and the others standing there as she passed, she made no sign of it.

Batthius turned to him as the murmur of quiet conversation began to break out in the hall. "I will have to stay," he whispered. "Please make sure she's all right."

Aether nodded immediately and stepped toward the doors. Beras shook Batthius's hand quickly and whispered something to his former crewmate that Aether didn't hear. Then he turned as well, and the two of them made their way quickly out the doors and back down into the castle grounds.

She hadn't gone far. She stood near the main gate, straight as a spear, hands clasped behind her back, staring out at the harbor that was visible from here only as a sea of masts sprouting up above the rooftops of the city.

"Pemana," Aether breathed as they came up behind her.

She turned quickly, her hands dropping to her sides, the braids at her temples, so similar to Lyrrek's preferred style, swinging out a bit as she spun. But she didn't look surprised to see them there.

"I wish I hadn't sent for you," she said. "I think I would have been happier if no one had seen this."

Aether didn't know what to say, and she wouldn't meet his eyes. So he simply nodded.

"What have you done?" hissed a sudden voice from behind her. Pemana's eyes widened in shock, and she spun back even faster.

An older woman, red-faced from the heat, or perhaps her emotions, and escorted by a distinguished looking man with graying hair and beard, were stalking in through the gate of the castle. Though Aether had never met them, it was obvious, just from the way Pemana resembled her father, who they were.

"Mother," Pemana said quietly, and Aether saw her shoulders tense in a way he'd only witnessed in his friend during the stress of a land-dragon hunt.

Her mother ignored Aether and Beras completely, both of whom took a couple involuntary steps back. But their presence caused Pemana's mother no concern or hesitation.

"Is this true, what we've heard?" she demanded loudly, stepping quite close and looking up at her tall, frozen daughter.

"I…wouldn't know what you heard," Pemana finally managed. Aether considered fleeing, but they just didn't get the chance.

"We heard you've been stripped of your commission!" her father said. He looked more astonished and unhappy than outraged, but Pemana seemed to flinch away from it nonetheless.

"No," she said, a little more strongly. "I was demoted and lost my command."

"Oh," he said, a tiny note of relief working its way into his voice. She could work to rebuild her career if she was at least still in the guard. Aether could see those thoughts plainly on her father's face.

But her mother was not interested. "You have shamed this family! How could you make such a mistake? What exactly is it that you did?"

Aether began to feel a burden of outrage himself.

"I didn't do anything," Pemana said quietly. "The charges didn't make any sense." She turned her head, then, and Aether saw her looking at him out of the corner of her eye. "Someone on the Council arranged this."

"The lords and ladies of the Council don't know who you are," her mother spat, getting even closer into her daughter's face.

Aether felt himself about to take a step forward, his own face going hot, unaccustomed to having to stand and watch one of his guildmates attacked and doing nothing about it. But he caught himself, knowing full well that there was nothing he could say to improve this situation. And before he could have said anything anyway, Pemana's mother stormed past her daughter and headed off toward the hall doors. "I'm speaking with Commander Ebrehar about this," she said, pointing her finger at the sky, her husband following her after a last sad look at his daughter.

"Mother, he…" she began, but her mother stomped quickly away and up the steps and vanished through the doors.

Pemana sighed. "He retired a year ago." She shook her head as her father gave her one last wave and followed.

"Pemana," Aether began again, but she held up her hand. A young man in a blue and gray tabard approached carrying a folded parchment, which he held up to her. She took it, and he nodded sharply, turned, and marched off.

She unfolded it, read for only a few seconds, then snorted in disgust.

"Captain?" Beras asked quietly. She turned to him, and the look on her face kicked Aether in the stomach.

"You can't call me that anymore, Beras," she said, a haunted note in her voice. "I've been demoted back down to recruit and assigned to harbor maintenance duty, per the orders of the Ruling Council." She held up the folded page.

Beras's mouth fell open, which prompted Aether to realize that his own mouth was hanging open as well. He closed it hastily, then stepped closer to her, trying to nonchalantly look around and see where the nearest guards were. He spoke quietly, meeting her devastated eyes. "Pemana, we both know something entirely corrupt is happening here, and we both know who's probably behind it."

She nodded without hesitation.

"Don't let them do this to you," he whispered. "We *need* you. You know you already have a better place to go than what they're trying to force you into here." He nodded toward the castle doors, toward her vanished parents...and vanished career. "Come with us. Don't let them waste you."

He emphasized the last two words distinctly. She had been starting to look away, but at those words, her eyes whipped back to his, and she stared at him for a long moment.

"You're right...Master Aether," she whispered quietly. Then she looked at Beras and nodded.

"Come with me," she said to them both, her voice strong again, and they had to step quickly to keep up as she wheeled and strode hard across the grounds on her long legs.

They re-entered the hall. There were still plenty of blue tabards milling about, but the hearings had ended, apparently. There was no immediate sign of her parents, but Pemana strode directly across the hall toward Lord Moredon, who was, just then, heading through beams of sunlight from the windows toward a side door, followed by an entourage of guards and servants. He saw her coming, and stopped, an unreadable expression on his face.

Aether and Beras hung back a bit as she walked forward, slowing as the guards nearest Lord Moredon looked on her rapid approach with a bit of alarm. She stopped and simply held the folded piece of parchment out in his direction. He nodded to his guards and walked over to her, accepting the document.

"I'm afraid that I will be unable to accept this new assignment, my lord," she said, calm and implacable. She grabbed the bottom of her tabard and dragged it off over her head. "I resign my commission in the Guard." Her voice carried, once more, through the great chamber.

Lord Moredon was not surprised. It was very clear on his face. He looked saddened. Then, for the briefest instant, Aether wondered whether he'd just seen a tiny, proud smile there. But it was gone so quickly that perhaps he'd imagined it.

Moredon nodded slightly at her and placed the folded parchment in a pocket of his robe. Then, saying nothing, he turned and walked away, the group of staring servants and guards following quickly behind.

Pemana stood there for another moment, silence having once again descended upon the grand hall of Castle Omen at her words. She turned and walked over to the nearest guard, handing the startled man her tabard, then walked straight out the door, without looking back to make sure that the others were still with her.

CHAPTER TWO
SHIFTING TIDES

P emana stood at *Horizon's* starboard rail, staring out at the sea from under the brim of her hat as they sailed northwest, on course for Vigil. Clouds to the west had turned purple and orange, and it looked like they'd be staring into a glorious sunset as they sailed toward the night.

The beauty of it angered her.

She heard light footsteps on the deck behind her and half turned. Lyrrek came up next to her at the railing, and put an arm up around Pemana's shoulders. Pemana managed a smile for her friend, but suddenly found herself fighting back tears.

She looked quickly away toward the sunset again.

"We had some sausages and cheese on board," Lyrrek said quietly. "So dinner won't be just dried fish at least. And I got out a bottle of brandy. I know that I could use some tonight."

Pemana nodded. They probably wouldn't reach Vigil until quite late, possibly even early the next morning, depending on the wind. Might as well make a party of it, she thought to herself, trying to ignore the bitterness.

Honestly, she would have loved nothing more than to collapse into a cabin with a proper bunk and just sleep for a few days, but *Horizon* was fairly small and didn't have extra staterooms. Aether had offered her the first mate's cabin for the night, since Orenna wasn't aboard. But Pemana, for some reason that now eluded her, had insisted that a crew hammock would be just fine.

"I'll probably take you up on the brandy, Lyrrek, thank you," she said quietly. "And dinner sounds like it will be perfect."

Lyrrek nodded, pleased, and gave her another quick squeeze before she headed back below deck.

Pemana sighed and turned, thinking for a moment. She shrugged and made her way toward the quarterdeck and the door of *Horizon's* captain's cabin.

Beras smiled down at her from the helm above, and she gave him a salute before leaning near the door and knocking quietly.

"Come!" she heard Aether call, and she opened the door.

He looked up from where he sat at his map table, a piece of leather spread out there, upon which he had laid the tools, bottles, and stones of a sharpening kit. The beautiful steel Silversea sword lay in the center, and he'd been closely examining the edge. The smell of tool oil filled the cabin.

Her eyes were drawn, as they always were, to the gleaming sword, and for some reason, the bitterness of the day swelled up in her throat again. She quickly swallowed it, and tried to make sure her expression was calm.

Aether smiled widely up at her. "Master Pemana," he said, leaning back, wiping his hands on a small cloth.

She nodded a greeting, and managed a small smile in return. She suspected that not hearing "Captain" before her name would probably never feel right again.

She swallowed that too.

Aether gestured at one of the chairs across from him. For the tiniest instant, she hesitated. It was the chair a captain usually gestured to when a subordinate came to chat. She knew he meant nothing by it, anymore than she ever had when she'd done it. But still, it just all felt so, so wrong.

She kept her composure and quickly took the seat, feeling him watching her.

"I've been doing some thinking," she began, and he nodded, still smiling. "What is it...what exactly is my job now, I guess?" She shook her head. "Sorry, this has been a strange day."

His smile vanished instantly, and he nodded. "It's a good question. I mean, to begin with, I'll just say it's whatever you want it to be. You're still on the Guild's Council of Masters, of course, so any way you identify to contribute is good enough for me. But if you're looking for ideas, I can catch you up on what you might've missed over the last few months."

She nodded, genuinely interested and glad for any distraction.

He paused, looking up above him, thoughtful, then met her eyes again and spoke quietly. "I suppose the first thing I should say is that Orenna and I have been speaking, and she thinks she's ready to move on from serving as first mate on *Horizon*. She's been working on other things that are more important to her recently anyway. I'd been thinking of offering the position to Beras, but, now…"

"No," she said abruptly, hoping that she managed to keep the sharpness from her voice. "It should be Beras. My official opinion as his former captain."

Aether nodded quickly. "Well," he continued, dropping the cloth on the table and leaning back to look up into the corner as if staring at his mental list. "As to the rest of the Guild, Orenna and Veytra, with occasional help from Kayd…" She saw his eyes flick toward her. "They've been doing a lot of coordinating of the various field teams, and trying to stay caught up on making apprentice bracers in their spare time. Kayd's been bouncing between helping them and traveling to visit the teams where they're working. And he always comes with us on *Horizon* for expeditions to the mainland, of course. We've been back a few times since I saw you last."

His eyes lit up a bit. "I have to admit I'm kind of excited for you to see the storerooms back at the guild hall. The hunting's been rather grand."

Pemana tried to nod pleasantly and waited.

He looked back up into the corner. "Both of Veytra's apprentices, Toliek and Mahlda, made Adept and went out on their own. They've been over in Cask, working among the beachsleepers there, which is where Veytra originally found them, if you remember. But they've turned up a few interesting leads, actually. And Amrelyn's still training Jyhnda and Neres, lately in New Brightwall, and has been working on some interesting things regarding…the network…"

Pemana leaned forward, staring searchingly at him. "You mean the Swordfish's network."

He nodded grimly.

The ship creaked around them as she rolled against a larger wave. Aether clapped his hand down on the sword to keep it from sliding.

Pemana stared at him.

"So tell me, what have Amrelyn and the others discovered about the Swordfish's network over the last few months, exactly?"

He met her eyes, and his grin returned.

"I wondered if this might be waiting for you," he said. He rose and stepped back to a corner cabinet and opened it, withdrawing a folio of documents, wrapped in a piece of leather and tied with a thong. He returned to his seat and held it out to her.

Pemana leaned forward, took it, and unwound the thong from the soft leather binding. She let the pile of loose parchments spill out onto the clear bit of table in front of her, and found what a practiced glance told her was a collection of notes, maps, and accounts of interviews.

She looked up at him.

"Amrelyn in particular," he said, "has had some luck tracking down...elements, I guess...of this organization we've been hearing about called the Depths."

She nodded. "I think that's his people."

"So Amrelyn told me." He looked at her. "We actually followed up a lead of hers this morning, and deposited a few of their hired goons with the magistrate in New Brightwall before we left to...come get you."

She tried not to wince. He hurried on in a way that made her wonder if she'd been that successful at hiding it.

"I haven't been able to make a lot of sense of the overall picture," he said, gesturing at the pile of documents. "But then, I'm not exactly a trained investigator."

She nodded slowly, and began sorting through the pages, before thinking better of it and simply wrapping them all back up in their cover for now. "Do you mind if I keep these?" she asked him.

"Of course not, please do. And just let me know what resources you need."

She stood and started to go, then hesitated.

"Thank you for coming to get me," she said quietly, half turning back to him. "It...I won't forget it."

He smiled at her, and gave her a half bow from his chair.

She managed a small smile back. "Sounds like Lyrrek's got some supper in progress down there," she said, gesturing back over her shoulder with a tilt of her head. "Buy you a brandy?"

"Sounds like an excellent idea," he said, and got to his feet, picking up the sword and sheathing it at his side in a practiced movement.

The early light of dawn burnished the waters of the sea, which lay relatively still that morning as *Horizon* drifted into a cove on Vigil Isle. Aether leaned closer to Pemana so he could speak quietly, given the hour.

"This location has been great," he said, pointing ahead of them into the small corner of sea that tucked behind a low hill, the waterline bristling with docks jutting out into the waves. This cove, which stretched deeper into the interior than a lot of the ones along this part of the island, was three coves north of Vigil's harbor. It was lined on both sides with smaller warehouses and traders, and many of the other docks were marked with Fishers' Guild seals. But as Aether carefully spun *Horizon's* wheel, they came slowly around the slight bend and he leaned toward Pemana again and pointed out the last spot in, a somewhat larger warehouse than the others that was built right down by the water, tucked away, out of sight from the sea, unless someone sailed all the way back into the cove. It was blessed with its own pier and a little dock, the pier just long enough for a smaller ship like *Horizon*.

"Ah, I see what you mean," she said. "You'd be hard-pressed to spot her, just sailing past."

Aether gave the wheel one last hard spin, and *Horizon* spent the last of her slight momentum on turning close enough to the pier that sailors could jump ashore with lines. They secured them, then turned to catch others thrown by their colleagues further aft, and hauled the ship the rest of the way in to bump gently up against the stone pier.

Aether breathed a sigh of relief that he and his crew had managed the tricky, close-quarters docking competently with Pemana standing there watching him. He grinned and followed her down the quarterdeck stairs, calling out a last few commands to the crew, thanking them for their hard work, and wishing them a relaxing couple days of leave.

There was a weary, but nonetheless enthusiastic round of applause at that.

Lyrrek emerged from below decks carrying a crate of food stuffs. He took it from her, earning himself one of her lovely smiles, then joined her and Pemana as they took turns crossing the gangplank the sailors had just laid across to the pier.

Lyrrek grabbed Pemana's arm ahead of him, exclaiming her intention to show her what they'd done with the place, and the taller woman allowed herself to be dragged off readily enough. Aether smiled and followed them into the old warehouse ahead that was, for now at least, serving as the guild hall for the young Wizards' Guild.

He turned into the near corner that he and Lyrrek had helped Orenna transform into a makeshift kitchen. It was a bit rustic, not too much more than just a stone-ringed campfire on the wide building's gravel floor. Smoke drifted up from the coals there, slipping out a small chimney in the slate roof directly above that a prior tenant had installed to vent some process or another.

But these days, surrounded by counters they had fashioned from planks laid across some old cabinets, the corner had become a fairly functional place to cook a lot of food. Orenna liked to throw small feasts to celebrate their return from a dangerous mainland expedition. It was an old Hunters' Guild tradition that Aether, for his part, had wholeheartedly approved of their adopting for the Wizards' Guild. And as the others had unanimously elected him Guild Master, it was, technically, up to him.

He set the crate of fresh produce down on one of the counters, and waved as he saw Veytra appear from one of the doorways leading into the deeper half of the warehouse. This frontmost portion of it was almost entirely open, a wide, columned space within which they had encircled small sections to serve as the kitchen, a lounge area where they could hold gatherings, and a few other spots for various purposes. The back half of the warehouse was a maze of smaller storage rooms, many of which the Wizards' Guild had converted into living quarters, and in the case of the chamber across the hall from Veytra's, a laboratory for working on magical projects.

Veytra was carrying a pile of the results of one of those projects in her arms as she came around the corner and spotted him. She bore a dozen pairs of sturdy leather bracers, new cut and stitched as a custom order through the local Leatherworkers' Guild, then modified by Veytra and Orenna once they took delivery. Now they were ready for the final step in their construction.

"Oh, perfect," she said, stopping in the doorway. "I was hoping the commotion I heard was you all getting back." She turned, gesturing deeper into the Hall with her eyes, then looking back at him. "Orenna and I are ready to enchant these, and we need a third. You have any plans this morning?"

"Nothing that can't wait," he said, yawning, and offered to take some bracers as he followed her back toward the laboratory.

He greeted Orenna as she smiled up from where she sat. She bent back to the bracer before her, into which she was lacing a last few stitches to enclose the pocket that held one of the enchanted stones that would give the bracer its function. He followed Veytra across the chamber, which though windowless, was still brightly lit by the glowing stones scattered around on various surfaces throughout the room.

He followed Veytra's lead and deposited his bracers on the long counter there.

Orenna stood, slicing off a last bit of spare lacing with a sharp bronze dagger, then carried the bracer across to add to Veytra's pile.

Veytra stretched, shaking her shoulders. Aether took a deep breath himself, calming his mind in preparation.

"Well?" Veytra asked, looking between him and Orenna. "Are we ready? We'll do the dragonskin stones first."

He and Orenna both nodded.

Aether closed his eyes.

He observed with his magical senses as he felt Veytra's cast begin. A fuzzy, sparkling veil appeared, emanating from where she stood just a few feet away. He felt Orenna's presence appear nearby as well, then, and began to cast the spell himself. What came next was a tricky act, taking quite a bit of concentration. He leaned his own magic *into* Veytra's, feeling the two efforts combine with a resonant vibration, a heightened sense of tingling power. And then he felt Orenna's cast lock into theirs as well.

The first time they had discovered this effect, Aether, Kayd, and Veytra had stumbled upon it out of curiosity, just playing around with what would happen if they combined their magical efforts. Two wizards casting together didn't seem to accomplish much more than both would have separately. But when three wizards' casts came together, something very different occurred. They had all three yelped like someone had startled them from behind, and had leapt away from where they had been standing, immediately losing their concentration and the cast they'd been attempting. It had been a hilarious few moments of them composing themselves before they'd been ready to try again.

But this morning, the three of them knew what to expect, and they kept it together. The compounding of magical strength that occurred when the three wizards cast the dragonskin spell multiplicatively rippled through each of them as a great surge of power. Aether felt Veytra gather the thrumming energy of it and shape it into a complex spell. The bracer she had picked up had two stones laced into it. For the first, Veytra gathered a pulsation of the dragonskin spell and emblazoned it into the stone. And then came the innovation that Orenna had discovered, as into the second stone, Veytra used their combined strength to layer a new magical effect over the first, something that Aether had recorded in his spellbook as a "permanence spell." Veytra welded the two magical effects together to produce a single, potent enchantment, one that would remain permanently bound into the stones. Then she released them from the cast.

All three gasped slightly, stumbling a bit. Orenna sighed and shook herself as Aether paced around, feeling the need to let the energy of the triplicate cast dissipate from him, as he often did.

"Phew," Veytra said, grinning. "Well, one down. Only a couple dozen more to go."

Aether chuckled.

"Seems like that turned out right," she said, peering closely at the bracer in her hand. "We'll do several in a row before I drop it next time."

Aether groaned, mostly joking.

"We'll take breaks," Veytra said, laughing, and tossed the completed bracer to him.

He caught it, and examined it with his magical senses. They had discovered early on that spells they enchanted into stones were powerful and flexible magic, but could be easily undone by any wizard who could sense them. This would be awkward if you meant to withdraw the magic from a lightstone or something and accidentally wiped the spells from a more complex working standing nearby, a problem that plagued some of their early experiments. Orenna figured out that the combination of the desired enchantment with the permanence magic, when laid down cooperatively by three wizards, resulted in an enchantment that was much harder for a single wizard to remove, even intentionally.

For the next half an hour or so, they pushed through the construction of the rest of the prepared bracers, switching to the healing spell for the second batch halfway through.

Finally, sighing, Veytra handed Aether the last one, and slumped into a chair.

Aether yawned and held the healing bracer up before him, examining it. The paired bracers, each bound with a single spell effect sustained by a permanence enchantment, had been the answer to a question that hung over the Guild's earliest days.

How would they know who they could trust with the enormous power of the magic that Aether had discovered?

Pemana had been the one to see that what they needed was the ability to hand someone spells they could use for the duration of a probationary period...spells they could use, but not necessarily keep, if they didn't earn the right to learn to wield the magic directly. They had come up with these apprentice bracers, one that provided the wearer with a perpetual version of the dragonskin protection spell, and a second bracer, worn on the dominant hand, that let the wearer cast a limited form of the Guild's healing magic. It wasn't a powerful enough spell to heal a person entirely of, say, their old age, as Aether had once done for Orenna by accident while dragging her back from death's door. But it would, with some concentration and sustained effort, let a Wizards' Guild apprentice heal wounds, or cure illnesses.

It had been a fairly successful experiment. Aether and Lyrrek had recruited a number of the sailors they hired to crew *Horizon*, people who, by that point, had already proven themselves. Veytra and Amrelyn had located candidates among compassionate people they'd found, as had Kayd and Orenna. Some of those early apprentices had already turned their bracers back in, having earned the right to learn magic directly.

It wasn't a perfect system, of course. There was always the possibility that an observant apprentice, carefully studying the nature of the magic enchanted into the bracers, would figure out how to cast magic on their own. After all, Aether had done something similar, and in far less optimal circumstances.

Gelkris had figured it out as well, just from studying Aether. And Gelkris was a man who, they now knew, had gotten dangerously close to delivering those magical abilities into some *very* wrong hands.

Veytra was staring at him. As if she could predict his thoughts, she said "I wish you would have given Emrek some of these, instead of, you know, making him the only wizard on the planet who isn't in the Wizards' Guild."

Aether sighed, but kept a patient grin on his face. It was pretty far from the first time this had come up.

"I probably would have," he said, "but we hadn't invented them yet."

She smirked at him. He'd used the same excuse before.

Lyrrek came around the corner and entered the room, followed closely by Pemana, who blinked in the bright light of the stones.

"And here's Veytra's laboratory," Lyrrek said, gesturing. Pemana nodded, looking around, appearing suitably impressed at all the various projects scattered about.

"Actually, I'm glad you two are here," Aether said, and met Veytra's eyes. "I've been meaning to tell you all more about this story."

Lyrrek and Pemana looked over at him.

"Which story?" Lyrrek asked.

"Veytra was just reminding me about Lord Emrek, and my teaching him magic," Aether said, trying not to sound defensive. "There's more to it, something I've never gotten around to telling you all." He met Pemana's eyes. "Since the Swordfish has…made things rather more personal lately…it's probably time you all heard the rest of it."

Lyrrek nodded, and sat down in a chair, a small smile on her face. She was the only one who knew the full account, and had suggested he share it with the others.

Veytra eyed him, leaning back against the counter behind her, arms crossed. Aether tossed the finished healing bracer back into the pile.

"You know I looked in Emrek's mind before I left him on that beach," he said. Orenna nodded. She and Lyrrek had kept watch from *Horizon* while he dug through the memories of the former ruler of Vigil. "There were…" he paused, looking up into a corner of the stone room. "I saw some things…about the Swordfish."

Pemana sat down in a chair next to Lyrrek, eyes locked on him.

"I saw how it all started," he said. "Looking at it with knowledge of how things turned out, it was obvious that the Swordfish was manipulating Emrek from the start. But Emrek didn't know that at first. The Swordfish found him when he was pretty young, younger than we are now, actually," he said, meeting Lyrrek's eyes. "Young Lord Emrek, still only his father's heir at the time, was already living a bit on the edge, sneaking off from his responsibilities now and then, sailing off into Cask to go drinking when he was supposed to be Contribution fishing, that sort of thing.

"The Swordfish saw who he was and played on his vanities, and ingratiated himself and some of his followers into Emrek's circle. Emrek loved the danger, loved the excitement of these impressive underworld figures wanting to spend time around him. The things they got up to were much more interesting than the boring work of learning to rule a major holding of the Lastlands, and the other things his father demanded of him."

Orenna was nodding. "Lord Derenat was a decent ruler, I think. Seems like he would have expected Emrek to work to become one too."

Aether nodded as well. "He did. Emrek resented it, thought he was smarter than everyone, and thought his father was holding him back. But he still wasn't really interested in the Swordfish's criminality himself. He just wanted to drink, waste time, and surround himself with people that made him feel...I don't know...special, I guess.

"But it came back to haunt him. One morning, he woke up, hung over, and found the Swordfish and several of his men there. They showed him a ring. It was his father's seal. They said they had the rest of his rings as well, because they had killed him."

Orenna gasped.

Aether went on, his voice quiet and neutral. "As he started to unravel, they told Emrek that they'd learned his father had been about to crack down on him, hard, and they had protected him from it by making him Lord of Vigil in his father's place. They told him that he would be a much better lord than his father had been. Then the Swordfish told him that he was quite sure Emrek would be better, because he would now be working for them. Because the Swordfish had arranged it so that if Emrek failed to do anything that was demanded of him, then information, including the rest of Derenat's rings, would be turned over to the magistrates, proving that Emrek had murdered his father to seize power."

Orenna shook her head, her eyes wide. "I remember when Derenat's ship didn't come back. The whole city was in an uproar for a month."

Aether sighed, and nodded. "I remember it now too, I'm sorry to say." He looked around at them. "The last thing the Swordfish did before they left was hand Emrek his father's signet ring. He spent the first two weeks of his rule with it in a pouch on his belt at all times, even while he slept. He was terrified someone would find it, and think his possession of it was proof he'd been involved in his father's disappearance. But it was something of his murdered father's, something he'd dreamed about having his whole life, and he cherished it.

"But the stress of what to do about the ring got to him, until finally, one night during a crossing when no one else could see what he was doing, he snuck out and threw it into the sea."

Pemana slowly put her hand over her mouth, shaking her head.

"He lived in terror of those other rings for the next thirty years, basically until we left him on that beach. In fact, the last thing I found in his thoughts, the thing he was thinking about as we arrived at Exile's Shore, was that at least he didn't have to worry about the Swordfish figuring out a new way to make his life worse, since it was about to end."

They all stared at him as he fell silent. Finally he sat down in a chair.

"All right," Veytra said at last. "I see why you taught him magic."

Pemana looked up at him. "I still think we were right to administer the punishment we did."

Aether nodded quickly. "I do too. Weirdly, I think even he thought so. He gave up resisting what the Swordfish demanded of him pretty quickly, and he was actively involved in his crimes for a long time, by the end. He thought I was a fool, but I don't think he thought that what we were doing to him was unjust. I found that interesting."

Pemana nodded. "The innocence of his younger self doesn't excuse the crimes of the man he became later."

"Exactly," Aether responded. "And I think he saw the younger version of himself the same way he saw me. He thought both of us were idealistic fools." Aether looked down, then chuckled and sighed at the same time. "I guess it remains to be seen whether he was right."

"I wonder if he's still alive," Veytra said quietly, after a moment.

Aether nodded, meeting her eyes again, and they all fell silent.

Pemana emerged back into the open half of the guild hall, trying to leave behind the melancholy feeling that chased her after their conversation. As she emerged from the corridor, another person was entering through a far doorway, nearest the road on into the city, carrying a crate.

There was no mistaking this person for anyone else. He was taller than anyone else in the Guild. He had already been a rather strapping young man when she'd met him, a couple years before, well fit for his rigorous apprenticeship under the harbormaster. But this last year, traveling, exploring the mainland, hauling on ships' lines, and fending off dragons…well, all the hard work had suited him.

She shoved hard on the thrill of feeling that leapt up into her stomach, stomping it back down where she tried to keep it, deep enough to pretend it didn't exist.

Kayd walked toward her, not noticing her there at first. When he finally did see her, he cleared his throat, shifting the crate a bit and slowing to greet her.

Whatever he opened his mouth to say, though, he apparently thought better of because he just paused for a moment, his mouth hanging open, then shut it, and merely nodded.

Finally, he managed a weak "hey," as he came up to her, his eyes full of emotion.

"You heard, then," was all she said.

"I'm so sorry I wasn't there," he said quietly.

"Oh," she said, too quickly, turning away. "I'm not. I wish no one had been there to see it."

He fell silent, just staring at her.

"Sorry," she finally said, pointing at the crate. "I don't want to keep you just standing here holding that."

He nodded, and started toward the kitchen corner.

"Well, it'll be good to have you around the hall, Pemana," he said over his shoulder.

She nodded, following him, almost without realizing she was. "Aether found me some things to work on, I think," she said. "Something to start on anyway."

"Feels like there's always plenty to do," he said, with a hint of exaggerated sigh. Then he looked up and met her eyes. "I'm...sorry you lost your ship," he said. "I know what she meant to you."

Tears suddenly burned around the rims of Pemana's eyes, and she fought hard to keep them there, willing them back into her eye sockets.

She just nodded at him, as no words seemed to fit.

"I'm glad you could come back here and have a place to go," he said. "The way the silver's been flowing lately, you'll probably make more here with us full time than you were with the Guard."

She managed a small, hollow laugh. "Lyrrek showed me the storerooms. You've been busy. You might be right about that."

"Well, every step forward is a victory," he said, but then he saw the expression on her face, and faltered.

"Yeah, well what are massive setbacks then?" she demanded. She did manage to keep *most* of the harshness out of her voice.

He winced. "Sorry," he said. "You're right of course." He looked down, then back up to her. "Still, I'll be glad you're around again, Pemana," he repeated awkwardly. Then he turned and headed toward the deeper chambers, leaving her standing there, watching him go.

Poor Kayd, she thought to herself. She didn't dislike him. Rather the opposite, honestly. But...it just...it couldn't be. She couldn't think of any way to explain to him why.

She sighed. She'd been struggling with this particular puzzle for a couple years at this point. There was no reason to think she'd suddenly solve it today.

She turned and looked out the door toward the waters of the cove. Before they'd drifted off to enjoy their leave, *Horizon's* crew had lowered the ship's two tenders down to the water and moored them at the hall's small dock. Aether had showed her where they kept some nets in the ship's hold. Maybe she could slip away and get in some fishing, or something. Just then, the solitude of a small boat on the sea seemed like a good idea.

Aether paused at the corner, waiting for Lyrrek to draw alongside him. Quehlo's outfitter's shop stood across the gravel road, and they had a rather large supply order to place with him. As Aether waited for her, his gaze shifted, almost of its own accord, across to the now-abandoned shipwright's workshop that had once been his old master, Norphret's.

Lyrrek came up beside him and took his arm. He turned quickly to smile at her, and let her lead him across to Quehlo's shop, happily ignoring the place where he had lived nearly a decade of his earlier life.

So much had changed that those almost felt like a different person's experiences. He grinned at Lyrrek again and followed her up the pair of stone steps and in the familiar door.

Aether had always loved coming to Quehlo's Outfitter. As a child, it had been the fantastical shop across the way, a place from where adventures were begun by lucky people departing on them. It smelled of leather, and oils, and wax, and many other, stranger things. He had occasionally slipped out after hours to stare in the dark windows at things he dreamed of saving up for: a dagger, or a spear, or once, for a month, a beautiful set of leather armor that Quehlo had kept on a dummy in the front, until a nobleman bought it.

Now, Aether was the guild master of a brand new, secretive guild that had perfected some fairly effective ways to bring in silver. In the first year of their existence as an organization, they had become the most efficient land drag- on hunters on Origin, far surpassing the Hunters' Guild in tactics and safety, and perhaps even volume. Already, in that short time, they had amassed a small fortune or two. And they were actually having a difficult time figuring out how to sell most of what they produced. It was all presently piling up in locked storerooms at their guild hall.

All that meant that these days, when he walked into Quehlo's shop, it was with a bulging silver pouch. He did promise himself that he wouldn't buy any armor, something that was, of course, more or less useless to him now.

As he followed Lyrrek through the door, his eye was caught by the armor stands in the corner that modeled some interesting looking leather sets, a few of which looked like ones he hadn't seen yet. He glanced at Lyrrek out of the corner of his eye.

He chuckled quietly and reminded himself that looking dashing wasn't an entirely pointless consideration…

"My lady!" he heard Quehlo sing out to Lyrrek from the door to the back. He came out behind the counter, setting down some small bundles, and walked to his usual spot at the center. He nodded at Lyrrek, and smiled at them both. "How are you?" he asked.

"Excellent, thank you Quehlo," Aether said warmly. "How are Nehldra and Sedren doing?"

"She's very well," Quehlo said. "And Sedren started pre-apprentice school this week."

"Hey!" Aether said. "I hope he enjoys it, school was one of the fun memories of my childhood."

He saw the way Quehlo looked at him and smiled reassuringly.

"Well, Sedren seems to be making some friends, I think. It sounds like it's going well."

"Great news, thank you Quehlo," Lyrrek said, leaning up against the counter and pulling a pouch from within her embroidered gray robes. "I actually have some more silver for Sedren's care today, as it happens."

"My lady," Quehlo said, patiently. "I've told you, that's really not necessary. Sedren's a good kid, even with everything he's been through. We're delighted to have him in our home and to get to take care of him."

"Well, even so," Aether said, "we take care of our own, and that includes all three of you at this point."

Lyrrek nodded and handed him the small pouch.

"And actually," Aether said, pulling out a larger pouch and a folded piece of parchment, "I have even more silver for you, for a resupply."

"Ahh," Quehlo said, nodding and grinning. "Getting ready for another trip then?"

"Yes. Endless Skies, this time."

"Oh!" Quehlo said, taking the list from Aether and unfolding it. "Well, now *that* will be interesting." Quehlo was one of the very few people on Origin who knew the full story of what Aether had experienced on the mainland during his exile, and knew that he had been to those ruins once before.

He glanced over the list, nodding, and making a few notes for himself. Then he took the pouch and hefted it, and nodded. "I can get that over to you in a day or two, will that be soon enough do you think?"

"Oh certainly," Lyrrek said. "We're not leaving for a few days, yet."

Quehlo nodded again. "I expect I'll have some change for you as well, my fine masters," he said, grinning.

Aether grinned back. Quehlo was also one of the very few people on Origin who knew about the existence of the Wizards' Guild.

"Let us know if you need anything, Quehlo, as always," Aether said, leaning in close. "And if you or Nehldra change your mind about those guild apprenticeships…"

Quehlo nodded slowly. "I think for now, we're best where we're at. The shop is very busy, and Sedren needs a lot of care." He suddenly chuckled and bent, stamping his leg on the floor enthusiastically and then standing upright to grin at Aether. "But my knees don't hurt for the first time in years," he said. "Sedren will grow up fast, I expect, like they always do. And I imagine we'll take you up on all of that sooner or later."

"Well, you'll be welcome, Quehlo. And thanks for everything, as always," Aether said, and waving, he followed a beaming Lyrrek back out the front door.

Pemana sat on an old wooden barracks bunk that had been moved into the small chamber she'd picked for her quarters in the guild hall. She sorted through a small stack of parchments, occasionally holding one up against a portion of the stone wall, trying various of them in various places. None of them felt right.

They were her drawings, mostly of architecture she'd found interesting during her years sailing around the Lastlands as *Champion's* captain.

These drawings had only ever hung on the bulkhead of her cabin aboard the ship. Maybe that was why they didn't feel like they fit anywhere here, no matter what she tried.

Pemana sighed and tossed the pile onto the bunk, and slumped back against the stone wall. After a moment, she gathered up the loose stack of parchments and stowed them back in the trunk by the door.

Kayd and Orenna had scrounged up some furniture over the several months they'd been here, and Pemana's little chamber did, thankfully, have a small table and a couple chairs, in addition to the bunk. She pulled a few stones out of a pouch and placed them around the room, casting lightstone spells into them until the chamber was plenty bright enough for reading.

She opened the trunk again and took out the documents that represented the Wizards' Guild's gathered intelligence about the Swordfish. She spread all of it out before her on the small table and sat down in a chair, rummaging through, trying to spot patterns, trying to isolate details with implications she might have missed.

Nothing of it added up to anything obvious yet. But as she stared over it all, her mind wandered to the things that had been done to her.

The Swordfish had to have been behind it. It was the only explanation that made sense. The charges against her had amounted to nothing more than a rather minor clerical error on her paperwork reporting the incidents surrounding Emrek's exiling. If there had been actual mistakes discovered (which happened all the time, of course), then as she understood the regulations, a captain would ordinarily be given the opportunity to simply correct the record. Demotion, and all the way back to recruit, was *not* how this sort of thing was usually handled.

One of the other Council lords had been a direct motivating factor in what had been done to her, she knew. His name, Lord Eglamon, had been the other signature on the order that stripped her of her command. And this collection of details before her painted a picture of something going on in and around New Brightwall, Lord Eglamon's holding. His city certainly wasn't the only one with substantial problems. But somehow she had a feeling that what was going on there was important and involved.

But there just wasn't enough here to make sense of it. She leaned back in her chair and stared up at the bare stone wall.

Aether had invited her to join them on the expedition to the mainland on which they were about to depart. She had been intending to go. But something about all this information, these clues with too many gaps between to paint a full picture of what was going on...the puzzle was eating at her.

She decided that she would have to stay behind. This work, finally getting enough blanks filled in that she could begin to identify the vulnerabilities in the Swordfish's operations…this was what really mattered. It was too important, and, she rather suspected, there wasn't anyone else out there working on it, now that the Swordfish had managed to have her so thoroughly removed from the Council's piracy investigation.

He was getting away with it. The Swordfish was getting away with what he had done to Emrek and his father, with what he seemed to be doing to the people of New Brightwall and several other cities around the Lastlands…with what he had done to her.

She grimaced, determined. She couldn't let it stand.

Kayd would be unhappy when he found out she wasn't coming on the expedition. Oh, he wouldn't object, really, and he would try to hide his feelings about it. But she knew that she was about to deflate his hopes. She knew he would have been looking forward to the time spent in close quarters with her, facing dangers together on the mainland.

Honestly, she admitted, a little uncomfortable…part of her had been looking forward to it as well.

But it wasn't going to happen. She had too much work to do.

Chapter Three
Risks

A ether steadied himself against *Horizon's* starboard quarterdeck rail, his right knee up on the bench there as he peered through his spyglass at the distant shore. It was tricky to focus, the image rising and falling with the ship's dance on the waves.

He breathed deep, and the earthy smell of damp jungle cut through to him past the usual notes of seawater, wet wood, and resin. He lowered the spyglass and watched the passing shoreline, as the coast began to turn northward.

Though the perspective was a bit off from his memory, of course, the location still felt familiar.

"I think this is it," he said over his shoulder, closing the spyglass and putting it in the satchel he wore as part of his gear on these adventures. "Bring us in, slow and cautious."

"Aye, captain," Beras said, and took a nervous breath.

Aether grinned, but turned quickly to hide it.

This would be a tricky docking, but they'd been over it, and Beras knew what to do. So rather than just watch over his shoulder and be a distraction, Aether nodded to him and started down the quarterdeck stairs, as Beras called out some orders to the crew.

He entered their cabin, and Lyrrek looked up from tightening a boot strap and smiled at him, standing and sheathing her shortsword as she turned.

"This should be a fun one," she said.

"Got a good feeling about this one, do you? If I remember right, you were pretty excited about Bastion too, and look how that turned out."

"Eh, I don't know if I'd go that far." She kissed him. "Maybe I'm just ready for an adventure."

"It's been a busy couple months," he agreed.

"Yeah, remind me to find us a chance to actually relax for a few days sometime." She tucked her braids behind her ears. "Well, are we ready?"

"I think so," he said, returning her grin. He retrieved his staff from the corner, then turned to follow her out the door.

They emerged back out onto the deck and Aether glanced to his right, now certain they were in the correct place. *Horizon* had entered a familiar bay, with a worn, ancient-looking stone pier barely hanging on at its north side. Beras had the crew drifting the ship slowly forward, carefully watching down into the water below them for obstacles that might hide in a harbor that hadn't been maintained for two centuries.

But the lookouts clinging to the rigging as they leaned out over the ship's dragon-carved bow managed to find them a safe route through, and the water was still deep enough, at least for a smaller ship like *Horizon,* to float right up to the crumbling pier.

They slowed near a section that looked the most stable, and sailors jumped over with long lines to tie off to the nearest trees they could reach.

Kayd stepped up to him, a look of concentration still on his face as he magically scanned the nearby jungle. "There are two stalkers up in the hills, five or six hundred paces, probably. No dragons in range that I can find. I think we're safe for now if we're not too loud." He opened his eyes, grinned at Aether, and turned to go get his spear.

Within twenty minutes, *Horizon's* small crew of sailors—nine men and women, plus the three wizards—all had pitched in and set up a base camp centered around the pier, encircling and protecting the ship. This was of primary concern for the whole mission, of course, as they couldn't get home without her.

Once everything was ashore and the most important preparations had been made, Aether called the group together and went over safety considerations.

He split the crew into three teams of three sailors each, and assigned each team to one of the three masters. No crew member was to be off on their own: all had to stay in the presence of one of the three wizards at all times.

Each member of the expedition wore a dragonskin spell protection bracer. Six of the nine sailors were also full apprentices in the Wizards' Guild, and had earned their healing spell bracer for the other arm. These six apprentices were also distributed evenly across the three teams. But though each crew member possessed some magical protection, and carried maces and spears as well, none of them had the ability to magically handle the worst threats they could face here. So each team would support and protect, while being protected by, a master wizard…just in case a dragon found them.

Thankfully, everyone here had been on at least one prior Wizards' Guild expedition, and all nodded, ready. Once Aether had finished the list of their usual safety reminders, the teams split up. For the remainder of this first day, Kayd would take two teams, his and Lyrrek's, and go after the stalkers they could still sense up in the nearby hills. As had been their usual practice on recent expeditions, in the early phases, Lyrrek would go with Aether and his three sailors while they explored the city's remains, looking for potential artifacts or treasures. Once they'd exhausted those possibilities, they'd split up into three full teams and rove more widely until they'd hunted enough land dragons to make the trip worthwhile.

So before the sun had reached its zenith, Aether led his small group, consisting of himself, Lyrrek, Beras, and two other sailors, into the jungle, heading in the direction of the small, shattered building he had once found here.

They left the sandy area near the pier where they'd camped and pushed their way through into the thick green undergrowth, the apprentices stepping ahead with their spears, scaring off crawling things, and pushing aside the lush foliage so they could all pass through. Lyrrek and Aether followed, half concentrating on their footing, half on maintaining a broader magical awareness for threats. The area seemed pretty safe at the moment, but they'd learned early on that sleeping dragons, including the small (and still very dangerous) terrestrial ones, don't generate much of a noticeable signature…until you wake them up, anyway. So it was necessary for them to keep their magical eyes constantly open, as it were.

Now that they had entered into it, the jungle air was warm and still, dense with humidity. Aether smelled something floral over the rich decay of the jungle floor, mingling with the ever-present odors of seaweed and salt from behind them.

The nearby birds and insects were loud in their songs today, adding to a general feeling of local safety. Aether nodded and led them further west through the thick undergrowth and trees.

They quickly found the building he'd seen during his exile. The others were properly impressed by the destruction that something, a full dragon by the looks of it, had wrought upon it. An entire corner of its mossy stone walls was ripped out and thrown to either side, a frightening reminder of the power of the creatures who truly ruled these lands.

They checked over the small, ruined building, Aether poking the lit stone at the top of his staff around into dark places. One of the sailors found a few small shards of pottery poking up from a corner. But there wasn't much else to be seen.

Kayd had discovered early on that most of these ruins of the old world, which had existed a lot longer than anything they knew in the Lastlands, often had quite a bit of history buried below the surface if you dug down a handspan within their ancient houses. But for this expedition, they were really more on the lookout for larger pieces of statuary or ornamentation, lingering artifacts that might impress the still-living human scions of this ancient lost city.

They moved on from the crumbled building, carefully picking their way through the thick trees as they tried to understand how the city of Endless Skies had been laid out two centuries earlier.

Lyrrek spotted a somewhat less dense line through the jungle that proved, on closer examination of the ground, to have enough stones lined up in various stretches to suggest an ancient stone-lined roadway of some kind. They oriented themselves to its path up into the hillier jungle around them, and began to follow it deeper.

Crumbled buildings began to emerge from the trees as they went. The thick jungle here was well into the process of reclaiming them. Everything was covered with moss, and plants and trees grew from within most structures, working slowly to eventually finish the work the dragons had begun.

They looked into what buildings they safely could. Some were too unsound-looking to enter. Even with magical protection, they'd still need to avoid getting buried in a collapsing stone building. But what buildings they did explore suggested that this place had been thoroughly ransacked by dragons in their…curiosity?

His people had never known for sure what drove the dragons to this destruction. But the Hunters' Guild and their explorations had long ago confirmed the ancient tales. When the winged dragons had first appeared, they had gone after anything that lived and immediately made it food. But after, they tended to linger in the area, and tore open most human-built structures, sifting through what they found inside. Most of what was left behind would have been pulverized by large claws.

So it was not surprising that the city of Endless Skies looked like it had been subjected to the same treatment.

But as they were passing over a fully collapsed building, Lyrrek spotted a small depression with an overhang at its edge. Curious, she dropped down into the hole, got down on her hands and knees, and glanced up into the overhang.

She gasped.

Aether dropped down next to her, crouching low, and held the lit end of his staff into the space to see what she had found.

The space under the overhang opened up and into the ruined stones of the collapsed building to form a small cave-like void. It wasn't a very large space. Aether dropped down on hands and knees on the mossy ground under him and crawled forward a bit into the darkness, raising the end of his staff up ahead of him to make sure there was nothing with more legs than him in the hole. He looked up into the space beyond to see what was there. By the smell it had been used by something musky as a den in the not too distant past, though it seemed empty now. And, he could see some interesting shapes protruding from the mud along one edge.

After a moment, he emerged, grunting, and holding a muddy piece of shaped stone in one now-filthy hand. "I think it was an oil lamp," he said. A deep depression had been carved into the top of it, with a shallow groove along the rim that could hold a wick. "There's several of them in there, and some other things that also look like they might be carved from stone. Don't know if it's the wares of a shop, or maybe just some collapsed steward's closet from an ancient house or something. It's mostly a muddy mess, and these carved stone things are probably all that survived. But there's more to pull out."

Lyrrek climbed up from the hole and turned, grabbing the staff next to his clean hand and pulling him up. One of the apprentices jumped excitedly down into the hollow in their place, accepted the lit staff from Aether as he held it down to her, then dropped down to crawl into the cave-like ruin. Beras climbed down to receive what she passed out to them, and before long, they had a couple dozen muddy stone artifacts laid out to examine.

It was mostly lamps and small, shallow bowls. But there was one statue-like shape, abstract and faceted, but beautiful, with a small carved depression on top.

"Oh!" Lyrrek said, picking it up and wiping some more mud off while looking it over curiously. "I think it's a candle holder!"

Aether whistled. Candles weren't unheard of in Lastlands society, but they were relatively rare, and expensive. Just the association with candles and the fact that only the wealthier nobility could afford them today might give the piece some added interest to the right buyer.

"Well, it's not a crown, exactly," Lyrrek said, grinning. "But it might be enough to get someone's attention, even if we don't find much else."

Aether helped the others gather plant fronds to wrap the muddy artifacts in, then they bundled them up and distributed the heavy stone objects among all their haversacks. Once they were all comfortably kitted, they stood, ready to depart.

"Hmm, I can't sense those stalkers anymore," Lyrrek said, turning back toward them. "I suspect Kayd's going to be ready for our help."

Aether nodded and pointed in the direction where he could sense the glowing group of apprentice bracers in the hills above them, and they all started off.

Aether spotted Kayd as he and Lyrrek dropped down into the rocky creek bed, the others following them. Kayd was covered in blood, but most of it seemed to be on his hands and arms as he waved up at them. "Everyone's safe," he called. "But, um…" he chuckled. "There were eight of them, actually. Six of them were sleeping and surprised us. It was pretty exciting."

Aether chuckled as he heard Lyrrek and Beras sigh at the same time. This was good news for their overall progress, but it meant a lot of hide-scraping and meat-slicing, even with all of them. They were in for a long night.

Aether turned to Beras. "Well, have 'em fan out and start looking for as much wood as we can find. We'd better get the fires going." He made his way along the creek to Kayd, who had bent to rinse a dagger in the small amount of water there, then stood to return to the large stalker carcass laying on the gravel.

"The others are just over the hill," Kayd said, pointing as Aether walked up next to him. He frowned, looking down at the large stalker. "A few of them were pretty big. I hope I brought enough salt."

Aether nodded. "I'll send Lyrrek back down to camp with her team to bring up the empty barrels."

Kayd grinned. "Eight more skulls for the storerooms, though. I'm telling you, they'll help this stuff sell, once we're parading rich nobles through."

Aether chuckled, drawing his dagger and kneeling next to the stalker. "No argument here. Besides, I'd wager that a lot of them will want to buy a skull for their trophy room."

Lord Eglamon, ruler of the city of New Brightwall, bent to smell the lavish plate one of the cooks laid before him. He reached out to grab a candle that stood near in a heavy silver holder and dragged it closer, so he could better inspect the complex pastry, which was wrapped delicately in lacy strands of some thin-sliced herb.

"Yes, very good," he said importantly, nodding very slightly to the cook, who backed away, bowing.

Eglamon took another sip of his wine and reached for a fork, ready to thoroughly destroy the cook's artistry. But before he could break into its structure, there was a sudden outbreak of murmuring at the main door to the hall.

"You know how I hate murmuring," Lord Eglamon said loudly, disgusted.

"Um," said a voice, one of the commanders, he thought, squinting at the hazy shapes of color on the far side of the room, too distant for anyone of his stature to have to be able to see.

"Forgive me, my lord," said the voice again.

Then Eglamon could see that other figures were entering the room. They weren't wearing the dark orange of House Brightwall's guards and servants. No, these figures were, despite his weak vision, quite easy to discern in their jarringly black tabards.

Eglamon gasped.

He quickly tossed the fork back onto the table before him and pulled himself to his feet.

He could see the orange shapes at the far end of the hall vanish out the door, replaced by a dozen new guards wearing black. He shuffled forward toward them, waiting.

The central dark shape appeared. As usual during such visits, Eglamon knew, he would be wearing a sturdy black cloak over a lavishly embroidered black robe sporting golden buckles.

"Your Majesty," he said quietly, coming close enough now to finally see that he was correct. He dropped slowly, wheezing, holding back pained groans as he went down onto one knee. The Swordfish stopped in front of him, staring down.

"To what do I owe the honor of your visit?" Eglamon said, struggling to keep his voice steady and looking up.

He heard someone approaching quietly from behind and knew it would be his chief servant. Bless the woman, she was brave, he thought. He heard her drop to her knees behind him, ready to assist with anything they asked of her.

"There have been problems in your holding," said the Swordfish, his voice, usually carefully warm, was flat and even. "I have received reports of interference with the work of my agents within your city."

Eglamon blinked. This was not good...rather desperately not good.

He bowed lower, looking at the floor. "Forgive me, Your Majesty, I had no knowledge of this. I will double patrols around all your underhalls immediately."

His knee was screaming, an agonizing song with which his lower back was beginning to harmonize. He gritted his teeth and tried to ignore them.

And then his servant shoved something that felt like a parchment against his hand where it trembled on the floor.

He snatched up the parchment and brought it close before his eyes.

Of course. She had mentioned it earlier that afternoon. He hadn't been in the mood and had waved her off when she brought it up...twice in fact. But he blessed her persistence now.

It was the information the Swordfish had been nagging him to get. His agents had delivered it this morning, he now remembered her saying.

She might have saved him.

"Your Majesty," he said, trying not to whimper. "I am pleased to report that we were able to track down the information you requested," he said, scanning quickly over what was written there.

He looked up at the Swordfish. "May I...may I call for the finest wine for you, Your Majesty, and relay the tale?"

He clung to hope. His knee cried out.

The Swordfish considered him a moment, then allowed a small smile and swept past, his black cloak dragging against Eglamon, who tried not to collapse over onto his ass in relief.

A few moments later, he was more comfortably seated and holding a goblet, hiding a relieved sigh as the Swordfish nodded approval of the wine and gestured for him to proceed, his face expressionless.

"My guards determined, Your Majesty, that the ship *Horizon* was originally commissioned by someone named…" He bent and peered at the parchment again. "Ah yes. It was a man named Brammus. From what my men have been able to find, he started off as a small-time swindler, but came into a minor fortune with some lucky timing on a few trade deals, though its likely there was some sort of…"

Eglamon froze, suddenly unsure, his mind reeling. "It's likely there was an…external intervention of some kind that resulted in that arrangement turning out so profitably for him. We're not certain of that part."

He'd almost spoken the word "criminal" to the Swordfish's face.

Eglamon swallowed hard and went quickly on.

"But we do know that this Brammus turned most of the proceeds into the custom order he placed at a shipyard in Empress Isle. Apparently he styled himself something of a dragon hunter, or fancied becoming one, at least. Though from what we can tell, he never made it to the mainland to try to hunt dragons. We know when he departed from Empress Isle with the vessel, and were able to track him to Cask where he apparently took on additional crew, but then we lost the trail after that."

"I know what happened from there," the Swordfish said, an impatient note in his voice, though he was nodding slowly. "I take it your agents are also unaware of the vessel's current whereabouts."

"I'm afraid so, Your Majesty," Eglamon said, trying to sound as sad as possible about this lamentable failing. "The ship docked in Vigil's harbor fairly regularly between journeys up until a few months ago. Since then, no one has spotted her in the harbor, though the Lady Lyrrek has been sighted at times in the city, and we have no reason to think the vessel was lost or something like that."

Daring, he risked a small chuckle. "My people have commented on their surprise at the number of dragon-carved ships there actually *are* out there, sailing around the Lastlands. It's been a popular motif the last several years, apparently."

He saw what looked like a trace of annoyance in the Swordfish's black eyes and rushed on, trying not to stumble over his words.

"But I will double our watches for the ship *Horizon* as well, Your Majesty. We will find her sooner or later, I am confident. The Lastlands isn't that big."

The Swordfish just stared at him and didn't respond. Eglamon swallowed, and lifted his wine to his lips, deciding that he should probably only pretend to sip until he knew he'd survived this encounter.

Finally, the Swordfish nodded and downed his wine. He set the goblet down and stood, stepping closer, looming above Eglamon where he sat.

"Notify me as soon as you learn anything," The Swordfish said, and then he was gone in a swirl of black robes.

Lord Eglamon watched him head for the door and sighed, very, very careful to make sure that sigh made no sound, and made himself a mental note to buy his chief servant a new house or…well, maybe give her an extra day off, at least.

He stared at the dark, blurry figures fading back out the hall door. He shook his head the tiniest amount and finally allowed himself a full, deflating sigh.

He had lost count of the number of times he'd cursed himself for the lapses that had landed him in this mess. There were a lot of them. Nonetheless, he added one more to the tally.

There was nothing he could do about it really, except hope for the best, and try to pretend this was all a situation he might still profit from. But by now he had come to doubt that he would ever gain what he really sought. And the relationship had persisted much longer than he'd expected it would already. The things he had seen, the risks he was taking…the things he'd been forced to do…all of it terrified him.

Pemana leaned back against the stone wall behind her, stretching her legs out, then shifted the small plank back on her lap and bent to the parchment once again. She looked up at *Horizon*, where the beautiful ship was docked at the pier before her, then back down at the parchment, where she swept several more lines into the drawing there, judging her rendering of the vessel.

She'd captured everything pretty well, she decided. Most of what she loved to draw tended toward buildings and castles. This side-on angle of the flagship of the Wizards' Guild in port had been a good challenge.

Or, at least, it had been a decent distraction.

She could hear the bustling noise of the small but lively feast celebrating *Horizon's* return from a successful expedition that was still well underway in the common space of the guild hall behind her. The music had finally stopped, but there was probably still plenty of eating and drinking to be done. It wasn't even fully night yet, sunset still working on darkening the sky past deep blue.

Kayd came out the door next to her, breathing deeply of the clean evening air, then spun when he spotted her there out of the corner of his eye.

"Oh!" he said, surprised, and stepped back. "You startled me."

"Unintended," she said politely, not looking up from her drawing.

He nodded and seated himself on the stone pier, looking back up at her. He was in her view of the ship now, but she'd really mostly finished the drawing anyway. Now she was just doing tiny touch-ups that were more about not having to meet his gaze.

She was probably going to leave, she had decided. And she had a feeling somehow that he would see it in her eyes if she looked into his.

"We missed your concertina," he said. "Veytra said it wasn't the same."

"Ah," she said, managing a tone of regret. "Sorry, just wasn't in the right mood tonight, I guess."

He nodded slowly, looking vaguely up at the building behind her.

She should just tell him she was leaving, she decided. Just get it out of the way, like yanking off a bandage. It would be over and she could just deal with the bleeding.

But as she opened her mouth to speak, Aether burst out the door, chuckling about something and shaking his head.

"Oh!" he said, when he saw them there. "Evening." He tipped his mug up and had a sip, then walked over to sit next to Kayd. He shook out the fingers of his left hand, wincing. "I haven't been playing guitar enough recently," he said. "That hurt."

"Brought it on yourself," Kayd said, nodding. "I warned you about those calluses."

"Yeah, I've been working on other ones instead," he said, staring down at his palms, at the tough skin fast-moving ship's lines had built there over the last couple years.

He grinned, then looked over at Pemana. "What're you…" he started to say, then his eyes widened as he realized what she was drawing. "Oh!" he said. "Is it too soon to come look?"

"No," she said, tilting her head to examine the drawing from a different angle. "I think it's probably done."

He stood and stepped forward, gasping as he came up next to her.

"Pemana! This is amazing!" he exclaimed, taking the parchment as she handed it to him.

She shrugged. "You can have it if you want it."

He stared at her, eyes wide. "I…wow!" he said. "Are you sure? This is a beautiful drawing. You really captured her!"

"I have plenty of pictures of ships," she said, which was a lie. Somehow she'd never drawn *Champion*. Now, failing to get around to that one felt like an anchor behind her.

"We'll put it up in our cabin," Aether said, awed. "Thank you Pemana, this really is incredible."

Better that than buried in a trunk in my chambers, she thought, but decided not to say it. Instead, she just nodded, standing and brushing off her trousers, ready to go find somewhere new to hide. She forced a small, rather unconvincing grin, and turned away to slip back into the busy guild hall.

Aether held out a hand to Veytra, who placed the small object in it.

"What is it?" he asked, looking down at his palm and examining it in the bright lights of Veytra's laboratory.

It was a small amulet, three rounded stones bound together in hammered copper, on a matching copper chain that fell loose and dangled from his hand as he admired it.

"Pretty, whatever it is," he said. "But I can feel…" He trailed off, peering at the amulet with his magical senses.

He snapped his gaze up to Veytra's after a moment.

"What is this thing?" he asked, eyes wide in amazement. "The magic is really interesting. It looks like…" he paused, looking over his shoulder to make sure they were still alone in her laboratory. "It feels kind of adjacent to the mind control spell," he said quietly. "But not exactly."

She nodded, gesturing to him to put it on, and pulled another one she was wearing out from under her tunic. "Go stand against the far wall," she said, and he complied while she stepped back to the wall opposite, behind her, and leaned against the counter there.

"Okay, you can hear me," she said. It was a statement, not a question, and the room was only about seven paces across. Then she clutched the amulet in her hand and stared at him. Her lips didn't move.

But suddenly her voice was in his head!

"But now you can probably hear me better," she said, her voice strangely situated, as if it had come from within his own skull.

"Woah," he breathed.

"I'm pretty proud of this one," she said, still in his mind, her lips only grinning.

He gripped the amulet around his own neck and reached for her mind. It made sense, once he tried it, the enchanted stones and their layered spells magically generating a linkage between his mind and Veytra's. "Wow, Veytra," he said back into her mind. "This is something else."

It was certainly strange, directing his thoughts straight into hers, but somehow it also felt…unsettlingly familiar? He wasn't sure how to put it or what that might mean.

"How far does it work?" he asked aloud, pulling the amulet off over his head and walking across the room to her.

"I don't know," she said, grinning. "Kayd and I tried them across town this morning, but that's as far as we've gone."

Aether grinned back. "Guess I'd better get to planning that next expedition then. We have to find out if they'll reach to the mainland." He looked down at the device, thoughtful. "Who do I see about ordering a hundred of these?"

"Yourself," she said with a chuckle. "You're *definitely* helping. These two were a lot of work."

He laughed and clapped her on the shoulder, shaking his head and smiling widely at her cleverness. He handed her back the amulet and turned to go.

"But Aether," Veytra said, her voice suddenly serious. "I've already been thinking about these. We uh…" she looked at the open door. "We should probably try to be careful who we talk to about them. Think about what the Council would do to get their hands on a capability like this."

He paused at her sober tone, then met her eyes and nodded. "You're right, of course. Just like all the rest of the magic."

She stared back, nodding. "Sooner or later, they're going to find out. And they're going to want to take it. All of it."

"I know Veytra," he said gravely. "I'm working on it." Then he grinned at her again. "Don't worry. When it's time, I'm confident we'll be ready for them."

Chapter Four
Empty Spaces

D eldrum held his bronze spear rigidly at his side, and tried hard to keep in step with the other three guards that were working as the Swordfish's personal escort that day.

He'd been surprised to be selected. He hadn't worked in the palace guard that long, and the Swordfish's personal escorts were usually handpicked from some of the more longstanding and loyal. But someone had weaseled out of work that day, and Deldrum found himself appointed to take one of the back positions.

And now he was walking behind the expensive black cloak that ran this place. He watched the Swordfish ahead of them, sliding through the corridors of his unfathomably costly palace, and wondered.

He wasn't sure what he thought about the Swordfish. He had heard the whispered stories of him for the first time years ago. Deldrum prided himself on his long experience, surviving the streets of Freehome. He'd only seen a few decades of life, but given what he'd been through, that counted as damn near wizened. The Swordfish's name was known on those streets, spoken of even by urchins, who scared one another with ridiculous tales of the man some of them called a pirate king.

He would never tell a soul, but…he'd been one of those kids once. The Swordfish's name had been out there for a long time. Deldrum had climbed far enough up amongst the real thieves to have learned that the Swordfish was, in fact, every bit as real as they were. If you learned too much about that without earning the right to know, it could cost you everything. But Deldrum had earned the right to know.

He'd been approached. That was how it worked, and no other way.

And now he was following the very real Swordfish through his own palace, and he'd be damned if the man wasn't an actual pirate king.

Seeing that throne for the first time had been…a revealing moment. There was a saying among the foolish that "there are no thrones in the Lastlands." But the fools were completely wrong about that.

There was admiration of the Swordfish among the petty thieves that Deldrum had known in his early days, of course. And among those more elite thieves he'd come to know, the ones he'd stumbled into impressing, and who had opened this door for him, the Swordfish was almost a revered figure.

But here, among those most intimately familiar, those who lived and worked most closely with the Swordfish himself, there was something else. It had taken Deldrum a while to see it, but now, he realized, it was everywhere he looked. Most of the people that worked in the palace, as guards or servants, were *frightened* of their pirate king.

He didn't understand it. What few tiny whispers he'd been able to coax out of people seemed like ridiculous lies, more akin, indeed, to alley urchin fantasies than the sort of thing you'd expect from the hardened men and women who had earned the right to be here. One older guard had whispered something to him about "the corpses" and underground thunder. Deldrum had listened politely enough, but privately decided that the man must have had a few of his mooring lines come loose.

It was stupid, of course. The Swordfish was an astonishingly gifted intimidator, obviously. They could all see that. It had made the man vastly wealthy.

But they were in on the racket. So what were they *actually* afraid of?

Deldrum watched the black-cloaked figure ahead, and turned his thoughts to the sword and dagger, wondering if there was some advantage to be obtained from all this lingering fear and superstition that might benefit his plan to depart this place with both weapons firmly in *his* possession.

Perhaps he should be worried about successfully stealing them? He had certainly wondered about that at first. Either way, it had been some time now since the Swordfish was gifted the weapons, and Deldrum had never seen them again.

He knew if…that is to say, *when* the weapons were his, *he* would wear them, and never let them out of his sight. He didn't understand why the Swordfish didn't do the same.

But he had heard mention of a private armory a time or two, something that sounded like it might be a separate location from the main guards' armory. He suspected that's where they would be found, if he could locate it.

They reached a staircase cutting below them into the deeper part of the palace, and Deldrum had to pay attention to stay in step and not fall as they marched down. It was several levels before they reached the bottom, the deepest part of the palace, not far above the level of the sea.

He did know a bit about what went on down here. It was one of the guards' main security concerns, so a lot of their operations circled around this deep part of the palace. He could hear the metallic tapping of heavy copper hammers pounding bronze chisels into stone, construction still under-way as workers struggled to cut the palace out from within the island's rock. This deepest level had the capacity to be the widest, of course, and the palace sprawled across the island down here.

From what Deldrum had heard, they had been at this ridiculous act of stonecutting for a decade, and might be going for a decade more.

Distant whip cracks occasionally sounded as flourishes above the rhythmic tapping.

The Swordfish slowed in the middle of the long corridor, though Deldrum could see no reason why they would stop at this particular spot. But then, in the light of the candle lantern carried by the servant, he saw that the dust of construction was beginning to be apparent on the walls and floor, and he realized, somewhat scornfully, that the Swordfish must be afraid of getting dust on his fancy black robes and boots.

He risked a tiny roll of his eyes.

Torchlight appeared down the corridor, approaching them. Two black-tabarded guards, each carrying a torch and a spear, accompanied a sweaty, red-faced man who looked as nervous as anyone Deldrum had encountered since he'd arrived in this generally nervous place.

"Your Majesty," the man said, breathless, bowing. "Progress proceeds well."

Deldrum realized who he was. The tale was a source of quiet amusement among some of the more brazen guards. This was the man overseeing the construction of the palace, an actual accredited master of the Builders' Guild that the Swordfish had found at one point, probably when Deldrum was still an urchin himself. The Swordfish had recognized in the man a weakness for drink and gambling, and had used those levers over a number of years to firmly lock down the man's services for himself. For years now, he had been overseeing work on this vast project, among others.

But not long before Deldrum had arrived at the palace, the master builder had turned up as a stowaway aboard a departing supply ship. The furious (and, presumably, fearful) captain had turned around and handed him back over to the Swordfish's guards.

After a couple weeks of imprisonment and whippings, the master builder had been returned to his work. The Swordfish had thanked him for his long service by appointing him a permanent honor guard, one that would never leave his side.

Deldrum was thankful he'd not caught that duty yet, at least. He'd heard the Swordfish had also informed the master builder that if he ever tried anything like that again, he would join the rest of his workers in chains. For Deldrum's part, he didn't understand why the Swordfish hadn't just proceeded to that step directly.

He viewed it as a weakness, a laxity. It gave him a certain amount of hope, that this place might not be as secure as it appeared.

The Swordfish and the builder droned on in some boring conversation about the logistics of carving out storage chamber six, and why it wasn't proceeding as quickly as the now profusely sweating builder had apparently promised. Deldrum let his thoughts wander, staring at the black-robed figure, and pondering some logistical matters of his own, such as just where in this sprawling subterranean fortress that damned private armory might be hiding.

Pemana shuffled along the graveled road that led through the small commercial neighborhood north of Vigil's harbor. None of the food she'd found in the hall's kitchen that evening had seemed tempting, at least not without a lot of work to cook something, so she'd slipped out to the Lights Out Inn, near the harbor, for some dinner. The inn's kitchen had been serving a decent fish stew that night. She was full and, by recent standards at least, even a bit contented.

The old warehouse that was their guild hall came into view as she rounded the corner. There weren't any lights visible from outside, though mostly this was because they had carefully blocked up any windows that might reveal to their neighbors the unnatural bright white of the magical lighting they used. Still, the place looked asleep, or even abandoned, and she sighed, already bored before she even made it home. She supposed she could continue working over some of the new information she'd gotten, but honestly, it felt like a bit of a dead end at the moment. It wasn't that late, and hadn't been dark that long. But maybe she should just call it a day anyway.

Motion drew her eye, something on the water out past the building, near the pier where *Horizon* was moored. She craned around to look, and saw a ten-pacer sailboat drifting slowly up to the docks, with three figures aboard preparing the boat for mooring.

"Amrelyn!" she called, recognizing her fellow master.

All three greeted her.

"Jyhnda, Neres," she replied politely, nodding and smiling at Amrelyn's apprentices. She jogged over to the dock and caught the line Neres tossed her, pulling the boat the rest of the way to bump against the wood. She handed him the line back once he jumped to the dock, and he and Jyhnda bent to finish tying up.

Amrelyn ducked below into the sailboat's cabin for a moment, then reappeared, slinging a haversack over her shoulder and stepping onto the dock to greet her with a grin and an informal salute.

"I'm glad you're here, Pemana," she said. "I think we have some information you might be interested in."

"Oh?" Pemana said.

"Orenna will want to get all this down," she said, starting up toward the hall. She turned back to the apprentices. "Once the sail's stowed, you two feel free to get set up in chambers and find yourselves something to eat."

"Thank you master," they both intoned, then chuckled with each other over the unintended unison.

Pemana grinned with them and studiously ignored the hint of guilt that she hadn't made everyone a big pot of soup that night. She hadn't chipped in to cook yet since she'd been back.

"I won't spoil it," Amrelyn continued as she and Pemana started for the hall, "but I think we might have a pretty solid lead for you."

Glad for the distraction, Pemana nodded and gestured for Amrelyn to precede her.

Before long, she had gathered up her notes and returned to the lounge area of the common room, where Orenna sat with Amrelyn, finishing up her list of their resupply needs while Amrelyn devoured a small tray of cheese and smoked fish with a tasty-looking, oily sauce.

Pemana smiled and nodded to Orenna and took her place, spreading out her notes and waiting patiently as in between bites, Amrelyn launched into the tale.

A line of investigation they'd been pursuing in New Brightwall had turned up a link to a small trader who, they had come to believe, might be an agent of the Swordfish. At the very least, they thought, he regularly did business with the Depths. And he wasn't really a trader at all, according to their contact. He was a smuggler.

Pemana blinked in surprised at this. There wasn't a lot of smuggling in the Lastlands, aside perhaps from an occasional rogue Hunters' Guild crew trying to hide from their Contributions or something like that.

"Smuggling?" she asked. "What does he smuggle?"

Amrelyn swallowed and met her eyes for a moment, her expression grim.

"People," she said.

"I'm sorry?"

"The contact said he smuggles people. He insisted he didn't really know what that meant, just that word was that a couple times, some of his cargo...got loose, and by the time other boats could catch up to try to help them, they had found...drowned people, bound at the wrists and ankles."

Pemana stared at her for a while, eyes wide, then bent to writing again.

"Neres is going to have to take a leave of absence for a while," Amrelyn said. "Some difficulties with his family's farm. He said he would turn in his bracers if he needed to. But he's been a good apprentice. I think he should keep them, and help where he can without drawing attention. Hopefully he can come back."

Pemana nodded.

"I'll check with Aether about that," Amrelyn continued, "but to more immediate concerns, this means that I have a good lead on someone that might be linked to the Swordfish in some way, and I'm down to just Jyhnda and myself." She met Pemana's eyes. "We could use a third, if we're going to try to bring this smuggler in."

"Oh, I'll come," Pemana said quickly. "We have to find out what's going on here, right away."

"My boat is a bit cramped for three," Amrelyn said, grinning. "But as long as you don't mind stuffing yourself in there with Jyhnda and I, we can leave first thing in the morning. We're pretty sure we know where he's bound, and we ought to be able to catch up to him at Eagle's End."

"I'll be ready," Pemana said grimly. She nodded down at Amrelyn's half-eaten food. "Thank you, Amrelyn. Enjoy your dinner and get some rest." She stood and nodded to Orenna, her thoughts already spinning toward what she'd need to pack, and how to get everything ready quickly enough to allow herself an opportunity to get some sleep before they departed, hopefully quite early in the morning.

This was what she'd been looking for. She had a course to follow now, and finally, a sense of momentum.

She wondered what she might be able to coax out of this smuggler. The Swordfish, she was now well aware, had sent many tentacles of his influence out into the world. She just had to get a firm grip on one of them, and pull.

Pemana swept into her small chamber and began gathering things up to throw in her haversack. She'd need all the documentation of the investigation with her, of course. She'd need her grandfather's sword, and she stood it up against the wall next to the bag.

She should probably take the first aid kit, one of the many Kayd had prepared for everyone traveling on various guild missions in the field.

The thought of Kayd brought her up cold for a moment. Would he be upset that she left without saying goodbye? Maybe she ought to go find him and tell him now, in case she didn't see him in the morning?

As soon as the thought passed through her mind, she sneered at herself.

What difference did it make if she left and he was sad about it? What nonsense. This was about getting her career back.

She looked down at her grandfather's sword.

This was about her honor.

She tossed her cloak over the first aid kit, disgusted, and continued packing.

Aether sipped his tea, staring through the beams of morning light that laced among the common hall's columns, and watched Lyrrek at the far end, where she stood talking to Kayd.

She gave Kayd a quick hug, then, and he waved across to Aether, before turning and heading out into the city.

Aether had been pretty sure just from Kayd's demeanor that something was wrong. It seemed he'd been correct.

Lyrrek came across and sighed as she sat down in a chair next to his. She picked up the tea he'd set there for her.

"Pemana?" he asked.

Lyrrek nodded. "She left with Amrelyn this morning. Didn't say goodbye."

Aether joined her in another sigh for his friends.

"Oh, that reminds me," Lyrrek went on, "I'm supposed to let you know that Neres had to put in for a leave of absence. Orenna and Amrelyn decided to let him take his apprentice bracers with him."

Aether thought about it for a moment, but then shrugged. "If they trust him, I'm fine with it."

She nodded again. "That's what I said too. But Amrelyn had a lead to follow up on, and needed a third, so Pemana went with her."

He hesitated, thinking about it, but again, had to admit that this was probably for the best. Pemana had taken over what had become a full-on investigation into the Swordfish, and this move put her right on the front lines of it. It made sense from a practical standpoint.

"Kayd seem upset?"

"I would say resigned. He started to say 'Every step forward is a victory,' but then stopped three words in and just shook his head."

"Well," Aether said, shaking his own head. "I imagine they'll work it out at some point."

"I don't know," Lyrrek said, suddenly quiet. She looked over her shoulder to make sure no one else was around. "I wonder sometimes, if something was going to move forward with them, wouldn't it have by now?"

Aether started to speak, but after a while, he just had to shrug and sigh again.

But then a thought brought a smile to his face.

"I don't know, my lady," he said. "Two years ago I might've asked myself some similar questions regarding the ridiculous impossibility of another long-simmering non-relationship I can think of. But…"

She smacked him on the arm, then leaned over to kiss him.

"So," she said after a moment. "Did you settle on a destination?"

"Peacelands, I do believe," he said, after sipping his tea.

She nodded slowly, thoughtful. "I was looking at the maps some more. This one might be tricky, right? Wasn't

Orenna saying that the Silver River isn't as big as the Red-water?"

"Yeah," Aether said, his lips pursed. "There's a good chance we're looking at doing some poling, or maybe even having to send the crew ashore with lines to drag us up against the current. Probably both."

"Oof," Lyrrek said. She looked at him. "So what we need is some wind magic or something."

He nodded immediately. "Probably so. I've tried a few things. So far at least, nothing has worked very well." He looked over at her. "I've been meaning to ask you and the others to look at it too."

She was thoughtfully quiet for a moment.

"I might have some ideas," she said eventually. "I'll talk to Veytra and Orenna about it later."

A few days later, the morning dawned cool and clear, and Aether was grateful. He settled the satchel containing his spellbook and other tools over his shoulder, and checked once more that his staff and the other potentially loose objects that lined their cabin were sufficiently secured. Then he grabbed his sword belt and buckled the Silversea sword around his waist.

He rotated around the cabin once more, and didn't spot anything else that wasn't ready. So he opened the door and exited out onto *Horizon's* deck.

He jogged over to the gangplank and across onto the guild hall's stone pier, to where Lyrrek was standing with

Kayd, watching the crew finish up their preparations for the ship's departure.

"Everyone reported in," Lyrrek said, looking up from the notes she was making in the ship's log. She handed him the book, her face a bit solemn. "I think we're ready."

"Well, Kayd," he said gently, "we'll miss you on the trip. But if anything comes up, contact us on one of the amulets." He pointed at his chest to the device below his tunic.

Kayd nodded and smiled, and did a decent impression of his usual affable self. "I'm sorry I won't be there for this one," he said cheerily. "But we're in pretty good shape on hunted products anyway."

Aether reached up to pat him on the shoulder. "It won't be a problem," he said. "If any of those rich noblemen wander in, make sure to show them the skull room."

Kayd chuckled.

"And don't worry, we'll be fine," Aether continued. "We'll just take this expedition a bit easier." He smiled and winked at Lyrrek. "Especially if we manage to get the new windstones tuned in enough that they can deliver on their promise. It'll be interesting to see how much help they are once we hit the Silver River."

"Well, as you said, Master Aether," Kayd said, grinning a bit sadly at them. "If you run into any problems..." He pointed at Aether's sternum. Aether nodded, and Kayd saluted them, then turned and strode back into the guild hall.

Lyrrek met Aether's eyes for a long moment, then turned and headed for the ship, signaling to Beras, who started calling out commands to *Horizon's* crew.

Chapter Five

Buried

A ether resisted the urge to shout in celebration, gripping *Horizon's* wheel as she surged forward. The Silver River's current leapt against the ship's carved bow, splashing water up as it tried to drag them along with it down toward the sea. But they had finally figured out how to summon and focus the wind with a series of enchanted stones embedded throughout the aft sections of the ship. And now, when Aether focused on them, he could summon a wind of great strength, and point it into the sails, exactly where he needed it for the best speed.

Horizon had raced across to the mainland, tacking instantly rendered a relic of the past. They reached the Silver Sea in only two and a half days, a personal best for everyone on board. Once they'd set course and sails, nothing really needed much further adjustment. Aether only had to keep the wind and ship aligned on the headings that produced the best speed along their course, and then just check the compass occasionally, maybe fine tune things a bit here and there. He didn't have to do much. The crew had to do even less, and they enjoyed the reprieve and got caught up on some maintenance, or just played dice and sang songs.

The Silver Sea had flown beneath them as well, and now they were cruising at a decent pace up the sinuous stretches of the Silver River, cautiously maneuvering through its twists and bends with their newfound magical control of the very wind itself.

Aether leaned toward Beras where he stood nearby on the quarterdeck, watching out over the crew and the ship.

"You sure you don't want to give it a go?" he asked.

Beras shook his head, eyes wide. "No way…uh, Captain," he said. He rubbed his wrists, where he no longer wore his apprentice bracers. Aether had officially promoted him to first mate before they'd departed. And with that promotion had come a second promotion…to the rank of Adept in the Wizards' Guild.

Aether could feel him occasionally pulsing the dragon-skin spell on and off, still frequently practicing his first real magic.

"I may be finally learning spells," Beras went on, "but if you'll forgive me sir, I'm not taking responsibility for steering the ship up a river with magic wind I don't understand until I've had a lot more practice at both magic and ship steering."

Aether laughed. "Fair enough. It is pretty fun though, I'll make sure you get the helm as much as you want on the way back."

"Once we get back down into the Silver Sea, we can talk about it," he chuckled.

Aether grinned and looked up at the shadows of the passing trees on the riverbanks, judging the light. "Looks like evening's not far off," he said. "We might as well start watching for a good place to stop for the night."

Beras nodded. "As you say, Captain."

A breeze brought a smell of stabled goats to Pemana, where she leaned against a stone wall next to the entrance of an alley near the harbor in Eagle's End. She wrinkled her nose at the smell and craned her neck, continuing to stare down the block.

If all went to plan, Amrelyn might be emerging from another intersection down that way. But so far, nothing.

She heard footsteps coming down the alley behind her, and deliberately made herself as nonchalant as she could, trying to feign a bored look.

But the light footsteps were Jyhnda's.

"Nothing?" Pemana whispered to her, as the younger woman emerged onto the street next to her and looked around.

"That narrows it down then," Jyhnda said quietly. She had lived in Eagle's End for most of her life, and she knew this part of the city well. She started off quickly toward another alley. Pemana followed her.

Jyhnda was right, too. As they stepped out of that alley onto another street, this one next to a market, Pemana saw the smuggler a block away.

He looked up, right as she realized that she was looking at him, and their eyes met.

She cursed to herself. This was the second time they'd seen him. Had he spotted them back at the harbor, closely observing his boat? She'd tried to look uninteresting at the time, but if he had noticed her then...

His eyes locked onto hers, and widened.

He knew.

She cursed again, this time out loud.

The smuggler spun and bolted into the market. Pemana burst into a sprint after him.

But he had a full city block's head start. She could hear Jyhnda's boots pounding the fine gravel of the street behind her, struggling to keep up with Pemana's long legs. But Pemana only ran harder, dodging shocked market-goers and stalls, struggling to make sure he didn't duck aside somewhere without her seeing it.

And then he did cut left, sharply, and disappeared up another alley.

Though she didn't slow her breakneck pace, she celebrated. If they were a little bit lucky, Amrelyn might hear him coming.

She rounded the corner into the alley, breathing hard. He was still pretty far down ahead of her, though she was gaining on him. But suddenly, as he passed another street, a shape leapt out into him, colliding hard with his shoulder and spinning his headlong momentum down to crash into a tumble of empty crates and rough sacks.

Pemana's pace slowed as she caught up, the smuggler swearing profusely as he tried to disentangle himself from the pile into which he'd dived. Amrelyn tugged her clothing calmly back into place as she hovered back, ready to intercept him if he tried to make a break for it again.

Pemana stalked forward, breathing hard, and reached down to grab the smuggler by the jerkin.

He stabbed up at her with a long dagger that he hid next to him until the last second.

She managed to dodge his strike, not that it would have mattered. She certainly had wardstones in place, ready for anything he might do. But the Wizards' Guild had collectively agreed, as a general rule, to limit obvious use of their magical abilities where others could see, at least for now. So, even though his blade wasn't much danger to her, she still avoided his thrust and reached in to catch the hand holding the dagger, squeezing hard in the right places and twisting his wrist until he cursed again and let it go spinning away back into the trash.

Jyhnda came up next to her, and the two of them bent to grab the smuggler's loose jerkin and haul him up onto his feet.

"Put your hands behind your back," Pemana hissed at him, stepping back and drawing her sword. "You're coming with us. Try that again, and it will cost you." The viciousness in her voice surprised her, as it must have Jyhnda, whose eyes widened a bit.

But the smuggler, though he stared at her with loathing for a moment, did finally comply, an oily expression distorting his features.

"Well, certainly, my noble ladies, why didn't you say so?"

Pemana stared him down while Amrelyn bound his wrists. He stared back at her from beneath greasy hair which had been pulled into a semblance of a style, but which the violence of his fall and capture had disrupted into a mess that revealed his actual filthiness. His beard was equally dirty, and the smell of him was pretty revelatory too.

He had begun to openly leer at her, so she grabbed him by the jerkin and spun him around, pushing him forward to stumble ahead down the alley. "Move," she said. "You're going to answer some questions for us. Whether that ends with you going free or feeding a dragon depends on you."

He laughed scornfully as he stumbled ahead. Pemana met Jyhnda's eyes and winked as she continued pushing him. It wasn't actually an empty threat. They did possess the ability to feed him to a dragon if they really, really wanted to. Jyhnda's eyes were wide, but she grinned as the smuggler's laughter trailed off.

It took several more alleys for them to reach the small apartment Amrelyn had scrambled to find that morning. The fact that it had a door opening out into one of the harbor district's alleys had been a selling point. They waited while Amrelyn unlocked the door.

"Ah," he said. "Finally time for a little fun, then, girls?" he asked.

Pemana shoved him face-first into the wall, and a muffled, sputtering curse erupted from where his face met stone.

"Nothing about this is going to be fun, I assure you," she whispered into his ear. Then she shoved him through the door.

He stumbled forward, acting like he had tripped, but it was a ploy. He used his momentum to jerk his arms free from Pemana's grip. He started to spin, ready to leap back at her and slam her into the wall with his shoulder.

It was a good idea, she supposed, to at least try to fight one's captors. She certainly would have, in his place. But she also fully expected him to try it. As he spun on one foot and tried to lunge at her, she danced aside and kicked at the other foot, the one he was clumsily holding up while he twisted.

She kicked that foot hard in the heel, and that foot kicked forward and tangled violently into the foot supporting him. His momentum carried him around in his spin and he hung upright in space for an instant, eyes wide, then teetered over to slap onto the stone floor.

This time he didn't curse, just roared in pain, rolling away from the shoulder on which he'd landed. She hadn't heard anything snap when he fell, so she let him carry on for a second, then jerked him back up onto his feet. At last, he was more compliant, gasping and cursing, but letting them shove him deeper into the apartment's backmost room, where Pemana forced him into a chair and drew her sword again, pointing the long bronze blade at him. He stared daggers back at her, but held still and allowed Amrelyn and Jyhnda to bind him firmly to the chair, both hands and feet.

"Now, that was all very uncooperative," Pemana began coldly. She turned to Jyhnda and Amrelyn. "Thank you my friends. Why don't you leave me to speak to him alone for a bit."

Something about the tone of her voice caused Amrelyn to meet her eyes, and for just a second, Pemana thought her fellow master was staring at her. But then Amrelyn just nodded and gestured for Jyhnda to precede her and closed the door behind them, leaving Pemana alone with the bound smuggler.

There wasn't much light coming through the small storeroom's single window, but it was enough. She sat down in the other chair that Jyhnda had dragged back here earlier, and stared at the smuggler.

"Your cargo hold was empty when we went aboard," she said quietly. "Where did you take them?"

An expression of combined rage and glee crossed his face. The rage at them having boarded his boat was obvious. But the glee told her that he had made his delivery before they had managed to search. He refused to say anything and simply leered at her some more.

"Thank you," she said. "Why don't you tell me who it was you delivered them to?"

He did finally respond, but it was just with more swearing.

She nodded at his various physiologically impossible suggestions, ignoring them, thoughtful. An idea had occurred to her, the one method she could think of that was guaranteed to tell her what he knew, with no chance of him deceiving her.

It was against their rules. One of the very few things that Aether had openly asked them *not* to do, was to employ the draconic mind control magic they used to protect their expeditions from dragons, but on people instead.

They maintained their skills with the technique by practicing it on each other, true. It wasn't done in anger, not even when used on a dragon that was planning to eat them. Still, Pemana had to admit that even as practice, just trying to demonstrate to a *friend* how this magic functioned…using it on another person felt quite…strange.

But really, she told herself, the main issue with the mind control spell was the terrifying prospect it would be for everyone else, to learn that these wizards now living among them possessed the power to just take over peoples' minds and read their thoughts. Someone that learned of that capability might become frightened of them, and frightened groups of people can become dangerous very quickly.

That was the main concern, wasn't it? Hadn't Aether said so? And he was quite right, of course.

But she thought of a loophole. There was a way she could do it, something that would allow her to get the information she needed without the smuggler knowing she'd taken it.

It would require some skill. She readied herself and nodded, standing up.

She had to time this just right. As he stared up at her, the first hints of fear beginning to show in his eyes, she hauled back dramatically, and threw a punch right into the smuggler's shocked face.

She didn't actually hit him hard at all, having no need to actually harm him. But just as her fist struck him, she cast the mind control spell, wrapping his mind in hers and squelching it into blank unconsciousness. He wouldn't remember anything from this moment until she released him. And as far as he'd know, she'd only knocked him out.

She had never used the spell like this before, with the intent to hold the opponent and raid his mind. She had never even been the one forced to redirect the wrathful attentions of a dragon before. She'd only gone on a couple of their expeditions, actually.

She didn't know how difficult a dragon might be, but she did know that it was a strain to hold the smuggler's mind in her magical embrace, and the strange feeling of discomfort was far stronger than she expected. The magic felt…off, somehow…even *wrong*. But she gritted her teeth and ignored all these considerations. She didn't know how long she could maintain the spell, and she didn't know what she was looking for. She had to focus and she had to hurry.

It took her a moment to figure out how to do it, because this was not something Aether had instructed them in. But she did finally figure out how to think *as* the smuggler, to sift his memories as if she had lived them. And finally, the reality of what was going on…the answers she'd been seeking…a great many of them tumbled out onto the dark, detritus-strewn floor of the smuggler's mind for her to sort through.

He was, indeed, working with the Swordfish's network. In fact, he had been smuggling for them for some years, since well before they'd begun referring to themselves as the Depths. That had only started rather recently, and while he thought it a bit silly, he was too intimidated by the Swordfish's agents to ever let anyone know that.

In the beginning, everything they'd undertaken had been pretty routine criminality. He'd buy stolen goods from some of the Swordfish's pirates for quite cheap and then re-sell them, or perhaps he'd handle some more traditional smuggling deals, helping them bypass Contribution tracking, that sort of thing. But several years ago, they had presented him with a new opportunity.

He didn't know what the Swordfish was doing with the people he smuggled. He only knew that the prices he was getting for successful deliveries were better than anything he'd ever run in his life. The smuggler wasn't much of a brawler himself, and was a coward to boot, and probably wouldn't personally be able to drag more than a decrepit beachsleeper into the chains they used for transport. But he would readily take deliveries from some of the Swordfish's pirates in one part of the Lastlands and keep the prisoners locked in his hold until they reached their destination. His fifteen-pacer sailboat was long and fast, almost a small ship, and pretty good for evading the scrutiny of house navy patrols.

And here it was. Here was the piece of information she needed.

Once his hold was full, he would sail as quickly and discreetly as he could, and would meet with a particular contact. This contact was either a member of, or had infiltrated his way into, the Eagle's End City Guard. The contact would meet him with a small force of armed men at his boat, all dressed openly in the Guard's golden tabards. They would drag away the men and women in chains and leave him with a good-sized pouch of silver. It was as simple as that. He didn't know, or care, what happened to the prisoners after.

And, she realized finally, he didn't know the Swordfish. He'd never met him.

Oh, he had heard things. And…this struck her hard…he seemed *terrified* of him. The shock she felt as she stumbled over the strength of that fear almost broke her concentration and caused her to lose the spell.

He had heard a lot of dark, strange things about what it meant to sign up and be a part of the Depths these days. He had heard things about what the Swordfish did to people, and forced people to do to others. He believed a lot of it was nonsense. But he didn't know which things were which. And if only a fraction of it were true…

She kept control of herself and kept searching far and wide through his memories, but he just didn't really know much more that was useful to her. At last, beginning to feel her power drain away into exhaustion, she had to release him.

He coughed and jerked his head up from where it had dangled while she'd held him unconscious. "What the…" he wavered back and forth, blinking.

She stared down at him, drained, wondering what to do with him.

There was no point turning him over to the local Council Magistrate. The smuggler knew, and so now she did as well, that the Magistrate here was corrupt. In fact, he'd even become a bit friendly with the old man, after bribing his way out of custody a few times in the past. He'd just get a brandy out of it and sent on his way, only a tiny handful of silver poorer.

There was no point. Disgusted, she bent toward the sputtering man and drew her dagger. His eyes widened, but she only sliced through the ropes binding his ankles, then his wrists to the chair. He gasped, and began to rub his hands.

She walked past him and jerked the door open. "Get out," she said quietly.

Amrelyn and Jyhnda looked up. They both got quickly to their feet as the smuggler stood up into the doorway behind her.

She stepped aside, pointing out toward the apartment's front door with the dagger she still held in her hand.

"He's useless," she sighed to the others. She stared at him as he made his way suspiciously past her, eyeing the blade. He glanced swiftly between Jyhnda and Amrelyn, then lowered his head and walked quickly to the entrance, vanishing with one last furious glance back.

Amrelyn and Jyhnda both stared at her. "I…" Amrelyn began. "Well, I guess I'm sorry we wasted your time on a worthless lead."

Pemana winced. "I'm sorry, I should clarify that he wasn't completely worthless," she said hastily. "I did get a few things out of him. I know that Eagle's End is important in all of this, for one." Then she looked at the door the smuggler had left standing open behind him. "Uh…" she looked at Amrelyn again, and silently cursed herself. "Sorry, though. I guess…well, we *should* probably set up a safehouse here in Eagle's End, now, but…this one's kind of…compromised. So I'll…I'll help you find a new one to use before you sail me back to Vigil."

Amrelyn nodded slowly. Pemana looked away, unable to meet her eyes.

This had not gone well. She couldn't say why she'd let the man go. She probably shouldn't have done so. But what could she have even done with him? *Actually* sail him to the mainland and feed him to a dragon?

Even if she didn't know what to do about it, she did at least have some information to go on now. The Swordfish was definitely up to a frightening amount. Now that she'd seen what the smuggler knew about the Swordfish's network, she was more sure than ever that the Swordfish was responsible for all that had happened to her. It's just that the smuggler himself was quite far removed from all of it. He didn't know that much about the Depths, except that there was a lot more to know than he was privy to. But he definitely didn't know anything about the Swordfish himself, or where to find him.

She sighed and followed Amrelyn and Jyhnda out the door of the now-useless apartment, quietly pretending she hadn't seen them trading bemused looks.

Aether stood next to Lyrrek and Beras as the rest of the crew fanned out a bit, checking the nearby forest for anything interesting looking. So far Peacelands hadn't proved that fruitful, at least in terms of what they'd seen among the ruins.

But the wizards among them were, nonetheless, all completely fascinated.

"I think we can get up this way," Lyrrek said, pointing up the thickly treed hillside ahead of them. The city of Peacelands had been in a region of hills, through which the Silver River wound. They had climbed up from the river and through a deep forest, where tumbled stone from ruins occasionally interrupted the shallow slopes.

"Even I feel it," Beras said, awe in his voice.

Aether stared into the woods around them, nodding. "We're getting closer," he said.

"Whatever it is, I think it's not too much further ahead," Lyrrek agreed. She pointed up the hill. "Over that rise, maybe."

Aether turned back to the others. "This way," he called, beckoning, and they climbed on.

As they topped the rise, he knew they had found it, and his jaw dropped.

There was a clearing on the other side of the hill, something of a tiny open valley. There were two sets of rocky outcroppings here, running in lines roughly parallel to one another, pointing across at each other to create a clear space in between swathes of heavily treed forest.

But the first thing Aether saw as he stepped over the rocks and out into the clearing were the strange boulders jutting up out of the line of outcroppings across from them. There were five of them, huge rocks that formed an interesting arrangement, tumbling down the low hill opposite.

But the rocks were very strange-looking, almost unnatural. And as Aether stared at them, he realized what he was seeing.

"Dragons have tried to destroy these rocks," he breathed. "What on Origin?" The boulders were absolutely *covered* with a crisscrossing pattern of deep, furious-looking claw marks.

But it was the bizarre gleam of the boulders in their magical senses that had drawn the wizards' attention. They shone, radiating magic with such intensity that they had felt it itching at the corner of their minds before they'd even docked *Horizon*.

"What is this?" Beras asked.

"I have no idea," Aether replied. He focused his magical senses on the boulders again, trying to understand what he was looking at. "But it looks like the dragons have been as confused as we are." He bent closer, examining the enormous damage dragon claws had wrought on the rocks. "Or maybe 'furious' is the word I'm looking for."

Lyrrek chuckled, nodding, and walked up to touch the mangled surface of the rocks. "Whatever this is, it's definitely good at attracting attention."

"You know," Aether said suddenly "I wonder…"

He stepped closer, placing his own hand on the rock. "I think that this might be magic that someone designed to do *exactly* that. I think it's a spell that's designed to attract attention."

"What?" Lyrrek exclaimed, eyes wide. "A spell designed by whom exactly?"

Aether shook his head. "No idea. Looks like the dragons have been puzzling through it themselves, and for a long time." He shrugged. "But if I figured out how a human could use dragon magic, maybe someone else did too at some point, I don't know." He stepped back, taking in the whole of the strange magical phenomenon. "It's not all the rocks along this edge, just these five big ones. It's strange, they kind of…"

He looked along the line of them. They formed some-thing of an arrowhead shape. If it had been intended as an arrow, pointing at something…he turned his head, looking across. If someone *had* made an arrow to indicate this direc-tion, then it seemed to point at the small corner in between rocky outcroppings on the opposite side. He jogged over that way.

The small open space formed a rather flat semicircle of ground up against the rocks of that edge of the low ridge, sheltered a bit from the surroundings by the rocky walls coming down on either side. Something about the little spot seemed kind of charming. It was just the sort of place he would select for a campfire, should he have been traveling through here, just him and Lyrrek.

Assuming that the boulders behind him weren't just some strange, natural magical phenomenon, or perhaps a bit of dragon mating behavior or something, then they did seem to point here. Was there anything here for them to be pointing at? Aether didn't see anything obvious. He intently studied the area with his magical senses, and didn't notice anything that way, either, rather disappointingly.

Or…wait…did he? He focused again, harder, then even harder still.

There *was* something there.

"Lyrrek, can you sense this?" he said pointing down at the ground before him. "It's like there's something really, really subtle here."

Lyrrek bent down, touching the dusty ground and con-centrating hard. "I think I see what you mean." She stood back up. "Vala!" she called to one of the sailors. "Can we borrow your spear?"

Before long, Aether had scraped a layer of stony dust clear from over the top of what did, indeed, look like something buried there; a wooden box perhaps, from the sound the butt of Vala's spear had made against it. The whole time he'd worked on it, Lyrrek had been sitting cross-legged next to the spot, focused hard upon it.

Aether leaned back, breathing a bit, and tossed Vala her spear back with a grateful grin. "What do you think?" he asked, turning to face down to where Lyrrek sat.

She opened her eyes and looked up at him, then stared across at the boulders. "Well, it's more a hunch than anything, I guess, but I think that maybe we're looking at two different forms of the same magic."

"Ahh," he said, nodding. "I see what you mean. Like the boulders are enchanted with magic that's acting to draw attention, while this thing is hiding under magic that's working to push that attention away."

She nodded. "Wild. What is this, do you think?"

Aether stared down at the spot he'd begun to uncover. "Well, there's only one way I can think of to find out." He sat down next to her and the opening he'd made in the ground. "Do you mind keeping watch while I study this? If I haven't cracked it after a bit, we'll swap."

"It's all yours, master," she said, grinning at him. She closed her eyes and began turning her head, watching, he knew, for dragons.

He smiled fondly at her, then closed his own eyes and bent again to the hole in front of him.

Something…was definitely buried here. He was fairly certain she was correct, and it was encased in a concealment spell. And yes, it seemed to be a variation of the similar magic that had lit the hillside behind them so clearly to overflying dragons.

But this magic was hiding something else that was also magical. It took all his concentration to get any sense of the presence of it, so he wasn't surprised to find that the dragons had ignored it, or even failed to notice it, parked here where it was, near the very distracting boulders behind him.

He pulled his spellbook out of the satchel at his side, and flipped to some blank pages. He dug out a pencil and quickly began sketching out some ideas and notes about the magic he was finding. He closed his eyes again, studying the spell carefully. Then he reached out and cautiously withdrew the magic of the concealment spell.

It worked.

"Woah," Lyrrek said, jerking her head to face down to the ground, her eyes still closed. "What is *that?*"

Aether grinned. "It's another protection spell, I think, that was hiding under the concealment one." He studied it closely. "This one, though…it's not like anything I've ever seen." He tapped the pencil on the spellbook thoughtfully, then jotted down a few more notes. "Is it…what do you think, does that feel like maybe it's got something to do with time? What am I seeing here?"

"Oh!" Lyrrek said. "Like it's protecting against the passage of time or something?"

"Ah," he exclaimed, breathless. "That would make sense." He jotted down a few more things, nodding. Then he read over everything he'd written, and concentrating, he cleared the...preservation spell as well.

Just to make sure he'd gotten the spell effects down correctly, he quickly replaced them, first the preservation spell, then the concealment one. "Fascinating," Lyrrek said, watching him work. He cleared the spells again, and looked up to meet her eyes.

"Well," he said, grinning. "Should we see what was so important?"

She nodded emphatically, then went back to scanning around them for threats.

He bent and began digging out the edges of the square shape. He slowly worked it out of the hole in the ground, and it proved to be a rather shallow, flat wooden box.

The outside of the box was in quite good condition. The wood didn't seem to have suffered any water damage during its time in the ground, which was amazing. "That preservation spell is really something," he said thoughtfully, inspecting the wood. Finally, he bent, looking around the edge of the box for clasps or hinges, and didn't see any. He brushed away some more dirt and spied a seam around the middle of the box, though, so he grabbed the upper half and lifted the whole top of it off.

Inside, there was a single piece of paper. Aether's mouth fell open in astonishment.

"It's paper," he breathed.

The smell of it was unfamiliar and intriguing. It's not that paper didn't exist at all in the Lastlands, but it was so much more expensive than parchment that Aether had never seen it before. Nonetheless, he realized what it must be immediately.

And it was beautiful, the color of fresh cream, smooth and crisp, and covered with an artful black script. In awe, he reached in and touched the page. And then he gasped. "I smell the ink!" he said. "Someone made charcoal ink to write this. I can smell it like they made it half an hour ago."

"That preservation spell is really something," Lyrrek repeated, chuckling.

He carefully lifted the paper, staring down at it, and then his mouth fell open again. "Oh my," he said, breathlessly. "It's a letter."

"Well, read it!" Lyrrek said, not opening her eyes. The others gathered close, all of them fascinated by this strange find.

Aether cleared his throat. "Um, well, all right."

He held up the page and peered closely at it. The handwriting was stylishly different than anything he'd ever seen. But after a moment of inspecting it, he had a feeling for what was being said, and he began reading.

"My…beloved," he began, somewhat haltingly. "I hope…beyond hope that you find these words that I've left for you here. The world has gone mad, as I'm sure you are well aware by the time you find this."

"What?" Lyrrek whispered slowly, opening her eyes.

Aether read on.

"I'm sorry I wasn't able to wait for you to catch up to me, but an urgent summons arrived this morning by courier, and I have to travel north immediately to join the…"

Aether leaned closer, frowning at the words on the paper. "To join the Pantheon's efforts…" he paused again, blinking, then looked up and stared into Lyrrek's eyes as he spoke the rest.

"To join the Pantheon's efforts in dealing with this dragon calamity."

Lyrrek gasped.

"This has been here for two hundred years?"

He bent to the page again. "I have received no official explanation as to the nature of this outbreak of attacks, though in my heart, I can't help wondering about things that we have only discussed in the quiet hours before dawn. I must depart our home immediately, but given what's been going on, I feel I can't trust this letter to remain undisturbed until you arrive here. Forgive me for forcing you to solve my little puzzle, my darling. I do hope these words find you. If they do, I would encourage you to gather all your servants and as many guards as you can convince and to follow immediately. Travel light, and with spells at hand. I will make first for the Pantheon's underhall in Sunset City. If you catch up to me there, we might have time for a walk along the banks of the river for the sake of old memories. Remember, near the market? That one spring when we were both stationed there?

"Be safe, Kohlia. If you see one of the flying dragons, use great caution. They are powerful wizards. They will attack with mind-stealer magic, and you must beat them to it.

"I hope that I will see you in Sunset City. Favor of the Shining One upon you, my heart.

"Yours for all, Vereden."

Aether fell silent, and for a long few moments, there was no sound but the wind in the broadleaf trees, as all of them stared off in different directions at the horizon, blinking, trying to process everything they'd just learned.

Later that night, Aether and Lyrrek sat by one of the campfires, Beras off to one side practicing his new magical senses by taking an early watch.

Lyrrek peered down at the letter, laid in her lap to angle it toward the firelight, re-reading it for probably the twentieth time. Aether stared into the coals, an idea beginning to circle around the periphery of his mind. He couldn't help a small grin.

"That preservation spell *is* quite impressive," he said. Lyrrek looked up at him, and saw his expression. She tilted her head at him, interested. By now, in their acquaintance, she had a pretty good idea what that knowing grin might mean.

"I wonder how much the nobility would pay for fresh land-dragon steaks, fresh as the moment they were cut," he said.

Her eyes widened, so much that she looked a little unhinged for a second.

"Remind me to have Kayd and Veytra design some special barrels for us," he said.

She shook her head, amazed. "Oh, that's a good one."

He chuckled. "I hope so. We really need to figure out some way to sell some of this valuable stuff we're piling up."

She looked back down at the letter in her hand.

"So I guess our next expedition is finally headed for Sunset City."

He smiled, nodding as he stared into the fire, thoughtful. "And soon. There were *wizards* on Origin before the Great

Flight," he said, his voice sonorous and dramatic as he proclaimed the fact. "This changes our history."

She held the page up and read. "I have received no official explanation as to the nature of this outbreak of attacks, though in my heart, I can't help wondering about things that we have only discussed in the quiet hours before dawn." She looked at him. "What do you suppose that means?"

"I'm not sure, he said, shaking his head slowly. "Something he wasn't willing to put in writing even though he'd hidden it so only another wizard could find it. So something he wanted to hide from the rest of this…Pantheon, I guess?"

"Hmm," she said.

"It sounds like he had a theory about…how did he put it? 'The dragon calamity?'" He shook his head. "We have to get to Sunset City, see if they left any more clues we can find. Maybe there will even be another letter."

She nodded, then fell silent for a moment, looking down at the page in her hand. She gestured toward his satchel and handed it to him, then let out a long sigh.

"There will be another letter," she said quietly.

"What's that?" he asked, looking back up from the satchel's leather flap.

"Kohlia, the wizard's beloved," Lyrrek said. "She never made it home to find this letter. She never caught up to him." Her voice was small.

He looked at her. Her face, the greatest beauty he had ever witnessed in the world, was drawn and sad in the flickering firelight.

He pulled his camp chair closer to hers and put his arm around her. She sighed again and leaned over to rest her head on his shoulder.

He enjoyed the privilege of her touch, as he always did, as he always would, and gently patted her arm. Then, after a few moments, he took the chance to help Beras magically scan the dark, forested hillsides surrounding them for approaching dragons.

Chapter Six

SLEEP

Pemana sighed and rolled over in her bunk, staring into the darkness of her silent chamber.

She couldn't stop thinking about the memories. They were beginning to haunt her. And they weren't even her memories.

She kept seeing flashes of what she'd taken from the smuggler's mind. She kept thinking about everything he'd seen, about all he'd heard.

More than anything, she kept thinking about the overwhelming *thing* that, she now knew, lurked out there. It was deeply dug into the fabric of society across the Lastlands. Whoever the Swordfish was, he had built something ugly underneath them all that was draining them down into itself, devouring them from beneath.

So much of what she had encountered over the last three years, most of it spent hard at work specifically investigating the explosion of criminality around this very problem, now came into sharper focus. And all of it just made her realize how completely out of their...well...depth, they were.

She rolled her eyes in the darkness.

They were up against something monolithic. The massive increase in crime in the Lastlands over the past two decades finally made a certain amount of sense, at least. The Swordfish had an enormous head start, and had, she was afraid, very nearly built himself a small empire. What chance did they have to root out this deep of an infection?

She sighed again, disgusted, and rolled over for what was probably the hundredth time, her cloak twisted around her legs, trying to force herself to…she gritted her teeth…to go…back…to…sleep.

Lyrrek sniffed her cloak, frowning.

"Do I smell all right?" she asked Aether.

He looked up at her from where he was bent, buckling a boot with shiny bronze fittings that reflected the morning sunlight streaming in through their cabin's small windows, an amused look on his face.

"What?" he asked, chuckling. "I saw you bathe with my own eyes, I'm sure you smell lovely."

"No," she said, "my cloak. It doesn't smell too much like a campfire, does it?"

He stood and stretched, looking at her with that warmth in his eyes that always seemed to transfer from him to her when he smiled like that.

He came close and bent gently in to smell her shoulder. Her pulse quickened, but he stood back up quickly enough, and spoke, leaning back to look down at her.

"Only a tiny hint," he said quietly. "Personally, I rather like it."

She swatted playfully at him, then nodded sharply. "Right, well, we'd better get going. We don't want to let the morning drag on too long."

"As you wish, my lady," he said grandly, sweeping his own light cloak aside in a wide bow and gesturing for her to precede him out of their cabin and onto *Horizon's* deck.

Beras stood waiting for them, next to the two crates containing the small bits of broken statuary they had found in Peacelands. It wasn't much of a find, but Lyrrek still hoped they might at least sell Lady Fehndala on a return expedition to look for more or something. And they had a good quantity of barrels and bundles in the hold, all ready for bargaining, in case the noble Council Lady proved curious about the small samples of dragon jerky or leather they carried with them. She and Aether each picked up a crate and headed off the ship.

She hoped this trip to Eagle's End would pay off in silver, of course. But that's not all this one was about.

She and Aether were both well aware of Pemana's recent adventure with Amrelyn and Jyhnda, and how it had ended up here in Eagle's End. Orenna had relayed it in detail while they were still on the mainland, during a very successful test of Veytra's amulets and their range. It had been quite a story when Aether had repeated it to her after he broke the connection with Orenna.

Their other purpose in Eagle's End, then, was to get a firsthand look at the city's ruler, Lady Fehndala, for themselves. They were to find out if anything seemed…off.

It took them a while to reach Castle Goldenhall, which sat on a low hilltop a distance from the harbor. Whereas some cities in the Lastlands had created a showcase of their beauty along the roads that led from harbor to noble seat, Eagle's End had not charted that course. The harbor and the castle were where they were, and that was the end of it as far as the House of Goldenhall had always been concerned. Between the two lay a sprawl of warehouse districts, markets, shops, and alleys.

They wound their way through the confusing tangle of streets, the brown stone towers of the castle rising up higher above the rooftops as they drew near.

At last they reached the castle gate, and stood waiting, crates on the ground at their feet, while guards in golden tabards watched them carefully.

"This is taking an abnormally long time," Lyrrek whispered quietly to Aether after several minutes.

"Mm," he whispered back. "Keep your eyes open."

At last a pair of golden-robed servants appeared, a bit out of breath, and bowed, apologizing for the delay and bidding their noble guests to please follow them to see the Lady, as requested.

They entered the castle's dim corridors, which seemed rather sparsely populated. Usually, at this time of the late morning, a castle would be bustling with preparations for serving lunch, with everything else also at its height of activity at midday besides. Yet Castle Goldenhall's corridors were almost deserted.

She did occasionally spot a yellow-robed servant. One met her eyes, and seemed alarmed and confused, freezing where she stood at the far end of a corridor until they passed.

Lyrrek leaned close to Aether.

"Something is definitely wrong," she whispered.

He nodded, but they both knew without saying that the other would want to keep going.

For her part, she had a feeling that they'd learn plenty in this meeting, one way or another. She checked her ward-stones again.

After a few staircases and grand halls, they reached a sitting room with doors that opened, it seemed, into Lady Fehndala's reception chambers. Once again, they placed the crates on the floor at their feet and waited as the few apologetic servants present informed them that the Lady would see them very shortly.

Lyrrek tried not to be too obvious about it, but she carefully studied their surroundings.

Castle Goldenhall was in a bit better shape than Castle Silversea, her own family's seat. Though in fairness to her ancestral home, she now understood, at least, why Em-rek hadn't been paying for maintenance for the last couple decades. The Swordfish's blackmail had stolen a great deal from her family in that time.

But interestingly, there were signs of something out of sorts here, as well. She didn't see as much in the way of crumbling mortar that should have already been repaired. But rugs were growing threadbare. There were odd empty places that looked like they had once held a piece of furniture, but the object was now gone. Broken and not replaced? Sold off?

The chambers they'd seen were all lit by lamps, not candles. She'd even seen a few rushlights here and there in servants' areas.

This castle felt like what Castle Silversea had been fifteen years earlier, as decline was just beginning to show itself.

At last the door opened and another golden-robed servant emerged, bowing, and apologetically waved them through.

Lyrrek entered the wide chamber and blinked a few times, taking it all in.

The chamber was quite colorful, lots of golden fabric draped over things, lots of tapestries and rugs in golds, reds, and blues. The peripheries of the wide chamber were crowded with statues and paintings. It all had a somewhat jumbled feel.

The room gave one the distinct impression that Lady Fehndala had brought most of the castle's remaining wealth of decorations to this one room.

Lyrrek caught herself and hid a shake of her head, turning to bow with Aether toward the figure in the center of the chamber.

Lady Fehndala sat on a short couch there, a piece of furniture that itself sat upon a strange, wide, circular dais just two steps high. In fact, Lyrrek suddenly realized, this whole room looked like it had originally housed a large statue in its center, and now it simply housed Lady Fehndala in her leisure.

The Lady herself was awash in embroidered robes of golden yellow, her hair aggressively styled into fanciful curls that looked both artificial and thin with age.

She peered at them coldly from her pinched, narrow face, her head back so that she could look down her nose at them, though she wasn't actually higher, since she didn't rise from her couch.

"My lady Fehndala," Lyrrek began.

But Fehndala interrupted her.

"You are the Silversea girl, then."

Lyrrek blinked. "Uh…yes, my lady. I am Lady Lyrrek of House Silversea,"

"Yes, yes," Fehndala said, her voice overly ostentatious. She was staring at Aether. "And who is this then?"

"My name is Aether," he said bowing. "I am…"

"I did not address you or give you permission to speak, commoner," Fehndala spat.

Aether blinked and fell silent. Lyrrek frowned, carefully containing herself.

She saw him glance her way, and recognized the gleeful expression he was presently trying to hide. He knew exactly what Fehndala had just initiated, and was preparing himself to enjoy a show, grinning, his eyes getting wider.

He did know her well.

Lyrrek stepped forward, drawing Fehndala's attention, cocking her head slightly.

"Thank you for seeing us, my lady," Lyrrek said, her voice very calm. "Were you expecting us?"

Fehndala stared back at her for an instant. Then she sniffed. "My guards informed me that you had arrived in that lovely ship of yours, yes."

Lyrrek glanced at Aether and saw his grin vanish.

"What brings you to my city?" Fehndala demanded.

May as well proceed and see where this wind takes us, she thought. She bent and picked up her crate, setting it on a low table nearby, and opened it to withdraw a packet wrapped in sheepskin. She unfolded it and pulled out a small, broken stone statue, the upper torso of a woman in robes. She laid it on the table in front of Lady Fehndala and stepped back to the crate to begin unwrapping another that proved to be a small stone jar, cracked and missing a chunk from the rim, but obviously of good workmanship. She placed it next to the piece of statue.

Fehndala stared at her. "You deal in broken pieces of stonework then?" she sneered.

"My lady," Lyrrek said, very patiently, "these items were retrieved, at great risk, from the grounds of the lost city of Peacelands, in the hopes of…"

"You!" Fehndala raged, spittle flying. "You went onto the sacred ground of my House's lost homeland! How dare you!"

She still didn't rise, though she gesticulated violently with each word.

Lyrrek knew immediately that Fehndala's outrage was planned. She didn't know how she knew, but she had no doubt that Fehndala had been preparing the words of this outburst for some time.

Her eyes narrowing, Lyrrek let Fehndala rage for a moment, raving about the sanctity of her dead ancestors.

"You're all nothing but a pack of thieves!" Fehndala roared in conclusion.

Lyrrek grinned and strode forward quickly enough that the guards at the walls grabbed their spears. Not that it would have helped them. But she only stopped at the edge of the small table in front of Fehndala, staring down at her, and pointing at the statue.

"It's a strange thief that brings the item in question directly back to its owner, my lady," she said, her voice cold and loud. She gestured at the crates. "These things are yours. We only brought back a tiny amount to show you what awaited you there, the lost, buried history of *your* ancestors." Fehndala started to interrupt but Lyrrek did not let her. "Pity," she said, even louder, "that you've just lost access to those homelands forever. Unless you can deal with the dragons yourself, that is." She spun and stalked back to Aether, who was no longer hiding his enjoyment of the show.

She turned to stare back at Fehndala one last time. "I guess we'll hope, my lady, that no one else wishes to contract with us to show them that which you have chosen to abandon today."

And with that, she spun and stalked toward the chamber door, Aether smiling broadly and waving at the sputtering Fehndala as he turned to follow her.

The guards at the door looked completely startled. Their eyes shot to Fehndala, awaiting orders, then back to meet Lyrrek's. She knew her determination was written all over her face. If the guards wanted to try to stop her, well…they could try. She glanced over and saw the look on Aether's face as well, the excited, amused expression that he always wore into battle. She'd seen it every time they sparred.

As she knew well, it didn't fill you with confidence, facing an opponent so obviously sure of himself that he looked like the confrontation was a game to him. The look on his face spoke volumes.

The looks on the two guards' faces, on the other hand, suggested that they understood the import of Aether's expression, and the eyes of both were quite wide, their postures rigid.

Fehndala didn't say anything though, and they swept past the two motionless guards and out into the corridor.

A servant outside the door looked panicked as they emerged from the waiting chamber, but managed to bow and hustle off ahead of them to lead them back to the exit.

She thought Aether did an admirable job of holding his laughter until they emerged back into the street outside the castle gate. He'd had to hold it in long enough that he only chuckled and sighed, feigning wiping away a tear as he shook his head at her. "That was a great one, thank you." He clapped his hands quietly as their pace relaxed a bit.

She rolled her eyes, but chuckled with him.

"So," he said. "What do you suppose all of *that* means?"

She was thoughtful for a moment. "Well, she was ready for us, obviously."

"Yeah," Aether said, his voice growing grim. "I didn't like the way she talked about *Horizon.*"

Lyrrek nodded. "Nor I. Do you think she knew we were coming? That speech she shouted at us seemed pretty well rehearsed."

He didn't answer right away, looking again over his shoulder.

"What is it?" she asked quietly.

"I think we're being followed," he said.

"To be expected, I suppose," she said. "You want to pick a place?"

"I'll keep my eyes open," he said. "For now, keep moving."

She nodded, now aware, and though she maintained her self-control and didn't look back, she did think she could hear some booted feet back there behind them.

After another block, they found a wider spot between two warehouses where sheep-drawn wagons could pull up and unload. "This looks good," he said quietly and slowed.

She nodded agreement. Now that they'd arrived at a good spot, there was no longer any need for pretense, so she spun, walking slowly backward, looking up the alley from which they'd come.

There was no one there.

"Do you think they gave up?" she asked him. "Or maybe we were wrong and they weren't following us?"

He shook his head, listening. "I think I hear them."

She listened carefully. Yes, she could just barely hear boots in gravel, a couple blocks over, pounding hard, and from a couple directions.

"They're deploying around us," he said. He met her eyes, grinning, the enthusiastic look appearing on his face again. "Ready?"

"Always," she said. She leaned forward and kissed him, then spun to put her back to his.

The first of them came from an alley to the west, pounding boots attached to vicious-looking men wielding bronze spears.

Lyrrek grinned and drew her shortsword. She heard the longer sound as Aether drew the Silversea sword behind her.

The attack reached her first. She deflected the first man's furious jab with her sword, pitching the attacker's thrust down past her. As he yanked the spear back, she shot her left hand down and grabbed the haft, letting him drag her back toward him with it. His eyes widened in shock as she flew toward him, and she added his momentum to her own strength and punched him in the face with the dragonskin fist that gripped her sword hilt.

He crumpled over onto his back, spear clattering away as she released it.

The one behind him roared and stabbed at her, but he overextended himself. She stepped nimbly aside to dodge the spear, then grabbed it too and yanked it forward at the extent of his thrust, pulling the large man off his balance so that he stumbled and fell forward with a loud curse.

She spared a glance behind her. Aether had three coming at him at once, but he swung the Silversea sword in a wide, hard arc. The swords she and Aether wielded were enchanted with the dragonskin spell, which protected them against damage and made them more effective at transferring sharp concentrations of force into a single point. If they'd been fighting swordsmen, Aether, with his strength and the longer steel sword, would probably be breaking right through their blades. As it was, one of the three men fumbled his grip on his spear at the force of his swing.

She turned back to the one on the ground, who was pulling himself up to lunge at her with his spear from his knees. She danced aside again, then jumped and kicked him in the face. He crumpled over backward on top of his comrade to lay in a motionless pile.

She spun and lunged forward to catch a second group of three coming in from the side. Even with a magical advantage, this would get tough if they got overwhelmed. She switched her sword quickly to her other hand as she dropped below the first spear thrust, blocking the spear up with her sword. Then she lunged forward and landed a solid dragonskin punch into the man's face, and he made a strange gargling noise and collapsed.

One of Aether's opponents rolled up next to her, flopping onto his back, and then Aether was at her side, the steel sword of her family's legacy flashing to smash away the next spear thrust. Side by side, the two of them lined up against the two remaining, who stared at them past their spears, eyes wide, both looking shocked and confused at how quickly the fight had turned.

Then the last two looked at each other, shook their heads, and started backing away. Once it was clear that Aether and Lyrrek were going to let them go, they turned and fled.

Aether stood upright, panting for breath but grinning, as did she.

"Well," he said. "That was a good workout. We can skip exercises today, I think."

She laughed, sheathing her shortsword, and looked down at the motionless men lying in the gravel.

"Nothing identifying," she said, nudging one with her boot.

"But notice all their spears match?" Aether said.

She squeezed her lips into a line. "So House Guard, then."

He nodded.

"I say we go pay Lady Fehndala a follow-up visit," she said, through gritted teeth. "Wouldn't she be surprised to see us?"

He chuckled, but then sighed. "I suppose there's no point really."

She looked around, then leaned closer to whisper. "Should we...you know...look at one of their minds, see if we can get proof that she sent them?"

She knew what he would say. She knew better than anyone that he hadn't felt good about taking Emrek's memories, despite what she, at least, felt were noble intentions and justifiable reasons. But he had been clear and consistent in his advice to the rest of the masters to avoid using the mind control magic on other people, except in teaching one another how to face dragons.

Still, to his credit, he did look like he was considering it for a moment. He'd proven to be a good leader over the last year; thoughtful, not always automatically assuming that he knew best.

He reminded her often of why she loved him, and that was one of the things she loved most about him.

But after he thought about it for a moment, he still shook his head firmly. "I don't think so. It wouldn't be proof we could actually use for anything anyway. And she's on the Ruling Council. Who are we going to report her to?"

"Fair point," she said, sighing. "Well, then we better get out of here before they send a bunch of fools with spears after the ship."

His expression hardened. "Agreed," he said quickly, grabbing her hand in his, and they started off toward the harbor at a jog.

Pemana weaved left, then right, then threw a combo of four punches in quick succession. She ducked, lunged, then weaved again, then came back to her first position, breathing hard.

They had left the center of the guild hall's columned common area as a wide open space, useful for exercises and training. It was early in the morning, and she hadn't seen anyone else up yet, so she'd been undertaking her workout alone this morning.

"Good morning," said his voice behind her as she weaved again, and she jumped, spinning quickly.

"Woah!" Kayd said with a grin, hands up, backing off a step as she landed facing him, still in her combat stance.

"Sorry," she said, and relaxed.

He had a linen cloth around his neck and was wearing simple garments, as she was. He nodded past her. "I was coming to exercise as well, I hope that's all right."

"Oh," she said calmly. "Of course."

She let him pass, then began running through her sets of maneuvers once again.

He tossed his cloth aside and stretched for a moment before beginning his own routines. She recognized them, of course, as the entire Wizards' Guild was still using combat training she'd passed on from her own early days in the Port Omen Guard.

The place he settled himself meant that she couldn't help watching him, right there in front of her, as he began working through the moves.

At first, she was just judging his technique, which had become pretty good over the last year. But she kept noticing the muscles of his calves, the way his back rippled as he swung his long, muscular arms around in practiced blocks and throws.

She cleared her throat uncomfortably and tried to focus on her own moves again.

His maneuvers brought him around to face her in a quick spin, and their eyes met.

She felt the heat of their locked gaze, and lost her place, cursing silently at herself and dropping her eyes as she started over from the beginning.

Aether looked down on his entire collection of maps and charts, which he had spread out on one of the tables in Veytra's brightly lit laboratory. Several of the other masters stood around the table as well: Orenna, Kayd, Lyrrek, and Pemana.

Veytra turned from looking down at the maps, thoughtful, and nudged Pemana who stood next to her.

"I don't know. What do you think?" she asked.

Pemana shrugged and looked a bit uncomfortable. "I'm not sure either," she said. "There's clearly more to follow up on in Eagle's End. But…" she looked up at Aether. "We can work on that. I think I have to agree, this thing about ancient wizards…it's hard to imagine what could be more important for you to figure out."

"Well, paying rent on this place, for one," Orenna said.

"A fair point," Aether said, nodding. "We're fine for a while, but it would be nice if we could move some more goods."

Lyrrek sighed. "I'm still disappointed that the artifacts from the last couple expeditions didn't return much silver. I thought that whole idea would work better than it has been."

Aether shrugged, smiling at her. "Eh, I'd wager we'll find some more interesting things out there somewhere. I still think it's a good idea."

He shuffled the maps, pulling out a reproduction of an old one that showed the lands west of the Dawn Sea and the cities that had once flourished there. He pointed to the mouth of a river, where it entered the Dawn Sea's westernmost extremity, the point marked on the map as "Sunset City."

"I have a good feeling about this one," he said.

"I am confused about one thing," Veytra said. "None of the noble houses descend from there. There weren't any survivors from Sunset City that made it to the Lastlands. Even if we were to find something spectacular, who would be interested in buying it?"

Aether nodded slowly. "You might be right," he said. "On the other hand, Sunset City was about as close to a capital as the Old World had. We could just as easily find some things that would be of interest to everyone."

Veytra thought about that a moment, then shrugged.

"The other benefit to that," he said, a mischievous tone entering his voice, "is that with no one alive today with a surviving claim to the lands around Sunset City…"

Lyrrek looked up and grinned.

"There wouldn't really be anyone to contest a claim by the Wizards' Guild to some choice lands somewhere," she finished for him.

He nodded. "Sunset City was supposed to be in some really beautiful country."

"Well," Veytra said, "I suppose that's good, but we've got a lot of work to do before we're ready to undertake re-settling the mainland, even as a long-term goal." She moved one of the maps to look at it more closely, but nodded. "Still, I suppose the rest of it does make sense." She stepped back from the table and looked up at Aether, then shrugged. "Go find that next letter. I want to find out what happened to the wizard."

"You're not the only one," Lyrrek said.

"We'll start getting ready," he said, and saw the look on Orenna's face. "But the Contribution feasts are in a few days.

There'll be a lot to do around here. We might as well wait until that's all calmed down before we try to sneak out of here again."

Orenna smiled at him, looking relieved. The feasts were always a very busy time.

Pemana started to wander out, but Aether called to her.

"Hey Pemana, don't forget," he said. "I still need to find a few minutes with you to go over the new magic we found up there."

She nodded distractedly, and he wasn't even sure she'd really heard him. She waved as she turned the corner and vanished.

Aether sighed. He hoped, and not for the first time of late, that she was doing all right.

Chapter Seven
The Contribution

L yrrek set her last crate down with a sigh and dropped into one of the chairs around the guild hall's kitchen fire. She poured herself a cup of the tea Orenna had left warming on the rough stones of the circular hearth.

Aether came up and set another crate down, and slumped into the chair next to her. He didn't look quite as tired as she felt, but they'd both been loading supplies and catching up on delayed tasks aboard *Horizon* all morning, and she was ready for a break.

"I know I keep saying it, but do remind me to work us in an actual day off at some point," she said between sips.

Aether looked at her and grinned. "A nice long sailing trip to a dragon-infested mainland doesn't count as relaxation for you?"

She rolled her eyes playfully at him. "That's work, and you know it."

"If you say so," he laughed. "Never feels much like it. I kind of love going up there."

She shook her head. "Now there's a twist I wouldn't have seen coming. Although I probably should have. You do seem to love an adventure."

He winked at her and performed a sweeping bow without rising from his chair.

The door at the other end of the common room opened and some people stepped in from the street outside. Lyrrek frowned. Two spear-wielding men in dark gray Silversea Guard tabards stepped inside, and met their eyes. She tensed.

But they merely stepped inside the door and made way for someone else who entered behind them, a man with dark hair and beard touched with gray, who wore a finely made gray cloak and short robe, the practical kind of garb worn by wealthy men of the Lastlands who needed the freedom to move around, say, the deck of a ship.

Her eyes wide, she shot Aether a look, and rose to go greet Master Tovold, her father.

As she went, she heard Aether take a deep breath and exhale, then rise to follow her.

Probably gathering his magic before battle, she thought grimly, though she tried to hide it behind a happy smile as she walked forward to greet him.

"Father," she said, hugging him. "Welcome."

He returned her hug, but not her smile.

Tovold looked around the wide chamber with its various rustic, almost campsite-like furnishings scattered haphazardly about, then looked back at her.

She coughed and tried not to look uncomfortable.

"Aunt Ilda said I could find you here. This is where you've been then?" he asked, staring at her.

Lyrrek blinked. She hadn't realized that her great aunt, now Lady Ilda, ruler of Vigil, was keeping such a close eye on her. "Well," she said, "actually mostly I've been at sea, I'd say."

He nodded. "It's a beautiful ship, I admit," he said. He raised his eyes over her shoulder as she heard Aether's footsteps crunching quietly in the gravel behind her.

Her father didn't greet him, merely turned back to stare at her again. She stifled a sigh.

"So what brings you this morning, father?" she asked. She turned and gestured toward the kitchen at the far end…which was, of course, just a bunch of camp chairs and makeshift counters around the stone-lined firepit.

She swallowed, sort of seeing their home for the first time. It was clean and tidy, but it did kind of look like a bunch of pirates had set up camp in the building.

"Can I get you some tea?"

He didn't answer.

She supposed she understood the strange look on his face as he regarded her. He was probably wondering where he'd gone wrong that his noble daughter had run off with a young rogue of a ship's captain who'd somehow turned her, in a matter of a few months, into a famous artifact hunter.

She hadn't had a lot of success in attempting to explain it to him thus far.

She saw her father's eyes flick to Aether once again, then he returned his stare to her.

"I am here for the Contribution feasts, of course," he said. "But while I'm here, I intend to deal with this situation."

She went instantly calm and cold. "And which situation is that?" she asked, her voice already hardening.

Once more, her father's eyes flicked to Aether, and she saw it and realized her fears were confirmed. It was, indeed, a battle that she had just entered.

"With the situation involving you and what you're doing with your life, young lady," he said. "Is there someplace private we might speak?"

"Father," she said quietly. She looked over her shoulder at Aether, who's face was calm and unreadable, and shot him a reassuring look. She turned back. "You must understand, that this…" She half turned and gestured to Aether, then met her father's eyes again. "This *is* a private setting. There is no me without him any longer, that's not how this works."

Her father blinked, eyes widening a bit, anger beginning to ignite there.

"Lyrrek," he said, beginning to hiss. "You know that I love you. But I cannot sanction this." Now he just gestured openly at Aether. "I will not allow my daughter to abandon her House and the plans we worked so hard for her to…"

"Plans for me?" she interrupted. "If you had plans for my life, this is the first I'm hearing about it." She pointed out the window, where *Horizon* was visible, parked at the pier, her dark gray House Silversea banners shifting in the light wind. "And as for abandoning my House, well…I just haven't done that," she said, shaking her head.

"But to fall in love with a commoner!" he exclaimed.

He'd gone too far. She saw that he knew it as soon as the words were out of his mouth. His eyes flicked to Aether again, then back to hers.

"He is probably the least *common* man I have ever met," she spat. "And that certainly includes you!" The last was practically a shout.

Tovold drew back, eyes wide.

"My lady, my lord," Aether said from behind her, his voice calm, the perfect tone to cut through aggressive conversations. It was something he'd gotten good at over the last year, trying to keep the group of unshrinking personalities that were his colleagues and friends on course.

"Before you harm your relationship, perhaps you'll let me speak for a moment," he said quietly. She met her father's eyes. He was still fuming…and now, by the look on his face, she suspected he might be angry merely because Aether was daring to speak to him.

And that was going to be the end of this conversation, because Lyrrek was about to explode.

"Please," Aether said, even more quietly, and met her eyes. She got control of herself and took a deep breath, then stepped back to stand next to him.

"Master Tovold," he said, looking to her father. "I know how much you care about your daughter. I have a great deal of respect for that, of course. She is a remarkable person."

Aether turned and looked at her, and she saw all the love he bore for her in his eyes, just then.

"You are amazed that she would choose to be with someone like me," he said, then grinned. "I understand completely, because I am amazed by that fact myself, every day."

He turned and met her father's eyes again. "I have loved her since the first time I saw her, you know, more than a decade ago. It was the very day my…former master…brought me to this city. I was only a child, then, but my feelings for her, my devotion to her, have only grown stronger ever since."

Tovold didn't speak, but his frown changed somewhat.

"You fear for my ability to provide for her," he said. "That is perfectly understandable. But…" he turned and met Lyrrek's eyes. "There are considerations of which you are not aware. Perhaps we should continue this conversation in one of our storerooms."

She nodded slowly. Maybe it was time her father was made to understand.

"This way," she said, stopping to pick up a small, lit oil lamp. Her father was still frowning, but now his head was tilted and he looked bemused, perhaps even a bit confused. He sighed and signaled to his guards to remain, then turned and gestured for her to proceed.

Aether led them back into the corridors to the deeper part of the hall. He got a set of copper keys out of his pouch and stopped at a door.

"This one, you think? he asked, meeting Lyrrek's eyes, as she carefully held up the lamp for them.

She nodded, and managed a grin. "It makes a good impression," she said, looking at her father.

Aether unlocked the door and opened it, and Lyrrek held the lamp high and entered.

She turned as her father followed her in, and saw immediately that this had been an excellent idea on Aether's part.

Her father's eyes widened. The lamplight shone off no less than forty-seven different gleaming white stalker skulls that were everywhere one looked in the windowless storeroom. They hung on the walls, they sat upon wooden barrels, and they were carefully arranged atop large bundles of hides that were stacked around the room.

Aether entered behind him, and they both watched as her father, awed, walked over to one of the great many bundles of dried stalker hides. He leaned to peer at the quality of the preparation. They would need tanned yet, but Aether had made sure they were preparing the hides in such a way that they'd be ready to sell. And dried into rawhide, they were lighter and better for storage and shipping.

Aether stepped forward and opened a barrel near the front that they kept unsealed. Lyrrek joined him and took one of the countless small sacks from the packed barrel. She opened it and pulled out a few shriveled, brown pieces of dried meat.

"Dragon jerky," she said to her father, sticking a piece in her mouth and then holding the sack out to him to take one to try, then spoke again around the food. "Well, land-dragon, technically. Stalker. But "dragon jerky" just has such a great ring to it."

To his credit, her father actually took a piece and put it in his mouth, his expression curious.

She watched his eyes. This part usually went well.

He turned to stare at her as he chewed, his eyebrows climbing his forehead. And then he turned to stare at Aether.

"I can't take credit for this one, really," he said. "Orenna came up with the recipe." He took the piece Lyrrek handed him and chewed, sighing. "It is delicious though."

Tovold nodded, eyes even wider. He stared around the room at the volume of high value luxury goods stacked around him, and Lyrrek watched realization dawn on his face.

"Our main problem, you see," Aether said, "is that we just aren't sure about the most effective way to move all this on to delicacy-loving Lastlanders with silver to spend."

Tovold continued to glance around the room, thoughtful. "How much do you have here?" he asked quietly.

"A bit over three more storerooms like this," Lyrrek said.

Impossible as it seemed, her father's eyes grew even wider.

"We seem to have the hunting down," Aether said. "But what we're lacking is a knowledgeable merchant to help us out with that last leg of the journey from dragon to drawing room, as it were."

Tovold looked at Aether, his eyes suddenly narrowing, as if he were truly seeing him for the first time.

Then he actually chuckled, a tiny smile beginning to form.

"Hm," he said. "I'm beginning to realize you might have the makings of a decent merchant yourself."

"You honor me, my lord," Aether said quietly, bowing to him.

Tovold looked back and forth between them for a moment.

"Very well," he finally said. "Which one of you is in charge of this operation, then?"

"Well, technically I am, I suppose," Aether said quickly. "But I defer to her in everything anyway."

"All right," Tovold said, and met Lyrrek's eyes. "Fifty-fifty."

Lyrrek laughed.

"Are you mad?" she said, grinning. "If it's going to be fifty-fifty, then *you* can figure out a safe way to hunt the land dragons. Ten percent."

"Remind me to ask you about just how it is you manage that. But now you're mad, my lady," her father said. "You know very well how much work will be involved in turning all of this into silver. Forty percent."

"You're right!" she said, triumphant. "I do know how much work will be involved. And I know exactly how much work's involved to get all this stuff here to the Lastlands, as well. Ten percent is probably about right, actually, or maybe even five." She grinned. "But I love you, Father, and I want you to like the man I've fallen in love with." She met Aether's eyes, and he grinned back and nodded. She turned back to her father. "So we'll offer you twenty percent, but that's our final offer."

Tovold sighed, but even he grinned. "Oh very well." He shook his head, and met her eyes, and for a second, Lyrrek could swear she saw something new there. Was he...proud of her?

"You remind me of your mother sometimes, my little lady."

He hadn't called her that in a long time. And he hadn't mentioned her mother in, probably, longer.

She did manage to fight back the tears, until Aether, who knew *exactly* what her father had just done to her, gently touched her shoulder, at which point she lost the fight.

Aether rose quickly with the sack of dragon jerky and drew her father's attention with questions about his ship and bringing his crew around to begin loading cargo, while Lyrrek turned to gain control of herself and wipe her eyes, no longer able to hide her wide, amazed smile.

Pemana opened the door and stepped out into the street, looking up at the sunset coloring the sky as it deepened toward night. She sighed and pulled the guild hall door shut behind her.

She was tempted to skip all this nonsense and keep working. But she also had to admit that there wasn't much more she could do with what she currently had in her possession about the Swordfish. She had been over every snippet of information the guild had collected so many times over the last weeks that she basically had it all memorized. And she hadn't been able to turn up any new leads to pursue, despite the insights she'd gained from the smuggler in Eagle's End.

So, she might as well go drinking. She couldn't really produce a good reason not to. But this still felt like a waste of time she ought to be using for something better.

The smells hit her first as she dutifully started down the gravel street, a complicated swirl of frying things and honeyed treats and ale. She followed it toward the muted roar of conversation and activity she could hear coming from several blocks over, from the vicinity of the harbor square.

It was quite a crowd, as most of the city's residents, and even a lot of the villagers and farmers from the rest of the island, came to town for the feast. But she quickly spotted the rest of her guildmates where they had said they'd be, at a table on the pier side. Even when sitting down, Kayd's height made it easy to pick him out among the expanse of round tables and chairs that got dragged out into the square and set up for the commoners to use.

Her friends were there, gathered around: Kayd, Veytra, Orenna, Aether, and Lyrrek. They cheered as they saw her weaving her way through the crowd and gestured for her to join them.

They had already been around to the stalls at least once, from the look of the plates on their table. Pemana managed a grin and nodded to them, but veered off to the edges of the crowd, where the city's inns and various merchants had set up their stalls with lots of delicious-smelling food options sizzling, bubbling, and smoking away.

She stopped at several of them, piling a large wooden plate with some fried fish, a few salads, delicacies, and smoked cheeses, and two different breads dipped in seasoned oils that oozed deliciously over everything else on the plate.

Lastly, she grabbed a clay mug of ale off the crowded stall nearest the tables, and made her way back to join the others, who cheered again when she arrived to sit down next to Kayd. She rolled her eyes at them, but grinned and got to work trying to catch up.

And she had to admit, an hour later, as she finished off another ale and finally pushed her plate away, that she was feeling considerably more cheerful.

Kayd returned with four mugs balanced in his two large hands, and sat them down for anyone to grab. He handed her one of them, meeting her eyes with a nod.

She smiled thanks at him, raising the mug in a toast of gratitude, and he smiled back.

There was a bit of commotion at the west end of the harbor square, near where the more exclusive tables for the nobility and wealthier merchants were cordoned off from the rest of the celebration. Lady Ilda emerged, wearing a fancy robe-like dress for the occasion, nodding to people she passed, smiling and taking the hands of others in greeting. She led her escort, half a dozen gray-tabarded guards who followed her slow march across the square to the decorated dais that had been set up as the focus of the grand event. A servant in dark gray robes stepped forward and lifted a small copper horn to his lips. Its shrill, nasally tone rang out over the buzz of conversation.

"The Lady Ilda, Ruler of Vigil!" he shouted.

The noise died down as Lady Ilda rather stiffly climbed the three steps to the small lectern at the dais.

"Welcome, my people!" she called.

She launched into a speech consisting mostly of platitudes about the Contribution, the Sky, and the people and their obligations. It was what you'd expect from a Council noble at a Contribution feast, and Pemana's attention wandered as she sat, quietly sipping her ale. Her view, given the seat they'd saved for her, was full of the ships in Vigil's harbor, and she found herself staring at them.

After several droning moments, she looked down at her mug, absently running her thumb over the Potters' Guild seal pressed into the side of it. A hush fell over the crowd, then, and she realized Lady Ilda had stopped speaking. Pemana looked back up at the dais.

Lady Ilda was gesturing dramatically behind her toward the wide array of oilcloth tarps that had been laid out on the ground there in advance. Wheels creaked as teams of servants grunted and strained, pushing the usual two large wagons into position above the tarps. The back wheels were chocked with stones, and a cheer went up from the crowd as half-a-dozen strong volunteers gathered around each wagon and lifted its front. The massive load of cleaned fish, freshly caught that day at House Silversea's expense, began to spill out onto the tarps in a waterfall of slippery, scaled bodies.

The people were ready. Families with children jogged forward, loading up several large fish in oilcloths or sacks, involving their children in the selection, and then receiving a small pouch of salt from several servants wearing bags of them. They began streaming back out into the city to take their bounty home, the children calling out "thank you Lady Ilda!" as they passed her, as their parents had prepared them to.

Ilda smiled at them as they went by for a few rounds, then turned back to the lectern.

"And let us also thank those who have brought this feast for us to enjoy," she said, and her speech continued by way of listing the various inns, merchants, and shops who had contributed food stalls.

"…and especially let us thank the one who made this feast truly festive with her donation of the barrels of ale we are all enjoying this year, my own kin, Lady Lyrrek of House Silversea."

Pemana saw Kayd's eyes widen, his grin turn mischievous as an idea landed in his mind. He raised his mug high.

"To Lady Lyrrek!" he shouted, lifting his mug high.

Laughter erupted around them, and the toast was taken up by hundreds of enthusiastic voices roaring it back into the night. It rang out several times, people drinking and laughing each time, and Ilda gave up on her speech and applauded her great niece with the rest as she slowly climbed down to return to the cordoned area.

The ale was really the Wizards' Guild's Contribution, as a group, of course. They had spent a rather enjoyable day as more traditional merchants, sailing *Horizon* out and sourcing several dozen barrels of fine Meritonian ale that they'd delivered for the feast. But they couldn't exactly put it in the name of the Guild, as they didn't technically exist in that sense yet. So they'd done it in Lyrrek's name instead.

Lyrrek looked stunned as the people of Vigil cheered her name. She gave Kayd a mock disapproving look, but a wide smile spread across her face as, for a moment, her hometown celebrated her as its hero.

Pemana watched her as she lifted her mug enthusiastically in return to anyone who seemed to actually recognize her and called out "to Lady Lyrrek!" Every time it happened, the cheers rang out through the crowd again, followed immediately by rounds of laughter. But no one seemed to get bored of it, presumably because of the drinking part.

Aether shouted with the rest, and clapped heartily for her every time as she bowed, still smiling and lifting her mug back.

But Pemana kept watching Kayd. Every time someone toasted Lyrrek anew, a small, delighted expression appeared on his face as he watched the joyful experience he'd created for one of his dear friends.

Servants frantically stacked filled mugs on the tables at the ale stall as people began to rise from the feast and make their way on to the next phase of the celebration.

"Well?" Kayd said, and she turned and he was suddenly there, leaned close to her. "Want to go look at the games then?"

She paused, but only for a second, before downing her ale and setting her mug back down on the table with an enthusiastic *clunk.*

"You know what, why not?" she said. "But we need to stop at the ale stall."

Fresh ales in hand, they followed the rest of the streams of departing, still-celebrating crowd up the castle road a few blocks until they reached the commercial district. The stalls at the corners, the first ones people encountered as they reached the games, were absolutely packed with lines of people excitedly waiting their turn, and cheering on other competitors.

Kayd nudged her and pointed out a stall where two older women were flailing ineffectually at each other with heavily padded wooden swords, to the hysterical laughter of themselves and the watching onlookers. They laughed with the others, then passed by a deeper area that had been roped off and backed with bales of hay, in front of which had been placed whole slices of precious trees, painted with targets. Competitors hurled copper throwing knives at them.

Pemana, curious, stopped and watched for a moment, but then Kayd caught her attention and pointed down the street further in, and she nodded enthusiastically when she saw what he was pointing at.

The line hadn't really started yet, and there were two open spots at the end, so they jogged the rest of the way and quickly set down their mugs on the wooden counter in front of them. The counter was divided into seven slots, separated by small wooden walls. Each slot was painted a different bright color, which matched a band of color on the bow leaned up in each slot, and the fletching of the arrows in the quiver next to it.

"Very well!" the barker called. "Next group, pick up your bows!"

Pemana was on the end, and picked up the red bow and pulled one of the red-fletched target arrows from the quiver. She stared over at Kayd next to her. "Wager?" she said.

"Ha! You're on. Five silver."

Her eyebrows raised, but she nodded. "Fine."

The barker raised the arrow he held in his hand as a signal, then dropped it.

"Fire your arrows!"

Pemana drew back and grinned. She'd always excelled at her archery training when she was in the guard. And while she'd had several ales at this point, she felt loose and confident, hopefully just shy of sufficiently impaired that it would affect her aim.

It wasn't a deep range, and the targets were fairly close. She released her first arrow and it landed only slightly off center. It was touching the edge of the bullseye, though. An auspicious start, she thought, and grinned, reaching for her next arrow.

Kayd's first shot, she noticed, was just as good. Her smile broadened. Excellent. She'd have to exert herself.

She did, too. By the time they reached their ninth and tenth arrows, gathering onlookers had begun cheering. The other five contestants were all over the place. But Kayd and Pemana both had tight clusters of arrows around the centers of their targets, and looked pretty evenly matched in score.

Each reached for their eleventh arrow, and Pemana glanced over, meeting his eyes. He smiled widely at her, then focused, drew back, and fired.

It was a great shot. Just a little finger's width outside the bullseye. The crowd cheered, then immediately hushed as Pemana looked thoughtfully at her target, then drew her bow.

The *twang* of her shot echoed, and with a *thud* her arrow wedged into the tight cluster on her target, dead center.

Cheers erupted as people around her grabbed her shoulders and shook her and hugged each other and laughed.

She grinned at the crowd and bowed with a flourish, then turned to see Kayd cheering and clapping just as enthusiastically as everyone else. She reached out her hand toward him, and he clasped her forearm against his, and they each nodded sharply at one another, smiling widely, and the crowd cheered again as they set down their bows and picked up their mugs.

He pressed some coins into her palm, laughing, and they stepped back to watch in a place of honor as past champions, toasted occasionally by other onlookers as the next group began firing their arrows off to cheers and more laughter.

She stood at Kayd's shoulder, cheering with the others. And then, off in the distance, a few blocks away, they heard someone yell "to Lady Lyrrek!" The toast rippled once again through the entirety of Vigil's commercial district in a chorus of shouts and laughter.

She shouted it just as loud as the others, and then, still laughing, she took a long drink of her ale, and leaned into Kayd where he stood, so conveniently located there next to her.

He caught her instinctively, his arm suddenly around her shoulders.

She felt warm, happy, surrounded by his patient strength. She half melted into the comfortable feeling of it, her head leaning over to pillow fondly against his shoulder.

And finally, she realized what she was doing and froze, her body going rigid.

He felt it, and removed his arm quickly, glancing over at her.

She stepped away from him, nodding and forcing a smile, holding her face carefully neutral, lest any of what was currently churning through her appear there.

She cursed silently at herself. She had to put a stop to this right now. She shouldn't be encouraging it. It was just cruel to Kayd. He really needed to move on and find someone who could...be with him.

For the thousandth time, she struggled to find a way to tell him. And for the thousandth time, she scoffed at herself. What was she going to do, just blurt it out?

You're not good enough.

That would, indeed, probably serve to put a stop to it.

It wasn't fair to him. It's not his fault that her family had an honorable legacy stretching back generations that was now hers to uphold. He had nothing to do with the fact that she already knew who she was supposed to marry one day. She didn't know specifically who the man was yet, but she knew what he would be. He would be a decorated and high ranking Port Omen naval officer, or perhaps, if her mother was astonishingly successful in her efforts, an actual nobleman of House Omen.

She looked slowly over at Kayd, staring at his chiseled features, at his hair, which he had been growing longer, as seemed to be the style these days. It suited him so well.

But he was a harbormaster's apprentice. He was a harbormaster's apprentice who hadn't even finished his apprenticeship. He came from a family of…well…peasants.

Her mother would flay her alive.

Sadly, she had, in fact, seen all the naval officers in the Port Omen Guard at one point or another during her service. And she was also pretty sure she had seen all the young noblemen of the house as well, unless they had a long-lost cousin tucked away in an estate somewhere.

None of this was fair to her either, as far as that went. But it was the reality. She had a duty to uphold, a legacy. She thought of her grandfather's sword, back in her quarters where she had left it…along with her judgment, apparently.

She sighed deeply, then leaned toward him.

"I'm sorry," she said quietly. "I have to go."

"What?" he asked, looking over at her in surprise.

"I just…I have to go, I'm sorry," she said, a little louder, and then she spun and marched away down the street in the direction of the secret guild hall of the Wizards' Guild, refusing to look back for fear of finding out what the look on his handsome face might teach her.

She almost made it out of the hall the next morning without seeing him. But as she was opening the door to slip out into the street, she heard him.

"When you said you had to go, I didn't realize you meant it like that," Kayd said. His voice was calm, emotionless.

She had frozen at the first word, and now she turned back to look at him where he had emerged from a corridor. He was dressed for his morning exercises, with a linen cloth draped around his neck.

He'd probably been hoping to find her there doing her own workout. She doubted he expected to see her heading out the door, fully dressed and wearing her cloak and brimmed hat, her grandfather's sword buckled at her waist, haversack slung over her shoulder.

She stared at him, unable to find any words to speak.

He returned her stare for a moment, thoughtful, then he raised one finger. "Will you wait here, just for a moment?" he asked. "Please?"

She nodded silently, sighing to herself, and he ran back into the corridor.

He wasn't gone very long, and she heard his footsteps pounding back to her. He appeared from the corridor, breathless, and stepped out, tossing something to her.

She caught it. It was one of Veytra's new "mind amulets," as they'd taken to calling them, on a copper chain.

"If you need to reach…anyone," he said, his voice, and face, still carefully expressionless.

She bent her head and put the amulet in a pouch on her swordbelt, then looked up and met his eyes once more.

Then she nodded once, turned and departed, closing the door behind her.

It was early, and the streets were still quiet as she marched toward the harbor, uncomfortably recreating her journey from the evening before. This time, she passed directly through what remnants of the feasting were still left to be cleaned up, and made her way to the harbormaster's office, which was just opening.

He only had one used sailboat available at the moment, so unless she wanted to wait around for one of the shipwrights to open so she could check with someone about a brand new boat she couldn't afford anyway, it would have to be the one he had.

She looked out the window at it, where his clerk pointed it out to her at the dock outside. She should go inspect it of course, but what was the point really? The sailboat was her only choice, unless she wanted to try and buy passage on a merchant ship, or throw away all her silver on charters for the foreseeable future. Neither were realistic options. If this was going to work, she needed the freedom a seaworthy ten-pacer would afford.

She asked the price, and coughed when told. She had the silver for it, but it was more than she'd hoped. If Aether hadn't paid them all last week, she wouldn't have been able to afford it. She sighed and carefully counted out the requisite coins, then signed the parchments with the harbormaster and took her copy. She nodded her thanks to the pleased harbormaster, trying not to think about Kayd, and headed out to her new vessel.

It was old. Minimal. Not inspiring or pretty. But it looked sound, at least.

She quickly released the lines from the cleats and stepped over into the boat's small cockpit. She lowered her head to peer down into the cabin below decks, and was relieved to see that it was clean, not filled with cobwebs and mouse shit, as she'd half expected. She gently tossed her haversack to the nearest corner, then climbed back up and began freeing sail lines in preparation for departure.

She raised the small triangular sail, sighing at having to follow her own orders.

But as wind caught in the boat's sail, and she began to weave her way skillfully out into the harbor traffic, she was forced to admit that the light vessel was very responsive and agile. She felt pretty good to pilot, especially to someone used to helming a full-sized house navy ship. Once she made the boat some windstones, it would probably serve her needs well.

Perhaps it was finally being back in command of something again, even if only a small sailboat. Or maybe she had just needed to get off by herself for a while, she didn't know. But she did already feel a bit better, now that she was cruising out into the swells, with a course to chart.

Aether took a deep breath, and walked over to join Kayd in the hall's kitchen where the latter was helping Veytra with preparations for that day's big pot of soup.

"You two want a hand?" he asked quietly as he came up behind them, and Veytra turned and nodded, unsmiling, but pointing to the small table next to a barrel of seawater for washing root vegetables.

"I wish I knew what her problem was," Veytra said finally, after a few moments of them all working in silence. "What did she actually say?"

"She actually didn't say anything," Kayd replied. "Not a word. Just went."

Veytra sighed and dumped a handful of cut vegetables over into the pot.

"I know you love her, mate," she said, looking at him sympathetically. "But I think there might be something wrong with that one."

Kayd actually laughed a bit, and Aether smiled. Veytra did know her oldest friend well.

"You're still welcome to change your mind, Kayd, if you want to come along with us," Aether said, looking up from the wet sunchoke he'd been scrubbing. "Crew ought to have *Horizon* ready to depart within the hour."

"Thanks Captain," Kayd said, with an only slightly strained grin. "But Veytra has some things I promised to help with, and Orenna needs help with recruiting. Plus, if…anyone…were to call in for assistance on something, I'd be…around to go…you know…"

Aether nodded and handed Veytra a big handful of damp pods and rhizomes to chop.

An hour later, he was aboard *Horizon,* standing in the sun as the ship finally reached a point far enough out from Vigil Isle that it wouldn't seem strange for her sails to be filled with a strong wind. He called the signal to the crew, then activated the ship's windstones and adjusted their heading against the compass.

Once everything was tightened down, their course steady, Lyrrek came up from where she'd been helping coil spare line and leaned against him to stare out at the island slipping away toward the horizon behind them.

"Feels good to be getting underway, this time," she said quietly, as he widened his stance a bit so he could support them both against the ship's gentle rolling. She turned at his movement and took his arm to stare out with him at the sea ahead.

"I know what you mean," he said, looking over at her. "It was a fun few days, but everybody seems pretty intent on getting back to work."

"Yeah," she said, with a sigh. "Exactly what I was thinking of, if by everybody you meant Pemana."

"Mostly," he said. "Pretty much how Kayd's dealing with it too."

"I hope they sort it out," she said. "I feel terrible for him. And I don't get why she'd just leave like that."

"Oh," Aether said. "That part, I do understand, I think," he said.

"How so?"

"She'd been sort of trapped there at the guild hall, you know?"

Lyrrek nodded slowly.

"I think if we lost *Horizon*, Sky forbid, the first thing I'd do is go try to find another boat. Otherwise you're just stuck where you are again." He gestured out at the ship's busy deck ahead of them, then widely at the sea and sun surrounding them. "I've gotten too used to this freedom, I'm afraid."

"I suppose I see your point," she said, "but I don't know. Maybe it's because I spent my entire childhood being dragged around the Lastlands on merchant ships, but I've just never really felt trapped like that."

"You always had the resources to go wherever you wanted to, if it came to it," he said simply. He hoped she understood what he meant.

She nodded without hesitation this time. "Very fair point."

"But think of it like this," he said, holding his hand out ahead of them. "Imagine a ten-pacer sailboat, loaded up with everything you need to tackle any adventure you could dream up. Imagine she's stocked with food, and a couple casks of water, and some camping gear, and maybe even some bottles of brandy tucked away in there in case you need to celebrate something. Now imagine that the whole world's yours to explore, and all you have to do to claim the chance is just throw up your sail and hold on, and you can follow any whim, go see what's over any horizon you choose. It's hard to go back once you've tasted freedom like that."

She was quiet for a moment. "I suppose I do see it, when you put it that way," she said. "But I don't know. You and Pemana are both ship's captains, of course. I wouldn't even know what to do with that ten-pacer."

"Nonsense. Well, if you'll pardon me for disagreeing with you, my lady," he said, grinning. "But I've seen how hard you've worked over the last year and a half. There isn't a part of this ship that you don't know how to crew."

She tossed her head a little, acknowledging the point.

He pointed out ahead of them again. "You know what headings to use and how to position the sails against the wind for best speed. You know how to tack. Even if you didn't know how to use windstones, you could get around, so you'd know how to not look suspicious while using them. You know how to find your direction without a compass, even. I mean, you've helmed this very ship plenty of times."

"Well sure, when one of you says 'here, hold this for a minute.'" He laughed and she chuckled as well, and went on. "But it feels like it would be a whole different thing to look at a sailboat tied to a dock and say 'I'm going to pit my wits, and my wits alone, with no help, against this finely tuned, complex example of human ingenuity and magic, in such a competent way that we both survive a dangerous passage over unpredictable seas until I can tie up to another dock on a whole different island somewhere else.'" She took a breath and shook her head. "It just sounds seriously *daunting* when you say it out loud."

He chuckled. "I suppose so." He looked over at her, and she met his eyes. "But I still have no doubt you could do it."

Lyrrek smiled back at him.

Pemana kept her eyes sharp as she spun the wheel, preserving as much of the boat's momentum as possible while she veered through the busy swarm of ships and boats that crowded the entrance into one of Freehome's several harbors. While the holdings were all carefully independent, this sprawling city was as close to a capital as the archipelago got, being the largest city by population, the largest city by overall economy, and the city where the Ruling Council kept its facilities.

The city's harbors were, as one would imagine, generally quite busy.

But Pemana had gotten fairly comfortable with the sailboat during the crossing. So she smoothly skimmed her way through the chaos, trying not to be too obvious about the boat's new windstones, to where she thought she remembered a public marina to be located.

She found a dock with an open slip whose rental fee didn't make her flinch too hard, so she paid the marina attendant and finished securing her new, but still rather old, sailboat.

She went into the slightly musty cabin below and finished stashing the last of the things she didn't need on her person away out of sight. No sense in making herself an easy target if someone snuck aboard.

She took one last look around, nodded, then turned and left the boat.

She strode up away from the marina into the sprawl of warehouses and commercial facilities that clustered around Freehome's harbors, connecting them into a tight mass that devoured the edge of the island, before the city climbed gradually up some low hills toward the fancier neighborhoods surrounding Redwater Castle.

But Pemana's course veered away from those rarefied parts of the city, heading instead in the opposite direction, northward toward one of the seedier parts of town on the far side of the harbors. It was a more neglected, less refined part of the city that grew brokenly over the island's rocky shores before crumbling, quite literally in some cases, off into the sea.

Indeed, many of the old stone buildings in this area weren't very well maintained, and had an unsound look to them. She kept her eyes open and her wardstones ready as she slipped into alleys that were jumbled with the lives of the residents of this part of town. Many people, a lot of them rather filthy, eyed her suspiciously, or even angrily, as she slipped through, but she ignored them.

At last, she reached the small junction where several of the neighborhood's mad web of alleyways converged into a single spot. She passed a few other people, ignoring their dark looks, and climbed the stone steps to the broken flagstones that served as a porch for the uneven looking building behind. An old sign hung at an awkward angle above the door, with clumsily carved letters that spelled out "The Toad's Hole." She sighed, pushed on the decrepit-looking door, and entered the dark, smoky space beyond.

The patrons of this tavern had a tendency to look up as one whenever a new person entered. It had been unnerving the first time she came here, several years ago. But she knew to expect it now and ignored them all, making her way to a shadowy corner where the barman frowned at her. But he pointed toward the back part of the wide, dingy room in answer to her quiet question.

She paid the barman a few coppers for a tiny misshapen mug of terrible-smelling brandy, and pretended to sip it while she walked through the mismatched tables and chairs toward the far wall. There, alone, sat an old man, his long, gray hair and beard a bit unkempt, even dirty, and his clothing the same. But he sat with his back to the wall, his sharp eyes, she knew, missing nothing as he watched her approach.

"You're looking well," she said quietly as she sat down across from him at his tiny table.

"Dragonshit," he said gruffly.

She shrugged and lifted her hands, half grinning, then took a sip of her brandy, trying not to wince at its harsh, truly unfortunate taste.

"Why are you here?" he asked quietly, lifting his own mug.

"I'm on a hunt," she said, even quieter. She tried to appear nonchalant as she moved her chair closer to him, and began to whisper. "Big prey, this time." She met his dark eyes. "The biggest of all, in fact," she said, this last barely audible at all.

He stared at her for a long time, unmoving, and said nothing. For a moment, she wondered if he knew what she meant, though she would be quite surprised if he didn't. He always knew. It's why he was still alive.

Then, for the briefest second, she saw his eyes flick around the room, considering the other patrons. Finally he leaned well back, facing the ceiling and draining his mug. As he rocked back forward, he bent over and placed the mug precisely on the table, drawing closer to her still.

"Tomorrow evening, probably around sunset," he breathed. "Follow the pretty one, but make sure you don't look so...pretty...yourself."

She rolled her eyes at him. Then she took one more pretend sip of her "brandy," before sliding it across to him with a grateful nod and rising to leave.

CHAPTER EIGHT

FAMINE AND FEAST

A ether pulled on the tender's oars one last time and let it coast up to bump against *Horizon's* hull. "Well?" Lyrrek called down to him from the deck. He looked up and saw her grinning down at him. "Did you get him sorted out?"

"He was a cantankerous one, that old dragon," he called back up cheerily. "But at the moment he's quite certain there's something important he needs to check out at the very far end of his territory, and he's flying north. We might get a day or two before he remembers to come back and we'd have to come up with something else for him to do for a while."

She grinned at him and took his hand to help him the last steps up the ladder to the deck.

"All right then," she said. "Get the rest of your things together." She turned and leaned against the rail, staring off northwest, where the ruins of Sunset City showed their presence in the jungle as uneven dents in the rich green of its canopy. "I can feel it out there."

"As can I," he said, a note of excitement in his voice as he opened the door to their cabin and stepped in to grab his staff and haversack.

She beat him back down to the tender, and had taken the oars. He grinned back at her, saluted, and took a seat across from her at the stern while she rowed them to shore.

He jumped out into the surf and dragged the boat up onto the pebbly beach, and they joined the rest of their crew of apprentices. While Aether had sailed north in the tender to deal with the dragon they'd sensed, Beras had gotten the rest through most of the work that needed doing to set up the expedition's campsite, and they were ready to proceed.

Six of the strongest crew were positioned to carry some new additions for this trip. There were three of the contraptions, each of which consisted of a rather special barrel slung under a long pole that two hardy individuals could carry between them.

As there had already been one dragon encounter on this trip, they decided they should keep everyone in a single group for the duration. So to begin, the whole expedition would head in the direction of the beacon spells that all three wizards could feel calling to them, not too far away, across the low hills to the northwest.

It didn't seem like it would take them long to reach the beacon. The jungle along the coast wasn't overly thick, for once, and it rather quickly gave way to even less dense broadleaf forest as they climbed up.

The forest was alive with singing birds flying about, and other than some small groups of swarmers that fled from their presence, there was nothing to delay them. Soon, they were all grinning as they emerged into the thinnest forest at the heights of the hills, where the trees gave way to occasional hilltop meadows that were dotted with scatterings of wildflowers. And some of the rockier hilltops afforded long views out over the surrounding landscape.

There was some discussion, as they saw the expansive views, of areas that might make a good place for settlement someday. But they were all excited to find the wizard's next letter, and kept moving.

Before long, they found themselves looking down on a narrow valley bordered by a long outcropping of broken rock that formed a low cliff at the valley's edge.

And once again, an awe-inspiring amount of destruction had been wrought upon that cliff by the claws of two hundred years of outraged dragons.

Over the centuries, the area at the base of the cliff had become a well-established clearing, as dragons landed and smashed trees over with their tails, or simply plucked them out of the ground and hurled them aside as they investigated the beaconed rocks. The ancient wizard had selected certain segments of the broken cliff face to enchant, once again forming a rough arrow shape that indicated a general direction. Some time in the past, one of the investigating dragons had managed to dislodge one of the enormous beaconed chunks of rock from the cliff itself, and it had tumbled down the face and rolled several paces before embedding itself in the mud. It lay there still, glowing brightly to Aether's magical senses, but out of alignment with the rest. Still, it wasn't too hard to discern where the ancient wizard's arrow was telling them to go, and he led the others to, once again, a smaller sheltered spot against some rocks.

A thrill of excitement made him shiver as he found the concealed box and stripped its spells, Lyrrek and the rest all drawing in close to observe, excited to learn more about this ancient mystery that had raised so many questions.

This time, the buried wooden box they found was much smaller, and smelled strongly of intriguing, unfamiliar spices as soon as Aether released the preservation spell and pulled off the top. Inside, he found a wrinkled, somewhat dirty piece of paper, folded in quarters to fit within the smaller confines. As he unfolded it, once again, the faint hint of charcoal from the wizard's ink joined the spicy smell.

The penmanship was sloppier than last time. This letter looked like it had been written hastily, or perhaps by an exhausted person. He squinted at it, the wizard's script a bit more difficult to make out this time. But once he had it, he sat down on the ground, and the others gathered in closer as he began to read.

"Kohlia," he began slowly.

"I waited as long as I could, my love. Forgive me for not waiting longer, but I must arrive at the underhall at…Head-waters…within the next week, and the journey thus far was treacherous, so I dare not linger. Hopefully I may wait for you there, while still aiding in the defense…or in the evacuation, such as the case may be. I fear the Pantheon's control may be collapsing under the weight of this assault, just from what I have encountered in my travels thus far. Things are going very poorly out there, as I'm sure you're aware."

Aether took a breath, and met Lyrrek's eyes, before bending again and continuing.

"On a positive note, my dear, I have encountered plenty of entertaining tales in my travels, and I am saving them up to share with you. The way these…"

Aether fell silent, reading ahead for an instant and blinking in surprise. Then he tilted his head to one side for a beat before continuing. "The way these fools scramble over themselves and each other when their survival is threatened can be quite amusing."

Aether looked up and glanced around, and saw that the others looked as confused as he felt in that moment.

He read on.

"Remind me to tell you some funny stories when we are reunited. Be safe, and I hope I will see you soon when you catch up to me. I think eventually we will all be recalled to the Great Underhall, and I long to stand in the Pantheon's Domain with you once again.

"Yours enduringly, Vereden."

Aether looked up and saw his crew looking around at each other and at him, and all were frowning.

"Um…" Lyrrek finally said. "Well, that was strange."

"Yeah," Aether said slowly, looking at the paper in his hand. "Strange is one word for it, I suppose."

After a while, they gathered themselves and set off to pursue a magical signal Lyrrek spotted that she thought might be a large swarmer nest. And an hour later, after a bit of excitement that provided the apprentices with some good training, Lyrrek went to work building a small campfire, while Aether prepared a few fresh swarmers to roast for when they had finished their work. Then, while Lyrrek tended to their lunch, he went and helped the crew with skinning and cleaning the rest of the several dozen small land dragons they'd just harvested. They tossed all the raw meat and scraped hides into the pole-slung barrels, which had been fitted with stones enchanted with preservation spells, to keep everything as fresh as the instant they placed it inside, for as long as the barrels' seals held.

Once they had all eaten and relaxed for a bit, they finished washing up in the small stream nearby and prepared to depart. Aether helped Lyrrek pour waterskins from the stream over the fire until it was out, then they started their hike back to the ship.

He drew up next to her at the lead of their long column, his staff thudding on the ground as he kept pace with her.

"Have you heard of Headwaters?" he asked Lyrrek.

"No, it's not ringing any bells," she said, watching where she stepped while they clambered carefully over a large tree's roots.

"Hm. Nor with me. I'm not sure what to do about that."

They hiked in silence for a moment, then Lyrrek shrugged and spoke.

"I guess it would be the Cartographers' Guild we need. There was a good cartographer's shop in Port Omen my father took me to, a long time ago. And there was a big one in Freehome as well, not far from that luthier's shop Veytra's always going on about, actually."

He nodded. It made sense. It was probably the best place to start.

"We have to find that next cache," he said.

"I don't know," Lyrrek said, and pointed at his satchel. "That letter was bizarre. I'm starting to wonder who we're dealing with here. Just what is this 'Pantheon' anyway?"

"No idea," he admitted. "But I still think we ought to proceed. There are some big questions here. But more than that, this 'Great Underhall' he referred to…if these ancient, secret wizards who once lived on our world had a central stronghold of some kind…" he turned his head, meeting her eyes as she looked over at him. "Well, just imagine what we might learn if we managed to find *that*."

Pemana smiled grimly, leaning even further back into the shadows to make sure she wasn't seen. She had to admit, he'd been right. The woman was pretty. And she wore her hair in a tight, complex arrangement of braids that would make her easy to pick out in a crowd.

Pemana, wrapped in a dirty old cloak and hood, her face dusted with ashes, had secreted herself in a small, deeply shadowed corner with a view of the entrance to The Toad's Hole. Around sundown, as promised, a lithe figure in leather armor and a fine light cloak appeared, looking quite out of place in this part of town.

Pemana watched the woman walk, catching herself to keep from nodding, lest movement give away her hiding place. The woman's gait looked like that of a trained fighter, and she moved through the threatening jumble of dark alleys without concern.

Interesting.

Pemana watched the woman enter The Toad's Hole. A moment after she disappeared through the door, it reopened, and several nervous looking men hastened out and scattered away in three directions. Pemana waited patiently, and after ten minutes, the woman exited again and stalked away down an alley that led back in the direction of the rest of the city.

Pemana timed her movements very carefully, and, checking her spells one last time, moved silently out of the shadows, maintaining a cautious distance to her target.

She followed the woman for the next hour as she traveled across the commercial district around the nearest of Freehome's harbors, stopping in at various shops and establishments for several minutes at a time.

Finally, the woman entered a much, much finer inn, one located at the transition where a district of warehouses turned into fancier shops. It took Pemana several minutes to find a dark corner to tuck herself into, here. Freehome had more than its share of beachsleepers, so she wouldn't be *too* out of place. But there were a lot more guards patrolling around this part of the city.

She sighed. This would take some luck.

After a while, though, she decided she was safe, as none of the guards she saw seemed to be regularly passing near her hiding place. But then five minutes of waiting turned into ten, then into twenty, and Pemana sighed again, finally realizing that being found by the guards wasn't her biggest problem at the moment. She might have lost her quarry. Or, if she was lucky, she would only have to sit here and watch until morning to make sure she didn't miss the woman departing.

She hadn't learned anything at all about who she was. She hadn't even really told her contact just who it was she was hunting when she got the lead from him. Perhaps he had misdirected her to get rid of her, and if she tried to speak to him again, she'd find him gone.

Her best bet, unfortunately, was to wait here and watch until the woman departed again, whenever that finally occurred.

Pemana sighed and drew the hood lower over her eyes, then recoiled as the act pulled the smell of it back into her face again. Washing the dirty old cloak would have rather defeated the point, but it stank. She closed her eyes for a moment, wiping her hand on her trousers and sighed again, careful to do so through her mouth this time.

Lyrrek dragged the last large bundle of rope aside into its corner, then leaned back against the bulkhead next to her, sighing, glad for the chance to just breathe for a moment.

Finally, she grinned, and kicked herself forward off the wall. It was good to be home, of course, but bringing *Horizon* in to dock was always a lot of work.

She jogged up onto the deck, waving back at the last few straggling crew members she saw finally leaving, making their way off into Vigil to go enjoy leave for a few days.

She looked around, trying to spot anything that still needed doing before she herself could go relax for a bit out of the heat of the afternoon.

"Um…Lyrrek?" Aether's voice called from inside the hall.

Something about his tone of voice made her move quickly, and she dashed across and up the low slope to the door, finding Aether in the kitchen with Orenna, who smiled apologetically as Lyrrek entered.

Aether held out the small parchment in his hand to her. His expression was somewhere between amused and alarmed.

She looked down at it, reading quickly.

It bore her great aunt's new seal as Lady of Vigil, stamped in ink at the top. It demanded the official appearance of one Lady Lyrrek of House Silversea and one Aether of Vigil, formerly of the Shipwrights' Guild, to attend upon Lady Ilda, Ruler of Vigil and Vigil Isle, as soon as humanly possible.

She looked up and met Aether's eyes.

"Wow," she said. "Um, yes, I suppose we'd better get going." She started to move, then stopped and looked back at him. "Aether," she said, looking down. "Leave the sword here."

He nodded quickly and unbuckled it, letting Orenna take his sword belt from him. She looked solemn as she turned and gave Lyrrek a quick hug.

Lyrrek grabbed a clean cloth from the stack of them near the washbasin and mopped the sweat from her face and neck, grinning and trying not to look nervous as she motioned for Aether to precede her out the door and into the street.

They reached Silversea Castle after a short hike, and the guards at the gate saluted them as briskly as they always did.

But were they, perhaps, staring at them? Or trying not to?

Lyrrek took a deep breath and increased her pace.

They found a gray-robed servant, who led them through the grounds to where Lady Ilda, attended by a number of servants and guards, was just rising from a stone bench near an arrangement of basins filled with potted flowers.

Lady Ilda looked up and saw Lyrrek coming, and her great aunt's gray eyes met hers.

Lyrrek saw those eyes narrow slightly.

"It is too hot to remain out here," the lady said loudly, gesturing to her and Aether to fall in line as the procession wound back toward the castle.

As they followed the servants ahead of them into the door, Lyrrek had to blink as her eyes adjusted, and she started as she realized that her great aunt was standing just a few feet inside the door, waiting for them.

"Thank you," Lady Ilda said, turning to the servants and guards. "Leave us, and make certain we are not interrupted, please."

Lyrrek noticed at least one of the guards with a sour expression on his face, but they all bowed and turned to go, closing the door behind them and leaving Aether and Lyrrek alone with Lady Ilda in the outer alcove.

"My lady?" Lyrrek said, bowing to Ilda, and seeing Aether follow suit out of the corner of her eye. "What may we do for you?"

Ilda came straight up to her and bent close. "We need to talk, young lady," she whispered.

"About what?" Lyrrek whispered back, alarmed.

"About what you've been up to lately," she said, her eyes shifting to Aether and back. "And about why I'm receiving missives from other lords on the Ruling Council, who will arrive here tomorrow for an audience with me about an official Council inquiry into the activities of a member of my house." Ilda was a bit breathless by the end of the recitation. "What in the world is going on?"

Wide-eyed, Lyrrek tried not to stammer. "Goodness, my lady, I assure you, I have no idea." She paused a moment, as something crossed her mind. "Um…if I might inquire…which Council lord is arriving tomorrow?"

"Lord Eglamon."

Eglamon, Lyrrek thought to herself, almost nodding. He was the Council lord who had been behind what happened to Pemana. And he was the ruler of New Brightwall. Their most recent operation there, capturing the thugs that had been shaking down shop owners, was only one of many things they'd done for the people of New Brightwall over the last year-and-a-half.

And now the noble ruler of New Brightwall, where the people seemed to face such a concentration of the activities of the Depths, was arriving here, with apparent concerns about their interventions.

Quite interesting indeed.

She kept all of this from her face, though, schooling her features into an expression of confused concern.

"I'm very sorry, my lady," she said quietly. "I assure you, I have no idea what this could be about."

"Who is this?" Ilda demanded, nodding at Aether.

Lyrrek looked at her for a moment, then turned to look at Aether. He was patiently watching them both, quiet, and he smiled slightly at her when he saw her look.

"His name is Aether."

"I know his name," Ilda whispered harshly. "Why is he always with you?"

"Well, for one, he's my captain," she said. Then her smile widened and she shrugged. "But above all else, he is my champion and consort."

Ilda blinked, her eyes flicking to Aether. Then she grinned, for the tiniest instant, before she caught herself and quickly frowned again.

"Well," she began, not quite sputtering.

"My lady," Lyrrek said quickly. "We are just a mercantile venture, investigating some…new methods of acquiring luxury goods for market. You should be aware of our Contributions over the last year, I expect."

Ilda stared at her. Lyrrek had a feeling that she was, indeed, aware of the amounts. It had been a busy year.

"And would you care to discuss just what these new methods are?" Ilda asked quietly.

"I'm afraid not, my lady, at least not at this time," she said, trying to look disappointed that she couldn't comply with Ilda's request. "They are a trade secret, for now."

"And which trade is that exactly, that deals in dragon leather and crowns?"

Lyrrek stared at her, wondering, for just an instant, if she ought to tell her the truth. She'd known her great aunt for as long as she could remember, of course. And as far as Lyrrek remembered, she'd always been gruff, true, but also pretty decent.

But no. The consequences of the world discovering what they had become were still too volatile an unknown to risk, at least with the Swordfish out there warping and twisting everything. Gelkris had taught them that. They had to remain silent and invisible for now.

So she only smiled regretfully.

Ilda sighed. "Very well," she said, drawing up and speaking louder. "Then *you* can deal with Lord Eglamon when he arrives here tomorrow evening."

Ilda turned and began to make her way slowly from the room, limping slightly.

"I'll expect your presence at the welcome feast," she said over her shoulder.

Lyrrek tugged a bit at her embroidered dress, getting it to settle better. It was still practical and allowed for good freedom of movement, as everything she wore did these days. But it was, nonetheless, one of the finer garments she owned. She needed to play this correctly, and was taking no chances.

Aether took her arm, his own dark robes a good complement to her dress. As they emerged from the warehouses into the evening darkness and started to turn onto the road leading up to the castle gate, he glanced past her out at the harbor, and pulled her to a sudden halt.

"Oh, that's probably not good," he said.

Eglamon had already arrived in Vigil, which they knew. They had seen the dark orange House Brightwall banners raised at the castle alongside Silversea's gray earlier that afternoon from the guild hall.

But they hadn't realized until now that Eglamon had arrived with fully four of his house guard navy vessels, in addition to his own larger ship, all of their orange trappings forming quite a contrast among the gray of the rest of the ships in the harbor. And spear-bearing guards in dark-orange tabards filled the harbor's docks, piers, and the harbor square itself, milling about, drilling, or sitting to sharpen weapons and work on gear.

"I…do not like this at all," Lyrrek said quietly.

He nodded, frowning, and followed her as she proceeded, more quickly, through the gate and into the castle.

They entered the hall and found that the feasting tables had been brought out, as expected. The wide chamber, bright with extra lamps, was already crowded with people, dozens of courtiers and dignitaries, as well as many more of her noble Silversea cousins milling about, already enjoying their wine. There were a few dozen more orange-robed servants, joining the gray-robed locals in various tasks. And then she finally spotted the cluster of dark-orange tabards near the front, close to the food-laden head table, that would undoubtedly be surrounding Lord Eglamon himself.

Well, she thought, no sense in dragging this out. She wanted to know what was going on.

She strode forward, looking over her shoulder at Aether to make sure he was with her, and seeing his surprise as she made such a direct course for Lord Eglamon.

As she approached, she rounded the guards and saw that Eglamon was, indeed, standing there, wearing a heavily embroidered, rather shiny robe of deep brown. He lingered near the end of the long table, where Lady Ilda sat in a chair, wrapped in an embroidered gown and cloak.

Lyrrek walked up, nodding to the guards who turned to watch them. Aether hung back, remaining respectfully behind her, ostensibly as an attendant, which is what everyone would assume in this company.

In reality, of course, he was her backup.

Lord Eglamon turned away from saying something to Lady Ilda at Lyrrek's approach.

"Ah," Ilda said, sounding relieved. "This is the object of your concerns, my lord. May I present my great niece, Lady Lyrrek of House Silversea."

She was certain she saw a startled look on the old man's face as his eyes shot to hers. Lord Eglamon had gray hair and beard, carefully groomed and extensively styled. His dark eyes, sunken in his wrinkly face, were wide, and his mouth opened slightly for a moment, as if the cogs of his mind were struggling to engage with the fact that the aforementioned object had just walked directly up to him.

"Well," he managed, his voice a touch tremulous. Then he stared at her for a moment, seemingly at a loss.

"What may I do for you, my lord?" she asked finally, meeting his eyes.

His wrinkled features hardened.

"I have no need to speak with you directly," he said. "You are dismissed."

Ilda's sharp withdrawal of breath was loud. Lyrrek grinned.

"Oh come now, my lord," she said, ignoring his breach of protocol. "Your concerns must be great, to have brought you here in such…" She glanced around at the dozen guards in orange tabards nearby, then met his eyes again before continuing, "…haste. Surely this matter, whatever it is, is best dealt with directly."

His face flushed slightly and he frowned harder. "We are here to discuss anomalies in the dispensation of property," he spat. "But these matters are not your concern."

"But my lord," she said quickly, "Lady Ilda just said that I was the very *object* of your concerns. Apparently whatever it is you seek here involves me directly, perhaps even intimately." She stared at him, unblinking. "And that, my lord, makes it my concern."

His eyes narrowed.

Ilda coughed and began to rise from her chair. Servants rushed forward, and she mumbled something to Lord Eglamon about apologies, and that she would return, slowly shuffling off with the assistance of a servant.

Eglamon continued glaring at her. "We will continue this when Lady Ilda returns," he spat. "Do not leave."

"I go where I will, Lord Eglamon," she spat right back, still staring into his eyes. "But as it happens, here is *exactly* where I'm going to be until I learn why *you're* here."

He sniffed, not bothering to hide his unpleasant expression. But he walked away from her, gesturing to one of his servants to bring him wine and a plate.

Conversation began to pick up again in their immediate vicinity, as those nearby who had fallen silent to listen went back to their discussions. She backed away a bit to wait for Ilda's return, and as she did so, she felt Aether come up close behind her.

"We're in trouble," he whispered. "When he said 'dispensation of property' he meant *Horizon.* That's why he brought so many guards. They're going to try and take her, and maybe us too."

She swore quietly, but nodded. "We can't start a battle in here. It would be a mess. You have to go, now. Get the others and get her out to sea." She turned over her shoulder and met his eyes. "I'll have to stay here and delay him from doing what he thinks he's going to do."

"Shit," he breathed. "I suppose you're right. Be safe."

She felt him gently squeeze her shoulder. And then he was gone.

After a few moments, Lady Ilda come back and resumed her seat. Lord Eglamon returned to her side, glaring at Lyrrek as if daring her to try to approach or speak to him again.

But Lyrrek wasn't really interested in trying to approach now. She was pretty sure Aether was right. Eglamon probably had a Council order to seize *Horizon,* or something to that effect. Now, her role was simply to stay here, within the lord's convenient view, to keep him from realizing that her escape was already underway.

She took a seat at a table and gestured for a passing servant to sit in the seat next to her.

"I'm sorry," Lyrrek whispered to the young woman, not taking her eyes off Eglamon. "Are you in the middle of anything that will get you in trouble if you don't finish it immediately?"

"I don't think so, my lady," she said quietly. "Not if it involves serving you in some way instead."

"Very well," Lyrrek said. "Well, I'm sorry to trouble you, but really the only thing *I* need is for that stuffy-looking Council lord over there to not notice that I don't have as many people with me as when I came in. Would you mind staying here for a few minutes and pretending to talk to me?"

The young woman grinned, a touch of mischief in her eyes. "Would I mind getting off my feet and having to do nothing for a few minutes, my lady? Not at all, I assure you, I am at your service."

Lyrrek chuckled and thanked her. They chatted about unimportant castle affairs for a few minutes, and then Lyrrek began asking her about her family and her life. They actually shared a rather nice conversation for almost twenty minutes, before Lyrrek saw Lord Eglamon glance her way, turn, then suddenly look sharply back and stare at her.

"Where is the young man?" he said, loudly enough for all around to hear him.

"Young man?" Ilda asked. But she immediately looked in Lyrrek's direction.

"Thank you, it was lovely meeting you," Lyrrek whispered to the grinning servant, then rose and strode forward as Eglamon, eyes widening, rose to his feet as well. "The young man that came in with her," he said, his eyes now darting around the hall. "Where did he go?"

"What business do you have with my captain, Lord Eglamon?" she demanded calmly as she approached them once more.

"Your captain?" he said. "Not for long." Lyrrek saw the upset look on her great aunt's face and knew Aether had been right.

"And just how do you propose to end our association, my lord?" she asked, a bit of a grin beginning to leak out onto her features.

She saw him hesitate. She had caught him unprepared once more. But then she saw him decide that there was no time like the present.

"I propose your arrest!" he shouted. "Guards! Seize her!"

A huge smile broke out on her face. It seemed that Aunt Ilda was going to discover the truth today after all.

So much for not bringing violence to the very seat of her noble house. She had done what she could to prevent it. But it seemed Lord Eglamon had removed the decision from her.

So be it.

The nearest orange-tabarded guards turned toward her, and by the grins on *their* faces, she knew that they were both ready for this mission, and yet also entirely *unready* for what was about to happen to them.

She laughed, and dropped into her best fighting stance, beckoning them forward, ready to put on a show that would live in the stories of House Silversea for ages.

Ilda's horrified shriek of "guards!" echoed through the hall. Conversation immediately died everywhere, replaced by the sudden clatter of spears and boots as the dozens of gray-tabarded Silversea guards stationed throughout the hall erupted into motion, finally driven from their frozen observation of the unfolding scene into action, rushing forward to defend a scion of their house.

The wide-eyed guards in gray and the equally startled guards in orange faced off against one another, the ones in orange tabards suddenly ignoring her to rush, alarmed, to surround Lord Eglamon, while a wall of gray-tabarded guards surrounded Lady Ilda.

Lyrrek watched it all, still smiling and shaking her head, but backing away quickly now that no one was paying attention to her.

"Stop this!" Lady Ilda shouted. "What on Origin are you doing, Eglamon? You fool!"

Lyrrek kept her laughter silent as she ducked behind a crowd of shocked courtiers and jogged lightly from the hall, unnoticed.

She raced quickly out of the castle, relieved to see that the orange-tabarded guards still swarmed the harbor, so Eglamon hadn't managed to get the word out this far yet. As long as Aether and the others had been quick, they ought to have been able to get away.

She jogged through the streets, slowing only as she reached the hall, where she found the street door unlocked.

Inside, there were signs of rapid evacuation everywhere. It looked like the place had been ransacked, which, she supposed, it basically had been.

Lyrrek sighed. It didn't feel good to see her home for the last several months gutted like this. But she was glad the others had gotten away clean.

She ran out the door to the pier, sliding to a stop and sighing again at the sight of *Horizon's* empty berth.

They'd done it.

She stopped, turning. She didn't know for sure what to do with herself, now. She supposed she'd better find herself a place to hide until Eglamon and his troops left Vigil Isle, at least, and then she could worry about figuring out how to find Aether and the others. Lady Ilda might even help her out, once Eglamon was gone. Lyrrek grinned fondly, thinking of her formidable aunt and the look of outraged wrath on her face, the last thing Lyrrek had seen of her before she fled the castle.

"There you are," said Aether's voice from behind her.

She spun, relieved, and ran to hug him.

"You got out of there so fast," he said, chuckling. "I doubled back to come help in case you needed it, but I guess you didn't."

"Remind me to tell you the story," she said, sensing that he was ready for them to keep moving. "It was really something."

"Well, excellent work," he said, grinning. "You gave us enough time." He pointed northward. "I parked a tender in the next cove over, just in case they came here directly. We'd better go find it and get out to the rendezvous."

She nodded and smiled, following him as he broke into a quiet run through the streets of Vigil.

They reached the tender where he'd tied it up and quickly loosed it and raised the sail. Aether took the tiller and line, activating the boat's windstones and slipping them quickly out of the small, poorly lit cove and into the perfect blackness of the night sea. He watched the stars, heading east. Then she saw him pull one of the mind amulets from below his tunic. He gripped it in his hand and closed his eyes for a moment.

"They're watching for us," he said. "We're just supposed to sail east until they spot us."

She sighed in relief, then looked back toward the lights of Vigil, receding over the dark water behind him. Her smile faded as she watched their home vanish behind them.

"I wonder when we'll be able to come back." she said.

"I'm getting tired of having to flee this place, if I'm honest," he replied.

"Yeah," she said quietly. "I guess we need to find the Wizards' Guild a new home."

CHAPTER NINE

ESCAPES

A ether tied off the tender's winch line and finished securing the small boat by the light of *Horizon's* deck lanterns. He drew in a deep breath of the cool sea air and let it out in a long sigh. It was a relief, under the circumstances, to be back aboard. But it was frustrating to find themselves in these particular straits once again.

They hadn't had a chance to try to rouse any of the crew, of course, who were all away on leave. So he had Orenna, Kayd, Veytra, Lyrrek, and himself as *Horizon's* only crew. And now they'd have to figure out a place to hide the ship where the Council couldn't find her.

He started toward the quarterdeck to join the others who were gathering there, standing or seating themselves near Orenna, who held the helm and steered them, for the moment at least, on a northerly course, away from Vigil.

He climbed up the steps, meeting the others' eyes.

"Well?" Orenna said. "Where do you think we head?"

"What are our options, do you think?" Aether asked, glancing around at all of them to make it clear he was asking for any or all of their thoughts.

"Mainland's one possibility," Veytra said. "Though probably not ideal. We're not really ready to start a re-settlement operation with just the five of us."

Aether nodded. "It's probably our 'if all else fails' option. But hopefully we can find something more practical."

"One of the tiny islands somewhere around the Lastlands maybe?" Lyrrek asked. "Up in the Silver Shoals, or even south around the Wastelands?"

"Hmm," Aether said, thoughtful.

"Eh, probably too easy for her to be spotted by patrols," Orenna said, staring out at the starry horizon and making a slight adjustment to their course. Lyrrek nodded, still thinking.

"Well," Kayd said, "we could…" He looked uncomfortable. "We could contact Pemana, see if she knows of anything we might try."

"It's a good idea," Aether agreed. Pemana's career as a house navy captain had taken her into places the others probably never imagined. "Why don't you see if you can raise her?"

Kayd saluted him and reached under his shirt, starting down the stairs and wandering forward into the darkness along *Horizon's* deck, hand raised to his amulet.

"Oh, that reminds me," Aether said quietly, reaching into a pouch and pulling out another amulet, which he handed to Lyrrek. "We should probably be wearing one at all times, with the way things are going lately."

Lyrrek nodded and took the amulet from his hand.

He looked around at the others, then watched Kayd for another moment before sighing.

"Well," he said, rising and starting toward the stairs. "I'd given an amulet to Beras, just in case, thankfully. I'd better go let him know what happened, and see if he can tell the rest of the crew to keep their heads down."

The sun rose the next morning, but they still had no answers. Aether and Orenna decided their best bet was to keep moving, so they wandered northward into the area of tiny islands known as the Wrecks. It wasn't a wonderful area to navigate, even with windstones, though it was safest during a bright day in clear weather. Thankfully, they did have that going for them at least, so they just kept carefully navigating about, avoiding the few other sails they spotted on the horizon.

Late that afternoon, after a frustrating, rather point-less-feeling day, Aether was at the helm, the others spread ahead to watch for hazards in the water. Kayd jogged up from below decks, grinning, and climbed to the quarterdeck.

"Pemana's got us something," he said as he reached Aether at the helm. "She's been in Freehome the last couple weeks. She said the harbors are really busy, and there are a lot of big warehouse complexes along the shorelines that have private sea yards, with gates. She'd seen some for rent, and thought she might be able to find one we could hide *Horizon* in." He pointed southeast. "She thinks she found one."

Aether sighed in relief. "Prepare for best speed!" he called out to the others. Orenna, Veytra, and Lyrrek all yelled "aye!" and started untying lines as he began to bring them about.

"There is one downside," Kayd said, turning to go help the others with the sails. "Rent on the place is a thousand silver a month."

Aether groaned, eyes wide.

"Well," he said at last. "We have to do what we have to do, I guess." He saluted Kayd as he jogged away down the steps.

A thousand a month? Sky, so much for their budget. And just when he thought he'd be in a position soon to push his most exciting secret project forward. The others didn't know about it yet, and he hadn't wanted to spoil the surprise.

Well, their guild hall rent alone ought to make sure he could never afford to put the plans into motion in the first place. He supposed that would indeed serve to keep the secret rather well.

He sighed, and with the others all forward, focused on their tasks, he gently rubbed his hand along the smooth wood of *Horizon's* polished wheel. A thousand silver was a huge amount just to rent a warehouse. But it was to protect their beloved ship, without which they couldn't continue earning silver at all, so anything they could afford was probably worth it.

And who knew, maybe they could get these messes sorted out quickly, and wouldn't be forced to hide the ship in Freehome that long.

Either way, the unplanned expense was frustrating. He decided, his expression grim, that it was but one more debt that the Swordfish, and now Lord Eglamon as well, owed them.

Aether gritted his teeth, his grip on *Horizon's* wheel so tight that his knuckles were white. He realized what he was doing and tried to calm himself, breathing deeply, and trying not to tense up.

Orenna stood next to him on the quarterdeck, a detailed chart of the area in her lap. Occasionally she uncovered a tiny lightstone to closely review the chart and compare it to the darkened world before them, as they navigated *Horizon* slowly through the crowded harbor waters of Freehome. Even now, in the middle of the night, parts of them were a complex maze of clusters of anchored ships and boats.

Lyrrek, Veytra, and Kayd were stationed forward, help-ing keep watch for hazards, and standing ready to quickly make changes to the configuration of the mainsail as needed.

Aether squinted into the darkness ahead. The blur of lantern lights strewn across the shorelines created little in the way of distinguishing features. Orenna's other hand was raised to her amulet, her concentration on communicating with Pemana at the moment, who watched from their des-tination, trying to spot their approach.

"She thinks she sees us." Orenna rose to her feet and handed him the chart. "I'll be right back," she said, as she jogged down the steps and ran forward to the bow of the ship. Aether watched her, by the dim light of *Horizon's* deck lanterns, as she raised her hand high. A small flash of bright white light pulsed from her hand. Aether, knowing what to watch for, saw an answering pulse of white light from between some lanterns on the shore, and breathed a sigh of relief. Now he knew where he was going, at least.

"I saw it," he called down to Orenna as she jogged back to the quarterdeck.

Orenna nodded, then turned forward and called a few orders to the other three, joining them to make some last adjustments to the sail.

As they slowly approached, the lantern lights on shore offered minimal illumination of the structure of the warehouse complex ahead. The barely visible facade of a large stone building rose above a broad set of sea gates that was more than twice as wide as *Horizon*. The gates themselves, wooden constructions seven paces high, cantilevered out over the seaside approach into the complex's walled sea yard, meeting in the middle. While shut, the gates enclosed any ships docked there in a small private harbor for discreet loading and unloading operations. It was an expensive feature, and the main reason why rent on this particular complex was so high.

But once they had managed this difficult docking maneuver, they could winch the gates back closed with their operating mechanism of pulleys and ropes, and only *Horizon's* two masts would be visible from anywhere outside, rendering her invisible against the backdrop of Freehome's sprawling forests of ship masts.

He could make out Pemana now, down on the rocky shoreline near the facility, just inside the small public sailboat docks that marked the edge of the property. She was waving her arms and gesturing one way or the other, and he made tiny adjustments to *Horizon's* wheel accordingly. Orenna watched their drift for a moment, then turned, gave him an encouraging smile, and jogged down to help the others with the docking.

It was a bit of a mess. With such a limited number of hands, the operation took a lot longer than it would under normal circumstances.

But the layout of this particular sea yard proved to be perfect. Kayd rowed a tender ashore and helped Pemana with the sea gates. As they crawled slowly open, Aether could see by the lit lantern in the center of the huge sea yard that one of the docking berths was quite long, and was cut straight back in toward the warehouse beyond, on the far right side of the yard from this perspective, approaching from the sea. The other was a bit shorter, and ran parallel to the shoreline, across the rest of the sea yard to his left. Both were lined with long, well-maintained stone piers.

Aether grinned. Expensive this place may be, but he could already see signs that Pemana had found them their money's worth.

He gave the ship one last small push with the windstones, then let *Horizon's* momentum carry them slowly straight ahead into the larger berth. Once they were close enough to the pier, Pemana and Kayd caught the lines that Veytra and Lyrrek threw to them. Orenna, Veytra, and Lyrrek joined them ashore then, and Aether bound the helm in place so the rudder would hold straight, and finally jumped down himself to help the rest. All together, grunting and occasionally calling instructions to one another, they hauled *Horizon,* stern-first, back around the corner to the other berth, which was long enough to hold a larger ship, and so had plenty of room for this one.

After much straining effort, they got her into position, and Aether helped the others secure her mooring lines to cleats. Breathing heavily, he finally took a moment to greet Pemana with a handshake and a wide smile, then accompanied her as she showed them all how to close the gate mechanisms. At last, they had the ship hidden, and Aether sighed as the nervous, hunted feeling that had been chasing him since Vigil begin to ease a bit.

Horizon was secure, positioned for a quick departure if they needed to execute one for some reason. They had done all they could.

"Thank you everyone," Aether called to his friends as they all finally began to relax. "It's been a really difficult couple of days, and you did a great job."

Veytra grinned at him, as did Orenna and Lyrrek. Kayd didn't, and neither did Pemana. But they were both standing uncomfortably, seemingly distracted by each other, as if uncertain how near one another it was acceptable for them to be. Aether ignored the temptation to roll his eyes at them.

"And great work on finding this place, Pemana," he continued. "Want to give us the tour?"

She looked at him for a moment, but finally grinned and nodded.

Aether jogged back aboard *Horizon* and grabbed his staff from their cabin, then joined the others as Pemana began to show them what she'd seen so far of their new home.

Besides their private piece of the harbor and the two docking berths, the sea yard itself mostly consisted of a wide, graveled space that would be useful for staging cargo and supplies for loading operations. There were high privacy walls along the outer edges that joined directly with the main structure of the warehouse itself.

All of it looked square, sound, and well-built. Aether nodded, relieved that they did indeed seem to be getting what they were paying for.

Pemana led them through a dark door into the warehouse proper, and Aether lit his staff, its white light revealing an open, columned space even larger than the one at their old guild hall. And, to top it off, this warehouse had a flagstone floor that would be easier to keep clean than the gravel of the old one in Vigil had been.

Everyone seemed pleased and impressed as they looked around, and Pemana received several compliments from the others on her find.

"This is wonderful, Pemana," Orenna said. "We'll find a good place in here for a kitchen, I think."

"Oh, it's better than you think!" Pemana said, an actual smile on her face. "This way."

She led them to a door and ushered them through, and all of them exclaimed in delight.

The room they entered wasn't huge by the standards of the main warehouse floor, of course, but it looked like it might have originally been a commercial kitchen of some kind. The chamber was lined with stone counters and lots of cabinets. There were multiple places with built-in firepits and stoves, and there was even a large stone oven.

Orenna whistled in awe as she looked around the grand installation.

"I'm not sure what this place was used for in the past," Pemana said, grinning. "But it looks like they cooked a lot of stuff in here." She nodded to Orenna. "I had a feeling you'd approve."

"Well, thanks after all, Lord Eglamon," Veytra said. She pulled a stone out of a pouch and it blazed into light. "I'm going to go explore the storage chambers." She pointed toward a dark door at the far side of the broad kitchen. "I'll need to find a good one to use for a new laboratory."

Aether nodded and smiled, gesturing for her to proceed. The others also began pulling out stones, and started wandering off to go explore on their own. The building echoed with them calling to each other about new things they noticed that were improvements over the old guild hall in Vigil.

"Pemana," Aether said quietly as he walked up to her. "This place seems perfect, thank you so much."

He saw Kayd watching them, silent.

Pemana nodded.

"It looks like there's plenty of space here, much more than the guild will need, for some time," Aether said. "If you need a place to work while you're continuing…your investigations, or whatever…please feel free to station yourself here, of course."

"Actually," Pemana said coolly, "now that you mention it, I do need get back to work." She pulled a small sheaf of parchments and a ring of bronze keys from a pouch and handed them to Aether. "There's an address in the documents, make sure you go pay them tomorrow."

"Right," he said, accepting the things she handed him. "Well, how's your search going? Do you need any help with anything? It looks like we'll be a lot more convenient to assist now, if you need us."

"Yeah," she said flatly. "Well, I'll let you know. Thank you. But I expect I'll be fine, and I really should get back to work."

And with that, she turned and walked away, headed for a door that opened from the large kitchen out into the dark alley outside. She turned and nodded briefly to him, and then closed the door behind her with a *thud*.

Aether met Kayd's eyes, shaking his head slowly, and they shared a sigh.

Pemana yawned, then squinted into the morning sunlight again, trying to spot the dangerous-looking woman she'd been studying for a few weeks now.

She seemed to return to Freehome every three or four days, and she usually traveled a route among a few dozen various shops, inns, and even a few local guild halls. It was usually the same places, but not usually in the same order. When she finished those rounds, she made her way back either to a local inn, or more often, to one of the harbors, to an expensive private marina there with rather better security than most. From there, Pemana was fairly certain the woman boarded a small sailboat and departed the city for a few days, leaving her with no alternative but to return to the Toad's Hole in a foul mood, there to wait, pretending to be a regular and miserably sipping foul brandy, until the woman showed up again and she could try to repeat the process.

Her contact had indeed vanished. This wasn't a surprise, really. But it was quite frustrating. She had wanted to see if she could get more information out of him, but she supposed she understood his reluctance to involve himself further in something this dangerous. He had, after all, retired years ago.

So she had gotten in the habit of frequenting a dark corner at the run-down tavern herself, until she spotted her target again and began the whole chase once more.

Today, though, she was determined to learn something new. She had managed to get a look at the exclusive marina the woman used, and thought she had a way to sneak safely inside so she could know for certain which boat belonged to her.

It might not be the most useful information, as once the woman departed, there was really no way Pemana could follow her, even in her own entirely unremarkable sailboat, without giving away to her target that she was being followed. But, if she knew exactly which boat was hers, maybe she could find a place to watch for the comings and goings of that boat instead. It might at least spare her the days she'd spent, bored out of her mind and disgusted, sipping sparingly at horrible brandy for lack of anything better to do.

She looked at the shadows on the street. The woman had gone into this weaver's shop more than twenty minutes earlier. That was a lot longer visit than usual, and Pemana suddenly cursed silently to herself.

There was an alley behind this row of shops. It was entirely possible the woman had slipped out the back.

Pemana sighed. She'd never figure out where she had gone next, only a few stops into the rounds. So she had probably lost her target. Again.

She frowned, then rose, determined. It would be a risk, but to her knowledge the woman had never had the chance to see her yet, so she shouldn't know Pemana's face.

She had to know for sure. Looking around and not seeing anyone nearby, she removed her stinking cloak and balled it up into the shadowy corner behind the tree trunk she'd been hiding in. She quickly wiped her face and tried to fix her hair, hoping she didn't retain too much of her beachsleeper guise, and headed out into the open street, nodding pleasantly at some others who ignored her as they passed.

She strode into the front door of the weaver's shop.

"Ah, how may I help you, m'lady?" A middle-aged man behind the counter looked up from one of his looms and smiled at her, waiting attentively for her answer.

It wasn't a large shop. She quickly glanced around. Unless the weaver was hiding her behind his counter, she had, indeed, gone out the back.

Shit.

"Oh," she said, meeting the man's eyes half-heartedly. "I'm sorry, my mistake, I've wandered into the wrong shop." She stared about, adopting a sheepish look. "My apologies," she said, then turned and strode out the door.

She stalked back over to the tree and picked up her filthy cloak, clutching it as a wadded ball as she began trudging back toward the small marina on this side of the city where she'd docked her sailboat.

Maybe she should just give up on this. Unless she found some way to figure out where the woman was going when she departed Freehome, this whole exercise was pointless.

Thus far, it had been entirely and exactly that.

She sighed. Reluctant as she was, there wasn't much more she could do but go back to the new Wizards' Guild hall.

The upside was that they did tend to work fast, her friends. In just the few days since they'd arrived, they would probably have the place transformed into something a lot more comfortable than her old sailboat with its hard bunk.

Her frustrated anger drained away into a flat, sticky sense of exhaustion, and she slunk back to her boat, trying not to smell the stink of her wadded cloak.

CHAPTER TEN
ON MAPS

L yrrek made a final notation on a piece of parchment, studied it thoughtfully once more, and nodded, stacking it with the others. Orenna had her helping with some of the reams of documentation that the Guild was generating these days. Their operations, with several teams of adepts and a master or two usually out and about somewhere, had been a lot to keep track of before the chaotic move from Vigil, and were threatening to get out of hand now.

The conversion of the large warehouse into a guild hall was going well, at least. Aether had, with a somewhat stressed look on his face, released more silver from the guild's treasury for them to use in buying some second-hand furniture. Orenna and Veytra had found a few good lots of chairs and tables, and some old sleeping bunks that would be a big improvement over the hall's flagstone floors. As it was, they had mostly all been sleeping on *Horizon* since the escape from Vigil.

She grinned. She and Aether would probably just keep using their cabin on *Horizon* as a bedchamber, as was their custom. But it would definitely be nice to have a bit of their privacy back.

Lyrrek neatened the stack of parchments and placed it in the cabinet they'd designated, relieved to be finished.

She was heading for the kitchen to get a mug of water from the cask when she felt the tingle inside her skull. She heard her name whispered there, like the peaceful monologue of her own thoughts, but in Amrelyn's voice.

"Lyrrek! I hope you're well. It's Amrelyn, if you're free to speak."

Lyrrek grabbed the copper chain around her neck and pulled it out from under her tunic, then gripped the amulet itself in her fist and cast the spell to return the connection.

"Amrelyn! I'm well, and I'm free. You have great timing, actually."

"Good," Amrelyn said, her voice becoming clearer now that they were both actively working to link their minds. "First, I should quickly report that we've completed the amulet deliveries, and we're settled in, back in Eagle's End. Everything went well."

"Excellent," Lyrrek said. "But I can feel your concern, so I take it there's more?"

"Oh yes," Amrelyn said. "This one's a big fish to land, and I wanted to get your thoughts on it."

"Well, that's me intrigued, then. What's the fish?"

"When we got back to the new hall here, there was a letter from Jyhnda's family."

"Oh?"

"She's been using the standard 'working for an institution that serves the struggling people of the Lastlands' line with her family. But it hasn't been doing the job."

"They don't believe her?"

"Oh, it's not that. Jyhnda's pretty fired up about actually *doing* that very thing. That's how I found her, she was one of ones we found bringing food to the beachsleepers."

"I remember," Lyrrek said.

"So it's not that they don't believe her, it's…" Lyrrek felt Amrelyn's annoyance at them through their connection. "Well, they think that sort of thing is a waste of time, and beneath their daughter."

"Ah," Lyrrek said. "Yeah, that's…unfortunate."

"So," Amrelyn sighed. "This letter says that they want her to take a different job, one with more opportunity. And they found her one."

"Well," Lyrrek said, thoughtful. "I suppose we can't really stop her going without doing the same thing to her that they are. What's the job?"

"That's the twist," Amrelyn said. "It's a servant's position…to be one of Lady Fehndala's handmaidens."

Lyrrek's eyes flew open.

"Jyhnda's grandmother was in the Eagle's End guard, and her family is known well enough to House Goldenhall that they were one of the few that Fehndala's servants approached about candidates. Her family want her to take the job, thinking it will ingratiate her with the House, or even Fehndala herself."

"What's Jyhnda think of all this?"

Amrelyn sighed. "She wants to take it. Only she wants to go in as an agent of the Wizards' Guild, so she can report to us on Lady Fehndala's doings, given all the weirdness that happened the day you and Aether visited her."

Lyrrek had been around enough powerful noble ladies in her own house to know how they spoke around their closest servants. In most cases, they spoke around them as if they weren't even there.

Amrelyn knew this too, of course. Nonetheless, Lyrrek could feel how uncomfortable the whole idea made her.

"What is it? Why don't you want her to go?"

"Just because it's so dangerous," she said, sighing. "And she's so young."

"I…" Lyrrek thought about it for moment. "I suppose, although she's only a couple years younger than I am."

"Fair point," Amrelyn said. "I've known you so long, sometimes I forget you're younger than me."

"And I will also say that Jyhnda seems pretty sharp."

"It's true," Amrelyn said. "And it's not that I don't trust her, to be clear. She can get a bit fired up talking about things she's passionate about, maybe. But I haven't seen any signs of indiscretion or being easily provoked or anything."

Lyrrek nodded, then remembered that Amrelyn couldn't see her.

"That's good." She paused a moment. "I don't know, Amrelyn. She's your apprentice, so I'll just say that I'll support whatever you decide. But I'll also say that seems like a pretty amazing opportunity, and we might be fools to pass it up."

"Yeah," Amrelyn said, sighing again. "I kind of thought that's what you'd say. And the problem is, I pretty much agree. I just don't like it."

Lyrrek was thoughtful for a moment.

"All right, let me ask you this, master to master," she said. "What is your official opinion of Jyhnda's performance as an apprentice?"

She felt Amrelyn's flash of happiness at Lyrrek equating them. Lyrrek wondered if Amrelyn felt the little surge of joy that brought her in return.

These amulets could be a bit...complicated.

"Well," Amrelyn began, "I'd say she's been an excellent apprentice. Not perfect, but very dedicated and willing to learn from mistakes, which is all anyone can ask, I think. And she feels like this is a calling to her, a lot of things she'd still be trying to do even if I hadn't found her, just with more risk."

"So she's Guild material then, is what you're saying?"

"As far as I'm concerned, definitely."

"Well, then I suppose you should just field-promote her to adept, and teach her some real magic, if she's going to be going into danger like that."

Lyrrek felt Amrelyn's relief.

"If you think that's a good idea, then I would agree. I'd definitely be happier about her going in there if she wasn't trying to hide apprentice bracers all the time. She's been picking up Pemana's exercises pretty well, too. I think if we made her a full adept, she could probably even fight her way out, if it really came to that."

"Well, I don't think it's established that you need any-one's permission to promote her if you believe she's ready. But if you want my opinion, I think it's a good idea."

"It's all new, my lady," Amrelyn said, and Lyrrek could feel her smile, even if she couldn't see it.

Lyrrek chuckled. "Well, tell Jyhnda congratulations from the rest of the Wizards' Guild, and we'll work out a belated promotion feast for her when we can all get together. Orenna will insist on it."

"Jyhnda's always really liked her. We'll make it happen," Amrelyn said, and took her leave.

Pemana deactivated her windstones and let the rough rope slip through her fingers as the old sailboat bobbed on small waves sent out by the wakes of the larger ships trundling through Freehome's busy harbor. She lowered the sail, letting the boat drift to one of the small public docks outside the new Wizards' Guild hall.

Unfortunately, she realized after a moment, she had misjudged the approach a bit. Sighing, she climbed up on top of the cabin and stuck out a leg, in entirely undignified fashion, catching the dock with a toe and dragging the boat the rest of the way over to bump into the salt-stained wood.

She bent quickly to tie the boat's mooring lines off to copper cleats, really hoping no one had witnessed her clumsy arrival.

Head down, she grabbed her haversack from the cabin and went to the alleyway door that opened into the former warehouse's columned main hall.

It was locked, but she'd figured that as one of the guild's council masters, she was entitled to keep a key. She unlocked the door and let herself into the sea yard.

As she entered the hall, she saw that they had indeed gotten a lot done since she'd been here last. They'd been forced to leave quite a bit behind in Vigil, of course. But there was plenty of *Horizon's* camp kit strewn about the large hall, enough to give the place a bit of a lived-in feel, at least.

It was mid-afternoon, but she didn't spot anyone around at the moment. She supposed that with only the masters presently occupying this larger building, the guild hall probably felt pretty empty most of the time.

She opened the door and entered the kitchen.

It looked like they had done the most work to transform the place in here. There were three decently-sized round tables ringed with chairs, obviously well-used, but still in good shape, probably enough to seat a couple dozen people all together. The counters were now stacked with some sundries, and there was a small pile of bags of dragon jerky, and even a bowl with some fresh fruit in it. And a delicious smell filled the air, presumably coming from the large pot keeping warm over a very low fire in one of the shallow stove pits.

She started across the room, headed for the soup, when his voice startled her.

"Oh. You're back."

She jumped and spun around.

Kayd was sitting in a chair by the far wall, a bench next to him stacked with the piles of books that represented the guild's small library. He held a book in his hands, closing it around a finger to look over at her.

"Hello," she said awkwardly.

He nodded, rising, and closed the book, placing it back down on top of one of the piles. "Is everything all right?" he asked.

"Oh," she said. The answer was no, of course. But somehow that didn't come out of her mouth. "Oh yes, everything's fine."

"Well," he said. He nodded.

Then he simply turned, pushed his way out the nearest door, and was gone.

She blinked.

That was fair enough, she decided. And certainly for the best.

She looked at the soup, and then decided maybe she wasn't that hungry after all, and headed for the sea yard.

Aether responded to her call, appearing from *Horizon's* hold and jogging up to greet her from the railing.

"Pemana!" he said. "Good to see you back, how are you?"

She glanced over her shoulder, then turned back and met his eyes. "Actually, I'm not…sure. I think I might need a fresh set of eyes or something. You in the middle of anything?"

"Nothing that can't wait," he said. "Just planning expeditions, as usual lately." He started to turn toward *Horizon's* captain's cabin, and then stopped, grinning. "You know what? Yes, please, come aboard. You can help me with this problem ale cask that keeps insisting on having ale in it, despite my efforts." He started toward the hold.

She chuckled politely and followed him below.

Once he'd seated them at the table by the galley, each with a full wooden mug, he took a long drink, then smiled at her. "Well, how can I help?" he asked.

She set her own mug down, swallowing, and thought about how to proceed. "There's…" she began, then paused. "I've been on a stakeout for the last few…well, years, it feels like, but basically since I left Vigil for here. It's been a few weeks I guess. There was only one contact I felt I could be absolutely certain wasn't involved with the Swordfish in some way. I did get one lead from him, though he's vanished now."

She took another sip. "Before he disappeared on me, he pointed me at a woman that I've been trying to follow. I suspect she's some kind of coordinator, or a deeper agent of the Swordfish's network in some way. She visits a lot of places routinely, so I think she's mostly out collecting protection money from shops, or coordinating something among some other locations. I've watched her having enough conversations with shady-looking characters at this point to be pretty certain that the lead is good."

She took another drink.

"So what's the catch?" he asked.

"I'm having a terrible time figuring out what she's up to," Pemana said. "I suppose I could try to take her in, but she looks dangerous."

Aether's eyes widened. "I've never known that to slow you down before," he said.

"Well, it's not that I'm scared of her," she said hastily. "It's just that she seems like the type that wouldn't be very cooperative, you know?"

He nodded gravely.

"My real problem is that I keep losing her," she said, sighing. "She parks a boat at one of the expensive private marinas with extra security. I wish I could tail her out of the harbor and see where she goes, but I can't figure out a way to follow her without tipping her off to the tail. Sailboats aren't very subtle, really, with all that bright white sail to give you away."

He was taking a drink as she spoke, and he set his mug down quickly, swallowing to free himself up to smile widely.

"I have just what you need," he said. He got to his feet. "Wait here."

He ran up the stairs to the deck, and she sat up, suddenly feeling a tiny surge of hope. If he had an idea that might actually help her...

She heard him jog across from his cabin and back down, and as he emerged from the stairway, she saw he had his spellbook in his hand.

"I meant to tell you about this when we got back from finding that first letter, but we never got around to talking about it," he said, flipping through pages in the book. He found what he was looking for and pressed it flat open, laying it down on the table in front of her.

She pulled it closer, looking at his notes.

"Let me just show you, first of all," he said.

She watched him as he closed his eyes in concentration for a moment. Then he opened them again and looked at her.

"Do you feel it?" he asked.

"Feel what?" she said, but as soon as the words were out of her mouth, she knew what he meant.

There was…a subtle tugging at her awareness…a sense of something nearby, almost buzzing at the back of her mind.

She closed her eyes and cast about with her magical senses. She spotted it almost immediately, turning to look up through the ship back toward Aether and Lyrrek's cabin.

It was the steel Silversea sword. She could tell from its shape. He had enchanted it with something, and its metal positively blazed with magic that seemed to be shouting for her attention. She could tell by its position that it was hanging in its scabbard over the back of a chair or something.

"We think it was intended as a sort of magical beacon," he said. "It's how we found the letters, the wizard was using this spell to leave markers so his wife would know where to look for them."

She saw the potential immediately. If she could just catch the woman sailing out of the marina long enough to cast the spell on some of the copper components of her boat…

"You won't be able to sense the spell if you let her get *too* far away," he said. But from the testing we've done, I'd guess you should be able to stay far enough behind with this spell to be out of sight to her, but not she to you."

Pemana let out a happy sigh, leaning back in her chair and lifting her mug to him in salute. "I think you just saved my investigation," she said, laughing and taking a big drink of her ale.

"I hope it helps," he said, smiling and raising his mug back to her.

Aether checked the slip of parchment in his pouch for the address he'd been given once more, and saw by the worn street sign hanging from the corner of a building that he'd reached the right place.

He saw the sign a few doors down the block that showed a stylized image of a map inside a circle, the marking of the Cartographers' Guild. Excited, he picked up his pace and hurried to the door of the shop.

He opened the door and stepped inside. It was a large shop, and filled with tables spread with maps and lined with bins, with rolled parchments poking up from them that were, presumably, more maps. It smelled quite similar to a book shop, which made Aether smile. A short, older man, with sparse but well-groomed hair, looked up from behind the counter and smiled back at him.

"Welcome," he said in a raspy voice. "What can I do for you, Captain?"

Aether had a feeling the shopkeep called everyone that. Most of his customers probably *were* ships' captains, as far as that went. But Aether still enjoyed hearing it.

"Well, I'm hoping you can help me," he said. "I have a bit of a strange request."

The shopkeep perked up. "Oh! I like those."

"I've been trying to help out a…member of my crew," he said. "He has an old family story about where his people are from, and I've been trying to keep an eye out for old maps that might show it."

"Ah, the mainland?" the cartographer said, a twinkle of professional joy in his eye. "That's always a fun hunt. Where are his people from?"

"Some place called Headwaters?"

"Hmm," the old man said, rubbing his chin. "Not ringing any bells for me, not that much does these days." He shuffled out from behind the counter and beckoned Aether to join him as he headed for the back wall of the shop.

"We don't have much in the way of actual ancient maps," he said. "But I do think," he said, rummaging through the forest of parchments, "that there's something…" He trailed off.

"Ah! Here," the old man said at last, and pulled out a thick roll. He stepped over to a table, Aether following closely, curious.

The cartographer untied the thong and unrolled the sheaf of parchments. Aether whistled.

"They're reproductions," the shopkeep said. "But they were a collection the guild made from ancient maps held by some of the greatest noble houses," he said, his internal salesman emerging a bit. "If there's anything likely to have an obscure Old World village on it, it would probably be in here."

Aether helped him carefully shuffle through some of the maps. But the cartographer flipped to the biggest one, and pulled it out to place it on top of the others.

Aether leaned in with him to look.

The old map was centered on Sunset City, and showed more of the smaller villages scattered about than most maps he'd seen.

He had a suspicion where he ought to start looking. His eyes traced a line from the city of Peacelands to Sunset City itself. He continued the line back northward up a tributary of the Gloaming River, on which Sunset City lay, and almost immediately, he spotted it.

Headwaters.

There it was.

It certainly looked like the ancient wizard's route had been taking him back northward toward the ancient Empire of Bastion, the capital of which they had actually visited once before, returning, famously, with the crown of the lost empress.

He grinned. Looking closely at the map, he suspected it would be a tricky navigation challenge for *Horizon,* even with windstones. But a smaller sailboat, on the other hand…

He was thoughtful for a moment, staring at the map.

"Well, Captain?" the old man asked. "If you're interested in the map, it does only come as part of this collection, I'm afraid."

"I'll want it, I think," Aether said. "How much?"

"Forty silver," the cartographer said calmly.

Aether managed to keep from cursing, and only cleared his throat.

"All right," he managed, his voice suddenly a bit raspy as well. "I'll take them."

Pemana sat, dangling her feet over the edge of a sea wall and holding a fishing pole, pretending intense interest in the bobber floating on the small waves five paces in front of her.

In fact, there was no bait on the hook.

And then, she saw the sailboat passing into her field of view, and the tightly braided hair, perfect for someone who spent a lot of time on the sea, of the woman who piloted it.

Pemana gloated and spat into the water. She had a place to direct her rage, at last. She had this agent of the Swordfish right where she wanted her. And maybe, if she was lucky, the pretty one would lead her to *him.*

Pemana closed her eyes. The small pulse of magic she could sense from the bronze dagger at the woman's hip had done its job. She grinned and withdrew the spell, feeling the tiny flush of the magic returning to her. She immediately began planting the beacon spell into the biggest copper and bronze fittings she could find on the woman's sailboat.

Once she had tagged half a dozen, and the boat had passed her to the point that she was out of her target's sight, she jumped to her feet, hauling the line back in. She walked over to the rather dirty young lad who watched her from the alleyway, and smiled, handing him the pole. He took it as she reached into a pouch and looked around, then leaned in closer to him.

"Don't tell anyone you have this now, okay? You buy you and your friends some good food, make sure you get your change like you're supposed to, and keep that money a secret, so you can get more later, yes?"

He nodded, wide-eyed, as she placed three silver coins in the palm of his hand. His eyes bulged so hard they looked like they were trying to escape his skull.

She gripped his shoulder and looked down at the boy, meeting his eyes. "You be careful out here, all right?"

"Yes'm," the boy said quietly. Then he dropped the fishing pole, turned, and sprinted off down the alley.

Pemana chuckled, picked up the fishing pole, and leaned it up in a corner where the boy would hopefully find it later. Then she broke into a run toward the public short-term dock where she'd left her boat.

Her target had slipped out into the heavy traffic of the main Freehome harbor. This harbor, the largest of the city's three principal ones, was at the far end of town from the slightly less frenetic one where the guild hall sat. It was one of the busiest pieces of sea that Pemana had ever navigated, and her target's sailboat had already vanished into the ever-shifting wall of wood and canvas formed by all the ship traffic crisscrossing the large bay.

But Pemana was unconcerned. She could easily sense the sailboat's location in the small glyph formed by the collection of beacons she'd bound into it. And since she had spread them across the boat, she even had a good sense of her target's distance. And she judged that she would need to let her get further away before she'd be at a sufficient distance to remain just over the horizon.

She freed her sailboat and raised the sail, looking around carefully to make sure no one was paying enough attention to notice that it was catching wind from a direction no one else's did. Everything looked clear, so she summoned wind and slipped quickly out into the churning traffic.

She weaved carefully among ships for a while, then finally got far enough through that the traffic began to thin. She had actually made up some distance on her target, so she lowered the output of her windstones.

As the boat slowed a bit, she found herself with a clear bit of sea ahead. She grabbed the chain around her neck and withdrew the amulet, then gripped it in her fist and concentrated.

She felt Aether's mind as her mental whisper of his name startled him. But she also felt a sense of relief from him, that she was well out there somewhere.

"Pemana!" he said once he'd joined the connection fully. "Good to hear from you. All's well I hope?"

"Aye," Pemana said, and for the first time in a long time, she meant it. "Just wanted to report in that I might be difficult to reach for a bit. That beacon spell works great, and I'm pursuing the woman I told you about north from Freehome as we speak."

"Perfect," he said. "Well, everyone's got amulets now, so if you need help, just tell us where."

"I will, Master Aether," she said.

He chuckled. "Be safe out there, Master Pemana." And he was gone.

Maneuvering to keep her target at the right distance occupied much of her attention for the next several hours. The weather was pretty, windy enough to keep her target moving, but otherwise a fairly lovely day. But the work of maintaining her course and distance did rather quickly become dull, and she found herself starting to dwell on things that it had felt good to ignore for a few hours.

Finally, for something to do, she deactivated the windstones and forced herself to stay at the right distance from her target using only nature's wind and her skill as a sailor.

The woman's destination had seemed likely almost immediately, though Pemana had begun to wonder if she'd been mistaken at one point as her target's course began to change. But after a while, she could tell the woman had corrected herself and was back on track to arrive at New Brightwall.

She found it quite interesting that once again, Lord Eglamon's holding was in the center of the target at which she had aimed their investigation of the Swordfish.

She was pulled away from her reverie about it when she noticed that she had gained on the woman's boat since the last time she'd checked. She started for an instant, but then realized that her target had simply arrived at the smudge of land she could see just beginning to emerge over the horizon, the white triangles of sails in the vicinity of New Brightwall's harbor just beginning to become visible.

Relieved, she reactivated her windstones, and felt the boat surge directly ahead.

It was approaching late afternoon, and the harbor was busy, but it wasn't the mess she'd gotten used to at Freehome lately. She veered quickly through it all until she came upon the high-end public marina where she could sense the bright glyph that was the target boat's collection of beacons.

And as she slowed to approach it, she finally laid eyes on the boat again, and realized her mistake with a loud curse.

The sailboat was docked there, but the sail was down and stowed, and there was no sign of the woman's braided hair.

And Pemana had cleared the beacon spell from the woman's dagger. So she had no way of knowing where her target would have gone.

What a rookie move, she thought, disgusted with herself. How fitting.

Why had she been so…distracted lately?

Sighing, she carefully picked out a slip several docks away from the woman's boat, one that would let her tie up at an angle from which she could watch for the woman's return through one of her own boat's small cabin windows. At least that way she could relax a little and keep herself out of sight at the same time.

She shook her head as she moored the boat, went and paid the expensive fee for the slip, then climbed back aboard and lowered herself against the bulkhead opposite the window, grumbling as she settled in for yet another indeterminately long vigil.

Chapter Eleven

PORTENTS

This was, Pemana decided, undoubtedly the worst part of the city of New Brightwall.

She was hidden on the dirty rooftop of a small, abandoned-looking warehouse, obscured from view by both elevation and the darkness of night. Her position afforded her a view of a complex of mismatched buildings that sprawled across an area of shorefront across the street from her, inside of which gleamed the braided-haired woman's beaconed daggers.

She'd spent a few restless hours watching the woman's boat, and dreading the possibility that she wouldn't return to it until she was ready to depart the city.

But just as Pemana was about to give up and go to sleep, the woman had reappeared and boarded her sailboat, looking like she might be making preparations to depart.

Pemana had groaned. She'd already been tired, and the boredom and frustration of waiting and watching was making her miserable. The idea of having to go back out to sea in that state felt potentially dangerous.

As soon as she'd spotted her, she had been able to quickly cast the beacon spell on the woman's dagger again, and this time marked her boot knife as well for good measure. And then, to her enormous relief, she'd seen the woman re-emerge from the cabin of her sailboat and head back up the dock and into the city.

Instantly, she'd felt better. Another long, boring sail had seemed like an awful idea. But an exciting, adrenaline fueled adventure, tailing her now easy-to-follow target through New Brightwall's maze of streets? That would wake her right up.

She'd quickly grabbed her cloak and a tightly tied leather bag with a long strap that she slung over her shoulder. Last, she'd looked at her grandfather's sword. This part of New Brightwall didn't feel that safe, and she decided she couldn't risk just hiding it in an out-of-the-way place she'd found in the cabin. She'd have to take it with her. She'd drawn the blade a handsbreadth and looked at it for a moment.

It would feel good to have it at her side, honestly. She'd buckled the scabbard onto her belt, slammed the sword back into it, and set off, pursuing at a comfortable distance, able to keep the woman well out of sight and still keep up without concern.

And the woman had led Pemana straight to this place, where she had entered and remained. Once it was good and dark, Pemana had scouted the surroundings, locating a few places that might make good vantages, depending on the time of day.

She had peered through the windows of this dark, some-what dilapidated warehouse a few doors up and across the

street from the target and was pretty sure it was currently unoccupied. So she'd scaled one of the sounder-looking
corners and crawled across the uneven slate roof to where
she could lay and observe the complex. The gleam of the
woman's daggers inside no longer had a vertical orientation
to one another.

Apparently Pemana's work was done for the day as well.

She looked at the rooftop around her, which would, it
seemed, be serving as her bed for the night. She'd lay awake
and observe for a while, see what kind of other activity she
might spot around the facility. But once she couldn't stay
awake, this would probably be the safest place to sleep and
remain unseen from the street below.

She sighed and pulled the strap of the leather bag over
her head and held its ties up in front of her, squinting to see
them in the tiny amount of light that reflected its way to her
from the nearest street lanterns a block away. She worked on
the knot until it came loose, and then, making sure to breathe
through her mouth, she opened the bag and pulled out the
filthy cloak that was her beachsleeper cover.

If a lookout happened to spot her there, sleeping on the
rooftop, and saw a woman wearing the sturdy, light-weight,
dark-colored cloak she was wearing now, and with a
fine-looking sword at her hip, then they might very well
recognize her as the threat that she, indeed, was. But if
they saw a lumpy form covered in the filthy gray-brown
beachsleeper cloak? Well, at worst, they'd throw something
at her and try to make her leave, rather than just, potentially,
clubbing first and asking questions later.

She hauled the tightly bundled cloak out of the leather bag, and the smell of it snuck through to her even though she was mostly breathing through her mouth. She exhaled in disgust, grabbing the visible corner of cloak and holding it while she flung the rest of it out away from her. It opened up, fanning out, and she released it to slide a few paces away from her across the roof. Maybe it would air out some by the time she needed to sleep.

She sighed again, a mistake in the lingering cloud of stink, and crawled back to the corner to watch, deciding that maybe she would stay up…and away from the cloak…as long as she could manage, even though she was already so tired.

Lyrrek started to grab her amulet again, for the twentieth time that morning. And for the twentieth time that morning, she hesitated and finally talked herself back out of it.

She sighed and rose from the table in the kitchen where she'd been trying to relax with some tea. Perhaps what she really needed was something more distracting to keep her occupied.

At the moment, though, the guild hall was pretty quiet. Everyone was away, out and about in the city. Veytra might still be there, asleep in her chamber, but Orenna, Kayd, and Aether had all headed out on various errands within a few minutes of each other. And there really wasn't much more she could think of that immediately needed doing around the hall.

Jyhnda had gone undercover into Lady Fehndala's suite of personal servants a couple days ago, now. It really wasn't that long, she tried to remind herself.

And she sighed again as she realized that her worries about Jyhnda had slipped back into her mind.

Sending her to spy on Lady Fehndala had seemed like a good idea at the time. And Jyhnda was smart and capable, or so Amrelyn said.

But Lyrrek was quickly growing nervous about not knowing how she was doing. If the Swordfish's people were in Fehndala's court, as they feared, then she had sent Jyhnda into a den of their enemy, and Lyrrek wasn't sure she'd fully considered that at the time. She'd begun to feel responsibility for that decision, and the weight of it was growing heavy.

She stood at the table, still unmoving, still unsure what to do.

Finally, she turned and looked at the guild's small library on the bench by the wall. It was mostly books that she and Orenna had owned before they'd all met, with a few new, more recent additions, as she and Aether, particularly, still loved to visit bookshops together.

There wasn't anything in the piles that she hadn't read yet.

On the other hand, that had never stopped her before. She shrugged and went to find an adventure she hadn't gone on in a while.

Pemana looked up from her lap, glancing quickly down the dark street, then went back to making herself small in the corner next to the pile of rubbish and broken furniture that concealed one of her observation spots. Having seen no one, she shifted the filthy cloak aside again, and scribbled a few more notes on the small stack of parchments on her thigh.

She shifted through the pages, re-reading, re-check-ing...re-thinking. It did all seem to make sense. After a couple days of watching, she thought she finally had an idea of what was happening here.

During the day, the complex was mostly quiet. But at night, people began coming and going, armed guards emerging to walk the perimeters of the complex's grounds and challenge newcomers. Occasionally, out in the harbor beyond the complex, a small, dark shape or two would ap-pear, barely visible in the darkness and quietly splashing. And though she didn't have a direct view of the place's seaward approach from her vantages, she had scouted far enough along the shore to see that the harbor side of the largest building did have a small sea gate. She was fairly certain that she could hear squeaking winches from time to time as that gate opened to admit those small boats.

Most of the people she had seen coming in or out over the last couple days had looked, frankly, like pirates. At first, she had started beaconing their weapons enthusiastically, before immediately realizing that this would create a morass of magical signals that would become impossible to read through. She needed to be able to keep her main target straight, even if she had become, apparently, boring and lazy for the last couple days.

And more than anything, the fact that the woman wasn't doing much drove the decision Pemana had come to now. She needed to go inside.

It really was the only way to progress further. She needed to understand what this place was, and what they did. Was there a link to the Swordfish here? Or had her contact sent her on a wild dragon chase?

The activity she'd seen around the location looked promising. But if she found out he had drowned her investigation with a false lead, she would…well, she wouldn't do anything, but she'd be very unhappy with him, she was sure of that.

She would need to make some preparations. There were a couple shops she should visit tomorrow, and she should probably get a decent meal in her stomach somewhere.

And hopefully, things would go well, and she would find something within the walls of the complex that helped her locate the Swordfish, or at least that refocused her investigation on something more productive than watching this woman laze about inside a warehouse with a bunch of pirates. Once she had her next lead, she would head back to the other end of the city to the Wizards' Guild, to check in and figure out where to turn next.

So it would be tomorrow evening, she decided. As soon as it was dark, she'd go in and find out what was really happening here.

Lyrrek jumped and dropped her book when she felt the tingle in her mind and heard Amrelyn calling her. She immediately felt a surge of the swirling nervousness that had haunted her the last few days, but tried to calm it so Amrelyn wouldn't feel it from her.

But then she felt a hint of Amrelyn's own disrupted emotions slipping through the half-connection as she reached for her own amulet, and she began to become alarmed.

"Is Jyhnda all right?" she asked quickly.

"Yes, she's fine," Amrelyn said. "Sorry, I'm sure you can feel my nerves. But she's okay."

"Good," Lyrrek breathed.

"Actually, I'd say she's doing quite well. She already has some interesting information for us."

"And it has you worried," Lyrrek said. "What's going on?"

"Jyhnda was in attendance on Lady Fehndala this afternoon, and the Lady received an envoy. From Lord Eglamon."

"Ahh, interesting," Lyrrek said.

"She said they spoke pretty quietly, like it was their instinct to be discreet, but Fehndala is a bit hard of hearing, and the envoy had to speak loudly enough that Jyhnda caught most of it. She heard them saying something about Council records and 'the exiling.' It made her ears perk up, since she knows the story of how the Wizards' Guild came to be. The way they were talking, she said, it made her wonder if they were talking about Lord Emrek, though she admits they never said a name."

"Hm," Lyrrek said.

"She was pretty specific about the details of what she heard, so I took notes. Fehndala told the envoy that while the exiling had been handled in accordance with Council laws, and adjudicated by one of Lord Moreden's guard captains acting with Council authority, that captain had now been stripped of her command entirely. Fehndala also discovered in the files that…a certain noblewoman, who she didn't name, was also mentioned as present in the captain's report. The envoy wrote all of this down while Fehndala was telling it."

Lyrrek swallowed.

"Lady Fehndala said she had a refinement to their plan that she wished him to communicate to Lord Eglamon. She wanted Eglamon to draw up official orders for the Council's other lords and ladies that their naval forces officially be on the hunt for *Horizon*. These requests were to include the specific detail that the rogue noblewoman in question had, in fact, stolen the vessel while in the process of illegitimately deposing the lord she exiled. Those now in possession of the ship were to be viewed as the perpetrators in crimes against a noble of one of the houses, and were to be hunted."

Lyrrek swore.

"There's more. The envoy was also supposed to pass along orders that this new information be spread among the common people too. She didn't say who those orders came from…but I know I have a theory."

"Wow," Lyrrek said, shaking her head.

"Jyhnda said she slipped out as soon as she could to pass along the information, but she had to return to duty right away. Does this change things? Should we pull her out?"

Lyrrek was immediately torn. She'd spent the last few days half-regretting sending her at all. But if they hadn't, they wouldn't know about this new threat.

"I've been worried about her, and I'm certainly tempted to say yes," she said. "But this is exactly why sending her was a good idea, right? It's already been worth it."

"I know she's excited it's working out, and didn't seem inclined to stop now," Amrelyn said. "But I can tell that this whole thing has you a bit…shaken."

"You are not wrong."

"Are you going to be all right?"

"I suppose so," she said. "I mean, what can they do to me, really?"

It was the right thing to say, probably, but it felt a bit hollow, and Lyrrek figured Amrelyn would feel that too.

"Well, I'll keep you updated when I hear from her again," Amrelyn said.

Lyrrek thanked her and they broke the connection. Then she sat, for a long time, staring at the wall.

Finally, though, she rose and shook herself. There was no sense in her wallowing in this. That wasn't going to fix anything. Their enemies were going to do what they were going to do, and she'd face what life threw at her, as always. What choice did she really have?

She shrugged and made a point of trying to feel cheerful, focusing on celebrating that Jyhnda was safe and doing well…at least for the moment…and went back to work.

Chapter Twelve

Implications

P emana checked the deepening color of the sky, judging the time. Night had mostly fallen, and as expected, activity around the small complex of buildings started to pick up.

She had chosen an opportune moment late that afternoon, when things were still pretty quiet in the area and no one was around to see, and sneaked up to a corner of one of the complex's warehouses to scale up its uneven stones to the roof. It had been a minor misadventure, and she had almost fallen. But in the end, she'd dragged herself, exhausted, over the edge and silently onto the slate of the warehouse's roof, which was hot in the afternoon sun.

This particular building of the complex connected to the others, and had a rooftop doorway, from which she expected a guard to emerge at nightfall. She had hidden herself in the small shade of the corner next to the door, ready to hit him from behind as soon as he emerged.

And then she had spent a miserable couple hours, crouched, trying to stay in the lengthening shadows, and wishing the evening sun would speed its journey along today.

At last, her long wait paid off. As darkness fell, she heard a thudding of footsteps on wooden stairs from inside the door, and it opened to reveal a scrawny man, barely visible in the dim lantern light from the street. He came out, closing the door behind him, and stretched, already looking bored, as he stepped further ahead of her to gaze down over the street below.

She crept silently forward, checking her wardstones.

Then, before she was in position, he turned to start back toward her and she gasped, surging into action.

His eyes widened as he saw the movement in the shadows. But before he could do more than open his mouth, she clubbed him on the forehead, hard, with her dragonskinned fist. He crumpled, and she tried to catch him and minimize the sound of his falling, lest it draw more attention.

She eased him down to the rooftop, then rummaged through his clothes, checking for keys or anything else that seemed important. But she didn't find anything beyond a few copper coins. She started to ignore him and move on, but as she looked down at him and stepped over, she realized that he was pretty young, barely more than a lad. She sighed and bent to cast a healing spell on his head, hoping he'd awaken unharmed…eventually.

She opened the door and crept onto a wooden catwalk with stairs that led down below. She found herself in a wide, columned chamber, as she'd expected. The space itself looked like it was mostly being used as, of all things, a warehouse. In fact, as she looked down at the dusty collections of crates and bundles in the dim light of a few lamps scattered around, piles that looked like they hadn't been disturbed in a long time, she began to suspect she had found another abandoned facility. But in this case, the braided-haired woman's colleagues had found it first.

At present, there weren't any other people visible, and the assortment of crates below beckoned, providing lots of good, dark corners to sneak around in while she figured out the interior layout of the place.

She made it down the creaky wooden stairs, cursing silently at every sound, and hid for a few moments among the crates. She turned and faced in the direction of the sea, and could feel the woman's beaconed daggers still subtly pulling her attention from within the largest building on the grounds. A connected row of old buildings wrapped around the corner from the one she was in all the way to that largest structure, so she hoped she could sneak through and, somewhere along the way, find what she was looking for.

She swallowed and took a deep breath, then began to move again.

She crept into the darker corridors, slipping from shadow to shadow, trying to find a route through the maze of storerooms she entered that let her remain undetected.

Once, she started around a corner and almost stepped on a ragged young man, who had three worn-looking, mismatched copper daggers on his belt. He was leaned against the wall, legs kicked up on a small pile of something, snoring softly. She caught herself from gasping and took a deep, slow breath instead. Then, nerves singing, feeling hugely vulnerable, she stepped over him, ready to leap away and draw her sword if he moved even slightly.

He just kept snoring, thankfully, and she shuddered as she moved on down the corridor past him.

She realized she'd passed into the next connected building when she noticed a change in the color of the stone walls. This one had two floors, and she crept up a set of stairs to the second level.

This building proved trickier to make her way through. She had to wait for a couple more thuggish-looking rogues to go about their business for several minutes before she was able to sneak past them. But thankfully she didn't have to knock anyone else out. The fewer unconscious bodies she left lying around, the better.

At last, she slipped through an old window that had once been on a building's exterior wall, but now led directly into another chamber, and knew she'd made it into the largest building, where her target waited. The beaconed dagger and boot knife were still above one another, and moving around what should be the building's large warehouse floor, so Pemana kept magically checking on the woman's location as she snuck cautiously through, wondering if she could find a place to observe from the upper level.

At last she did find another room, near what should be the outer wall, where the warehouse would overlook the sea. In that corner of the building, there was a second story room with a wide, empty window that opened out to her left, letting in lantern light from a space beyond. The small room itself was full of dust and old furniture. It looked like it might have been an office at one time, judging by the old scraps of parchment littering the corners. But it didn't look like it was being used for anything by the current occupants.

She snuck quietly through the dark room to the window, and looked out onto the warehouse floor. As soon as she peered up over the sill, she stifled a curse and dropped down to crouch out of sight.

She pulled herself silently aside, below the low window sill to the corner, careful to make sure she was deep in the shadows. Then she raised her head up until she could just peer over the edge.

This largest main warehouse floor was huge, and the space among its many columns was a jumbled mess of old crates and bundles...and activity. Dozens of men and women, all of whom looked like pirates to her experienced eye, were hard at work.

In here, there were plenty of signs of crates that had been torn open and looted. Lots of the wide, columned hall had that same dusty look she'd found throughout. But many of the crates had been shoved together and aside into awkward piles to make room for new pockets of activity. And finally, as she watched, the pieces of the puzzle began to assemble themselves for Pemana.

The warehouse's sea gate wasn't very large. But unlike the one at the Wizards' Guild's new hall, this gate actually opened into the warehouse building itself, and there was a short canal cut into the floor, where boats could pull inside to be unloaded. They wouldn't fit a ship in here. But they had, apparently, already admitted a couple tenders, because a number of men were unloading two small boats, while cursing and joking with each other.

The braided-haired woman's voice rang out, telling them to shut up before she cursed them for real. Typical pirate-sounding banter, Pemana supposed. But she was quite surprised when the roguish men *did* fall immediately silent.

In her experience, she would have expected jeers from this type. It felt anomalous. She made a note of it.

Crates repurposed as tables had been laid out in some of the spaces cleared of old cargo, and more rough-looking men and women sat at them, sorting through a varied assortment of goods and products. And at one spot a bit nearer to her, she saw a couple men, guarded by a particularly large fellow who loomed over them, sorting piles of copper and silver coins.

It all seemed to fit what she would have expected. They were likely processing pirated or otherwise stolen goods, figuring out what they'd hauled in that they might be able to sell, and re-routing currency back up to the top. She'd seen a similar pattern a few times in her…former…career.

But one thing did catch her eye here that was unusual. In a rather prominent location, out on their own and convenient to the sea gate, sat three long, large crates. She noticed that on the short end of each crate, a strange hole had been roughly chiseled…a small horizontal rectangle.

They reminded her of the holes left in dungeon cell doors for passing bowls of gruel to prisoners.

She saw the braided-haired woman, then, as she strolled out into the open from somewhere deeper among the stacks of old crates.

A grizzled older man near the boats made his way toward her, and leaned near to say something quiet. But she held up her hand and shushed him. Then she turned and began leading him toward the quiet corner of the warehouse…the one from which Pemana watched.

She ducked quickly down, cursing silently to herself again, and desperately hoping they hadn't spotted her head there in the window.

Then, she heard booted footsteps crunching in the warehouse's fine gravel floor, and quiet words from below.

"I'm supposed to return and report to his highness, you fool!" the woman was saying. "If I don't have some progress to give him…"

"Aye," the man whispered back. "But I don't know what you want us to do. They seem to have vanished into thin air, the lot of them. And no one's seen the ship anywhere for weeks. Maybe it sank and they're all dead. Or maybe that's what we should tell him, anyway."

There was a loud *slap* and an intake of shocked breath.

"Next time you cross *that* line, it won't be *me* correcting you," Pemana heard the woman hiss. "Remember that."

She slowly raised her head to dare a glimpse down below. The grizzled man and the woman were facing each other, and staring. The man was rubbing his cheek and apparently trying to decide whether he was sufficiently afraid of the admittedly dangerous-looking woman in front of him that he would let her survive what she had just done.

Evidently he was, for after a moment, he simply dropped his hand and looked sullen as she went on.

"There will be more workers coming through tonight," she said, a bit louder. "Make sure there are no repeats of last time, understand? And get your crews off their asses and find that ship. Or you'll all be joining them in their chains." She stared at the bemused man in front of her, who only nodded and looked away.

The woman stalked off, and Pemana watched the pirate watch her go, gripping the hilt of the dagger at his belt as he stared at the woman's retreating back.

Pemana dropped down, chilled and newly concerned. She considered for a moment.

Enough was enough. Maybe…

Maybe it was time that she and the woman had a bit of a private chat.

And for that, she'd need time, and to get that time, she'd need help.

She began slowly making her way back out, retracing her steps as quickly as she dared and as quietly as she could.

Aether jogged down *Horizon's* gangplank and across the guild hall's sea yard, bursting into the common area.

"Woah!" Veytra said, stepping back and looking alarmed as Aether slid to a stop to avoid crashing into her.

"Sorry!" he said. "I just heard from Pemana. We all need to talk."

Veytra must have seen something in his face, because she didn't have a snarky comeback for once. "Lyrrek's in the kitchen with Orenna," she simply said. "I'll grab Kayd and meet you there."

He nodded and headed for the kitchen.

Once Veytra and Kayd joined them a moment later and they'd all sat down around a table, he told them what Pemana had found in New Brightwall.

By the time he finished the story, all four of them wore the same combined expression of anger and concern that he could feel on his own features.

"Workers?" Kayd said.

"That's how Pemana put it," Aether said. "She didn't stay on long," he added hastily, trying not to give Kayd a sidelong glance.

"What does she want to do?" Orenna asked.

Aether looked around at them, wanting to gauge their responses. "She thinks we should go in and take them down."

That was met with momentary silence, but Lyrrek, at least, was nodding slowly.

"Did she say how many...well, pirates, I guess?"

"She estimated about four dozen all told, maybe less during the day," Aether said. "And she's worried about the woman departing. She wants us to go in at first light tomorrow morning, if we can make it there in time."

"I've got the first of the new sailboats Orenna found pretty much ready to go," Kayd said. "I can have us ready to depart within the hour."

Aether looked at the others. "It sounds pretty straightforward. Pemana said she worked out a story to tell the local magistrate to get a troop of guards to check the place out tomorrow, around mid-morning, to clean up the aftermath."

"What's she going to tell them?"

"Something about anti-aristocrat plotters meeting there, supposedly trying to plan something to do with Lord Eglamon."

Veytra and Lyrrek chuckled. But Orenna frowned. "That's a little unlike her, isn't it? Lying to a Council magistrate?"

"She said she had reason to believe we couldn't trust the magistrate in New Brightwall. But she figured his guards might actually rouse themselves for an impending threat to Eglamon himself, if she tipped them off about it early, before the magistrate turned up for the day."

Orenna considered, and shrugged.

"Well?" Aether said. "What do you think, do we have any objections? Anything I'm not seeing?"

The others were thoughtful, but they all shook their heads.

"I'll make sure the boat's ready," Kayd said quietly, and Aether nodded, then watched him go.

The darkness of night was leaking away, replaced by a dim blue of early morning light. The air was cool and fresh, thanks to a breeze coming in from the sea, and Pemana took a deep breath of it and positioned herself in front of one of the warehouse's ground level doors.

Her attention felt strangely divided, as the other five masters reached out to her amulet through their own at the same time. Once all of them, Aether, Lyrrek, Orenna, Veytra and Kayd, had told her they were ready, she took a deep breath, cast the spell back to them, and said "now!"

There was an instant's disorientation as the connection broke, and she shook her head. Then she drew her grand-father's sword, and, checking her wardstones one last time, kicked in the door in front of her.

Some of the shoddy-looking masonry shattered, blasting fragments and dust into the hall beyond as she stormed through the door. She charged the very surprised pirate that tried to leap up at the violent disturbance. He didn't have time to do more than reach for one of his long daggers before she was on him, so she just clubbed him with her empty fist, and he crumpled where he'd been trying to rise from his wobbly chair.

She raced down the corridor she'd entered, now starting to hear shouts echoing through the complex as the rest of the Wizards' Guild burst in and began their attack.

But Pemana had chosen her position carefully. She had to be the first one to reach the braided-haired woman. She'd decided she didn't care about Aether's prohibitions against using the dragons' mind-control magic on humans. Pemana *had* to know where to find the Swordfish. That woman's mind was the only place she knew of where she could acquire that information.

So she had to get there first, and before one of the others found her. Once she had the information, she would deal with whatever consequences arose from how she'd acquired it.

She slid through a doorway at the end of the corridor and burst into the wide, columned warehouse floor where she'd seen the woman the day before. She was on the opposite side of the main chamber, and had emerged into another space that had been cleared among the crates. Two pirates roared and lunged toward her from the makeshift corridors formed of crate piles, daggers out.

She quickly disarmed one with a flourish of her sword, his dagger flinging over to embed in a crate. The other stabbed at her, and she simply let him fail at it, goring her shirt, but doing no harm to her dragonskin ribs. She stabbed him back in return and he fell with a cry.

The first roared and leaped to put his hands around her throat. But she leapt toward him at the same time, and his eyes widened in shock even as his hands reached her neck. She landed on his forward foot, stamping it hard to the floor and letting her body weight crash over onto him, feeling him try unsuccessfully to squeeze her throat through her dragonskin spell protections. But as he lost his balance and fell over backward, he let go, arms waving wildly, only to crash onto the back of his head with a *thud* and go still. She climbed up from his motionless form and jogged on past, headed further in.

Crates here had been arranged to form chamber-like spaces, some with pallets on the floor, where people had been sleeping in the small, makeshift rooms.

This is where she'd last seen the woman's bound dagger, but now she found the spaces back here empty.

She wasn't here, where Pemana had expected to find her.

And then, with a draining horror, she realized that, in the chaos of meeting the others and working out the plan of attack over the last couple hours, she hadn't checked recently to see where the woman was. She'd been so fixated on finding her here and getting what she needed from her. And she'd been busy fantasizing about the fight to come, and finding the Swordfish, and tracking him down, and staring into his eyes while she put her grandfather's sword to the purpose for which it had been crafted.

Pemana closed her eyes and glanced quickly around, searching frantically with her magical senses.

But just as quickly, she confirmed that she couldn't sense the woman's daggers anywhere nearby.

Groaning, she turned her attention in the direction of the marina where the braided-haired woman's boat had been docked, where its spell-beaconed components had been glowing to her senses for the last several days while Pemana figured out what to do.

The boat was gone. Wherever it was now, it had gotten far enough away that she couldn't detect any hint of its location or direction.

Pemana's screamed curse echoed off the warehouse's ceiling, blending in among the other shouts and crashing sounds that filled the morning.

Aether couldn't help but grin as he looked over the large group of unconscious pirates, laid out on the floor not far from the sea gate, bound at the wrists and ankles. Lyrrek and Veytra were attending to the five weary-looking men they'd found chained up inside one of the large crates. Kayd, a dark look on his face, had punched the locks on their thick copper chains until they'd broken, earning amazed, confused looks, but also gratitude from the freed prisoners for his trouble.

But Aether noticed the way that Pemana was simply standing, arms crossed as if she was clinging to herself, staring over the scene. She looked exhausted, dark circles under her eyes giving her a hollowed look.

"Pemana," he said quietly, coming up beside her. "You did really well. I think we struck a blow here."

"We didn't do a damned thing," Pemana whispered. "She wasn't here."

Aether remained silent a moment. Pemana had been hoping for more leads, he supposed, which made sense.

He looked over at her and pointed.

"I don't think those men over there would agree that we did nothing," he said. "One of them has children, did you hear? The Swordfish's thugs took him off a beach where he was mending nets. Snuck up and clubbed him from behind."

She was silent, staring at the men, one of whom had fallen to sit on the floor, and was trying not to weep in relief at the apparent end of his ordeal.

"We better get them out of here," Pemana said quietly, looking up toward the light coming in from an exterior window. "I hope the magistrate will deal with these," she said, pointing to the bound pirates. "But we don't want to be here to answer their questions."

"Well, I can't argue with that," Aether said, and, casting one more surreptitious glance her way, he went to round up the rest.

Deldrum stared, eyes wide, at the woman tied to a chair below the Swordfish's throne.

He'd seen her led into the palace that morning, and recognized from her attire that she was probably one of the Swordfish's field agents. He knew not to pay too close attention to any of them, but this one, he couldn't help watching as she'd walked lithely past.

On another day, perhaps she would have noticed his smirking stare, and might have stabbed him or something, from the way the other guards talked about the agents. But this woman had looked totally preoccupied, even worried, as she arrived. It was quite a difference from the usual confident bluster Deldrum would have expected from the Swordfish's top people.

He supposed that her concern must have been justified, given that she was now gagged and bound to that chair, while the Swordfish stared down at her from the throne.

A couple other agents stood nearby, careful not to look at her as they quietly explained details of the astonishing story that had been circulating through the palace all day.

Someone had attacked one of the Swordfish's counting houses in New Brightwall, and the losses had been heavy. Some zealous idiot of a commander in the Council magistrate's local guard had arrested a couple dozen of the Swordfish's people there, before the magistrate himself, who was thoroughly the Swordfish's man, had been able to intervene.

Now, the whole thing was a big mess, apparently. And to top off the strangeness of it all, people kept saying the attackers had been the Lady Lyrrek and her crew.

Deldrum didn't know what to make of that. If his theory that she was a skilled con artist was truth, then surely she had heard of the Swordfish by now, and would know not to cross him. And why would she involve the Council magistrate? It sounded like the magistrate's guards had seized most of the assets and silver on site, which would have meant that Lyrrek's crew left it behind. That didn't fit either.

All they had done was liberate a handful of captured workers that were supposed to be bound here to the palace for stonecutting duties. What would the point of that have been? Deldrum had no idea.

Whatever the Lady Lyrrek was, he thought, it didn't matter now. The Swordfish's people had told the Swordfish that she was behind his losses. She was probably doomed at this point.

Pity, that. But maybe, once he had his swords and was on the run himself, he could track her down and they could hide out from…or take on…the Swordfish together. And then the Swordfish's kingdom would be theirs.

He pulled his attention back as the other agents finished their accounts of what they'd learned, and silence fell across the throne room. The Swordfish just continued to stare down at the beautiful, terrified, braided-haired woman, his face cold and unreadable.

Finally he spoke.

"Clear the throne room."

Deldrum was immediately filled with conflict. He knew he was supposed to wait somewhere outside, like the others. But he'd been appointed to a different, smaller side door into the throne room than he had been in the past. And as he joined the others in saluting and abandoning their posts to step out into the corridors, he realized that he was, for the moment, entirely alone on that side of the palace.

Glancing up and down the long hall, he confirmed there was no one else around, and realized that given his location, he ought to have a chance to hear approaching footsteps before anyone could actually see him.

If he was very cautious…could he peer through the crack in the door, and see what was going on in there?

It was foolishly dangerous, but so much about this place didn't make sense, and he couldn't resist his curiosity. He silently stepped back closer to the edge of the door and tried to see through.

The angle wasn't great. He could see the Swordfish on his throne, but his view of the woman was blocked unless Deldrum opened the door again. That would undoubtedly be a deadly mistake, and he was taking enough risk already. So he just watched the Swordfish as the last sounds of guards and servants departing the throne room fell silent.

After a moment, the Swordfish spoke again. Deldrum was at one of the closer doors to the throne itself, and though the Swordfish spoke softly, he could make out his words.

"You've been in my service a long time," the Swordfish said. "Do you know how old I am?"

She made no answer, of course, with a gag in her mouth.

"I am about seventy of this world's years."

Deldrum frowned.

The Swordfish looked like a man of about thirty summers, close to Deldrum's own age. He decided it was true that he must be older than that, given how long he'd been working to build all of this. But seventy? That was ridiculous. Another lie?

"Oh, I may not look my age," the Swordfish went on, and began rising to his feet. "But I confess, I have been feeling it a bit lately." His cold stare hardened as he began climbing down the dais. "I feel it most especially when fools that I trust *fail* me."

The Swordfish began tugging at one of his black gloves, just as he stepped close enough to the bound woman that he disappeared from Deldrum's line of sight. He cursed silently to himself, and turned to put his ear closer to the crack, wondering grimly just what he was about to hear.

At first there was nothing. But then, after a moment, he heard the woman's voice, muffled by the tight gag, begin to scream.

He heard her feet scuffling against the floor as she started to struggle. Then he heard the legs of her chair jumping and clattering against the stone floor as the violence of whatever was happening shook her.

Was he strangling her or something? It didn't sound like it. Her scream grew louder and louder, still muffled by the gag, but obviously not otherwise restrained between there and her lungs.

He listened in growing horror to the bizarre cacophony of her gurgling scream, which began growing weaker, then weaker still. Finally, it faded into a low, crackling moan, and then silence.

And then, after another moment, he heard the Swordfish take a deep breath, and release it in a long sigh.

He heard the Swordfish's bootsteps, suddenly slapping the stone, and froze in horror. But thankfully, they headed away from him, and he looked again and saw the Swordfish enter his field of view, striding to the door in the far wall. He tore it open and shouted out into the hall.

"Get someone in here to clean up this mess."

Deldrum watched, awed, as the Swordfish calmly climbed up and resumed his seat on the throne. He sat there, motionless, watching disinterestedly as a handful of his most highly ranked guards entered the room and made their way to where the woman sat, still out of Deldrum's sight.

He heard them take hold of her chair, heard a *honk* of wood against stone as they pivoted it and began dragging her from the chamber. He heard their scuffling efforts, the scraping of the chair legs against the smooth, carefully carved floor.

They re-entered Deldrum's view, and his mouth fell wide open. He only barely prevented himself from letting a loud gasp escape from his mouth.

The woman was still bound to the chair, sightless eyes wide and bulging as the guards dragged her tilted form along by the chair's back. But if not for the frazzled shock of braided hair atop her head, Deldrum wouldn't have known it was her.

Her corpse looked like she had been dried into jerky. She had become shriveled, her flesh drained and shrunken.

Deldrum only barely managed not to yelp as he hastily crept backward from the door. He kept going, confusion and terrifying questions rippling through his mind as he backed all the way across the corridor and bumped into the wall, startling himself into yet another near-yelp.

He clapped his hand over his mouth and leaned back against the wall, frozen.

He thought of the disturbed older guard who had whispered something about "corpses" to him, the one Deldrum had immediately dismissed as a mad fool.

It seemed he might be forced to re-examine that assessment.

Chapter Thirteen

A Burning Glow

Pemana drifted into the guild hall's kitchen. She ought to eat, she supposed, though she was struggling to motivate herself to do it. Lately, nothing seemed worth dealing with.

Perhaps she was just feeling dejected at finding herself at a dead end once more. She had no new leads. The last one she'd found had cost her several weeks of boredom and frustration, and in the end, had led to nothing.

Well, perhaps they had struck a small blow against the Swordfish, she allowed. But it hadn't done anything to move *her* toward regaining what *she'd* lost.

The others had seemed pretty pleased with themselves over the last week since they'd returned to Freehome. Pemana supposed it was true that the counting house had been the biggest of the Swordfish's toys that they'd managed to break. But she couldn't escape the nauseating feeling that, for starters, what they had done would be no more than a bruise to the Depths as a whole. It would, however, likely outrage the Swordfish. And then what would *that* bring?

Her attitude had begun to wear on the others after a few days. They had started leaving her alone, as if unsure how to deal with her dark mood.

She sighed. She did feel bad about that. She didn't want her friends to feel like they had to walk on eggshells around her. But she also just felt bad generally, and didn't really know what to do to move things forward once more in a way that would cheer her up.

The door to the alley suddenly banged open and Pemana started, spinning, only to draw in a breath in relief as Orenna entered.

She came in and shut the door behind her, and turned to face Pemana. And Pemana's relief vanished.

Orenna stared back at her, visibly upset.

"I need to talk to everyone, right away," she said quietly. "Will you help me round them up?"

Pemana raced off immediately, the feeling of foreboding and despair swelling in her.

In a moment, they were all gathered, most of them too alarmed by Orenna's obvious distress to sit.

"What is it, Orenna?" Aether asked, his voice full of concern.

She blinked hard, gathering herself, and began to speak.

"I heard it at the market," she said. "Everyone's talking about it."

She took a deep breath and went on.

"There was an attack on a village on Vigil Isle last night." Now that she'd begun, the words began to roll out of her like rocks tumbling down a slope. "Boats came from the sea in the night. The attackers wore black masks and shot flaming arrows into everything flammable they could see. Then they came ashore and attacked the people that turned out to fight the fires."

Lyrrek gasped. Pemana clapped her hand over her mouth, fighting a sudden urge to vomit.

"There were survivors," Orenna went on. "But not many." She looked at the floor as she spoke, not meeting anyone's eyes, her voice flat. "When others arrived to help after the attack, they realized that most of the able-bodied residents of the village were missing, except a few who had…died."

Stunned silence followed her words. It sounded like something out of a history book, something from their people's bloody, violent past. Nothing like this had happened in the Lastlands since the dragons had come. The Lastlanders often told themselves, rather pridefully, that for all their struggles, at least they had grown beyond their ancestors' warlike ways.

Perhaps they were mistaken about that.

Aether's eyes were wide when at last he broke the silence. "Was this the Swordfish? Did we do this?" he whispered.

"I don't know," Orenna said, still not meeting anyone's eyes.

"What village," Kayd asked.

Orenna looked up. Pemana saw the look in her eyes as she met Kayd's.

"Everblue," Orenna said quietly.

Kayd leapt to his feet, his chair crashing back onto the flagstones. "I have to go," he said, his eyes wide.

"I don't think any people or farms outside the village itself were attacked," Orenna said, "just so you know. But I don't blame you."

Veytra and Pemana both got up at the same time.

"I'm coming too," Veytra said.

Pemana nodded, and looked quickly between them. "We'll take my boat. It's already prepped to depart."

Kayd met her eyes, for the first time in weeks. She didn't know what she read there. But he nodded.

Pemana had her sailboat's windstones blasting them forward, at such a clip that the boat slapped its way through the swells, cutting hard against the sea as they raced northwest.

Vigil Isle was a rather long sail from Freehome. Even with the windstones and Pemana's skill, the trip would take several hours.

Kayd sat up on top of the cabin, his back to the mast, staring ahead and not saying much to anyone.

Veytra sat next to him, occasionally patting him on the knee.

They'd been friends forever. And Veytra understood what he was going through, of course. Pemana on the other hand, had never met his mother.

But for some stupid reason, whenever Veytra touched him, Pemana bristled.

The third time it happened, she became outraged at herself. She had heard over ales more than once the laughing explanation about Kayd and Veytra's friendship, how they had bonded over music and books as kids and been fast friends ever since. They both seemed dismissively amused by the suggestion that their friendship ever could have been anything more. They were more like siblings than friends.

But Pemana thought Veytra was very pretty with her straight black hair, so different from Pemana's own wind-blown mess of practical tails or occasional braids. And Kayd just always seemed so comfortable around Veytra. So much more…himself, perhaps.

And none of this mattered anyway, she quickly remind-ed herself, feeling a harsh annoyance that her foolish mind kept dragging this nonsense out onto the floor for her to clean up. If Pemana were to become romantically involved with a harbormaster's apprentice, there was no doubt that her mother, presumably after having summoned the outraged souls of her grandfather and great-grandmother back from the Sky, would hunt her down. What cursed difference did it make to her whether Veytra had her hands on the harbormaster's apprentice in question?

She sighed and glanced down at the sailboat's small compass, making a very slight adjustment to their heading. Then she stared once again up at Kayd's broad back where it was bisected by the mast, and wished she could get the boat to cut through the waves even faster.

Pemana sat uncomfortably at the small, charming farm-house's kitchen table.

The chair itself was comfortable enough. But she sat next to Veytra, watching Kayd's relieved mother hugging him for the ninth time, and wondered just what she had been thinking in jumping up to volunteer to bring him here.

She had seen the look in Kayd's mother's eyes as he awkwardly introduced them. His mother knew who Pemana was to him. That much was obvious. She seemed fascinated to meet her.

Most importantly, his mother, who had shaken Pemana's hand and introduced herself by her name, Sehkla, was just fine, despite the attack. It had everyone in the area quite rattled, of course.

"Well, I hope you'll think about taking my parents up on the offer," Veytra continued. "They wanted me to let you know they would love to have you, and think you'd be safer in the city with them for a while. They have plenty of room with me not being there."

Sehkla smiled fondly at her. "Thank you dear," she said. "I still don't understand what's happening though. How in the world is this related to you all, and why are we in danger?"

"We don't know for certain that it's us they're after," Kayd said, a bit unconvincingly. "But I do wish you'd go stay with Veytra's parents. I worry about you here, out on your own."

Sehkla leaned her head against her son's big shoulder, and he patted her gently on the back. "Oh all right," she said. She looked at Veytra again. "It would be nice to spend a bit of time with your parents. How long will this danger go on, do you think?"

"It's…hard to say," Veytra said. "But hopefully we can…get to the bottom of it…quickly."

Sehkla nodded, finally, and turned back to the kitchen counter, opening a drawer and looking within, then glancing around the room as if taking stock. She seemed like she might be a little lost, trying to imagine what she might need to take with her.

"Kayd," she said, as she opened a cabinet and peered inside. "If you're all concerned about your families being in danger…have you spoken with your father?"

Pemana watched him.

He shook his head. "Not…recently," he said. "He was still up in Cask, last letter I got from him. I haven't visited him there in…a while."

"We can stop in at Cask and check on him," Pemana said, speaking up for the first time. "We should probably warn him."

Sehkla looked at her with an expression that was both grateful and…something else.

"What about your family, dear?" Sehkla asked her kindly. "Where do they live, are they safe?"

"They live on an…uh, they're just outside Port Omen," Pemana said quietly. "I…suppose we probably should stop in there as well."

She swallowed. *That* ought to be an interesting visit.

Aether looked down at the maps spread out on the table, then back up into Lyrrek's eyes.

"I suppose you're right," he said. He leaned back in his chair. "Deep, I'm more than half tempted to set it all aside and just go help Pemana hunt the Swordfish down."

Lyrrek nodded. "It's one possibility."

"But she doesn't have any idea where to look next," he said, staring down at the old map that showed where Headwaters lay. He gestured toward it. "The other half of me thinks we should just race up there and try to find out what the next letter says."

He didn't voice the other consideration. The stronghold of the long-lost wizards was up there somewhere, too. He felt certain of it. If they'd had the magical knowledge to preserve simple letters for one another in the way they had, then imagine what wonders might still lie preserved within their actual *home.*

But they had discussed that enough times in the last few weeks. He didn't want Lyrrek to think he was becoming obsessed.

He watched her rise from the table in the guild hall's kitchen and start for the counter where they'd been keeping some dried herbs for teas. Before she could reach it, though, there was a knock at the door that led from the kitchen out into the alley.

Lyrrek opened the door.

"Oh!" she said, and smiled widely, stepping back to usher someone in.

It was Toliek, Veytra's former apprentice, who'd been working in Cask since he'd graduated to adept. He saluted Lyrrek as he stepped past the door, and as he entered the room, he turned and spotted Aether and smiled, saluting him as well.

But then Lyrrek was exclaiming and stepping back to welcome her father, Master Tovold, as he strode through the door, smiling and with his arms out to hug her, followed by a couple of his guards, who shut the door behind them.

Aether rose quickly, and went to shake hands with Lyrrek's father, and then with Toliek as well.

"Well done!" he said to Toliek. "I'm impressed that you were able to find him so quickly."

"I'll have to credit the Sky for that one, Master Aether," he said. "It was good fortune that I stumbled on Master Tovold's ship where I did."

"Thank you so much for finding him," Lyrrek said, the relief evident in her voice, despite the fact that it was a bit muffled as she clung to her father in a hard hug.

"I'm here," he said, patting her on the back. "We're all fine. Toliek told us there was some concern for our safety."

Lyrrek stepped back, nodding. "It's everyone. There's dangerous things going on out there."

Tovold nodded gravely. "I heard about Everblue." He met Aether's eyes briefly, then looked back at his daughter. "I was relieved to hear that all of you were well. When I found out you'd vanished from Vigil, I was worried enough. But then to hear about the attack…"

Aether nodded with them both, his mouth a small, straight line. It was weighing on all of them.

"But," Tovold said after a moment. "At least I come bearing some good news."

"What's that?" Lyrrek asked.

Tovold turned to the door. "You'll see. Open the sea gate for me, if you would."

Aether looked at Lyrrek, and she raised her eyebrows. He shrugged with her and followed.

After a few minutes, they had winched open one of the sea gates far enough that a pair of tenders from Master Tovold's merchant ship could row their way into the hall's private harbor. They pulled up next to one another against the empty pier and began tying up.

Four large sailors from Tovold's crew positioned themselves in the bottom of each tender. Then, grunting, they struggled to lift some crates up onto the stone pier.

Aether stared, wide-eyed at Tovold, who was walking back over to join them.

He bent to open the top of the first crate and reached in to pull out a bag, which he handed to Aether.

Aether felt the heavy, malleable bulge of coins as he took the bag, grunting, surprised by the weight. He opened the bag and looked inside.

It was full of silver coins.

He looked down, mouth falling open. The crate was filled with bulging bags.

He looked over at the two boats, counting crates.

They weren't that large, the mismatched assortment of wooden boxes.

But there were twenty of them.

"I'm glad I found out where you are." Tovold said. "I can't keep your cut on my ship any longer. It's in the way, it's not secure, and it seemed like it was even starting to affect her balance at speed."

Aether met Lyrrek's eyes. Hers were perfectly round circles.

Tovold grinned. "Oh, and my compliments on the dragon products," he said. "They're quite a hit. Let me know when you have more ready to move."

"I…" Aether began, but that's as far as he got, his power of speech thoroughly compromised, his eyes trying to escape his skull as he stared out over the fortunes accumulating there in the guild hall's sea yard.

CHAPTER FOURTEEN
COMPASS

Pemana finished cinching the last of her sailboat's mooring lines to an old copper cleat with a broken horn, the pink metal of the break reminding her of the exposed flesh of some mortally-wounded green-skinned creature. She shook off the strange thought and straightened up, turning to follow Kayd and Veytra down the worn, uneven dock to the shoreline of the city of Cask.

Visiting this place had always been an adventure, in her experience. Many of Pemana's investigations over the years had led here at one point or another. The fact that her current direct pursuit of the Swordfish hadn't led here in any way was unexpected on its face, perhaps, but Pemana thought she understood why. Cask's underbelly was a tangle of inter-gang territorial conflicts, and had been for…a long time. From what she had seen of the Swordfish's operation, it was much more organized and efficient than the loose associations of thugs and lazy pirates that tended to scrabble over scraps in Cask's back alleys.

Hopefully that meant the Depths weren't very active in Cask, and they'd find Kayd's father perfectly safe and just where they expected to.

And of course, as they walked, she kept one hand over the pouch that held her coin purse, and the other lightly gripping the hilt of her grandfather's sword.

She stepped off the worn pier onto the muddy gravel street. The city's usual smells, its persistent notes of overripe garbage and waste, mingled with the scent of wet gravel from the short summer rain that had arrived in Cask not long before them.

Kayd leaned down to speak quietly with Veytra as they started off down the road, his head close to hers, and Pemana reminded her clenched jaw that it was very likely they were quietly discussing the suspicious-looking lads eyeing them from a few docks over. She resisted the temptation to jog forward and walk more closely behind Kayd and Veytra, and forced herself to just keep moving.

The tavern they sought wasn't far from the harbor. It was a nondescript stone building. Pemana decided she probably wouldn't have noticed it was a tavern if Kayd hadn't pushed his way in the worn wooden door. If there was a sign on this side of the building, she didn't see it.

But, as she entered behind the other two, she did find a smoky, sour-smelling room with a bar and a barman at one end, and a dozen sailors spread around uneven tables with mugs on them. So she shrugged and followed Kayd and Veytra to the bar.

"Get 'ya?" the barman mumbled at Kayd.

"Oh, nothing thanks," Kayd said mildly. "Looking for Ehkud, he still working here?"

The barman spat. "No," he said, speaking a bit more clearly. "And if you find him, you tell that bastard that he ain't gettin' his last wage until I get my key back."

"My grandparents were wed, actually," Kayd said, still perfectly mild.

The barman stared up at him for a moment. Then he spat again.

"Sorry lad," he said finally. "I haven't seen him in…a couple weeks. He just didn't show up one afternoon."

"Do you happen to know where he was staying?" Kayd asked.

The barman just shook his head.

Kayd sighed and dropped a couple silver coins on the counter. He nodded to the surprised barman, then led them back out to the street.

"I had my father's address on a letter…a while ago…" he said quietly, staring out at the horizon as he stood motionless in the road outside the tavern. "I didn't keep it. I don't know where he was living here."

Veytra patted him on the arm. "Let's go by the little hall Mahlda and Toliek set up. We can give them a description of him and ask them to keep an eye out."

He nodded and let her lead him down the street.

Adept Mahlda was excited to see Veytra when they arrived at the door of the small converted apartment. Pemana had met Mahlda once before, early on, when she was still Veytra's apprentice. She thought she remembered her being middle-aged, but if she had been once, she'd obviously mastered the healing spells since.

Veytra returned Mahlda's hug, and Kayd her handshake. She saluted Pemana as she greeted her, and Pemana returned her salute, smiling. She also remembered Mahlda being friendly, but the animated excitement that seemed to pulse from her was new.

She led them all in and closed the door behind them.

"Um…" she said, looking over the empty counters in the kitchen, then turned back to them with a sheepish expression. "Sorry, we actually gave away what food we had left earlier this morning."

"That's all right," Veytra said, her smile fading. "We can't stay long anyway. We just had some information to leave with you, to ask you to keep your eyes out for someone for us."

She explained the situation with Kayd's absent father. Mahlda became appropriately solemn as she understood, and with a compassionate look at Kayd, and a hand on his arm, she promised that they would do everything they could to help find him.

Kayd's smile was thin and a bit forced, but he thanked her graciously.

Veytra started to take their leave, but Mahlda interrupted her.

"Actually," she said, "I'm glad you stopped by, I had been meaning to reach out to you. While you're here, I should tell you about a strange thing we heard recently." She stepped quickly over to a small side table and opened a drawer, withdrawing some scraps of parchment. "Some of the beachsleepers know that we're associated with the famous Lady Lyrrek," she said. "So when this happened, they remembered and made a point to tell us."

She read her notes. "They told us that a strange man's been coming and hanging around the beaches now and then over the last few weeks. Sometimes he'd share fish, or trade for little things, but mostly he was just odd and quiet, and didn't say much. But he did, at one point, ask if anyone had heard rumors about a particular noblewoman, and he named Lady Lyrrek and House Silversea. And he asked something about a ship associated with her too. They didn't remember the name of the ship, but when I asked if it was *Horizon*, they said they thought that sounded right."

Kayd met Pemana's eyes, and he looked alarmed.

"They described him as looking like any other beach-sleeper, with long, tangled, dark hair and beard. But he wore a strange, rough-looking short robe of a dark-colored leather. The beachsleepers were arguing about whether his robe was made of stalkerhide. One swore it was, and the others were making fun of him over the idea that a beachsleeper like them would sail around in a tiny, broken-looking boat, but sit with them at their fires wearing a robe worth a small fortune." She looked up. "It was all so strange, I wrote it down. I don't know if it means anything, but I wanted to make sure you knew, since they mentioned Lyrrek."

"That is bizarre," Veytra said, turning toward Pemana. "One of the Swordfish's agents, you think, trying to track us down?"

"I wonder if…" Kayd began, trailing off thoughtfully.

Pemana had a sudden flash of insight.

"Lord Emrek?" she said, incredulous. "You think he made it off the mainland?"

"If he did," Kayd said flatly, "then he'd probably be one more out there hunting us, wouldn't he?"

Lyrrek waited as Aether unlocked one of the deepest store-rooms in their new guild hall, one of the ones that lay furthest away from any outer wall. He lit the stone on his staff as he entered the room ahead of her, then leaned it up against the wall to illuminate their work.

"I don't mean to try to start an argument," she said, joining him in the storeroom. "But I do think we ought to talk about it, at least once more. It's going to be an enormous amount of silver."

"I know, Lyrrek. I don't disagree." He smiled gently, and accepted the haversack she held out to him. "We can certainly talk about it more, or even argue about it if we need to." He set the haversack down on top of one of the twenty crates of silver they had, with a great deal of effort, dragged back to this secure chamber. Then he turned to face her, an expectant look on his face.

She appreciated that he didn't just proceed with the task, that he was actually giving her a chance to try to talk him out of it, if she could.

It wasn't that she was convinced she wanted to talk him out of it. But it was a weighty matter, pledging to spend such a huge chunk of their profits on something speculative.

"I think it's just making me nervous, that's all," she said. "It's not that I think it's a bad idea. It's just so…quick, maybe."

He nodded and looked up, contemplating. "It's true, I suppose." He gestured toward the expanse of crates, and spoke quietly, even though they were alone, and deep inside their own guild hall. "Although the counter-argument to that is that it's probably not ideal for us to be sitting on this giant pile of treasure. It's a lot to guard, and so far, we don't really have the capacity to protect it as well as we should, even if we are wizards."

She nodded. That was a fair point.

"So I'd argue that if we're presented with an opportunity to turn some of it into something productive that's easier to protect, we ought to go for it. And, as I've said each other time we discussed it…" He winked, and she understood that he wasn't being harsh. "Imagine how much of an investment it will be in our future, if we actually manage to pull this off and convince the rest of the world to help us rebuild…the world."

She grinned and walked over and hugged him. "You're right, I suppose." She looked across the crates of silver. "Maybe it's just that it feels good, you know? Looking at it all and knowing how…set we are, I guess. I mean, what is this going to cost. Ten of these crates? Fifteen?"

"I hope it'll be less than half," he said. "But I admit that I tried to count two of them, and it was a workout. So I estimated a total. Wouldn't surprise me if I'm off by a few dozen bags." He kissed her. "But I am pretty sure there will be more than plenty left."

She sighed, but nodded. "We're going to need a lot more apprentices. I wish the Swordfish would just get out of our way and let us get back to work."

"Yeah," he sighed with her. She released him and picked up the sturdy haversack, nodding down at the crate.

He stood and lifted the top of it, and she crouched, placing the bottom of the haversack on the flagstone and holding it open while he began lifting out bags and dropping them in. After several, he lifted it, testing the strain of the weight on the haversack's straps, and decided that they'd have to stop there.

"I guess that will have to be enough," he said, grabbing her extended hand and helping her upright. "Hopefully they'll take the job with this much down."

"You'll charm them," she said, smiling at him. "You have that way with people."

He bowed to her at the compliment, and came back up grinning. "Sure you don't want to come with me? It's been pretty...tense lately. It might be a nice distraction."

Her smile faded at the reminder of Everblue, as it had each time, the last few days. And yes, he was probably right. She probably could use the distraction. But she had other work to do.

"I promised Orenna I'd stay available in case anyone reached out while she was away, so she could relay back to me if any immediate needs came up." She kissed him again. "You'll be gone all day. But you should go and try to enjoy yourself."

His smile had faded as well. "I'm not sure whether to expect a good time or not. It might just be strange and uncomfortable," he said, sighing. "But I guess I'll find out."

Aether focused on the magic in the little tender's windstones, relaxing the force of the wind that was inflating the sail, and felt the small boat's speed lessen slightly. It had been a rather adventurous trip around the island in such a tiny boat, all the way around the easternmost point, from Freehome to the city opposite on the southern shore, Savage Seas. Aether didn't have to rely on natural wind conditions, as long as no one was observing him too closely for use of his windstones. But today was a bright, windy summer day, and that meant the sea was…exciting. And there wasn't much the boat's magical modifications could do to help with that.

He and the little boat had taken a bit of a beating on the long sail around to the south side. He probably would have made it quicker if he'd just walked across the island, honestly. But the heavy haversack in the floor of the boat would have been quite a burden on a long hike. And anyway, it had been rather fun, leaping the little boat with its small sail up and down some good sized swells on the way.

Clusters of stone buildings with slate roofs finally began to appear on the shoreline ahead, as he continued west along the island's southern coast. He was still enjoying the refreshing, salty spray and the windy day, but it would be a relief to get off the choppy water for a while, while he took care of his business in Savage Seas.

He dodged through the ship traffic entering and leaving the city, crossing past the main harbor without entering himself. His destination was on the western corner of the small bay around which Savage Seas had sprung up long ago. Aether watched in awe as the impressive sight came into full view.

There, on the shoreline, was the largest shipyard Aether had ever seen.

He spotted a large sign at the western end of the yard, where there were a couple public docks. As he dropped the power on the windstones to let the tender drift lazily in on a light breeze, he stared, bemused, at the wooden sign bearing the glyph of the Shipwrights' Guild that stood, a full two paces tall, next to where the dock met the shore.

He didn't know exactly what he was expecting. He had, over his lifetime, been around other shipwrights' yards aside from the pathetically small one in Vigil at which his former master had employed him throughout his childhood.

But he had never been anywhere near a shipyard as huge as this one.

He'd long known of this particular yard's achievements. It was one of the most famous in the Lastlands, and probably the gold standard of the Shipwrights' Guild. At one point, he would have been thrilled by the opportunity to come see this place.

But Aether hadn't thought of himself as a shipwright for more than a year, not since he and the others created the Wizards' Guild. Technically, he'd never formally withdrawn from his apprenticeship as a shipwright. But he wondered how he would feel about this walk back into that world.

Would it dredge up troubling memories for him? He had worked pretty hard at forgetting his former master entirely.

Aether lowered the sail and tied the boat to cleats, then took a deep breath, lifted the heavy haversack to his shoulder, and stepped up onto the dock.

The shipyard did, indeed, feel huge. He was at the western edge, and the other side, to the east, was what…two hundred paces away? He wasn't sure of the distance, it was so far. Along the shipyard's section of shore, the natural depth of the sea had been transitioned onto a low slope of land that was fitted with huge ship winches and long, flat rows of thick poles, laid out together, ready to help roll a ship's entire hull up onto land for servicing. Each of the four wide ship bays could accommodate a truly massive vessel, and there were lots of lesser bays around the peripheries for working on smaller boats or other projects.

The scale of the place took his breath away, and he was almost disoriented for a moment.

But as he stared around, astonished, it began to register that something was wrong.

Finally, after glancing around, he spotted it. While the wide yard was crowded with the shipyard's infrastructure, there wasn't actually much going on that he could see. The whole, huge place was far too quiet for an active shipyard.

This facility was large enough that there ought to have been hundreds of laborers swarming over large ships' hulls in a row before him, pounding, sawing and scrubbing away at their work. It should be an absolute cacophony. But though he could hear a few things underway here and there at the peripheries, it wasn't much, and sounded mostly like sharpening of tools perhaps, or a few other maintenance tasks being done.

Three of the four large ship bays lay empty. Aether slowed, staring up at the fourth, at the disconcerting sight of the nearly completed stern of a large ship, its wood all mid-construction fresh and bright. It only had bulkheads rising up from the keel until a point about two-thirds of the way toward the bow of the eventual ship it was meant to be. It looked strangely skeletal from there forward. And as far as Aether could see, no one was at work on the ship at all just then.

What was happening here? Hopefully he hadn't wasted his time lugging this heavy bag of silver all the way around the island for nothing. Because it looked like this shipyard was mostly shut down.

He spotted what looked like a small village of buildings tucked away in a back corner of the yard, and figured that's where he'd find someone in charge. He supposed he ought to at least try to figure out what was going on.

A gruff, strong-looking middle-aged man looked up from a box of tools as Aether approached the nearest stone building.

"Hello," Aether said. "Pardon for interrupting, but I'm a shipwright's apprentice, looking for the master, or a master, or however this place…"

The man looked up at him as he trailed off, wearing what Aether would have sworn was a pitying expression.

He jerked his thumb over his shoulder and said "the big building," then turned back to his tools, shaking his head slightly.

Aether refrained from frowning and just headed for the largest of the nearby stone structures.

As he started up the steps, shifting the uncomfortable weight of the bag on his shoulder, he noticed that the door was ajar, presumably to let some air circulate on a warm summer day. He knocked politely and pushed the door open some to peer inside.

"Come in," said a man's voice. He saw someone gesturing from a desk across the chamber and stepped inside, blinking as his eyes adjusted after the bright sunshine outside.

"Thank you," Aether said, crossing the office. There were two chairs in front of the desk, and the man gestured toward one, closing a drawer and giving Aether his attention.

"What can I do for you?" the man asked him.

Aether carefully set his haversack down next to one of the chairs, suppressing a relieved sigh, and took a seat. "My name is Aether," he said. "I'm actually a shipwrights' apprentice…"

"Well, I'm sorry lad," the man interrupted with a sigh. "There's no jobs here, I'm afraid."

"Oh!" Aether said. "What's going on? I did notice that this place seems a lot quieter than I would have expected."

"Aye," the man said with a sigh, leaning back in his chair. "There's been a downturn, the last couple years. It's finally caught up with us." He stared at Aether. "Surely you've noticed it, if you've been working as an apprentice."

"Ah," Aether said, nodding. "Actually, I've been away from guild work for the last year or two. I hadn't realized things were bad these days."

"Well," the man sighed again, "They have been that. Whatever you've been up to recently instead, I'd recommend you stick with it." He gestured around his office, a bit of a bitter expression slipping onto his features. "I don't know what's going on with the world lately, but it's like people have stopped buying new ships."

He stood and looked out the window toward the half-completed hull in the yard. "We thought we had some work, finally, but the buyer's finances collapsed, and now I can't afford to pay my workers, much less buy the supplies to finish the build myself." He turned and stared at Aether, shaking his head. "Sorry lad, I don't know why I'm telling you all this." He returned to his chair. "Well, was there anything else you needed? Like I said, I got no jobs, that's for certain."

"Oh, I fully intend to keep doing what I've been doing," Aether said. "Actually, I'm here to talk to you about buying a ship."

The man's eyes and mouth both flew open.

"What?"

"Sorry, yes. I *was* a shipwright's apprentice, but that's not what I do anymore." He looked around at the wonder of the giant shipyard outside the windows. "Although I have to say, this place is absolutely incredible!"

"Uh...thanks," the man said, sounding bemused. "Well, what kind of ship are you looking for?" Aether could sense the shipwright's nervousness. He knew well that he looked quite young to be showing up and ordering a ship like it was a fish dinner at the inn. Aether could sense the suspicion forming in the man's mind, that perhaps this day had decided to compound his sufferings by delivering him a criminal or something.

"I'm sorry," Aether said, standing up and holding out his hand for the man to shake. "Master...was it?"

The shipwright didn't stand, but he did shake Aether's hand. "Master Emeled. You said..."

"Aether," he repeated, smiling and taking his seat. He reached down and opened his haversack, withdrawing a short roll of parchment.

"I have something particular in mind," he said. He unrolled Pemana's drawing of *Horizon* and handed it over.

The shipwright immediately whistled, turning the page upright, eyes wide as he studied the rendering. "Now *that's* a beautiful ship. Dragon-carved, huh?"

"Yeah, she's a gem," Aether said proudly. "But she needs a sister. She's only about thirty paces. I was thinking about something with a matching design to this, but more like fifty paces long. We need a bigger ship to add to our fleet."

The shipwright looked up from the drawing and stared at him for a long moment. Finally he spoke. "Are you conning me, son? Are you someone I'm going to regret meeting?"

Aether laughed. "No. It's all right, I do understand, I'm probably not what usually walks through that door with money to spend on ships. But I represent an organization that has need of one, nonetheless. And we want a *pretty* one. And you're the best." He looked around, grinning. "I've been hearing that my whole life, it seems."

The shipwright continued to stare at him. But now his eyes were occasionally flicking over Aether's shoulder, out the window at the partially completed hull in the yard.

Aether wasn't surprised. He wasn't an expert shipwright, exactly, but he did know enough to suspect that the large, partially-built ship out there was probably going to be about a fifty pacer once all was said and done.

And he liked what they'd already done with the stern just fine. They were the best, after all.

The shipwright swallowed. "Just what kind of financial resources do you have then? How much are you willing to pay for this pretty ship?"

Aether bent and pulled out one of the bags of silver coins, opening it and handing it over. Master Emeled stared at the heavy bag, reached in and pulled out a handful of coins. While he did, Aether continued piling four more of the large bags onto his desk, until the shipwright's eyes bulged and his mouth fell open.

"I know this won't be nearly enough to cover the whole cost, of course. It's probably just enough to get you started. But I didn't figure I could wear the whole of the price all at once. So hopefully this will be enough to get your workers' pay caught up and cover raw materials until I can make it back over with the rest." He chuckled. "I think I might need to rent a sheep wagon and bring some friends to help on that trip, though."

The stunned shipwright finally looked up from the pile of bags of silver on his desk, and Aether pretended not to notice that he was trying to blink back tears.

"Well!" Emeled said, finally, leaping to his feet. "Allow me to welcome you properly, Master...Aether was it?" He stepped forward and shook Aether's hand, with enthusiasm this time, a huge smile breaking out on his face. He reached into his desk and withdrew a couple glasses and a bottle of brandy, immediately pouring himself a large one that he downed in a gulp, gasping slightly as he poured two more and handed Aether one. "To...whatever it is you do!" he said, and clinked glasses with Aether, who laughed and took a drink, beginning to catch some of the shipwright's excitement.

Master Emeled took a sip of his second brandy and set it down, picking up the picture of *Horizon,* a pencil, and some extra parchment. He handed Aether the drawing to carry, then pulled him toward the door with him. "Let's go walk the hull so you can see the work we've done so far," he said animatedly. "You can let me know what you want, and we can fix you up...uh...hopefully without having to change what's already there too much."

Aether chuckled. "I'm sure it'll work out fine, I already like what I see." He followed Emeled across the yard toward what would, apparently, soon be his new ship's hull, grinning as the shipwright described how excited his carvers would be when they saw the gorgeous bow work they were about to get to do.

"Great news everyone!" Master Emeled suddenly roared out across the yard to his workers, glee in his voice. "Turns out today's payday! And we're getting back to work!"

Lyrrek gasped, grasping her amulet tighter as Amrelyn's words woke her the rest of the way up, and she sat up from where she'd nodded off under her book.

"I'm here," she said back to Amrelyn's mind, once she'd cast the spell herself. "Sorry, I'd dozed off, apparently. I'm awake now. You said Jyhnda…"

"Hi," Amrelyn said, chuckling quietly. "Sorry to wake you, but it's urgent. Jyhnda slipped away to contact me. She was in attendance on Fehndala when she…uh, when Fehndala, I mean, received a message. She was talking to one of her advisers and when he saw the look on her face, he asked who it was from. She said 'him,' and the adviser said 'Eglamon?' And she said 'no. *Him*.' And Jyhnda said the adviser looked like he was going to faint. Then Fehndala said everything was confirmed, and they were to report to Eglamon with 'the delivery' at the time they'd all agreed."

"Delivery of what?" Lyrrek asked.

"They never said. But Fehndala did say they were supposed to bring three particular guards that she named, and she seemed very annoyed, and said that she'd *known* they were agents of *his*."

Lyrrek drew in a sharp breath.

"Fehndala got salty about being ordered around like a servant for a while, then gave orders to have her ship ready to depart at first light tomorrow, and said that they may as well complete other business she had to do on the way."

"Oh wow," Lyrrek breathed. "Do you think we can get Jyhnda on that trip somehow?"

"She's already been told she's going," Amrelyn said.

Lyrrek was silent a moment, pondering what she could read of Amrelyn's feelings through the connection.

"Do you want to order her out?" She asked.

"No. We've been over all of that," she said bluntly. But Lyrrek could also feel that she wasn't resentful. She was just feeling the weight of responsibility, much as Lyrrek had been. "Jyhnda's all for it," Amrelyn went on. "But there's a problem."

"What is it?"

"I don't have any backup. I beaconed the chain on Jyhnda's mind amulet, so I can follow them in my sailboat. But...I need another set of hands. Preferably wizard ones."

Lyrrek froze.

Amrelyn was right of course. It was imperative they have someone handy in case Jyhnda needed extracting for some reason. And they should have already found Amrelyn more help, since she was still out in the field, trying to hold things together in that regard for them. But everything had been so...dicey, lately.

So Lyrrek had to send someone to help her. If someone left Freehome right away, they could probably be in Eagle's End by nightfall, or at least not too long after.

But there was no one else here.

Aether was off buying a ship. Orenna had taken one of the three sailboats she'd found for them over to Empress Isle on an errand. And Kayd, Veytra, and Pemana hadn't yet returned from warning family.

There was only her.

It was fitting really. This mess was kind of her fault. She could have backed Amrelyn up from the beginning and kept Jyhnda from being in this situation at all.

On the other hand, she did have the remaining two of Orenna's newly acquired sailboats.

Lyrrek swallowed, hard.

"You all right?" Amrelyn asked her.

"I...think so," Lyrrek said. "I'm just thinking through the fact that I'm the only person that can help, and that it looks like I'm about to embark on that solo sail everyone keeps telling me I can handle." She didn't need to explain how nervous she was about it. She was quite certain Amrelyn would be able to feel it.

"You *can* handle it," Amrelyn said immediately. "I believe in you, my lady."

"Thanks Amrelyn," she said quietly. "Well...all right then, nothing for it. I guess I'll see you tonight."

"You will, Lyrrek. I promise. Call for me if you have any problems."

"Yes master," she said, grinning. And she broke the connection.

She stared at the wall for a long moment, feeling panic start to bubble up in her, trying to figure out what to do first. She leapt to her feet and raced for their cabin on *Horizon.*

Once she'd dressed for an adventure and packed everything she thought she needed in a haversack, she belted on her favorite shortsword, then sat down at the map table with a parchment and pencil.

She'd thought of contacting Aether on his amulet. But she hated to interrupt him during what she hoped was a really interesting experience, to say nothing of the potential awkwardness for him of trying to explain to strangers why he needed to have a private conversation with his necklace.

Besides, this was all likely nothing but a precautionary measure, and they wouldn't really learn anything useful or be in any danger anyway. So she just wrote him a note and laid it on the map table where he'd see it when he returned and looked for her.

Then she jogged off the ship and over to the door that led out to the public dock, where the two new sailboats were moored, locking the door behind her.

She had helped Orenna with loading the boats up with supplies and equipment, and knew that both should be ready for sail. One was actually a twelve-pacer, but she decided on the smaller ten-pacer, which felt less intimidating, if only slightly.

She finished one last look at the route to Eagle's End on one of the boat's charts, and laid it where it would be handy. Then, taking a deep breath, she decided she was as ready as she was going to get.

She untied the boat and raised the sail, then sat down at the small helm and took a deep breath.

"Well, little lady," she said to the boat, then stopped as she realized she'd used her father's diminutive for herself.

She grinned. "Why not. Let's go, little lady. We can do this." And looking around to make sure no one was near enough to notice, she activated the sailboat's windstones, gripping the wheel and feeling a thrill of nervous excitement as she and the boat surged into motion together out into Freehome's busy harbor.

Chapter Fifteen

Departures

Pemana burst out of the front door of her parents' estate house, firmly denying herself the loud curse that wanted to erupt from her, and stomped down the stone steps two at a time.

Kayd and Veytra rose from one of the benches near the small pond in front of the house, looking understandably bemused. Pemana hadn't been inside that long, maybe fifteen minutes. But when her parents had met her at the door, they had pointed at the benches out front as a place her friends could wait while they discussed some things with their daughter.

She could hardly blame Veytra and Kayd for feeling awkward under the circumstances. It was a pretty long sail from the hospitality that *both* of their families had separately shown to *her* in the last couple days.

"I am so sorry for that," she said, not bothering to hide her exasperation and disgust from them. "I don't know if I ever really noticed it before, but my parents aren't..."

Kayd actually patted her on the shoulder. Then he looked embarrassed and jerked his hand away. But she managed to smile at him, at least a little, and led them quickly off down the lane back toward the road. While they went, she couldn't help imagining that she could feel her parents' stares following them from around a curtain somewhere behind.

"So, how did it go, then?" Veytra finally asked. Her tone made it a bit of a joke, and Pemana did feel some of the tension in her ease as she chuckled.

"Predictably, I guess," she said, with an exaggerated sigh. "They only wanted to talk about that ridiculous job scraping barnacles off hulls, how maybe if I stuck it out and worked really hard for a few years…a few years, I reiterate, of spending every day scraping barnacles off hulls…how I might be able to start rebuilding my career."

"Ugh," Veytra said. "I know I'd pass on that, thank you very much."

"That's what I told them. But when I tried to change the subject, to tell them there was danger…" Pemana fell silent, trying to think of how to word it.

"What?" Veytra asked after a moment.

She sighed. "They scoffed and said that whatever 'nonsense' the locals were getting up to on Vigil Isle was no concern of theirs." She looked at Kayd, hoping her expression looked apologetic. "For what it's worth, I was…suitably offended, on your behalf."

Kayd, who had been starting to frown, relaxed.

"I told them I'd just met your mother, who was from right there near the attack, and she was amazing."

He actually grinned at her, which made her stomach flutter. She hadn't seen his smile much recently.

She quickly went on. "They ignored my warnings, I think. Just kept veering back at that stupid job."

"What did you say?" Kayd asked.

She looked at him and grinned. "I stood up and told them I liked my new job far more, and the pay was better anyway. They demanded to know what my new job was."

"What'd you tell them?" Veytra asked.

Pemana grinned. "I said 'dragon hunting,' and then marched right out. They both looked completely shocked."

Kayd and Veytra both applauded.

"Oh well done," Veytra said.

Kayd's smile faded, though, and his face fell. "I'm sorry your parents don't support you," he said quietly, staring up the road ahead of them toward the harbor. "That's not fair."

She stared over at him for a moment, then nodded and continued on as silence fell, the only sound the crunching of their boots in the road's crushed stone.

They reached the dock and Pemana's sailboat at last, and Kayd and Veytra each untied a mooring line.

"Well," Kayd said as they stepped aboard, the sailboat bobbing a bit with Veytra's added weight, and quite a bit more with Kayd's. "I guess we're headed back to Freehome then?"

Pemana nodded. "I suppose so. There's certainly nothing more we can do here."

"What *are* we doing now?" Veytra asked. "Lately…" Pemana saw Veytra cast her a sideways glance. "Well, it kind of feels like we're on the defensive, you know?"

Pemana sighed, adding her breath to the windstones' effort as they inflated the sail. "I do know." She was silent a moment, then met Veytra's eyes. "I'm not sure where to go next. The last lead I had…got some people killed."

"Sorry," Veytra said quickly. "I didn't mean to bring that up."

"It doesn't matter," Kayd said quietly, before Pemana could respond. "We have to keep going, no matter what the Swordfish does to get back at us. We have to find him."

Pemana and Veytra both turned to look at him. He was staring out at the horizon ahead of them, and spoke again, his voice firm.

"There are people out there, trapped, prisoners, or Sky knows what. One of them might be my father. And no one else is coming to help them."

Aether sat down in the chair at the map table in their cabin on *Horizon,* Lyrrek's note in his hand. He read it over once more, then frowned, thoughtful, looking vaguely in the direction of the public dock outside their sea yard.

At least now he knew why there'd only been one sailboat left there when he arrived back.

He'd come inside and discovered he couldn't find any-one at the hall just then, including Lyrrek.

Now he understood. Her note wasn't particularly long, but it said a lot, nonetheless.

She'd written that something came up with Amrelyn and Jyhnda, and they needed more help quickly, and she was the only one here, so she had to leave right away. But she said not to worry, and that she'd contact him on his amulet once she knew more about it. She said she hoped he was right about her sailing skills, because she was taking one of the sailboats and leaving for Eagle's End, and she'd have her amulet if he needed to reach her.

He leaned back, staring up at the bulkhead. He wasn't *too* worried. He did trust her skills, and certainly her intelligence. And she was a stronger swimmer than he was, and he was pretty good.

He knew Orenna had gotten a good set of charts for each boat, and from the same cartographer he'd been to, in fact. Lyrrek knew to consult them carefully for known hazards and how to watch for surprises. And the weather was fine, too. She'd be fine.

He thought about contacting her, just to check in, to tell her that he was proud of her. But he was fairly certain that at least some part of his motivation was just to make sure she was still okay. And so he chose to trust her all the way, and lowered his hand from his amulet.

He looked around for a minute, thinking about what to do with himself, and decided a distraction would be beneficial. Trusting her didn't change the fact that it was her first solo passage, a risky endeavor, even for a wizard, and he didn't want to sit around worrying about her.

And that brought his eyes back to the second part of her note. She said that she'd thought a lot about what he said, right after the Contribution feast, about the freedom of going off in a boat alone. She had decided she was excited to try it. And she'd also thought a lot about the importance of them finding the next cache the wizard had left. If he wanted to go on a little solo adventure of his own, since everyone else was, maybe he ought to think about taking that twelve-pacer and trying to go find the next cache while she was away. She trusted his skills too, and knew he would be safe, even in a land of dragons.

He stared at the bulkhead of their cabin for a while again.

He had to admit, her idea held a certain strange appeal.

His solo excursion, in exile, along the southern coast of the mainland had been traumatizing in some ways. But it had also been the most amazing adventure of his life, at least once he'd figured out how to use magic by observing some land dragons. The idea of going back, alone, of facing that perilous wilderness again, just him and his wits, but this time with magic and a boat…it sounded, somehow, remarkably enticing.

Nonetheless, he hesitated. He would be gone for a while, days away if something went wrong. What if she needed his help?

But he quickly reminded himself that she was on her way to join Amrelyn, and the rest of their very capable friends would still be relatively close, if they needed help.

And she was right about one more thing. Finding the wizard's next letter was crucial.

At last, he talked himself into it. He wrote Orenna a second note from him, explaining where he and Lyrrek had gone, leaving a few guild-related instructions, and letting her know she could contact him anytime she needed to. Then he left both notes in the kitchen for Orenna to find when she returned.

Grinning, he jogged to *Horizon* to gather everything he'd need to take along.

Soon, he had everything well-secured aboard the twelve-pacer sailboat, and had checked over her supplies and necessities. He even inspected her carefully for structural soundness, just to…assuage his nerves. Once a shipwright, always a shipwright, it seemed. But everything looked fine. Orenna had a good eye for boats herself, of course.

He untied the sailboat from the dock and clambered aboard, and after only a few moments, was racing northward, cutting through the salty spray.

Evening was fast approaching, the sky darkening and the air growing cooler, when Lyrrek finally saw masts beginning to bristle up over the horizon, and knew she'd made it to Eagle's End.

Relief blossomed in her. The long sail had gone fairly well. It had somehow been both thrilling and boring.

The harbor was quiet, and she only saw one other ship moving, a Fishers' Guild vessel passing her on its way out. There were a few cheers and whistles from a pair of the sailors aboard as they looked down and saw her at the helm of her boat.

She just ignored them and sailed on, trying to spot a sign for a public marina somewhere.

At last she spotted the cluster of smaller masts that probably meant a public marina, and sure enough, she finally saw the sign and breathed in relief. And while she did see a lad up on the hillside lighting lanterns, there didn't seem to be anyone else around to watch. She picked an empty slip and, checking around behind her, adjusted the sail and let the windstones puff her gently forward.

It wasn't a particularly pretty effort, but it was successful. She got the sailboat well secured, and climbed back aboard to finish stowing the sail. At last, breathing hard, she dropped onto the bunk in the cabin to rest for a moment, pulling her haversack over and checking that she had everything ready.

Finally, she climbed out onto the dock. The sound of her boots drew attention as she approached the small stone house on the shoreline. Its door opened, and an old woman appeared, rubbing her eyes.

She took Lyrrek's silver for a few weeks of slip rental, and gave her a gap-toothed smile when Lyrrek wished her a more peaceful remainder of her night.

She made her way quickly through the streets of Eagle's End, the spires of Lady Fehndala's castle rising up before her once more. She climbed, tired, up to the apartment, and the door, once again, opened to the sound of her bootsteps.

A relieved-looking Amrelyn emerged and grabbed her in a smiling hug. "I knew you could do it," she said, then stepped back, looking her over. "How was it?"

"Good enough," Lyrrek said, truthfully. "Definitely not perfect, but somewhere around good enough."

Amrelyn smiled. "Well, you look tired, and I've got some bread and salted fish to feed you, so you can relax for a few minutes. But we've got work left to do, I'm afraid. Once we've got everything set up and out to my boat, you can take the bunk and rest, and I'll keep watch, make sure we don't miss Fehndala's departure."

Lyrrek couldn't help a small sigh, but grinned, nodding. "I'm up for it. But I'll definitely take you up on something to eat first."

Aether watched the dawn light tinting the horizon from the east, smiling at the beauty.

Lyrrek had contacted him the evening before to let him know she'd arrived safe. He had been relieved enough that he had anchored at a tiny passing rock of an island to get some sleep.

The wind had really died down overnight, and this morning, the sea was like glass, especially to the east where the black was becoming blue, and beginning to cast sparking highlights of color against the smooth expanse of glistening water. Under ordinary circumstances, he'd have been becalmed in this weather, bored and frustrated, despite the surreal beauty. But with his windstones and sail set up just right, his keel was cutting through the calm water with efficiency he'd never experienced before. With so little resistance from the usually choppier sea, he felt the twelve-pacer sailboat rising up onto the surface of the water at the bow.

It felt like his sailboat was flying across the sea, probably faster than he'd ever gone in his life.

He held tight to the wheel, suspecting that the speed was getting high enough that if he lost control, he'd stand a chance of capsizing the boat, and then he'd be in for a bad day or two until his guildmates managed to get to him. So he kept a firm grip. But he did reach down and pick up a cup of the tea he'd made at dinner the night before and sipped it, watching the beautiful colors of the awakening sky as he raced northward upon a nearly perfect sea.

Chapter Sixteen

Gathering Clouds

P emana followed Veytra into the kitchen back at the Wizards' Guild hall. Orenna turned from a counter, startled, then smiled when she saw who had joined her.

"Ah!" she said. "Glad to see you lot. It was getting pretty lonely around here." Orenna looked around past Veytra and Pemana. "Kayd still with you?"

"Yeah," Veytra said, pointing back over her shoulder. "He's fine. Took some things to his chambers."

"Where's everybody else?" Pemana asked.

"They've gone," Orenna said. She told them about Lyrrek and Aether and their solo expeditions.

Kayd came in during the explanation, and she had to start over. By the time she finished telling them, Kayd looked a little worried.

"Is everything all right with them?" he asked. "They've been inseparable, since…well, since Emrek, I guess."

Orenna grinned. "I think so. If they were having problems, I have a feeling I'd know."

Veytra started catching Orenna up on the details of their short journey, and Pemana found herself facing Kayd.

He looked up at her.

"Are you headed back out?" he asked her quietly. "Need your boat set up with anything before you go?"

She stared at him for a long moment, then slowly shook her head. "I...don't think so. I'm afraid I'm out of ideas, at least for today."

Veytra turned back to them. "Do you two mind helping me out? I should probably take advantage of having a couple spare master wizards standing around without commitments for a moment. If we got a bunch of stone sets enchanted, I'd have plenty to work on for a while, fabricating amulets and bracers."

"Of course," Kayd said, gesturing for Veytra to precede him out of the kitchen. Pemana nodded, then followed the others as they turned to head back toward Veytra's laboratory.

She'd probably prefer some privacy at this point, honestly. She'd been stuck with these two for several intimate days now. It wasn't that she minded their company. But it would be nice to get some quiet rest.

She knew full well that in the end, though, she would just lay on her bunk, pointing sharp mental reminders of her own failures at herself. So she might as well help them get *something* useful done.

She caught her head and shoulders sagging, and jerked herself back upright, lest anyone else notice.

———◆———

Lyrrek held tight to the mast of Amrelyn's sailboat, peering ahead under the sail, with a hand shielding her eyes against the sun.

"I think that one will work," she said, pointing in the direction of an empty slip around the side of one of the public marinas in Dawn's Hope.

Amrelyn nodded and steered the boat in the direction indicated.

Lyrrek climbed down into the cockpit, then ducked forward into the boat's small cabin. She picked up Amrelyn's spyglass and settled herself into the bunk, taking a comfortable position.

"How's that?" Amrelyn called down quietly after a few moments, just as the boat finally bumped up against the dock.

Lyrrek extended the spyglass and pointed it toward the small side window. She was far enough back that she ought to remain almost impossible to see from the outside.

She had to adjust her angle in the bunk, and stay pretty still for the alignment to work. But she was reasonably comfortable, reclining there, and had a decent angle with the spyglass of what was happening on the deck of Lady Fehndala's flagship, across the way, where it was docked at one of Dawn's Hope's guarded naval yards.

"I think this should work," she said back to Amrelyn.

"Stay down there," Amrelyn said. "We don't want to risk anyone on board her ship recognizing you."

"Ugh," Lyrrek replied. "But you're right. Aye Captain, guess I'll take first watch then."

Lyrrek felt the boat bob as Amrelyn climbed onto the dock to tie up and go pay the fee.

Lyrrek kept watch for a long time, while Amrelyn returned and eventually strung up one of the hammocks and
tried to get some sleep. Lyrrek felt strange about laying in
Amrelyn's bunk while her friend settled uncomfortably into
the hammock, but the bunk had become the post of the one
on watch by necessity. So she just lay there, watching and
waiting, occasionally smacking her cheeks to make sure she
stayed alert.

She didn't really know whether Lady Fehndala herself
was still aboard. She easily could have gone ashore before
they got themselves docked and in position to watch. Other
than a few sailors doing work that looked to Lyrrek like
maintenance tasks, there wasn't much going on aboard the
ship.

Finally, though, things did pick up. A pair of men in
rich-looking short-robes and boots arrived, escorted by some
of the lady's yellow-tabarded guards. They stood on the deck
for a few moments, and then the lady herself finally appeared
from below decks, escorted by a few more guards and a
couple of her yellow-robed servants.

Sailors produced a rather fancy camp table and four
chairs, and Lyrrek watched as Lady Fehndala, one of her
advisers, and the two gentlemen all sat around it and were
served wine.

They discussed something, occasionally with a lot of
gestures, for a good twenty minutes. Then everyone rose,
and the gentlemen bowed and departed, this time without any accompanying guards. So perhaps they had been
fetched? She didn't know if that meant anything, but she
jotted down some notes about the event on her parchment,

just in case. None of what happened seemed interesting enough to wake Amrelyn about, at least thus far.

Eventually, as evening drew near, there was a bit more activity. A group of boisterous men emerged onto the deck, no longer wearing their tabards, and began making their way off into town.

She made a brief note of it. But she was pretty sure she knew a group of sailors headed for an evening at the tavern when she saw it.

Amrelyn suddenly started awake.

"Wha…?" she mumbled. "Oh…" Then she awoke fully, shaking her head, and withdrew her amulet from her tunic.

Lyrrek kept watching Fehndala's ship, but couldn't resist glancing over at the hammock now and then.

Finally Amrelyn nodded and tucked her amulet away.

"Jyhnda says there was nothing much going on today. She said the men who came aboard were just merchants?"

Lyrrek nodded. "A couple well-dressed men had a meeting with Fehndala on deck. But all they did was talk and drink a bit of wine."

Amrelyn nodded. "She said it sounded like it was just about some textiles deal or something." She grinned. "She said she was sorry she didn't have anything interesting to report, but that she's really glad we're here in case something happens."

"Well, I have nothing more interesting to report than that either," Lyrrek said. "Unless you count eight or nine sailors wandering off to go to the tavern."

Amrelyn nodded, then shrugged and yawned. "Well, I'm probably awake for a while, if you want to swap."

Lyrrek yawned back. "Stakeouts always this much fun?"

Amrelyn chuckled, swinging her legs out of the hammock. "So Pemana says."

Three days later, Lyrrek had gained quite a bit more perspective on the enjoyableness of stakeouts. In her considered opinion, they were dull, stressful, and at times, rather miserable.

They had followed Lady Fehndala's ship from Dawn's Hope to the city of Eastwind, where a further considerable amount of nothing interesting occurred. Time was starting to feel slippery to her, long periods of staring through a spyglass broken by fitful sleeping, and extremely boring confinement in the tiny cabin of Amrelyn's sailboat. In the heat of the day, it was a lot worse, even with the windows propped open.

She fantasized about ideas to relieve their watch. They should rent a room in an inn and just let Jyhnda tell them when they were leaving. Or at the very least, perhaps she could disguise herself as a hunched old woman with a shawl over her head while they slipped out to find something better to do, even if it was only an evening in a tavern with some hot food and cellar-cool ale.

Maybe they should just trust that Jyhnda would be fine, and sail back to the guild hall until she called in with something interesting to tell them.

She knew Amrelyn would feel terrible about those ideas, though, to say nothing of what Jyhnda would think. She didn't mention any of it out loud. And they weren't things she would really do anyway, she was…fairly certain.

She sighed. At least Amrelyn got to leave the boat occasionally to go get them supplies and fresh water.

Lyrrek felt herself slipping again toward drowsiness, and was quite relieved when Amrelyn returned with news.

"Heard from Jyhnda," she said, stowing a few sundries in their places, and starting to grab up things that had gotten scattered around the cabin the last couple days. "She thinks they're getting ready to leave."

"Thank the Sky," Lyrrek breathed, looking back through the spyglass.

She could see a few more sailors moving around, now that Amrelyn had pointed it out. It looked like they were making preparations to depart.

She hadn't noticed. But in fairness, it had been a really long few days.

"Jyhnda thinks Fehndala is nervous about something," Amrelyn went on. "She's been holed up in her cabin, just drinking wine and nibbling at plates of snacks. And she's been a lot more likely to snap at servants over little things than she was before."

Lyrrek sighed. "That sounds…bad," she said.

Amrelyn nodded. "I think even Jyhnda's worried about it."

"Well," Lyrrek said, "at least we'll be back out at sea. It seems to me that if someone was going to notice us, it'd be likely to happen in port somewhere. Following from over the horizon where they can't even see us seems much safer."

"Long as the weather holds," Amrelyn said, "you're probably right."

The weather, unfortunately, did not hold.

"This is not good!" Lyrrek yelled over the wind and the pulsing rain that pounded them. Night had fallen more than an hour ago, and the weather had grown threatening not long after. Yet Jyhnda's beaconed chain had just kept on moving out ahead of them, even as the rain turned into a full-blown storm. It seemed Fehndala's ship had finally stopped moving now. Hopefully that was a good sign and not a bad one.

Lyrrek held the sailboat's wheel hard, terrified that her limited sailing skills were being put to this extreme of a test so soon as she guided the struggling sailboat up and down swells she couldn't even really see. She would have much preferred to let Amrelyn helm her own boat in these conditions, but Amrelyn was huddled just inside the cabin, a lightstone in her hand, trying to study a detailed navigational chart while keeping the parchment as dry as possible. The rain was coming in from some entirely unreasonable directions at times.

"I think I know where we are!" Amrelyn called back. "And Jyhnda's signal still hasn't moved. I think there's an island just over the horizon, and they must have known they were close, so they pushed on."

"What do we do?" Lyrrek felt her words snatched away in a particularly stiff gust of wind, and wondered if Amrelyn even heard her.

Amrelyn vanished deeper into the cabin for an instant, stowing the chart, then came carefully back out, just visible in the dim glow of the tiny lightstone mounted near their feet. Lyrrek relinquished the wheel to her and pulled herself across to the other seat, not daring to let go of the rolling boat in the process.

She felt a surge forward as Amrelyn opened up the sailboat's windstones. She leaned Lyrrek's direction a bit. "We have to get off the sea! We'll have to risk that Fehndala's guards are sheltering from the storm, not watching for pursuit."

"You're right," Lyrrek called back to her. "We can't stay out here. Take us in!"

A large wave suddenly lifted them, and they both cried out at the unexpected upward lurch. But the boat crested the wave and slid down the other side, and kept moving forward, the windstones and Amrelyn's solid grip on the helm keeping them stable.

Fear threatened to overwhelm Lyrrek, but she forced herself to breathe regularly. She focused with her magical senses on the tiny, gleaming speck of magic that was the chain of Jyhnda's amulet. It was, blessedly, getting closer. And it gave them a steady heading to pursue in this terrifying dark swirl of wind and waves. It gave them their singular hope of surviving this.

After a few minutes, the worst of the wind gusts seemed to have passed, and the storm became more of a sustained pounding of wind and rain. They were still miserable, the swells still terrifying, but it felt a bit less dangerous, at least, as the unpredictable wind tried to capsize them less often.

But then, as they were tipping down the side of a big wave, an awkwardly timed gust *did* hit them, and from the worst possible angle. Amrelyn's strangled yelp of a scream as she felt the disaster unfolding galvanized Lyrrek's consciousness in her terror, and she both saw and felt what was happening.

Amrelyn's face was frozen with horror. They were going to flip into the black sea. It would be the end of them. No spells they knew offered protection against drowning.

Lyrrek's mind snapped reflexively into action, and the magic to operate the boat's windstones ripped through her, empowered by her fear and instinct. The magical wind blazed up into the saturated sail, blasting it back out away from the direction of their plunge with a loud *snap* of wet canvas, and pushed back hard against the storm that was trying to swallow them just then.

The boat lurched back upright as the hull slipped sideways down into the trough between the waves, wrenched straight by the force of the magical wind filling its sail, and then they buoyed back up the other side of the trough, jerking into the direction of their momentum as the keel caught and yanked them back on course.

Lyrrek saw that Amrelyn was still frozen in fear and reached out to put a stabilizing hand on the wheel, just in case. But her motion broke Amrelyn's instant of paralysis, and she gasped, then started steering again.

"You saved us," she croaked. "That was…that was brilliant!"

"Are you all right?" Lyrrek croaked back.

Amrelyn nodded, a look of grim determination coming over her rain-soaked face. "Hold on," she said.

"Trust me, I am," Lyrrek said.

Amrelyn began trying to guide them through the swells by feel, trying to work with, rather than against the waves. Lyrrek could feel her using the windstones to change direction and actively counter the wind when it was a threat. And in this fashion, they stumbled along through the storm.

And soon, Lyrrek saw lights on the horizon, and quickly withdrew the magic from the small lightstone near their feet, just in case.

She stared through the rain and blackness, trying to make sense of the arrangement of small lights that flickered in and out as the roiling sea tried to hide them. There were only a handful, maybe five, so sparkly with distance and rain that it was hard to tell. But as they drew nearer, she could finally make out that a pair of them were the lanterns on the deck of a ship, Fehndala's she presumed, though Jyhnda's chain was no longer aboard. She could sense it further ashore somewhere, not too far away.

Lyrrek gripped the cabin so she could half stand and lean nearer to Amrelyn, not wanting to yell and risk being heard as they drew closer. "We can't really just sail up and dock, right?"

Amrelyn glanced down and held her hand over the compass. The small, plain stone on her ring pulsed into light, letting her see their heading, then she let it go out and returned to staring ahead into the darkness. "If we're at the island I think we're at, this should be its southeastern corner. We might be able to get in the lee of the land mass and be sheltered a bit, if we go north along the coastline from here. Maybe we can find a small bay or something."

"I don't know how we'll do that in the dark, but yeah, we have to try," Lyrrek said, and dropped back to her seat, clinging hard to the wet wood in front of her.

They sailed around the cluster of swinging lantern lights, which provided a reference point, but no real useful illumination to them in the storm-lashed darkness. But the wind did seem to lessen some as they passed northward into the lee of the island.

Fehndala's ship, Lyrrek could now tell, was some distance offshore, riding its anchor and dancing with the storm, but not tossed about too much there, in the lessened wind.

But as they passed around the ship and the lantern-lit shore, the waves began to come in from a different angle, now that they were within the unpredictable eddies of the island's lee side. A large wave, almost cresting already, tipped them unexpectedly sideways, back in the direction of shore.

It wasn't enough to capsize them, and Amrelyn responded with the windstones to balance it. But as the boat righted, plunging ahead, a loud *crack* suddenly sounded and Lyrrek smashed face-first into the bulkhead in front of her.

Amrelyn cursed, then grabbed her. "Are you all right?" she asked, her ring lighting again. She looked completely terrified in its tiny light.

"I'm fine," Lyrrek said, rubbing her wet face reflexively, her wardstones having protected her. "You?"

"I'm all right," Amrelyn said, but suddenly grimaced. She had released both sail and wheel when they'd hit. But the boat was, at least, upright, not trying to tip too far in the wind.

Amrelyn grabbed the top of the cabin doorway and swung herself down and in. Lyrrek heard her boots splash into water when her feet hit the deck.

"We're going down," Amrelyn hissed, the light from her ring staggering about the cabin as she lunged for something. She whirled back around, thrusting Lyrrek's haversack at her. Then she spun back inside, and Lyrrek saw, from the wildly flailing light, that she was getting everything she could grab into a haversack of her own. And Lyrrek, by that light, could see how quickly the water was rising up, already at Amrelyn's knees.

She watched, helpless, knowing she'd only be in the way, as her friend worked frantically to keep at least some of her possessions from drowning along with her poor, doomed sailboat.

The water was already sloshing up Amrelyn's thighs as she waded back and took Lyrrek's offered hand, letting her pull her up to where she stood in the cockpit, ankle-deep herself.

"Well, after you, my lady," Amrelyn said, extinguishing her light as she pointed into the darkness in the direction of the island's shore, to the right of the cluster of swaying lantern lights. "I guess we're swimming for it."

Lyrrek sighed, turning to regard the black waves into which Amrelyn's boat was quickly descending.

Sharp rocks might not have posed as much danger to her, with all the wardstones protecting her. But still, there was something primally awful about the feeling in her guts as she leapt forward off the sinking boat into the black water.

CHAPTER SEVENTEEN
ARRIVALS

P emana jerked awake, eyes wide in the echoing darkness. It took her a confused instant to remember she was in her small bedchamber in the Wizards' Guild hall in Freehome.

She closed her eyes and struggled to concentrate for a moment, until a small lightstone finally began to gleam on the table. She slowly opened her eyes, blinking against the brightness, and peered blearily around.

Nothing was out of place.

A loud clap of thunder sounded, startling her so she ducked, and she sighed. At least she knew what had awakened her.

"So much for sleep, I guess," she whispered to herself.

She kicked her cloak off and sat up to stick her feet in her boots, letting the lightstone behind her fade as she felt her way out into the dark corridor that led toward the kitchen.

Once there, she lit a couple of the stones they kept scattered around on shelves and counters, and got a mug of water from the cask and downed it.

She looked around, then. She didn't think she'd seen an ale cask.

No. Just the water.

She started opening cabinets, and after a few, came upon a couple brandy bottles. She took the open one and drained the last drops of water from her mug before pouring some brandy in its place.

She wandered out into the dark common area, with its windows that looked out onto the sea yard, where they kept a single oil lantern burning. By its dim light, she found a seat in one of the chairs they'd brought in, and sat with a grunt and a sigh.

She sipped her brandy and stared out at the lantern, where it swayed slightly in the wind and rain that swirled in the walled sea yard. She watched the sky brighten momentarily with distant lightning.

After a few sips, she caught her mind starting the spinning dance it had fallen into lately, thoughts of Kayd spiraling into thoughts of her family and her fallen naval career, which led inevitably to the Swordfish, to revenge, by which, she hastily reminded herself, she really meant justice…

She snapped her attention away with an exasperated sigh. But as always, the next turn of the spiral pushed forward into her mind anyway. *Her* mistakes had wrecked some people's lives, and were indeed actively wrecking more now, in the case of the ones that she knew the Swordfish had taken.

Some people had died.

Pemana had no new leads. She had no hope for finding any that she could see. She had no hope of figuring out where to find the missing. She had no resources behind her.

Well, that wasn't entirely true, she thought, chastising herself. Her guildmates certainly counted. Their efforts were admirable. But they weren't an ancient noble house's powerful navy, with the mandate and resources and labor of tens of thousands of souls living in a lord's holding behind them. Yes, she and her guildmates had magic. But they didn't have the people, beyond a handful here and there. What power did they truly have to stop the Swordfish? Because he seemed to have the people, the resources…and apparently, even the Ruling Council itself on his side.

They were basically trying to overthrow the order of their society.

Granted, the Swordfish had done so first. That was true. But he had done it over decades of slow, festering infiltration. Rooting that out now would be a monumental task.

The weight of what they were attempting settled in on her until she felt immobilized.

She sighed, closed her eyes, and took a larger drink of her brandy.

Lyrrek dropped to rest against the stone wall of a building, just in from the rocky shore, and huddled in the darkness, breathing hard. There wasn't much of an overhang on the building's roof, there at the back. But it did let her and Amrelyn have their heads out of the miserable chill of the rain for a moment.

"I would prefer to never do that again," Lyrrek whispered, slumping back, pulling her wet limbs up into the smallest ball she could make of herself.

"Me too," Amrelyn whispered.

"I'm sorry about your boat," Lyrrek said, feeling awful for her friend. But then she quickly brightened and chuckled. "I guess the only good news is that I already have a nice new one waiting for you in Eagle's End, and with a few weeks of slip rental paid, besides. She's a good boat, too," she said, and sighed, then shook her head. "Now we just have to figure out how to get Jyhnda and get out of here."

Amrelyn nodded. Then she jerked her head up, and whispered "oh, speaking of…" and grabbed her amulet.

Lyrrek watched her for a few moments, then Amrelyn whispered "be careful," and tucked her amulet back under her wet tunic.

"I told her about the boat," she said. "She's worried. She says there's something off about this place, something creepy about it. They were all moved into a guest-house which seems nice enough, but the servants that were already here are all wearing black robes, and there are guards in black tabards. And Fehndala seems almost ill with nerves."

"Oh my," Lyrrek whispered, frowning.

None of the noble houses used black for their liveries.

Was it the Depths?

"She said she's tried to look around a bit, but there are a lot of guards posted around certain areas. There's a whole complex of buildings, stretching across to a second pier around the southwest corner of the island. Most of the guards seem concentrated around the south end, where the guest houses are, so we might find some sheltered place where we could hide more northward, toward the center of the island a bit. She said there are some larger buildings there, though she didn't get a very long look, and only by torchlight as they loaded in."

Lyrrek nodded. "I'm freezing, even with my wardstones. Let's keep moving, and maybe we can find a shed to hide in or something. And…I guess we better be watching for a boat, too."

They rose, keeping low, and scurried along the wall of the building, looking northward up the dark, brush-covered slope, struggling to see anything at all in the tiny amount of light that made its way this far over from the lanterns nearer the pier.

Aether shielded his eyes against the morning sun ahead of him, and peered up the small river where it wound eastward. He'd gone so far up the Gloaming River that there wasn't much left of it. He'd even felt the boat's keel scrape bottom a couple times, and wondered how much further he'd be able to proceed.

Surely Headwaters had to be around here somewhere. There would barely be room for two boats to pass each other in the channel at this point, so the river was at risk of becoming impractical in terms of access for a village. He kept his eyes out for anything that looked like it had once had something to do with civilization of any kind.

The river took a northward bend ahead, and he watched the small sparkles of insects dancing in the sun beginning to gather out over the water as he rounded it. As he brought the boat around the bend, he realized what he was seeing beyond, and grinned in relief.

Just north of that last bend, he could see rocks protruding, and the water was broken up into some light rapids. Below them, the river widened out to the east in a small backwater, with the crumbling remains of an ancient-looking pier built along one edge of it.

He'd found it, at last.

He let the windstones sigh away their output as he drifted off into the backwater, pushing the boat slightly one last time until it *clunked* into the rocky pier. He quickly lowered the sail, then leapt ashore with a long mooring rope he'd prepared, paying it out as he jogged a dozen paces to a stout tree, which was the nearest thing he could find that looked sturdy enough to be secure.

He ran back and dragged another long rope to a second good tree, and once the boat was tied up, he stepped down into the cabin to sort through his things.

He checked the map again, peering closely at it, and deciding its indication of Headwaters' location had done the job. He could sense something whispering at the edges of his mind, and was relieved to know that he had found the next beacon.

He'd hesitated to employ his magical senses too aggressively as he'd drawn closer to Headwaters, because the land thereabouts looked like it might be good country for dragons seeking their prey, and he didn't want to attract more attention than the beacon itself might already draw. From what he'd come to understand of dragon minds, thanks to the half-dozen he'd encountered now over the last couple years, they didn't wander into one another's territory very often. But younger dragons that hadn't established themselves yet would be forced to pass through from time to time, and would usually only receive a harsh warning delivered via their mind-control magic, then be allowed to move on.

It meant that you could never be absolutely certain there wasn't another dragon passing near, even if you had already located the owner of the territory you were in. And he hadn't seen any dragons yet on this trip.

He did finally allow himself a bit of a glimpse outward with his magical senses, now that he wouldn't have to be dealing with the boat at the same time, should he call in a dragon by mistake. He spotted another cluster of beaconed boulders not far up into the forest, gratified that he'd found the place, and that the ancient wizard had managed to make it here as well.

He quickly dropped his effort, once more minimizing how much he radiated magically. He grinned, grabbed his satchel and reached for his staff, excited to find out what new revelations might be waiting for him here.

Lyrrek sighed. "Why am I finding myself staring out windows through spyglasses so often lately?"

She focused Amrelyn's pocket spyglass out the window of a two-story storage barn they'd managed to climb into before morning. The building was a way up the slope, and at the far north end of the complex from the guest houses where Fehndala's people were staying. It was a couple dozen paces higher in elevation, as well, and so this barn had proved to be the perfect vantage.

After peering in a few ground-level windows, Amrelyn had found a back door on the far side of the building in the damp, dark, pre-dawn, and they'd managed to shove it open without making too much noise. Inside, they'd found storage for landscaping tools and what looked like remnants from construction at the site. They'd climbed up a narrow staircase to a storage loft above, where some small windows looked out. From there, they could watch both the south dock where Fehndala's ship was moored, as well as the western dock that, at that time at least, was empty.

Lyrrek had still been miserable in her wet clothing, though at least the rain had washed out a lot of the seawater's salt. But it was dry inside the small barn, and someday, she thought, they might be again too.

Amrelyn had pulled out her second spyglass and handed it to Lyrrek, and they'd each taken a window, determined to figure out what was going on here while they worked on getting Jyhnda out.

A second ship had arrived not long after the gray dawn, docking at the other pier to the southwest, and neither of them was surprised that it bore banners of Lord Egla-mon's House Brightwall orange. Soon, both orange and yellow-robed servants were making their way around the grounds. And, occasionally, they saw a black-robed servant among them as well, or a small group of guards in black tabards.

It didn't feel like anything they observed was telling them much, though.

"Wait," Lyrrek said. She was at the western window, and could lean around to get a bit more northward of a view. And there, she saw another set of sails coming south, headed, it seemed, toward one of the empty spaces next to Eglamon's ship.

Lyrrek whistled, recognizing what she was seeing as it came into focus. She knew a bit about ships, of course, after a lifetime of helping her father aboard his merchant vessels. And this was a big, beautiful one. It bore no banners, and flew no flags. But it was long, with three masts, and she could tell that whatever it was, it had been quite expensive.

"Hello, who are you?" she said aloud.

"What?" Amrelyn asked, and came over to her.

Lyrrek pointed, and they both stared out at the ship.

As it got closer, she could see the black tabards of the crew and guards on deck, going about their preparations for docking.

"Sky preserve us," she whispered.

CHAPTER EIGHTEEN

IMPENDING

A ether lifted the carefully folded bit of paper from inside the small coffer he'd just dug up, brushed off the knees of his trousers, then lowered himself slowly onto a nearby boulder. He laid the paper on his knee and took a drink from his waterskin, staring out at the surrounding forest and listening to the gentle sighing of the breeze among the leaves.

Once he'd rested for a moment, he lifted the paper once more and examined it closely.

This letter was pristine-looking, quite unlike the mess the last one had been. The wizard's script was once again careful and controlled. But the message was short.

Aether flattened the paper on his knees and began to read.

"Kohlia, I hope you are well, though I fear for your fate at this point. I have waited as long as I dare, and this place is not safe. If you are still following me, do not remain here long. Several dragons seem to be fighting over this region.

"And worse, what gutter rats do remain in these lands have become near-feral as this fancy civilization of theirs gets devoured. They are starving and desperate. Take no chances.

It seems that Bastion is the epicenter of this catastrophe, and we are journeying to the heart of it. The scum get worse the closer I get. If you encounter anyone who is a not a member of the Pantheon, it may be best to destroy them at your first opportunity, just to be safe.

"My plan now is to make directly for the Great Underhall. It's possible there is safety to be had there. Or perhaps it will just be accountability. I know not. Perhaps I will be able to tell you what I mean when you finally catch up to me.

"And if we are fortunate, we might even find a means of escaping this nightmare.

"Be safe, my love. Find me soon."

Aether dropped the letter back to his lap, staring out at the shifting leaves of the trees ahead of him, lost in dark thoughts.

Lyrrek counted the masts they could see through the barn's various windows.

"That looks like it makes five ships all together, then," she said. "I wonder what that means?"

Amrelyn just shrugged and shook her head, then kept staring, spyglass up, out her window.

The large, unmarked ship had soon been joined by a second one in Eglamon's dark-orange, and later one more in Fehndala's golden-yellow arrived as well. It wasn't clear to them what these other vessels were doing, but the grounds of the complex were now crawling with servants and guards wearing those same colors, though most of the buildings themselves were guarded by groups in midnight black.

Lyrrek watched several of the black-robed servants closely as they moved between buildings. But nothing about their appearance or actions told her anything new. She sighed.

Her stomach gurgled in reply. Amrelyn tossed her the waterskin and she took a small sip. They'd have to sort out what was going on soon and get Jyhnda out, or they were going to have to start worrying about provisions. The boat's small cask had gone down with it, and they only had the one waterskin.

As Amrelyn caught the waterskin Lyrrek tossed back to her, her head suddenly jerked up and she almost missed it. She took out her amulet and concentrated for a couple minutes. Lyrrek watched her face grow increasingly alarmed. Finally she gasped, and then spoke.

"Sky, Jyhnda. Be careful," she whispered.

Amrelyn opened her eyes and let her amulet fall against her chest, staring for a few seconds.

"What is it?" Lyrrek asked quietly.

Amrelyn met her eyes.

"She snuck away to tell us. It's…all the black robes and…" She took a deep breath. "That other ship is the Swordfish's ship. The Swordfish is here."

Lyrrek looked at the floor and sighed. She'd begun to fear it might be the case.

Amrelyn didn't look away. "We're getting Jyhnda out," she said firmly. She actually grinned, and somehow, it made

Lyrrek's trepidation ease a bit. "And just think how excited Pemana is going to be when she hears we found him."

Lyrrek snorted quietly. "The look she's had in her eyes lately? I'm not sure 'excited' is the word I'd use."

Amrelyn nodded solemnly, sliding her amulet back into her shirt, and lifted the spyglass back to her eye.

Pemana stared over the array of parchments spread out across the table in her chamber. It was every broad map she had in her possession, every detailed navigational chart, hundreds of pieces of written notations of interviews and documented rumors, not to mention pages and pages of her own speculations and summaries.

She didn't bother with making second copies to throw off anyone who might find her evidence, these days. She trusted her guild-mates and their collective ability to protect their premises. And they weren't operating in public. But more than anything, there was just too much, this trove of information about the Swordfish. It represented hundreds of hours of work that she and others had put in on this investigation, if not thousands.

And it had amounted to nothing but setbacks.

She should just give up. The Swordfish had won.

They had thought that the magic Aether discovered made them special, that it somehow gave them an edge in any endeavor they undertook. Well, that was foolish and wrong. They were still just game pieces in their world, and people like the Swordfish were the only ones actually playing the game.

She leaned over in her chair and picked up the satchel she'd begun to use for storing all of this useless parchment. She held it open and reached across the table, about to sweep as much of the junk in as she could in one pass, no longer really caring about keeping it organized or neat.

"Pemana!"

She jumped, so startled she dropped the satchel and nearly yelped. It was Lyrrek's voice, in her thoughts.

"Pemana, are you there?"

She fumbled to pull the amulet from under her tunic, finally getting it untangled and into her hand. "I'm here, sorry Lyrrek!" As she spoke, she felt Lyrrek's anxiety flood through their connection. "What is it, what's wrong?"

Lyrrek told her quickly, that they were fine, but their boat had sunk, and she, Amrelyn, and Jyhnda were trapped on an island with Lady Fehndala, Lord Eglamon, and…

When Pemana heard Lyrrek say "the Swordfish," she nearly fell over.

"Where?" she demanded, dislodging a few maps to fall to the floor as she bent and flipped through the navigational charts, quickly finding the one she wanted.

Lyrrek described it carefully, a small cluster of islands nestled offshore, east of New Brightwall, the northwestern of the three small islands there.

It wasn't marked as inhabited on Pemana's chart, but most of these navigational maps were more concerned with what was in the water than what was on land. This map, in particular, was one she'd had for a long time, a high-quality chart she'd gotten while still captain of *Champion*. It marked the east side of that island as a navigational hazard.

Lyrrek quickly explained what they'd been able to learn of the complex's layout, and Pemana sketched out a fast map on a piece of blank parchment. Lyrrek tried to estimate how many guards they'd seen, but emphasized that they hadn't made a thorough count.

Once Pemana had everything down, she tried to calm her rapid breathing and think.

"All right, Lyrrek, I think I have it," she said. "Are you three safe?"

"I think so, for now," she replied. "Amrelyn and I are hidden away in a barn. It's Jyhnda I'm worried about, she's still inside, pretending to be one of Fehndala's serving girls. We haven't figured out how to extract her, but I guess we need transport off this rock before we can really do that anyway."

"I'll be working on it, and I'll call for you again if I come up with anything I need you to do. We'll be coming."

"Thank you Pemana," Lyrrek said quietly. "I'm sorry for this mess."

"Don't be ridiculous, you brilliant hero of a wizard," Pemana said, and for Lyrrek's benefit, she let herself feel every sparkle of the dark joy in her heart that she'd been trying to hide from her friend. "You found him for me. Now let's go get that murderous asshole."

She felt Lyrrek's relief, and told her to be safe before she tucked the amulet back in her shirt.

She started to run one way, then froze, turning to start running another, then stopped herself again.

She couldn't panic. She had too much work to do, and not enough time to do it. She took a deep breath. Priorities.

She spun and leapt for the door, racing out into the hall and shouting.

"Kayd!"

Aether cinched down a knot, securing the last bundle of his supplies firmly in the sailboat's cabin. He glanced around, giving everything his customary last check. All was in place.

The day was already half gone. He probably wouldn't get very far this afternoon before he'd have to start looking for a place to camp. But now that he'd found the letter, this trip felt like a waste of time. He'd already known he was looking for these wizards'…Underhall. All he'd really gotten here was confirmation of something he'd begun to suspect anyway.

He missed his friends. He *definitely* missed Lyrrek.

Maybe he'd been wrong about this solo adventure idea.

He climbed out onto the stone pier, about to begin untying the boat, when suddenly Lyrrek's mind clashed into his.

"Lyrrek?" he nearly shouted back, grabbing for his amulet. "Are you all right?"

"I'm all right," she said quickly. "We all are. And I don't want you to have to worry, all the way up there where you can't do anything, but…I do have to tell you that we're in a bit of trouble."

She told him where they were and what had happened. And as his shocked mind grappled with it, he knew she felt his fury at himself for not listening to his intuition when it told him going off alone like he had might be a bad idea.

"I'm so sorry," she said, pained. "This is my fault, not yours. Amrelyn didn't want to let Jyhnda do this at all, and I talked her into it. And I sent you up there."

He caught hold of his emotions immediately, sucking in a deep breath. "No, I'm sorry Lyrrek. We're going to be fine. Besides, you told me it was Jyhnda's idea."

"Yes, that's true, but..."

"Listen to me," he said, feeling calm wash over him. "Everything is fine. You've all done wonderfully well. Pemana and the others will get to you by this evening?"

"Sounds like it."

"I trust you Lyrrek, you know that." He laughed a bit in his thoughts so she could hear it. "If the Swordfish knew how much danger he was in, with you three there with him on the same island? He'd flee like a roamer from a dragon."

"I love you," she said. "Remind me to tell you about the storm sometime. It was wild."

"I will. I'm glad you're all right. Do what you have to do to get the others home," he said. "I love you too, and I'll be there as soon as I can."

She told him not to worry once more, and then she was gone.

He dropped to his knees on the stone, stunned. Now that he no longer had to control his emotions for her sake, they pounded over him like a gale.

What could he do? It would still take him several days to get back, even if he didn't sleep and somehow figured out how to navigate rivers in the dark. But one mistake, and he'd be stranded until someone could come for him.

This had been such a foolish thing to do. He never should have come up here alone.

If only he had stayed behind.

If only he could…

His body froze, his eyes widening. But the idea blazed onward through his mind, singing with implications.

It was, without a doubt, the stupidest idea he had ever had.

But why wouldn't it work?

Even as the ridiculous plan crystallized in his mind, he tore it apart, trying to figure out where the fatal flaw was.

It would be hard. It would be fantastically dangerous. He'd have to prove some magical theory in the process and invent some new types of spell stone.

But he couldn't find the thing that meant it *couldn't* work.

He swallowed, hard, and leapt to his feet. In but a few seconds, he had raced to the boat, grabbing one of the maps.

He peered closely down at it, studying the fine detail as well as he could. It might work. If he got everything right, it *should* work.

What choice did he have? He had to try. For Lyrrek.

He spun and began yanking knots loose, ravaging the sailboat's well-stocked supplies and emergency gear, blessing Kayd and Orenna for their thoroughness as he did so. If he survived this madness, he'd have to remember to pay them both a big, fat bonus out of the Guild treasury.

Soon he was slashing strong leather hides into wide strips, and frantically stitching pieces together with the strongest waxed cord he had onboard. It turned into an enormous project quite quickly, and spread out across every horizontal surface in the cabin.

He was sweating profusely, and trying to remember to get a drink now and then. The work took him nearly two full, frenetic, agonizing hours. But when he was done, he had managed to bundle everything together in such a way that he ought to be able to wear it all as a bulky, makeshift backpack while he traveled. He added an extra waterskin to his haversack and made sure he had everything he'd need, including an assortment of good, smooth stones, in addition to the several he had already stitched into the seams of the complex leather construction. New spells sparkled firmly within them under one last magical glance.

It could work. It *had* to work.

He checked over the boat once more, then made sure that Lyrrek's sword was as secure at his waist as possible, literally lashed into its sheath at his belt. He grabbed his staff and leapt ashore to the pier, starting off immediately at a jog, headed eastward in the direction of the wide gap between the hills, and the flat stretches of gracefully ascending grassland he could see beyond them.

As he went, he scanned the surrounding landscape with his magical senses, looking as far and wide as he could, no longer concerned with hiding himself from the wrong kind of attention.

Chapter Nineteen
Going In

Pemana leaned forward at the helm of her sailboat, will-ing it to carve even faster through the calm water of the moonlit sea. The sharp sound of stones drawn across blades punctuated the slapping of the hull against the waves, as her guildmates prepared their weapons and checked one another's gear in the cabin below.

She closed her eyes for a moment, focusing on the tiny gleams of magic at the horizon. She could sense the chain of Jyhnda's amulet, as well as Lyrrek and Amrelyn's wardstones.

Pemana opened her eyes again, focusing ahead. The first golden glimmers of lantern light were beginning to crest the horizon, and she adjusted their course west. A lot of those lanterns were on the decks of five heavily-guarded ships, and it was vital that they avoid drawing their attention too early. At sea, wizards or no, they were just a handful of fools on a sailboat, as vulnerable to being run down and drowned as anyone. It was only once they reached land that she and her colleagues would become the most dangerous threat those poor pirates would *ever* encounter.

She grimaced. Some of them would never encounter an enemy again after tonight…unless, perchance, they found themselves in the Deep. But that was between them and their souls.

She tightened the angle of the wind, driving them even faster on as they skirted the lights, headed westward up the coastline, where her charts showed a safer approach that hopefully wouldn't try to sink her boat.

They circuited far enough northward to be able to turn toward land, and Pemana began easing off the wind. She raised up from her seat to stare out at the moonlit water ahead, hoping if there were any rocks, she'd be able to spot them.

Kayd emerged from the cabin below, and she saw the look on his face.

"What is it?"

He met her eyes. "Jyhnda didn't make it out."

Pemana swore.

"Is she all right?"

"Lyrrek thinks so. But they saw her get caught trying to sneak out a window and hauled back in. They watched them move her, but haven't heard from her. Lyrrek and Amrelyn are holding near the building they took her to."

Pemana stared at him for a moment. Then she focused and the windstones whipped their clothing around them as the boat launched forward. She veered, pointing it directly at the closest bit of island shoreline.

"Tell the others to be ready. I'm dropping you as close as I can, and I'll have to go find a hidden anchorage and catch up."

"Aye, Captain."

She didn't correct him, or even wince. Why bother? It felt right to her too. She just nodded sharply, and he bent to enter the cabin and tell the others, while she stared ahead at the rapidly approaching rocks, determined to get this exactly right.

Lyrrek peered into the shadows along the dimly moonlit trail, wondering if she had just seen movement. A few of the shadows moved again, and she saw three of them detach from the darker backdrop of the underbrush.

As the shadows drew closer, they resolved into the outlines of people she recognized…Kayd, then Veytra and Orenna.

She whispered Kayd's name, and they froze, startled, but then joined her quickly in the deeper shadows where she huddled next to a small building.

"Sorry," she whispered to Kayd as he crouched next to her. "Amrelyn's still ahead, watching." Lyrrek looked at the other two. "Pemana with the boat?"

"Yeah," Kayd whispered back. "She said she'll find a place to hide it and catch up, but not to wait for her. If Jyhnda's in danger, we're supposed to give her a quick idea of the layout, then go straight in."

Lyrrek swallowed, and nodded. "Then we'd better move." Orenna and Veytra both nodded their readiness as well.

She ran as quietly as she could on the gravel of the path, leading them forward past a couple small outbuildings to a sheltered spot of dark shadows along the side of one of them. They all crouched there, and Amrelyn greeted them with silent nods, holding a finger in front of her lips and pointing.

Lyrrek leaned carefully out and looked down the wider gravel road that ran through the center of the small complex. A few buildings away, on their side, a pair of guards in black tabards stood near one of the lanterns, leaning tiredly on their spears and mumbling about something.

Kayd patted Amrelyn's arm in acknowledgement and leaned close. "Where is she?" he mouthed.

Her face grim, Amrelyn pointed to the building with the lantern…and guards…out front.

Lyrrek looked at the building again. She'd only glanced at it earlier before heading back to meet the others. This building was a bit different from its neighbors. It had a lower roof than the rest, low enough that it looked like there were probably steps down into the space when you entered.

Unlike the freestanding structures surrounding it, this building backed directly up to a spot where the rocky outcrops that ran from the ridge's height at the center of the island terminated in a short cliff. It was the only one built directly up against the rock face itself.

She closed her eyes and looked magically for Jyhnda's amulet again. It was still there, gleaming brightly, inside the building, near the back wall, though the chain was jumbled into a wad, as if Jyhnda had hidden it in a pouch.

"Has anyone managed to look in the windows?" Orenna asked.

"No," Amrelyn breathed. "The guards have been there the whole time."

"Someone should sneak around the other way and do something to distract the guards, let you get a look," Veytra said. She looked at Orenna. "Want to come with me?"

Orenna nodded.

"Try not to take out the guards," Kayd said, "but…you know…don't let them raise an alarm either."

They both nodded grimly.

"Give us a few minutes," Veytra whispered and followed Orenna off into the darkness.

After those few minutes, they heard a distant crash that sounded like breaking pottery. The guards jerked around, spears held up in front of them, and jogged off in the direction of the noise.

"Now," Amrelyn hissed quietly.

Lyrrek followed Kayd as they crept silently along the front of the closer buildings, necks craned to watch the progress of the guards jogging away, until at last they reached a point where they could see through the windows into Jyhnda's building.

Lyrrek leaned to peer through the nearest window. She knew where to look, right where her magical senses were telling her Jyhnda would be.

She saw people moving inside, all guards in black tabards. She looked for the yellow robe Jyhnda would have been wearing.

But she wasn't there. Lyrrek stared through the window at a bored-looking guard who stood in a less-than-disciplined slouch, leaning on his spear next to a wooden door set into the rock wall itself.

Jyhnda's amulet was in the guard's belt-pouch.

Pemana gave a last tug on the anchor line, and was fairly certain the boat wouldn't drift free. She checked the loose arrangement of canvas where the sail was piled, ready to be hauled quickly up. Hopefully, if it came to it, she could get the boat underway in just a handful of frantic seconds.

She checked her sword and her magic, nodded, then took a deep breath and jumped into the black water.

It came nearly to her shoulders, and she gasped, gritting her teeth and ignoring her discomfort at the thought of what she might not be able to see below the waves as she waded, as fast as she could, through the shallow water and toward the slick rocks of the island's shoreline.

As she stepped free, seawater streaming from her, she suddenly heard Kayd's voice in her mind.

"Pemana, are you all right?"

She felt the grim rigidity in his thoughts, and quickly grabbed her amulet.

"I'm fine," she sent back. "Is everyone else okay? What did you find out about Jyhnda?"

"She's been separated from her amulet. We don't know where she is."

"Damn," she said, and stepped carefully along the rocks, trying to squelch some of the water out of her boots as she went.

He quickly explained the layout of the buildings on the western edge of the complex, and the fact that the building Jyhnda's amulet was in seemed to open into the low cliff itself. She thought she could almost see it in his mind's eye as he described it.

"Amrelyn's panicking," he said. "She wants to go in now. We can't sense Jyhnda using any magic anywhere. But Amrelyn says that given where the guard that has the amulet is posted, it stands to reason that Jyhnda would be deeper in through that door."

"Makes sense to me," Pemana said. "I'm at least several minutes away. Don't wait for me."

"If you're sure," he said.

"Go. I'll be fine. I'll call for you if I need help."

She felt just a hint of the pained feeling that surged in him at those words, but he broke the connection immediately. It left her thoughtful as she squeezed more seawater from her clothes, then began to jog quietly up the shoreline in the moonlight, hoping it was enough to spot any tripping hazards.

Chapter Twenty

Metal on Metal

Lyrrek steadied herself, crouched low and in the shadows, but ready to move. She shifted from one foot to another, trying to stay comfortable.

Orenna and Veytra finally both nodded that they'd caught their breath, and Kayd leaned closer to them all.

"Remember," he whispered. "Metal on metal will be loud. Use your fists, if you can."

"We have to go now," Orenna said. "We sent the guards off the other way, but they'll be headed back anytime."

"Follow me," Kayd said, and moved fast.

Lyrrek was right at his heels as they crept quickly around into the shadow of the low building.

Kayd went straight up to the window, which was lower than normal, meaning that nearly the whole upper half of his body was framed by it as he reached toward one of the shutter-style window's panes of glass and tapped.

The nearest black-tabarded guard flinched, startled, then stepped to the window to peer out into the night, looking for the source of the sound.

His eyes went wide as he realized that he was staring up into the face of a large, muscular young man who smiled grimly through the window at him.

Before the guard could react beyond a widening of his eyes, Kayd lunged forward with all his strength focused into both dragonskin fists, aiming them at the center. The tiny copper latch burst and the windows slammed inward into the guard's face with a *bang* and the sound of cracking glass. The guard stumbled back several steps with a cry, grabbing his nose, and Kayd dove through the window after him.

Lyrrek's eyes were almost as wide as the guard's as she watched Kayd's dive. He soared through the window, angling forward to fall the extra arm's length down to the lower level of the floor inside. He caught himself on his hands and rolled, somersaulting back up into a crouch and launching directly into another two-fisted punch aimed straight into the guard's chest.

The unfortunate guard crashed back into the nearest of his fellows behind him, both men's spears clattering as they flailed and fell.

It was a great move, quite agile for someone Kayd's size, and all the guards were frozen in astonishment for a moment. But that wouldn't last, and Kayd would be surrounded immediately. Lyrrek could see that. There were probably another dozen guards in there. Swallowing and taking a deep breath, Lyrrek watched Kayd for a split second, and as she saw him continue moving, clearing the space inside as he leapt into his next attack, she dove through after him.

It started to feel like a long fall, but thankfully, she caught herself well with her hands, mimicking Kayd's move and tucking to let her body collapse forward, rolling over and bringing her back up into a crouch.

She had aimed a bit left of where Kayd had landed, and her momentum brought her up facing the shocked-looking guard by the wall who had Jyhnda's amulet. She leapt forward into another dive, straight at the guard, hands out to grab for his spear.

He was so surprised that he only managed to hold it up between them, and she caught the haft, slamming it back into his chest, the momentum of her collision into him pitching him back to crack his head against the stone wall.

She yanked the spear away from him as he fell, but he had lost his grip on it, and she saw his eyes roll back into his head as he tumbled into a heap at her feet.

Lyrrek spun, dropping the spear, and raced toward Kayd, who had knocked out another, but was about to be stabbed at by seven or eight spears at once.

Orenna swung through the window, feet first, then bounced forward into an immediate attack towards some of the ones lunging at Kayd. Between Lyrrek, Kayd, and Orenna and their quick efforts with their fists and feet, only a few of those spear thrusts got through, and the ones that did all *thunked* off Kayd's magically protected skin.

And then Amrelyn and Veytra were in the chamber with them as well, and the remaining guards didn't last long, falling quickly under the dragonskin fists of the five master wizards.

The front door of the chamber burst open, and the two guards from outside crowded through together, shocked expressions appearing on their faces as they realized that their fellows were all lying in various crumpled poses on the floor inside.

Veytra was closest to them. She lunged up and grabbed them both by the necks of their black tabards, and ignoring their awkward, confused attempts to slash their spear blades at her, she dropped and fell backward, yanking them both to tumble headlong into the chamber with a yelp and a hissing gasp.

Their flailing landings at the bottom of the steps weren't so graceful as Kayd and Lyrrek's had been, and they both sprawled along either side of Veytra onto their faces. Kayd stepped over and helped her knock them both out before they could recover themselves.

Amrelyn yanked Jyhnda's amulet from the fallen guard's belt pouch, scattering a handful of coppers and some tiny scraps of parchment about as she did. Then she stood, spitting down at him, and examined the amulet closely in the light of the nearest lantern.

"No blood," she said quietly.

Kayd patted her shoulder, then slipped past her to open the door into the rock face. With Lyrrek and Amrelyn only a step behind, he disappeared into the dark tunnel beyond.

Deldrum sighed, *thunking* the end of his spear softly on the trail as he slouched along on sore feet. He was thoroughly tired of this patrol.

They were a pointless exercise, these nighttime watches. Nobody actually lived on this stupid island, which was, as far as Deldrum could tell, a place the Swordfish used for meetings with people who weren't worthy of knowing the location of his palace. The only people who visited regularly were the Swordfish's servants and agents.

Patrolling the island seemed quite pointless to him. But there had been some excitement today when someone discovered a sunken boat offshore, and now everyone was supposed to be on alert.

He rolled his eyes. Sunken boats were everywhere in the Lastlands.

He turned the corner toward the lanterns outside the entrance to the underhall itself, and couldn't help gazing curiously at it. No guards stood outside at the moment to frown at someone getting too close.

The new guards aboard the Swordfish's ship had been informed upon arrival that the underhall itself was *extremely* off limits. It was guarded at all times, and by some of the most loyal.

Wait.

He stopped, looking back and forth.

The underhall was, indeed, entirely unguarded at that moment.

That was very unusual.

And was that an open window? What on Origin?

Deldrum trotted curiously over to the window and looked inside, and then his mouth fell open. The antechamber was full of crumpled men and women dressed in black tabards, lying where they had fallen. A couple of them were beginning to make groggy movements, groaning in pain.

The door that led, apparently, deeper into the underhall itself stood ajar.

Deldrum gasped and spun, cursing as he burst into a run on his sore feet, sprinting hard for the Swordfish's ship.

They were under attack.

Lyrrek followed close at Kayd's shoulder as he crept down the long, dark corridor. Occasionally there were a couple steps lit by a lantern, the only illumination.

The tunnel had been carved from the rock, and was impressive, with arched architectural features down the length of it. They had gone several dozen paces into the island, she estimated, before they finally reached a closed door.

She could see light coming from under the door, and crept quickly up to it, dropping down to one side so Kayd could do the same. She cautiously pushed the door open a bit, peering through the crack.

She saw Jyhnda almost immediately, and sighed in relief. She looked fine. She was sitting on a chair, still in the yellow robe of one of Fehndala's servants, though they had taken her shawl and belt pouches.

Lyrrek turned and met Amrelyn's eyes in the dim corridor. "She's fine," she whispered, and saw Amrelyn wilt a little as relief washed over her. She nodded.

Lyrrek looked back in at Jyhnda, who was sitting with an admirable level of calm, looking like she was trying to be patient with someone.

"With respect, my lord, I don't know what you're talking about," she said.

"We found your wrecked boat," spat a nasally male voice, and an older man in a long black robe stepped into Lyrrek's view. "We were watching for you to make your move, fool girl. Now you *will* tell me what I want to know. Who is your target?"

"Forgive me my lord," she said, and Lyrrek could see her trying to act the right amount of worried. "There's been some sort of misunderstanding. I arrived on Lady Fehndala's ship, with the rest of her servants. I'm sorry I was trying to sneak out, I didn't mean anything by it, I was just going to…" She paused, and adopted a convincingly embarrassed expression. "Well, there was a…rather handsome guard, you see, and I was…"

He stared at her as she trailed off, then barked a single laugh.

He stalked over to the desk nearby, and yanked open a drawer.

Lyrrek watched him withdraw a long bronze dagger from within.

She grabbed Kayd's shoulder. "This is my responsibility," she mouthed. He nodded.

She stood and slammed the door open as she strode through it. The noise made the black-robed man jump, and he spun to face her, the dagger gripped in his hand.

His eyes widened as he saw her stalking toward him, with what she knew was probably a grim expression on her face. He raised the dagger.

But before either of them could do anything, Jyhnda leapt from her chair at the black-robed man, who had turned away from her toward Lyrrek. She aimed a hard punch directly at the elbow attached to the hand that held the dagger, and a resounding *crack* echoed in the chamber.

The dagger flew from his nerveless grasp, its metallic clanging into the wall an accompaniment to his great, hissing intake of breath. And then he began to scream.

Lyrrek punched him hard in the face, and silence descended once more, broken only by the thudding of his crumbling fall.

"Oh my," Jyhnda said, looking down at his arm, motionless where the man had awkwardly landed. "That felt like something broke." A worried look came over her face, and she bent next to him, hands over his elbow. Lyrrek felt the gleam of her healing magic as she tried to undo what she'd done.

Lyrrek looked over and saw Amrelyn had followed her in, and they shared a proud look for a moment, then stepped over to help amplify her spell.

"Well done, Adept," she said quietly to Jyhnda as they finished and were helping each other up.

"Thank you, Master," Jyhnda said shyly.

"Is that the Swordfish?" Kayd asked from the corridor, where he was keeping watch.

"No," Jyhnda said. "Just a head servant or something. But I think I figured out what they're doing here."

"What?" Lyrrek asked.

Jyhnda met her eyes. "I think it was a prisoner exchange. From what I heard some guards saying, it sounded like Fehndala and Eglamon emptied out their magistrates' dungeons and brought all the prisoners here on ships. I think they loaded them all on the Swordfish's ship earlier this evening."

"They did what?" Kayd demanded, stepping forward.

Jyhnda shrugged. "They wouldn't let us watch or anything, but I think that's what was going on."

Veytra and Orenna returned from checking the corridors that branched off, shaking their heads. "No one else that we can find nearby," Veytra said, "though we didn't explore that far."

"We better go," Amrelyn said. She handed Jyhnda her amulet. "Are you all right? Did they do anything to you?"

"I'm fine," Jyhnda said, grinning. "The creep that took my amulet nearly got caught talking to me. He didn't manage to get anything else he wanted. Not that I would have let him."

"Well," Amrelyn said, a grim look on her face. "We'll talk about it later. And you can kick him on the way out if you want, Lyrrek took him down for you."

"Thanks again, master," Jyhnda said. "I'm fine. But yeah, I think I'd like to stop being Fehndala's servant, now, if you don't mind. She's a mess."

"I believe you, let me assure you." Lyrrek said, chuckling. "I've seen where she lives. And yes, let's get the Deep out of here."

Pemana, out of breath, dropped from her bent-over run into a crouch in the shadow of a building. The gravel trail cut sharply left and widened, so this was probably the main road Kayd had described. The building they'd gone into should be just around the corner.

She crept slowly up to the edge of the wall, peering around. She didn't see any black tabards. And after a second, she spotted the open window on her side of the shorter building.

Nodding, she started to step around the corner when the *twang* of a bowstring alerted her, and she stepped back just in time for an arrow to *thunk* into the stone wall, its bronze head bouncing off, a spray of fine sand from the mortar striking her warded skin and causing her to flinch.

"Intruder!"

A man's voice screamed it from the darkness behind her somewhere, and she heard immediate yells, followed by the stirring of boots on wooden decks of ships and building floors across the complex, a cacophony of motion beginning from all directions.

With a curse, Pemana drew her sword. She started to head toward the window, ready to dive in and try to catch up to the others.

But then she froze.

No. She couldn't do that.

Another arrow flashed past, skittering off into the darkness.

Kayd and the others had to escape. She was the one who had messed up. She had alerted the entire island.

Their only hope of breaking out was if she didn't lead the horde of guards that was about to descend on her straight to her friends.

She exploded into motion, sprinting in the direction the arrows had been coming from, sword out, ready to try to break through and draw them away.

But she skidded to a halt as she rounded the corner. The archer had seen her coming and pulled back.

He had retreated to join the fifty additional black-tabarded guards running to join him, torchlight and shining spears blazing from their ranks.

Pemana gasped and raised her grandfather's sword.

Chapter Twenty-One

CLASH

Lyrrek helped Jyhnda strip off the yellow servant's robe, revealing practical trousers and a tunic that she'd been wearing underneath.

Jyhnda tucked her amulet away, wrapped the black belt and pouch she'd taken from the unconscious chief servant around her waist, then slid his bronze dagger into the belt. "I'm ready." She said.

Kayd started toward the doorway, then suddenly froze, holding up his hand. "Do you hear that?" he asked quietly.

Lyrrek listened hard. And she did hear it. Shouts. A scream.

Battle.

"Pemana," Kayd gasped, and burst into a run.

"I'm sorry I got you into this," Lyrrek said to Jyhnda between strides as they chased after Kayd.

"This was my idea," Jyhnda said. "I'm sorry I got *you* into it. But it will be an honor to fight at your side, my lady."

Lyrrek held up her shortsword, and Jyhnda clanged the long dagger's guard against hers in a ringing salute as they burst into the open chamber behind Kayd, who was already sweeping startled black-tabarded guards off their feet and shoving them over into one another.

She helped Jyhnda quickly dispatch one sword-wielder, then stepped back as the others streamed in around them and joined the fight.

Lyrrek heard more shouts and screams from outside, and ran over to stare out the window through which they'd come in.

She could see Pemana in a gap between buildings! She was several dozen paces through the complex, back toward the western pier where Eglamon and the Swordfish's ships were docked.

Lyrrek gasped. Pemana fought valiantly above a pile of fallen black-tabarded figures. She was being pushed back their direction, but seemed to be trying desperately to avoid that for some reason.

Why wasn't she falling back to join them?

"Kayd!" Lyrrek shouted.

The guards pushed Pemana back again, and then again. Exhaustion reared up within her, and she stumbled away from them, leaving behind more fallen in black tabards to slow the enemy's advance. But there were so many of them. And she knew there would be more coming from behind her soon.

Her grandfather's sword was heavy. It had always been too long for her, really. It had never been that big of a problem. But she had never faced so many enemies at once who were trying to kill her, either.

Tears of frustration and exhaustion leaked at the corners of her eyes. She had to divert this attack away from her friends. But they were cornering her backward, straight toward the low building.

And then she heard Lyrrek's voice, from within the building, shout "Kayd!"

Cursing, she quickly stabbed another two, stumbling back after, letting the sword drop between waves, now, grabbing at any rest she could get, her shoulders on fire.

And then she heard a new voice shout.

"Halt!" the voice roared. It came from the direction of the ships.

The black tabards parted and pulled back from her immediately.

A *bang* sounded behind her, a door slamming open, and she heard Kayd roar her name.

The guards that were drawing in around the door he emerged from were running away when she spared a glance over her shoulder. But it didn't seem like they were running from Kayd. As they fled, they were staring back, terrified, beyond *her*.

She spun back, and saw a dark-haired man in black robes and cloak trimmed with gold step into the gap the guards made for him. He raised a gloved fist toward her, his eyes locked with hers.

It was him.

She turned to face him, grim determination driving away her exhaustion.

But then the world exploded in blinding blue-white light, an instantaneous *boom* smashing into her ears, into her whole body.

Every muscle seized at once, from her toes to her eyelids. Her entire being clenched, so hard that every fiber of her screamed.

She felt herself lose contact with the ground, blasted over backward in an involuntary leap, her view of the world wheeling wildly overhead. As she spun over, upside down, she saw Kayd, where he'd been behind her, connected to her heart by a brilliant blue-white bolt of lightning that was hurling him away from her.

And then the world came back up at her face, and she crashed into agonizing darkness.

Lyrrek screamed and leapt back through the low building's doorway as she watched the lightning blast through Pemana and into Kayd. It rippled into the ground around him and arced to their building as she managed to fall backward inside.

A deeply unnerving feeling that every hair on her body was standing on end flashed over her.

She gasped, falling to a crouch, the others staring between her and the door in open-mouthed silence.

She jumped immediately back to her feet and ran for the doorway.

"Kayd!" she called. He had fallen next to the building, sliding in the gravel, and lay there in a fetal position, moving slowly as if he was trying to untwist himself.

She glanced, shocked, over at Pemana, who lay on her face, completely motionless, a dozen paces away.

The Swordfish stood beyond her fallen friend, staring at her. Then he lifted his hand and pointed at Lyrrek, and she closed her eyes.

But instead of another *bang*, she heard the guards around him roar and start to rush forward.

Lyrrek burst grimly into motion herself. She spun down to Kayd, slapping healing magic into him with everything she was, grabbing him by his large bicep and pulling hard.

Suddenly, Veytra was there, and Orenna too, and she felt their magic expand her own into powerful, blossoming life, and the three of them flowed all of it through Kayd like a waterfall.

She heard bowstrings *twang* and hoped that her wards would hold, because she couldn't release her concentration on the healing spell until they had him on his feet. He was starting to move, starting to unwind and breathe.

There was a skidding of boots on gravel as Amrelyn and Jyhnda slid in between them and the whistle of the oncoming arrows, batting them aside as, at last, Kayd groaned, and started helping them pull him to his feet, bent over and limping, as they all dragged him back toward the door.

Lyrrek spared a glance toward Pemana.

It had taken them too long to get Kayd up. The Swordfish's men had already surrounded her, had her by the shoulders, and were dragging her limp form away from them back toward the ships.

"No!" Lyrrek cried, tears erupting from her eyes as she struggled to keep Kayd from falling, while they all stumbled awkwardly back into the antechamber and toward the tunnel.

Chapter Twenty-Two

Blades

L yrrek fell back against the stone wall in the head servant's chamber, catching her breath. Amrelyn took her
place at the doorway with Veytra, and they readied themselves for the next assault.

Orenna and Jyhnda bent over Kayd, who was now
sitting cross-legged on the floor, concentrating on casting
the spell with them, helping create the triplicate amplification
for his own magical healing. Hopefully he'd be back on his
feet soon.

Lyrrek, Jyhnda, Amrelyn, Veytra, and Orenna were taking turns holding the ground here at the doorway into the
long, carved tunnel. They were tiring, but so far, none of the
waves of guards trying to push through to them had been that
successful. Several of the black-tabarded guards had fallen,
though their fellows were trying to drag them back and up
the corridor when they did, lest they create an impediment
to their progress with their own wounded.

They had struck back enough of their attackers that she
had begun to see dark-orange and golden-yellow tabards
among the fighters as well, whatever that might portend.

"I think I'm all right," Kayd said, pulling himself slowly to his feet with a groan, and reaching for a spear. He managed to pull himself upright, but had to use the spear to support himself. "Not sure how much use I'll be in the fight, though," he said, his voice tired.

"We can handle it," Orenna said firmly. She turned to look at Lyrrek, and Lyrrek met her eyes.

Orenna's expression was carefully neutral. "Why don't you see if you can reach Aether while we're between waves," she said quietly. "He would want to know what's going on."

Lyrrek nodded and took hold of her amulet.

She thought of him and cast the spell, reaching for his mind.

She found him, but could tell immediately that something was drastically wrong. She couldn't tell what she was sensing, and called his name again, alarmed.

She felt him cast the spell from his end and their connection erupted into strange emotions.

His mind felt exhausted, as if he was being pushed to the very limits of his endurance. But he was also…excited beyond measure? And very proud of himself, perhaps?

What on Origin was going on?

"I'm all right!" he mind-shouted at her. "Hold on, I'm coming!"

And then he was gone.

She gasped and opened her eyes.

"What?" Orenna asked her, startled.

"I don't know," Lyrrek said, in wonder. "It felt like he was enduring something intense, and his emotions were crazy. But he says he's coming."

Orenna frowned, then suddenly her eyes widened, her mouth opening. But before she could speak, Veytra shouted.

"Here come more guards, too! There's a lot, get ready!"

Lyrrek grabbed her shortsword and pulled herself to her feet.

Pemana felt the first light of the world returning, and groaned.

Everything hurt. Her body was a storm of agonized sensations.

She was close to death. She hadn't known she had the capacity to know that, but she felt it now. It felt like she had torn every muscle in her body, like all that kept her going had been drained away.

She tried to stay calm, her mind swimming in body-wide agony and near-terminal exhaustion. She had one chance, and she didn't know if she had the strength. But she strained to reach for the concentration to cast the healing spell, carefully balanced on a blade of consciousness, trying not to pass out. The slightest hint of the magic trickled through her.

It didn't feel a lot better, but as the magic flowed, the feeling that she was about to tip off the ledge of life and fall away into the comfortable peace beyond eased some, the swirling vertigo retreating a bit.

Sensation returned, the pounding of her heart in her ears lessened, and she realized that part of her discomfort came from the awkward angle at which her head was hanging. She was tied to a chair. That was the problem. She groaned and straightened her neck, which hurt in new ways, but relieved some others, and on balance felt better.

She cast a bit more of the spell before feeling that she'd exhaust herself out of consciousness again if she wasn't careful, and relaxed for a moment to just breathe.

She was in the cabin of a ship, she realized, from the sound and the feeling of motion beneath her. And from the familiar slap of waves against hull, and the rate of the gentle rocking she felt, she knew that it was a large vessel and they were at speed.

Pemana cracked her eyes open, and lantern light blinded her anew. Gradually, her eyes adjusted. It was a ship's cabin all right, but a larger one than she'd ever been in. And it was much, much finer, the appointments looking like they belonged to someone of great wealth. Her chair was facing aft, toward a fancy map table in the center, not unusual for a sailing vessel. But there were also framed paintings on the walls, rich drapes of luxurious fabric surrounding an actual bed, not a bunk like most ships would have. And there was even a stone statue, carved in the form of a beautiful woman standing in an unnatural pose, built into the highly polished wood of that corner so that it wouldn't shift while they were at sea.

She must be on the Swordfish's ship.

The realization chilled her through as memories returned.

The Swordfish was a wizard.

The reality of it hollowed out what little solidity remained in her world. He had nearly killed her with powerful magic, magic that none of them had even dreamed was possible.

He was a much more powerful wizard than she, or any of them.

And now he held her captive.

She remembered the last thing she'd seen, Kayd's face, contorted in agony as he flew away from her.

She wondered if he had even survived. She wondered whether any of them had. Despair began to cry in her heart.

They would have been at a great disadvantage if they faced him. The Swordfish's spell had blasted straight through her best magical protections.

A sudden thought distracted her. If any of them had survived, someone might be trying to locate her. All her magical items were gone. She wouldn't be generating any magical signature for them to find.

She stared at the statue in the corner. It would take most of her remaining strength. And the Swordfish might just notice and remove it. But she had no choice, she had to try, she had to give herself a chance, even if only the slimmest one.

The beacon spell was a strain, but she managed it, and the statue sparkled in her magical senses for an instant, before exhaustion overcame her again, and she had to collapse all efforts and just breathe some more.

She looked down at herself as she did so, eyeing the rough ropes binding her into the fine wooden chair.

The knots looked formidable. She sighed, but then suddenly, something registered, and her sigh became a tormented gasp.

Her grandfather's sword…it was gone too.

Pain and desolation washed over her, and she spent her last bit of strength hissing a curse, straining at her bonds until she was dragged back down into the darkness again.

Lyrrek clashed swords with another guard that lunged for her through the doorway. She was able to redirect his blow into the wall, then whip her shortsword toward him along his arm, stabbing into his shoulder. He jerked back with a cry, stumbling into the other guards behind him.

Good, she thought to herself grimly. Her tunic was getting pretty well ventilated from all the slashes that had gotten through her defenses. Her wardstones held, she was unhurt; but she was nearly exhausted.

And she had seen some maces appear among the guards.

Perhaps some of them had finally figured out that they were fighting dragons here.

Kayd had insisted he was recovered enough to fight again, and was taking a turn at the doorway. He met her eyes, breathing hard, and both of them leaned on the nearest wall as the attackers pulled back again, shouting curses, and dragging the latest group of their wounded back up the tunnel.

"You'd think they'd get the hint and give up," Kayd whispered grimly.

"I do wish they would," Lyrrek sighed, not managing to get much humor into her tired voice. "You doing all right?"

"I think so," he said quietly. "You healing yourself as we go? It helps."

"Thanks for the reminder," she said wearily, and let some magic flow through her. He was right. It did help a little.

"They just keep coming," Kayd said, squinting down the corridor. "There were a lot of ships full of guards here." He looked over his shoulder at the others, then met her eyes. "I'm not sure we can stop them all."

"Maybe we need to push our way out," she said, feeling a bit better as she cast another pulse of healing magic through herself. "Make for Pemana's boat?"

Lyrrek regretted saying her name immediately, as the despairing look that flashed across his face broke her heart.

She started to step across to him, intending to put a hand on his shoulder and tell him that she believed Pemana was alive, and none of them would stop until they got her back. But she didn't make it to him, stepping back to irritably bat aside the hail of arrows soaring down the corridor at her, several of them getting through to bounce off her hip and leg, one getting caught in her tunic.

Lyrrek cursed and pulled back into the chamber, tugging at the arrow dangling from her perforated clothing.

"They're coming again," Kayd said grimly.

She took a deep breath, threw the arrow to clatter into the corner, and readied herself.

Before the next wave reached them, though, an enormously loud sound pierced down into the depths of the tunnel from outside, echoing wildly off the parallel stone walls.

She and Kayd met each other's eyes, astonished. Distorted by distance and echoes, it was still, unmistakably to this experienced group, the roar of a large dragon, the very first time one had ever been heard in the Lastlands.

She looked back up the corridor. The guards that had been charging toward them had frozen, expressions of horror on their faces, and were turning to dash back out in response to screamed orders from behind them.

"So," Orenna said, a huge smile on her face. "That *is* what he was doing."

Jyhnda looked quite alarmed and confused, staring around at the grinning faces of her guildmates.

"That will be Aether, I think," Orenna said, patting Jyhnda on the shoulder. "Let's go see what he's gotten himself into now." And she trotted off up the corridor ahead of the others.

Lyrrek's delighted smile widened as she followed at a run.

By the time Lyrrek caught up to the others in the antechamber, the guards had all scattered. Bowstrings and shouted orders echoed through the grounds from all directions outside.

From the shouting, it sounded like a lot of the orders involved pulling back to protect the ships.

Suddenly, a great *woosh* of wind thundered through the building, nearly blowing out the torches. They all ducked instinctively, and outside, they heard screams, and the gravelly *thuds* of bodies hurling themselves to the ground. The lanterns out in the road swung wildly, casting crazy shadows as she and the others carefully approached the door. The pounding of booted feet picked back up again, but it was drawing away from them, occasionally accompanied by another roaring dragon scream from somewhere above.

And then, as they stepped out into the road, not seeing any guards within view, the rhythmic blast of wind from a landing dragon's wings began to pound through the street. The silhouette of the great beast appeared from the moonlight above, dropping to land in the widest spot of open clearing nearby. The tremendous wind of its landing blasted grit all the way back to where they stood watching, amazed. At last, the dragon came into the light of the swinging lanterns as it stalked toward them.

It was a big dragon, more than a dozen paces long. Its indigo scales, blending to a lighter gray on its belly, sparkled reflections of the lantern-light at them, but Lyrrek barely noticed it. Her eyes were entirely focused on Aether.

He was sitting up from where he crouched on the dragon's powerful shoulders, and she saw him unwinding leather straps that seemed to lash him into a complex arrangement of them wrapped around the dragon's neck and torso, like a cart-sheep harness.

Amrelyn drew up next to her, watching the dragon approach. "Huh. I guess you were right, he actually did it."

Lyrrek grinned, remembering, and nodded. "Yeah, that counts."

The dragon stopped some distance from them, flipping its wings neatly to its back, and slowly sank to its belly, its sleek, fanged mouth hanging open, long tongue lolling a bit, as it panted for breath, clearly winded from its recent efforts.

Aether finished unstrapping himself and swung his legs carefully over his staff, where it was bound to the dragon's harness, then dropped from its back the short distance to the ground. And then he was running to Lyrrek, and she held out her arms, and he was, finally, there.

"I'm so glad you're safe," they both whispered, clinging to each other.

She looked over his shoulder at the intimidating sight of the dragon lying there, staring at them. Aether had bound leather up and around its head into a halter of sorts, as well, and she could see the bulges of stones within, indeed could sense the intricate magic bound into them that was keeping the dragon passive. She shook her head and drew back from the hug to meet his eyes.

"Well done, you madman," she said proudly.

Kayd stepped up to them, and Aether grinned up at his friend. But his grin faltered as he saw the look on Kayd's face.

"They took Pemana," Kayd said quietly.

Aether's eyes widened. "Where?"

"We don't know," Lyrrek said. "We had to pull back after the Swordfish...he's a wizard too, Aether."

"He hit Pemana and I with a lightning spell."

Aether's mouth dropped open. And then Lyrrek saw a look come over his face that she hadn't seen often.

He was usually such a kind, even calm person. But once in a while, he'd get a look in his eye, when talking about his abusive former master, for example. That look flared hotly there now.

"The only thing we know is that we saw his ship coming from the north when he first arrived," Lyrrek said.

"Can the dragon carry us both?" Kayd asked.

Aether stared at Kayd for an instant, then sighed.

"Maybe. But I don't think she could manage both of us and Pemana."

Aether stepped up to his friend and put his hand on his shoulder, his mouth a thin, determined line. "I'll bring her back, Kayd," he said quietly.

Kayd nodded, dejected.

Aether saluted him, then turned away from them, running to the dragon, who watched him curiously.

He climbed up on its back and started securing the straps around himself. "Do you have a boat?" he asked her.

"We think so," Lyrrek called back, not too excited to approach much closer just then.

"It looked like all four ships were heading out as we came in to land. Get on the sea and use the confusion to slip through, then head back for the hall."

"We will," she said. She felt Orenna and the others draw up next to her, watching in fascination as a look of concentration came over Aether's face, and the dragon rose up onto its four feet, flipping out its wings into a stretch.

Aether met Kayd's eyes once more. Then he bent and gripped the straps as the dragon lifted its wings high and leapt into the night sky, blasting grit in all directions again.

The others jogged off in the direction in which they thought Pemana had hidden her sailboat. Lyrrek lingered a moment longer, watching the silhouette of Aether and the dragon disappear back into the moonlit sky above, then finally broke into a run, racing to catch her friends.

Chapter Twenty-Three
Engulfed

T he light returned, slowly, and this time, Pemana remembered to straighten her neck, easing the pain
there. The rest of her body still certainly hurt, but it had
eased a bit. She pulsed a tiny bit more healing magic through
herself, then took a long, rattling breath.

"Good," said a cold voice behind her, and she froze. "You
will answer some questions for me."

She heard boots on the deck, the creak of the ship. They
were still at sea. She pulled her eyes slowly open. She was still
tied to the chair, still in the cabin.

Black robes filled her peripheral vision as he walked by,
then turned to face her, sitting down at the map table.

He stared at her as she tried to hold her head up and
return his gaze. He had long, straight black hair and dark
eyes. He was almost handsome, but there was a strangeness
to his features that she found…unappealing.

"I watched you during the battle," he said. "I saw you
take many hits but suffer no injury. I know who and what
you are."

She blinked, but said nothing.

"Were you seeking me directly, or have they expanded the scouting effort?"

Now she only stared back at him, trying not to frown.

He, on the other hand, did not resist frowning at her. "When did you arrive here?"

She saw the anger begin to kindle in his eyes when she didn't reply.

"You *will* tell me what I want to know." He reached into a pouch and pulled out her mind amulet. "What is this device?" he demanded. "I'm not familiar with it."

What on Origin was going on here?

She had to keep him talking. As long as he was talking, he wasn't harming her further. Her body couldn't sustain much more damage.

"Forgive me…my lord," she croaked, unable to manage much more than a whisper. "I am permitted to say nothing."

Now the Swordfish looked confused. "Why? On whose authority?"

Something was odd about the look on his face. He looked frustrated and angry, as before, and the irritated confusion was new, but there was something else.

And then it registered. It was fear she saw on his face.

The Swordfish was afraid of her.

That was strange. She was certainly no threat to him in this state. But his eyes kept flicking about her person, like he was watching for signs of her about to do…what exactly?

Suddenly, she was overwhelmed with the desire to examine him with her magical senses.

"I…my lord…" she choked, and made a display of weakly coughing, letting her words fade. But she'd faked it, to give herself a few seconds.

It was a strain and a risk. If he noticed, it might mean her life. But she had to know. Her magical senses revealed…

Nothing.

The statue behind him still blazed with its beacon spell. But the Swordfish had no magical signature that she could sense. He wasn't even warded, which was very strange if he was a wizard, and, for some reason, afraid of her.

Or…wait. Was there magic there? She coughed weakly once more, then focused intensely on the Swordfish himself.

There *was* something there, barely detectable! And then she realized that it must be the concealment spell Aether had learned from the caches. The Swordfish was hiding from her somehow. He was…

She froze mid-cough.

Aether had learned that spell from caches left behind by an ancient wizard living on the mainland before the Great Flight.

How did the Swordfish know that spell?

She focused her magical senses on him even harder. There was a faint echo slipping through his concealment magic. There were definitely other spells underneath, so she was certain he was warded.

And there was something else…a slight concentration of barely glimmering magics, near his hands…

It was too much. She felt herself passing out, and released her sensing, gasping and shaking her head.

"Forgive me my lord," she mouthed again, seeing his frustration grow.

He started to rise.

"You *will…*"

An explosion of sound erupted above them, a blasting, trumpeting roar that startled them both so much that the Swordfish fell to his knees in his scramble to duck, and Pemana would have joined him if not for the ropes holding her bound.

Shouts and curses erupted out on the deck, and were followed in a few seconds by singing bowstrings.

The Swordfish got back to his feet, tripping a bit on his robe and cursing. He looked into her eyes, and his were wide…panicked.

She managed a weak smile, nodding slightly. "A colleague of mine, I think," she whispered.

He stared at her, gasping. Then he reached into his black robes and withdrew a long, bronze dagger.

She closed her eyes, gathering herself. She was pretty sure she would only have enough strength to cast the dragonskin spell once, so she had to time it carefully to…whatever he was going to do. She listened to his boots, ready for him to come alongside her.

But he stopped a bit short. She opened her eyes quickly, but he was bending down. She readied the spell, but he only began sawing at the ropes binding her ankles.

He got those loose and cut the ones at her wrists, then the ones around her torso.

Pemana gasped as blood flowing freely again caused new sparkles of pain throughout her extremities.

He grabbed her by the tunic and hauled her out of the chair.

He wasn't that large a man, and she was definitely not a dainty waif herself. But somehow, he managed to leverage her up and get her own feet under her, nearly dumping her face-first onto the deck in the process.

He dragged her, weakly stumbling, back toward the door out onto the main deck.

She tried to gasp the word "please," to beg him to let her rest a moment, but it didn't come out of her mouth, and she almost fell.

The Swordfish shoved her out and to the edge of the deck with one hand and looked up into the night, the dagger held high in the other, reflecting the lantern light.

Pemana doubled over in agony, watching the Swordfish above her, gasping and desperately preparing the dragonskin spell, but needing to wait until the last possible second.

She heard the flapping of great wings in the moonlit darkness, and then looked up and spotted the darker shape moving against the dark sky. The dragon screamed again and grew larger, continuing its swooping turn back toward them for another pass.

The Swordfish waited until the dragon got close enough to see them in the lanternlight.

Then he shoved Pemana over the side.

She barely had time to suck in a breath as the black waves slapped up to meet her.

She heard the dragon roar again, the sound muffled through the sea water, as she struggled to get back to the surface.

She broke through, gasping air. Her strength was very nearly gone.

Carefully, agony in every limb, she managed one more weak kick and got herself floating on her back, trying to move as little as possible, as the blackness of unconsciousness threatened to drag her down with it into the depths.

And then she heard the great flapping of wings, felt the harsh spray of the sea blasted across her face. She saw the great shadow blotting out the moon, and holding her breath, cast the dragonskin spell.

It was all the strength she had.

The dragon's claws struck her torso and hips, folding her into the sea. Then, she was violently unfolded as the sea was ripped from her.

The black water below her plunged away, and she surged into sudden motion, an intense sideways lurch that felt like it was going to remove her head from her body. Her arms and legs flailed weakly in an impossibly loud roar of wind.

She started to scream, but the scouring wind ripped it from her mouth, along with the last of her consciousness.

Lyrrek sat with Kayd, who held very tightly to the wheel of Pemana's sailboat, holding their course firm as they raced across a calm sea toward Freehome. The first light of dawn glazed the eastern horizon, but as beautiful as it was, she couldn't appreciate it this morning.

The others seemed to understand, and had left her and Kayd to their shared vigil, retiring to the cabin to get what rest they could.

She thought, for the thousandth time, of trying to reach Aether. But she didn't want to distract him in the middle of something intense, when he might need his concentration to…

She refused to allow herself to consider the idea of Aether out there, battling the Swordfish's terrifying magic, alone.

She stared out at the horizon, determinedly keeping her mind on their course. Maybe another hour until they reached Freehome?

They had been sailing for quite a while, even with the ideal conditions and windstones. The longer it went on, the harder it became for her to ignore the desperate horror trying to slip into the back of her mind.

What if Aether didn't come back? What if they just never heard anything from either him or Pemana ever again?

She choked back another sob and forced herself to breathe, staring ahead at the horizon.

Suddenly Kayd gasped, and she jerked her head toward him, and saw his expression transform.

Relief.

All of her pain drained instantly away, and with it her tears flowed, streaming down her cheeks.

She had them mostly wiped away a few minutes later when Kayd finally released his amulet, turning to look at her.

"They're all right," he said quietly. "It was Pemana. She said to tell everyone sorry they took so long to let us know they're safe, but she was nearly…gone. Aether had to have the dragon pluck her out of the sea after the Swordfish threw her overboard, and by the time he got her back onto land, he had to spend a few hours panic-healing her just to keep her alive."

He paused to release a shuddering sigh, and went on.

"By then, Aether was worried about getting the dragon into the sea yard before the sun came up, so they had to just race for the hall. They got there, and they're safe. Aether asked her to contact us while he got the dragon a barrel of water. Apparently she's thirsty."

Lyrrek blinked, stunned. "There's a dragon in the sea yard of our guild hall?"

Kayd chuckled weakly. "It would seem so."

"There's a what, where?" Veytra asked, appearing in the cabin door, eyes wide.

Pemana eased into a different position in her chair in the guild hall's common room, sighing.

A rotating trio of her friends, including Amrelyn and even Jyhnda, before they departed back for Eagle's End, had taken it in turns to spend time pouring healing magic into her until she gained enough stamina to help with it herself.

Today, after all of that, she felt immeasurably better. She was still tired, but just having the freedom from all-encompassing agony was a blessed relief.

Kayd had sat with her several times over the duration of her healing. He seemed to have suffered less damage from the Swordfish's lightning himself. And Lyrrek and the others had started healing him almost immediately after he was struck. So sometimes he helped the others heal her, and sometimes, later through the next day, she and the others had returned the favor and healed him some more as well. And occasionally they just tossed some healing magic around to everyone else, because all had been through a lot in the last few days, and each of them could use it.

Everyone's eyes had gone wide when Aether asked if a couple of his friends would mind helping him heal the dragon some as well, as after all, she had flown him an enormous distance yesterday. But Kayd and Lyrrek, once they'd gotten over their shock, had both said they'd be happy to help.

Pemana, though, had insisted one of the three be her. She was feeling a bit better by that point, and after all, if it weren't for the dragon, she'd be dead. She probably owed her just as much as she did her friends. So, late that afternoon, she and Kayd flanked Aether, and the three of them had walked slowly toward the snoozing dragon where she lay, curled into a large, heaving, scaly mound, comfortably napping away the heat of the day in the gravel of the walled sea yard.

She'd watched Aether concentrate and gently take control of the dragon's mind to wake her. The dragon lifted her great indigo head, blinking her sparkling eyes and looking at them.

"She doesn't understand what we're going to do, but I did manage to convince her that it will be good for her, I think," he'd said. "The mind control stones are holding her steady, so we should be safe."

The dragon's dusty smell was strong, but not unpleasant. The sparkling irises of her great eyes had flared as she focused on them, as did her nostrils as she sniffed the air. But she'd remained calm, just staring at them, as they began the healing spell.

As the healing washed over the dragon, she had cooed, a rumbling ripple of tiny trumpets that definitely sounded like she was enjoying their gift of magical refreshment.

This morning, the second after her rescue, Pemana was unsure what to do with herself. It had been an eventful couple days, and she was ready to get back to work. But all the questions lingering over that work remained, so she found herself staring out the window at the snoozing dragon, wondering.

She still didn't know where to find the Swordfish. And now, she knew that if she did find him, they had no way to defeat him. His magic was so much more powerful than theirs, and until they figured out how to replicate it, they would stand no chance of defending against it.

And worst of all, she had lost her grandfather's sword. She was trying not to think about that. It was far too…disruptive.

She sighed and rose from her creaky camp chair, headed for the kitchen.

Lyrrek was inside, sitting at a table with a cup of tea and a book.

"Morning," Pemana said. "Aether find anything interesting last night when he took the dragon out?"

"No," Lyrrek said, placing the book down on the table and smiling up at Pemana. "He said he flew some big circles north from the island, but couldn't find any signs of the statue on the Swordfish's ship anywhere."

"I suppose it's likely he finally noticed it and cleared the spell," Pemana said, sighing as she sat down at the table with Lyrrek. "Ah well."

Kayd came in the other door and stopped, looking a bit surprised to find them there. But after a moment's hesitation, he headed toward them.

"Orenna back yet?" he asked Lyrrek.

"Not yet, she said she wasn't sure how long it would take."

"I promised I'd help her pack everything away," Kayd said, and went to get himself a cup of tea as well.

And then he turned, and met Pemana's eyes with a bit of a sheepish look. "Cup of tea?" he asked quietly.

She hesitated, but then something shifted.

Why not?

No reason why not was forthcoming. So she nodded, even managing a bit of a smile. He looked away, but poured a second cup for her.

As he was setting the tea down on the table next to her, a knock sounded at the alleyway door, and they all turned sharply toward it.

Maybe Orenna had her hands full? She wouldn't usually knock on the door to her own guild hall.

Kayd frowned at the door suspiciously as well, and walked swiftly over to it. He yanked the door open, then grinned.

"Toliek," he said, holding out a hand for the adept to shake. "Orenna mentioned you might be in for resupply today."

Toliek entered, nodding and smiling at the others as Lyrrek and Pemana greeted him. "I think Veytra's supposed to have me some new apprentice bracers to take back to Cask, too. Mahlda's got her eyes on a couple new candidates."

"Oh good!" Lyrrek said. "Sky knows we need apprentices."

"Oh," Kayd said, holding out a hand to Toliek's shoulder to stop him as he started toward the common room door. "Um…yeah, don't barge out there just yet. There's a dragon in the sea yard."

Toliek's eyes burst open wide, and he stared around at them. "A what?"

"Aether sort of…befriended a dragon a couple days ago," Lyrrek said, chuckling. "It's a long story. You going to be around for dinner this evening? We can tell you the whole tale in proper fashion."

Toliek stared at her, then opened the door to peek through, his mouth dropping open as he caught a glimpse of the dragon through the window.

He turned to look back at them, a stunned expression on his face. "Damn right I'm staying for dinner. This I *have* to hear."

The door to the alleyway opened once again, and Pemana chuckled, turning to look, expecting to see Orenna.

But it wasn't Orenna that stepped through the door.

Her mind took a few seconds to process what she was seeing. It was a man, with long, unkempt black hair, and an equally untidy beard. He wore a strange leather short robe that looked like it had been handmade by someone without a great deal of leatherworking skill. And it was a dark, dark gray that looked suspiciously like stalkerskin.

The man looked like he was about her age, and for some reason, he looked very familiar, but she couldn't place it.

And then, as Pemana's mind finally registered that someone uninvited had just walked into their kitchen, Lyrrek spoke.

"Greetings, cousin," she said, not moving, her hands clasped on the table before her.

Kayd rose immediately to his feet.

"*Lady* Lyrrek," the bearded stranger said, a bit of a sneer in his voice, and at last, Pemana had it.

"Emrek?" she blurted, stunned, then jumped to her feet too, her mind filling with magic as she dropped into a loose, ready pose, silently cursing the absence of her sword.

"You made it off the mainland, I see," Lyrrek said, still calm, still unmoving.

Emrek barked a short, quiet laugh. "Turns out wizards don't tend to stay exiled, do they, my lady? A lesson we've *all* learned."

"What brings you here, Emrek? Followed Toliek over from Cask?" Pemana demanded in her steeliest tone, meeting his eyes as he turned to look at her, and took in her obvious readiness for combat.

He stared at her, and Pemana remembered the soft, weak, corrupt fool that she'd sent with Aether to leave on that beach at Exile's Shore. That man was gone, replaced by a younger, stronger, fitter man who stood before her now with a dangerous glint in his eye, wearing the evidence of his skill in both magic and combat as a literal robe.

What had Aether done in teaching this man magic? As if their world didn't have enough complicated problems.

She focused hard on Emrek with her magical senses. And she realized immediately, to her surprise, that he wasn't warded. She stared closer, looking for signs of concealment magic, but didn't find even those subtle hints.

It seemed that Emrek was standing there, completely unprotected, vulnerable, in their kitchen.

A hint of amusement flickered on his face as he felt her magically probing him.

"Well, are you done?" he asked after a moment.

Confused, Pemana relaxed her effort, and just returned his stare.

Then Emrek looked over at the others, at grim-faced Kayd and startled-looking Toliek, then back to Lyrrek, meeting her eyes.

His voice was softer when he finally spoke.

"I came here because I need your help."

Chapter Twenty-Four
Surface Tension

A ether leaned against the wall of the corridor, around the corner from the kitchen, and listened to Emrek's words. He'd been holding himself in reserve for his friends, ready to dash in from behind and finish the fight in one swift stroke if he had to. But it didn't sound like that fight was going to materialize, thankfully, so he might as well join the conversation. And this seemed like an opportune time.

"What do you need our help with, Lord Emrek?" Aether asked, stepping out and entering the room, hands clasped behind his back, but a spell at the ready.

Emrek turned to look at him, and Aether saw his eyes narrow slightly.

"I haven't been a lord for a while, boy."

Aether grinned. "As it happens, I haven't been a boy for a while."

Aether thought he might have glimpsed the smallest hint of a smile through Emrek's overgrown beard.

Emrek turned back toward the others, where Kayd and Pemana both still stood in loose, dangerous poses, ready to leap into a fight if they needed to. "I'm not going to attack any of you," he said gruffly, looking at Pemana in particular. "None of you have any reason to attack me that I'm aware of. So maybe you could all just relax."

Kayd grunted, shaking his head slightly, and lowered himself back into a chair, joined after a moment by Pemana, who picked up her tea and sipped, not taking her eyes off Emrek.

Lyrrek just smiled at him, looking unconcerned where she still sat at the table.

Aether looked back at Emrek. "Pardon our manners," he said calmly. "You caught us unprepared for guests. Come in." He gestured to one of the tables. "Have a seat. Cup of tea?"

Emrek stared at him for a moment, then shrugged, moving toward a chair nearest him at one of the empty tables.

Aether poured a couple more cups of tea at the counter, and came to deliver one to Emrek, sitting down a few seats away, but at the same table.

"So, you were saying you needed our help?"

Emrek ignored the cup of tea. "Yes," he said. "One could say you owe me that much."

Aether stared back at him, and hoped he managed to keep a skeptical look from appearing on his face.

Emrek looked around at them. "I don't know what exactly it is you're all engaged in here, but I did enough digging while looking for you to get the sense that you're at war with the Swordfish."

"He's at war with us, at least," Pemana said, and Aether heard the trace of bitterness in her voice.

"Well, that's *my* war you're fighting," Emrek said grave-ly. "The Swordfish is *mine*. The things he did to me..." His words trailed off.

"We know what he did to your father," Pemana said quietly. "And to you. You're not the only one who needs to see him destroyed, either. He's done a lot...to a lot of us."

"Then I'm joining your war," Emrek said.

A long, thoughtful silence descended over the room as they all stared at each other.

"It isn't much of a war," Lyrrek finally said. "We don't know where he is, or where he goes. We've been hunting him, trying to track his networks, but we don't know where he hides, so he's been free to slip away and plot retaliation. He's done some terrible things. We're right in the middle of trying to prevent him from doing some more, in fact."

"But we don't know where to find him so we can stop him," Pemana said. "He keeps getting away."

Emrek took a deep breath. "Well, I can't claim any direct knowledge of his location," he said. He lifted his tea and took a sip, before meeting Pemana's eyes.

"But I do know where his palace is."

Pemana gasped and looked up from one of the kitchen tables that she had spread with all her maps and charts.

"He's doing *what?*"

Emrek stared at her from where he stood next to Aether across the table, arms crossed. "I thought you would have figured that out by now," he said. "How did you manage to catch *me*, anyway?"

"Sky knows," Pemana said grimly.

"I pieced it together, things I heard from beachsleepers at Cask and New Brightwall," Emrek said. "It sounds like there are dozens of missing people."

He turned and sat down in one of the chairs, leaning back in it. "I found someone who knew some things a few weeks ago. Apparently someone managed to slip away last year. Story they told was that the missing people wake up locked in chains in the cargo hold of a ship. After a few days, they find themselves offloaded at a rocky island with nothing on it but a long pier. Then someone opens some doors and they don't see the light again. They work at hard stonecutting labor deep inside tunnels cut into the island, and are caged when they're not working."

Emrek stared up into the corner. "It sounded familiar to me. The Swordfish made me attend him at his court a few times. It's hidden, cut into the rock of a barren island. But I was always escorted in, and only taken in through the front entrance, which is a ways up the slope on the southwest corner. I was never allowed into the deeper areas. But it still sounds like the same place to me. I'd wondered how he'd found the place. Never occurred to me that he was having it built himself."

"We caught Eglamon and Fehndala delivering the contents of their dungeons to him a few days ago," Aether said.

"You caught him?" Emrek said, sitting up straighter. "Did you try to kill him?"

"We were planning to face him," Pemana said quietly. "We didn't really get the chance." She stared at him. "He's a wizard too, you know."

Emrek's eyes widened. "What?"

"He blasted Kayd and myself with lightning. It nearly killed us."

Emrek turned to look at Aether, then back at her. "That something *you* know how to do?"

"Not that we've been able to figure out so far, no," Aether said with a small sigh.

"His spell went right through my defenses," Pemana said. "We'll have to figure out what to do about that if we're going to face him again."

"Hmph," Emrek said. "I'll add it to my list of things you don't know, then."

Pemana rolled her eyes and looked at Aether, who just shook his head slightly.

"We did see recently that the Swordfish has a fondness for tunnels," Aether said. "We were just at an island complex of his that had some carved tunnels and chambers. It didn't sound exactly palatial, though."

"Where is this palace of his?" Pemana asked. "Most of the Lastlands doesn't offer a lot in the way of tunnelable land, aside from some places like Eastwind, but that whole island is pretty full of mines at this point."

"There are some smaller islands, far northeast, that are rockier and have higher elevations," Emrek said. "Never get out that far?"

Pemana shook her head. "No, pirates from Vigil kept me busy at the northwestern end of the archipelago for most of my naval career."

Aether cleared his throat.

Emrek just stared at her, then went on. "It's a rocky island, northeast, out past Fool's Gold.

"Hmm," Aether said. "Yeah, I hadn't flown out that far."

"What?" Emrek asked, frowning. "Flown?"

"Oh," Aether said, chuckling. "Right, sorry. I suppose I should warn you, don't stumble out into the sea yard."

He walked over and opened the door that led out to the common area. "I think, if you lean to your right a bit, you'll be able to see her out the window…"

Emrek did, and Pemana watched his eyes bulge as he processed what he was seeing.

"Uhh…" he said, frozen.

"She's a friend of mine," Aether said, grinning. "And she's good about following instructions. She ought to sleep through 'til nightfall, if I don't wake her up."

Emrek flicked his gaze to Aether briefly before returning to stare out at the sleeping dragon, shaking his head slightly. "Well, then I won't do any screaming. I hope."

"Eh, she's pretty laid back, for a dragon," Aether said.

"How many guards does the Swordfish have in his palace," Pemana interrupted, grudgingly making an effort to not sound rude.

Emrek finally broke off staring out at the door, and Aether closed it again.

"A few hundred on-site, I'd expect," Emrek said. "I don't really know for sure."

Pemana was silent for a moment. "So, let me see if I can sum this up." She took a deep breath. "We need to find a way to free dozens of chained people from the Swordfish's subterranean palace, and help them escape from hundreds of the Swordfish's armed guards, while also destroying this evil pirate lord who seems to want to be king of the Lastlands, but who is also some kind of dangerous wizard whose magic we don't understand."

"That sounds about right," Emrek said, staring back at her with a bemused expression. "I'm glad I came to the only other wizards on this planet, then." He looked around at the large kitchen. "What is it you people do here again? Catering?"

Aether laughed. "With fast dragon delivery anywhere in the Lastlands in two hours, guaranteed." He shook his head. "It will be the Wizards' Guild, once we figure out how to get the Ruling Council to register our charter without trying to capture us, or kill us, or…you know…forcibly employ us."

Emrek stared at him for a long moment, eyes narrowing, then said "Yeah," in a tone of voice that told Pemana he wasn't unaware of that last consideration himself. She supposed he would know, as he'd been on the Council himself before she and Aether exiled him.

"Well," she finally said, breaking the uncomfortable silence, "we'll get started working on a plan."

"I'll see if I can rouse Beras," Aether said. "Sounds like we'll need *Horizon* for this, at least, if we're going to rescue a large number of people."

"From what I've heard, there's no way they'll all fit aboard…*Horizon*," Emrek said, and Pemana heard the trace of bitterness in his voice, saw the sour expression on his face, even through his untamed beard.

She could relate. It was surreal, but here they were.

"Sounds like we might need a second ship," she said, pondering her old connections, wondering if they might even be able to persuade Batthius to help or something like that.

She saw Aether's eyes flick to her, and suddenly he stood back up.

"Yes, well, we'll be working on a plan," he said quickly.

Emrek got to his feet as well. "I'm going to do some further scouting of my own. I'm sailing out there, see what I can find out about sneaking onto his island at night or something. Maybe I'll even get lucky and bump into him."

He took a couple steps toward the door, then turned back. "If I learn anything useful, I'll return in a week or two."

"Oh, wait," Aether said suddenly. "Before you go, I should show you something we figured out that'll be a big help."

"What?" Emrek asked, turning again.

"We've been calling them 'windstones.'"

Lyrrek hastened through the bustling market, slipping between fragrant stalls, the large woven sack of produce on her back serving to keep the vendors from bothering her as she passed through. She looked like either a worker or a servant, she hoped, and not a rather famous someone that a number of less-than-friendly individuals were hunting.

She still attracted the usual complement of stares, mostly from the men. That didn't bother her the way it once had, now that she had the capacity to protect herself so thoroughly.

But, though it had felt good to get out of the hall to run this errand for Orenna, now that she was here, she felt more vulnerable than she'd expected.

As she drew near the edge of the market, she passed a large message board, where locals tacked up parchments offering or seeking various things.

She'd walked by this one a few times since their move to Freehome. Usually she didn't pay much attention to it. But this time, something drew her eye.

It was her own name.

She stopped, shocked, and stepped over to the board, reading quickly.

It was a public notice of bounty warrants, bearing the Council seal. It listed herself, Aether, and Pemana by name, as well as any of their associates, as wanted for questioning regarding crimes of piracy against the Ruling Council, and one of its lords, here unnamed, in particular.

It offered a hundred silver for information leading to their capture.

Stunned, she started to reach for the parchment, to bring it back to the others. But she froze, realizing what an enormously stupid thing it would be for her to be caught tearing down her own bounty poster.

She was famous…and lately, even infamous. Suddenly she felt like every eye in the city was staring at her.

She never should have come out here.

She ducked her head, shifted the heavy sack of food, and walked away as quickly as she possibly could without breaking into an actual run.

She desperately tried to avoid making eye contact with others she passed. She sighed in relief once she got several blocks away, and found the foot traffic somewhat lessened.

She turned from the narrow cart track onto another, one of the longer ones that stretched from the market to eventually intersect one of the alleys that ran near the guild hall. She still had a way to go, but began to feel like she'd almost made it home.

She focused on steadying her breathing, taking long, calming breaths.

As she came around a corner, she had to step around a man who stood there, holding some parchments in an open folio, its strap dangling loose as he flipped through the documents. She cleared her throat, not wanting to startle him from behind, and quietly said "pardon me," as she passed.

He muttered irritably, like he was about to say something rude, but then he froze.

She saw his head jerk up out of the corner of her eye.

"You!" he roared.

It had been a strange year and a half. Lyrrek from two years ago would never have imagined the turn her life had taken.

But she had spent those last two years learning some unexpected things, acquiring some quite unforeseen skills. She'd become an adventurer…a dragon hunter. Her guild-mates, Pemana especially, believed in regular physical training to keep their reflexes sharp and bodies strong, even with the magical advantage they took into battle. After all, their land-dragon prey brought the same.

Lyrrek's reflexes had actually become rather good, and she was proud of the fact that she'd turned out to possess some natural skill at the fighting that was such a central part of their work.

It certainly proved useful now, as the large man, face contorted with rage and glee, stuffed the documents back under his jerkin and lunged for her.

She ducked instinctively away and down, the large sack of produce swinging off her shoulder as she whipped it his direction.

He jerked back with a curse, thankfully. She didn't really want to wreck Orenna's vegetables by using them as a blunt weapon.

But it did buy her the moment she wanted.

She swung the bag free to slide gently clear across the gravel, unbruised and far away from what she was about to do to her attacker.

She spun back to him, using the instant of his reflexive jerk away from the bag to drop into a ready crouch directly facing him, hands out in front of her. She carried wardstones, of course, but magic flared in her as well, as she took all the advantages she could grasp.

The man blinked for an instant as he seemed to recognize someone who might possess some training in her stance. But then he grinned menacingly, and drew a long bronze dagger.

"Thanks for deliverin' yourself to me," he said scornfully. He looked at her empty hands "But ya probably shoulda brought a *weapon*, my lady, if you were gonna fight back."

His eyes slid down her body. She saw his sneering smile begin to grow.

An answering grin spread across her own face.

"Oh, I'm always well-armed," she said, her voice rich with humor.

He lunged forward again, and she saw right away that he was quick, despite his size. He wasn't as big as Kayd, but close.

But she trained regularly with Kayd. Nothing about this man intimidated her. And as he charged forward, she saw that he wasn't aiming the blade at her. He was simply charging at her with his mass, probably hoping she'd cringe backward and he could overwhelm her.

So she lunged forward at him, instead.

His eyes widened, but he had his arms out to try and engulf her. It was a mistake. They were out of position for him to use to defend himself.

She hatcheted her own flat, dragonskinned palm in a chopping motion, hard into his throat.

A gurgling *crunch* echoed in the road, and he collapsed forward as his legs gave out under him. She felt him start to fall onto her, his eyes bulging in horror and agony.

She dropped swiftly into a squat, and let his collapse drive his forehead hard into her shoulder, the choking gurgle squelching to silence as the momentum of his own fall knocked him unconscious.

His limp form tumbled against her and knocked her aside, but her stable stance meant she was able to keep her feet and slide away from him as he fell.

She watched him crumble onto his face in the road, tiny pebbles spraying away as his arms and head flailed into the ground, then fell still.

Lyrrek slowly stood up, staring around to see if anyone had witnessed the short fight.

For the moment, at least, it looked like she was clear.

She stared down at the motionless form, at a loss.

She knew she couldn't move him, not very far at least. She didn't know if the damage she'd done would be fatal, but she didn't have time to do anything about it. She had to get the Deep out of there.

Quickly, she bent and grabbed his jerkin, hauling hard to roll him up enough that she could grab the folio from within and yank it free.

Then she raced the few steps to the bag of Orenna's produce and hauled it up with a grunt.

She took one last look down at him, then back in the direction of the guild hall.

She couldn't go straight back. Pemana's lessons rang in her mind. She'd need to wind her way home, taking a wandering path, to give herself a chance to spot anyone else that might be pursuing her without leading them back to her friends.

Cursing under her breath, she started quickly on her way, struggling with the temptation to burst into a panicked run.

Pemana looked up from the folio of parchments Lyrrek had handed her, unwinding the strap around it.

Lyrrek was starting to look a little calmer. Aether and Kayd had been in the kitchen when she burst in, carrying a large bag of produce and a stunning story.

From her description of the encounter, it sounded like she had acquitted herself quite well, though she was still understandably wide-eyed at first. It seemed that being back in the safety of the hall with her guildmates was helping her calm down.

Pemana was glad they had called for her. A little breathlessly, she began flipping through the pages.

The documents appeared, unfortunately, rather similar to the notes that *she* tended to produce when she was investigating something. There was a lot of detail here, too. And it seemed to point rather uncomfortably near to them.

Their pursuers were sniffing around their very neighborhood, it seemed.

And then Pemana flipped a page and gasped.

"What?" Lyrrek asked quickly.

"That explains a lot," Pemana said, extracting the page she'd just uncovered and sighing as she reached across the table and handed it to Lyrrek.

Lyrrek took it from her and flipped it around to look.

Aether and Kayd stared down at it with her.

It was a drawing of Lyrrek's face. Quite a good likeness too, Pemana had to admit. She'd never been that good at drawing people herself, and she recognized that whoever had rendered this had been somewhat skilled.

"I recognize it," Lyrrek said quietly after staring down at the drawing for a while. "It's a copy of a portrait from a few years ago. The original's in one of the parlors in Silversea Castle."

She raised her eyes, and Pemana saw the hint of tears in them.

"I really can't go outside anymore, can I?"

Aether put his arm around her, a dark expression on his face as he tried to comfort her.

Pemana looked away, but in doing so, met Kayd's eyes.

It had been awkward for a long time now, when it was just the four of them together, and something happened to draw attention to Lyrrek and Aether's happy relationship.

It was worse these days, of course. Kayd looked away, and she hid her own uncomfortable sigh, turning her gaze back to the folio of documents and notes.

It was clear from what she was seeing here that this pursuer had been hunting them in Freehome for some time. She didn't see anything that pointed exactly to them, and maybe he had just gotten lucky to stumble upon Lyrrek the way he had.

But it still left Pemana feeling truly vulnerable. She had a feeling she wouldn't sleep very well, later that night.

And then some words on the parchment drew her full attention, and she frowned, leaning closer.

She flipped through some pages. She flipped through them again, then back, confirming what she'd seen, making sure it meant what she was afraid it meant.

"Shit," she said suddenly.

"What is it?" Aether asked, looking up from whispering quietly to Lyrrek.

"Kayd," she said, breathlessly.

He looked up and met her eyes. "What?"

"There's...they..."

She swallowed and took a deep breath.

"There's information here. I think it means they found your father in Cask."

Kayd jumped up and ran around beside her, looking down, as she pointed out names, locations, including Cask...referenced events, and a notation of date.

He saw it too. She was probably right. The Depths hadn't known Kayd's or his father's name yet, but the details added up, filled in the gaps in their own understanding of his father's disappearance.

It was likely him.

"Well, that's why he was missing, then," Kayd said weakly, deflating. He slowly sat down in one of the chairs. "The Swordfish has him."

Lyrrek sighed, and looked wide-eyed again. Aether looked like he wanted to say something, but couldn't think of anything.

Pemana's own expression became steely.

She stepped closer to Kayd and bent down to put her hand on his shoulder.

"Listen to me," she said quietly. He looked up and met her eyes again, surprised.

"We're getting him back, Kayd."

Chapter Twenty-Five
Night Skies

A ether dried a last dish with a damp cloth, relieved to be finished with cleaning up after their dinner. It had been his turn to cook that night, and honestly, he'd been tempted to skip it. After that day's events and discoveries, none of them had seemed like they were in the mood for dinner.

Orenna, though, had quietly pulled him aside and suggested he go on and do it anyway. It would do all of them some good, she'd assured him.

And so, he had headed to the kitchen, thinking about a quick soup or something. But in the end, he'd come up with an idea that made him grin. Maybe it would lighten their spirits.

So, when he'd called for them to come to dinner, they had arrived to a spread of fried breakfast cakes with sweet syrup, and a big skillet of mutton sausages.

It was a favorite breakfast of theirs, and it had been a while since they'd had a chance to have a big breakfast together. Veytra at least, had chuckled at the choice.

They'd all dug in heartily, and acquitted themselves well. There was little left of what he'd laid out when they were done.

As he was putting away a few last things, Lyrrek came back in, followed by Pemana.

Lyrrek poured out some cups of herbal tea, and Pemana sat down once more at one of the tables. She had the agent's folio, and was still flipping through it.

"There's more," Pemana said. "I think that this agent was getting some of his information from Eglamon and Fehndala's people. I'll have to check it against some of my older notes, but I'm pretty sure I recognize some of these names."

Aether finished drying his hands and hung the cloth on one of the bars. He came around to sit down next to Pemana, staring intently at what she pointed out in the documents.

"I don't know if this will be enough to serve as direct evidence against them on its own," she said. "But with everything else we know?"

"It's a pretty good start," Lyrrek said grimly, settling into a chair herself.

Pemana nodded.

Aether smiled coldly. "Then maybe it's finally time they face Council justice too."

"Do you think there is such a thing as Council justice anymore?" Pemana asked him.

Aether considered for a moment, then shrugged. "I don't know. But I think we still have to provide them an opportunity to decide that for themselves."

Pemana stared at the wall. "I think it's become more important than ever that we get someone to the last site, to that 'Great Underhall,' or wherever this trail is leading. And we need to do it as soon as possible. We can't really proceed until we know what to do about the Swordfish being a wizard."

She stared vacantly, eyes dark with her memories. "I don't know if he actually *is* one of the ones who were here before. But there were similarities to what I could sense from him and some of the spells you've been finding at these caches." She looked up at Lyrrek. "I hate to take him away from you again with everything that's going on, but I think Aether has to fly up there on the dragon, and right away." Pemana turned back to him. "He can get there and back much quicker, if you think she'd be up to the flight."

Aether nodded slowly. He had basically sworn to himself that he wouldn't go off alone like that again. But yes, the dragon could do it. And Pemana was right. He and the dragon could be there and back again in a few days. Their first trip to Bastion, aboard *Horizon*, had taken weeks.

"It's fine," Lyrrek said. "I'm going too."

He turned to look at her, surprised. "Are you sure?"

She nodded, a determined expression on her face.

He thought about it for a moment. "Well, she was able to carry myself and Pemana all right, and she was pretty tired by that point. It might take a bit longer, and we'd have to stop more often to let her rest." He stared up into the corner, considering. "But it would still be far quicker than sailing, of course. And the best boat for that is still up in *her* territory anyway."

Lyrrek swallowed, looking like she might already be reconsidering the idea.

"You can back out if you need to," he said, touching her wrist. "It's intense, the wind pounding on you." She looked up into his eyes. "But I will tell you, it's so, so worth it, seeing the world from up there…"

Pemana cleared her throat. "Do you think there will be anything at Bastion we can use? I *really* don't want to get blasted by that lightning again. It…hurt."

"I can only hope so," Aether said.

Lyrrek nodded, swallowing again.

"All right," Aether said, grinning. "We'll start packing, and head out tomorrow night."

Aether stood next to the dragon where she crouched patiently in the yard, turning her neck to watch them. He and Veytra tugged on straps and tested the durability of the modifications they'd made to the saddle to make absolutely certain it would hold in the wind of flight, with two adult humans clinging to the dragon's scaled, muscular back. Those muscles would be pulsating for the duration of the journey, and they had to make sure their movements couldn't work anything loose.

So they had gone over the entire saddle and made some upgrades and reinforcements. It seemed like it was all holding up well.

"It looks good to me," Veytra said, tugging at a last strap herself. She still seemed quite nervous around the dragon, understandably, but she was doing a good job at ignoring it to help make sure he and Lyrrek were safe. "I hope she doesn't tire out, carrying you both."

"I think we'll be fine," he said. "She's quite strong. And it's pretty easy to feel how tired she is when I connect to give her directions."

He turned toward the dragon's head, and she obeyed his thought and leaned down toward him, craning her long neck to let him reach the halter. He ran his magical senses over the reinforced pouches containing the enchanted stones that enabled their communication, and which were keeping her from remembering that she would usually devour these strange creatures and destroy their unnatural caves.

They had replaced Aether's original stones with more secure triplicated enchantments. These and the other additions they'd made to the halter all seemed firm and stable.

Finally, he concentrated, taking over the dragon's mind for a moment and feeling the sensations of her long body. She had grown accustomed to wearing the saddle, comfortable enough with the slight restrictions it placed on her usual freedom of movement. Nothing felt out of place or awkward from her perspective.

He released her mind, and she blinked, then looked over toward the approaching forms of Lyrrek, Pemana, and Kayd.

Lyrrek was bundled up as he'd recommended. It was summer, but not a particularly warm night, and she'd been as surprised as the others to hear that the air grew colder as you headed upward into the sky. He'd assured her that once they reached the mainland, they'd find a place to camp until morning, and spend the rest of their trip flying during the bright heat of the day.

But for now, they did have to depart in darkness, and it would be chilly in the hard wind of flight. He adjusted his own jacket and scarves, pulling on one of the leather caps he and Orenna had fashioned for them.

"Ready?" he called out to Lyrrek, whose eyes were locked on the dragon.

She only nodded.

"It's not so bad," Pemana was saying as they drew close. "It's pretty intense at first, but once you get through those first few wingbeats, it's kind of amazing." She grinned. "And I felt terrible at the time. I'm looking forward to trying it again sometime when I can enjoy it."

"You'll get the chance, I suspect," Aether said, grinning.

Lyrrek and the others slowed as they drew within a few paces of the dragon.

Kayd, saying as little as usual lately, stopped earlier, eyeing the dragon carefully. Veytra went over to stand next to him, happy to be a bit further away.

But Pemana seemed unperturbed. She threw an arm around Lyrrek and half-encouraged, half-pulled her the rest of the way.

Lyrrek met his eyes.

"You sure about this?" he asked her gently. "You really don't have to come."

"I'm not putting us through that again," she said, and her voice was firm. "So...how do I do this?" She reached for the straps.

Aether bent and made a stirrup of his hands, and helped her step up and throw her leg over the dragon's back.

The dragon moved under Lyrrek's weight, adjusting to the sensation. Lyrrek gasped at the unexpected motion and fell forward, clinging tightly to all the straps she could get her hands on.

"It's all right," Aether said, patting Lyrrek's knee. "She'll get used to your weight and calm down, hang on."

Once the dragon settled herself again, Lyrrek sat up, and though she was breathing hard, she helped him and Pemana strap her safely in.

Aether turned to face away from the dragon's shoulder, and jumped up backwards to sit there. The dragon moved again, but he quickly threw his right leg over her neck and gripped, and patted her as she settled under him.

Once they had Aether's straps secured as well, Pemana punched them each lightly in the leg. "Good fortune!" she said, stepping back. "Find something we can use to beat that monster."

"We'll try!" Aether said, cheerfully. He looked down at the others, watching Pemana return to Kayd and Veytra, the three of them jogging back over to the hall door, ducking around the corner to be protected from the wind of their takeoff.

He felt Lyrrek press herself into his back.

"It's going to feel pretty crazy at first, while your guts catch up with us moving," he warned her over his shoulder. "But once we get going, it feels great."

"If you say so," she said into his back.

He chuckled. "All right. Remember your amulet if you need to talk to me. It's pretty loud up there."

He felt her forehead move against his spine as she nodded once.

Well, Lyrrek was as ready as he could help her be. It was time. He sent that thought to the dragon, and she stood up.

She raised up to her full height, craning her neck skyward and spreading her great wings. Aether felt Lyrrek gasp as the dragon crouched, suddenly pointing them upward as well.

And then she jumped with her mighty hind legs, propelling them into the sky.

He heard Lyrrek begin to scream into his back as the sensations of the dragon's powerful first wing beat blasted through their bodies. It was kind of like diving off the highest deck of a ship into deep water, but more intense and ongoing, pulsing again and again as the dragon's wings hurtled them swiftly up to speed.

The roar of the wind in Aether's face became deafening, and he couldn't tell if Lyrrek stopped screaming, or he just lost the ability to hear it.

But then, as they began to level off, he felt her turn her head against his back.

The lantern lights of their neighborhood in Freehome plummeted swiftly away, the sparkling vista of the city at night spreading out below them.

And then he knew that Lyrrek *had* stopped screaming, because the sound of her joyful shout of amazement and celebration at what she was seeing cut through the wind, and he heard it.

Smiling, he turned the dragon northward with a thought, letting her carry them as swiftly as she wanted back in the direction of her home.

Deldrum managed not to gasp, but only barely.

The Swordfish released the hilt of the eating knife he had just slammed into the chest of one of his black-robed servants.

The stunned man, who had accidentally tipped a goblet of wine on the table while serving the Swordfish during dinner, collapsed backward onto the stone floor with a short cadence of *thuds.*

The Swordfish had seemed…different…since they'd all narrowly escaped the dragon attacking his ship. He seemed distracted and ill-tempered.

And he was overreacting to things with some regularity.

The Swordfish, frowning, picked up a napkin and used it to push away some of the wine that had run toward him across the library table at which he'd decided to dine that night. Other black-robed servants, after a moment's frozen shock, came hesitantly forward to clean up the mess for him.

The Swordfish ignored them. To Deldrum's alarm, he turned and stared straight into his own eyes.

"Get this out of here," he said coldly.

Deldrum nodded and rushed forward, suddenly confused and unsure what to do with his spear.

One of the other guards in the duty with him that night stepped forward, a strange but sympathetic look on his face, and to Deldrum's relief, reached out for his spear, then stepped back.

Deldrum bent over the motionless black-robed form, trying to avoid looking down at the wide, horrified eyes of the dead man as he grabbed him by the hands and dragged him away from where the Swordfish sat, at one of the tables in the center of the palace's expansive library.

Deldrum kept his eyes up as he strained backwards, trying to keep silent as he undertook his efforts. The angle meant that he stared across the library, past the Swordfish, past the rows of tall shelves of books to the far wall, toward the impressive greatsword display that hung there.

Under normal circumstances, he'd be in trouble if he was caught looking at this one for too long. He didn't need anyone to warn him about this. And oh, how he'd been longing to stare anyway.

But at this moment, all the other guards, the servants, and the Swordfish himself were distracted with other matters. The Swordfish nibbled at food with a gloved hand while watching his servants closely.

So Deldrum was free, for the first time, to just stare at the shining steel greatsword that hung on the wall on the far side of the library chamber.

He still wanted the matched sword and dagger for himself more than anything. But so far, he hadn't been able to locate the armory where they were stored.

He knew where *this* steel sword was kept, though.

It looked unprotected. Perhaps the Swordfish, who Deldrum, like the rest, finally understood to be some kind of wizard, had cursed this sword, and that's why it was left in the open? Who knew?

Who knew wizards were even real?

At least he finally understood the strange way everyone in the palace behaved, the awkward fear that seemed so close underneath every quiet conversation.

Still, it might be worth finding out whether the greatsword was cursed, he decided, once he figured out a way to leave…assuming he hadn't yet found the sword and dagger he preferred.

He backed through the door and had to turn into the corridor, and so was finally forced to give up staring at the long, steel sword.

Unfortunately, he forgot not to look down at the lolling head of the dead servant he was dragging, and he found himself almost vomiting.

With a silent curse, he swallowed hard a few times and kept shuffling backward, keeping his eyes up and staring down the candlelit corridor.

It was well past time that he got out of this terrible place. What if *he* was the next person to accidentally anger the Swordfish? Would he just get blasted with lightning or something, like that unfortunate swordswoman that night?

He shuddered, and kept dragging, trying to ignore the red streaks the servant's blood-soaked robe was beginning to leave down the center of the corridor's polished floor.

The ruins of the city of Bastion looked quite different from above as Aether, Lyrrek, and the dragon soared over.

Aether felt Lyrrek slap his hip, and looked back to see her pointing out to their left.

Trying to peer through the wind, he looked where she indicated and realized she was pointing at the ruins of the ancient palace, where they and the others had found the lost Empress's crown last year.

He grinned, looking back out at the mountains toward which they flew, and loosed a hand from the straps to pull his amulet out, careful not to let the wind rip it away as he gripped it and reached for Lyrrek's thoughts.

"Looks different from up here!" he said.

He felt her movement as she reached for her own, then she responded.

"It's beautiful, but kind of sad," she said.

"We'll try to look around a bit up in the mountains, see if we can spot something that might be this Underhall of theirs. Are you sensing anything yet?"

"No," she said. "I've been looking."

"Me too. If we don't spot anything fairly quick, we'll find a place to put down and rest for a bit."

He slipped his amulet back under his jacket and nudged the dragon westward from their present course, trying to study the terrain of the hills leading north out of Bastion's ruins.

While they had certainly become overgrown with forest in the two centuries of their abandonment, it wasn't hard to tell where the cart tracks and roadways had likely been, just by the topography. He picked one of the routes and turned the dragon once more to follow its path.

Bastion had been right under the foot of the mountains, at the edge of the hills at their base, so before long, the rushing wind was growing colder as the dragon climbed them higher.

A few of the likely tracks quickly ended in small enclosed valleys, or once, at the ruins of what looked like a small mountain village. But nothing they saw seemed much like what they were looking for, at least from the air.

He was just about to reach for his amulet to say they should stop for a rest and to warm up, when he felt Lyrrek let go of her straps with one hand.

"Look west!" she called into his thoughts.

He jerked his head and stared along the mountainous terrain, trying to see what had caught her attention.

And then he saw it. There was a flat area in the distance, looking something like a pass between two lower peaks. And on the edge of it, tucked up against the far mountain…

It looked like the ruined remains of what must have been a grand castle.

He grinned into the wind. Something about the location felt right.

He swung the dragon over with a thought, and felt her relief. She was about ready for a rest too.

It only took them a few minutes to reach the rocky, flat expanse in front of the ruin. The ancient roadway here was more obvious, as it was just above the tree line, and the track was still evident, where it crossed through the pass and continued northward into the mountains.

But here at the height of the pass, a fortress had stood, guarding the mountainous road. It sat next to a small lake surrounded by boulders that tumbled into one end of it from the ridge against which the ruined castle had stood.

The dragon adjusted her course toward the lake as she saw it, and he let her pick a spot to land carefully on the rocky shore. Aether sent her the thought to let them climb down, then she could go run and get a drink, but to try not to get her saddle wet.

The dragon obliged, and once he and Lyrrek were standing next to her, he untied his staff and removed it, and tied all the loose straps up into the saddle. Then he slapped the dragon gently on the shoulder, and sent her the thought to go help herself.

She jumped up and trotted the few dragon paces to the water, reaching out with her long neck to bend her head to drinking, careful to stay back from her own splashing.

Aether grinned, then turned to Lyrrek, who had dropped her haversack and was unwrapping her scarves and stripping off her jacket.

"You holding up all right?" he asked, joining her in removing his outer layers. It wasn't a hot day, exactly, up here in the mountains. But being out of the scouring wind made the dry mountain breeze feel balmy by comparison.

"I'm fine," she said, returning his grin. She stretched, then looked toward the ruined castle.

He joined her. Dragons had mostly torn the place down over the centuries, unsurprisingly. But there were some thick bases of the outer wall that were still recognizable as a human structure. The mass of the pile of rock rose up in a slope, winding toward the natural pile of the mountain behind.

He closed his eyes, concentrating with his magical senses.

There was nothing. But he expected that, and only focused harder.

There. It was very subtle, perhaps even more subtle than the caches had been. But there *was* a trace of the concealment magic coming from within the pile of rubble. Subtle as it was, it seemed to be, nonetheless, everywhere below them.

Excitement kindled in him. This might be it.

He focused harder, straining. The outline of the spell was beyond what he could sense. It might cover an enormous area below the fallen castle. But finally, as he was growing tired, he thought he spotted a bit of structure to the form of the spell. Maybe it was encircling a doorway there, or something to that effect?

Gasping, he released the effort and opened his eyes. He made sure to note some physical landmarks in the rubble pile above the anomaly in the spell, and turned to Lyrrek, who was picking up her things.

"Let's move. I'm bringing the dragon over."

She took his hand and they jogged aside. Then, while she watched, he took a comfortable pose, and reached out for the dragon's mind.

Once he had settled himself in her consciousness, he opened her eyes and blinked up at the pile of stone, pacing forward on her feet to the spot where he and Lyrrek had been standing. He looked for the landmarks he had noted earlier, and had to lower her head a couple paces, more to the level of his own eyes, to know for sure he had spotted them.

Then he cantered forward a few dragon paces, until he approached the spot, and looked down on the rubble.

Tilting the dragon's head, he judged the likely angle, thinking of the location where the spell's structure faltered. If there was a doorway there, they'd want to approach the spell from a corridor leading to it.

And as he glanced along with her eyes, he spotted some parallel lines, still visible in the rubble, and realized they might be a couple steps from a stone staircase, barely protruding from the pile.

He stepped the dragon several paces back and carefully cast the dragonskin spell. It was strange to cast the spell *as* the dragon. In fact, he wasn't sure whether he was using her magic, or his own. But he supposed it really didn't matter.

He reached down with the dragon's powerful, almost hand-like front paw, and began digging at the rocks above the staircase with her claws, shifting stone effortlessly aside with her enormous strength, kicking up a great cloud of dust.

He felt his consciousness divided for an instant as Lyrrek pulled his human body back away from rolling rocks that tumbled down the slope in their direction. Once he focused back into the dragon's mind, he was careful to send them the other way.

After a few moments of dragon-digging, he had cleared a small crater into the spot he'd picked, and still seen nothing. He had no way of knowing if the few steps he'd found were the bottom or top of the ancient lost staircase. The dragon didn't seem to be tiring, but it might be pointless effort, and he didn't want to waste her energy.

As he was considering trying a different spot, though, one of his swipes caused the rock he'd reached for to collapse away from him, and he yelped excitedly from the dragon's mouth.

"What?" Lyrrek asked. She couldn't really see into the crater from her vantage.

Aether peered closer at the small, dark hole he'd made, then quickly scrabbled out some more around the edge, enlarging it.

It wasn't too difficult to create a big enough opening for a human to enter. He peered down into the hole through the dragon's eyes, and saw what did look like steps leading down into darkness, though they were covered with enough rubble to make it difficult to discern much.

Before he withdrew the dragon, he reached up and pressed some of her great weight onto the piled rocks above the hole. He didn't want to start climbing in and have it all collapse on him. It seemed sturdy, though, and held the dragon's weight.

He pulled her back a bit, then withdrew his mind, sending her back to the lake to wash her feet and relax for a while.

He opened his human eyes, disoriented for a moment, taking tighter hold of Lyrrek's arm as he swayed briefly.

"I think I got it," he said. "Come on!"

He released her arm so they could navigate the rubble, which was trickier on human feet than it had been on dragon ones. But soon they stood over the impressive hole, and he lit his staff and peered into the darkness below them.

The staircase did continue down into the darkness, and he grinned. He lowered himself into the hole a few steps, and bent to peer deeper within.

There was an impressive archway there, which extended downward into a vaulted corridor a few paces beyond.

He looked up and met Lyrrek's eyes, grinning. "This is it."

She smiled and slung her haversack on her shoulder. "After you," she said.

The air was cooler, still and cave-like, as he ducked his way far enough down the stairs to stand up and walk the rest of the way down to the corridor below.

Once Lyrrek made it down and joined him, they continued slowly down the ruined corridor, eyes on the vaulted ceiling, watching for any sign of instabilities.

They passed a few doorways and peered in, finding small chambers whose purposes were long lost. There was a lot of dust and detritus, and signs of centuries of water damage and decay. Very little they found was recognizable as anything.

But as they progressed along the vaulted corridor, Aether spotted a glint of something ahead of them.

"What's that?" he asked, raising the staff's light. He hurried forward.

And then he stopped, in awe, Lyrrek coming to stand next to him.

"Woah," she said, breathless.

Before them stood a grand set of double doors, carved from wood into beautiful abstract designs, and polished to a sheen that reflected the magical light back to them.

"They're not damaged," he said, amazed. "There's no water damage, no rot, nothing."

Lyrrek stepped forward and closed her eyes.

"It's magical," she said. "Look. The concealment magic is still active, too, but I think it's the preservation spell beneath it, on a grand scale."

He closed his eyes, focusing his magical senses, and immediately saw she was right.

"This has to be it," she said, stepping forward and reaching for one of the doors.

He caught her shoulder, gently stopping her. "Hang on. I think we're safe, but let me make absolutely sure there isn't some nasty surprise hiding underneath, some trap or protection."

She swallowed and stepped quickly back. "Yeah, that is a good idea."

They both examined the doors intensely for a couple minutes.

"I don't think I see anything else," Aether said, still a bit hesitant.

Lyrrek took a deep breath, then pulled her haversack off her shoulder and knelt to open it.

"Well," she said. "Someone has to walk through the door and make sure." She lifted aside the few things she'd brought with them that weren't still strapped to the dragon's saddle, and withdrew a small bundle of thin rope.

Aether watched her, confused for a moment, as she uncoiled the rope. Then she lifted the end of it around her chest in a loop, and began tying the rope off under her arms.

"Wait, it should be me," he said.

She handed him the other end of the rope. "Don't be silly. You're stronger than me. If something happens, you'll be able to haul me back out and heal me. I'd have a much harder time returning the favor."

Now it was Aether's turn to take a deep breath, frowning. But he couldn't argue with her logic.

He held out the staff to her, and she took it, nodding and meeting his eyes with a smile. "I'm sure I'll be fine."

He held the end of the rope tight, paying it out as she walked forward to the doors, clunking his staff on the cracked flagstones.

She approached the doors and reached out to touch them with the base of the staff. He held his breath as she touched the right door with a soft *tap,* and then pushed it open.

It swung with silent ease, opening to reveal a black void beyond.

She poked the lit end of the staff through.

Nothing happened. The magical light was unaffected.

"Looks fine," she said quietly, turning back to smile at him, and he saw the nervousness on her face.

But she turned, took one more deep breath and held it, then stepped forward through the door.

He held his breath with her.

"I'm fine," she said. "I..."

And then she spun to look at him. "Woah," she said. And then her eyes widened. "Woah," she said again, dragging the word out. "I'm fine. And now that I'm inside the spell, I can sense...wow!"

He stepped closer, still clinging to the rope, ready to yank her back through.

"This place feels like it might be holding an absolute treasure trove of magical artifacts!" she said. "I sense them *everywhere*."

Eyes wide, he nodded and stepped through the door after her.

She was right of course. As soon as he stepped within the concealment spell, he felt them, itching at the back of his mind. And when he closed his eyes and peered around with his magical senses…

Sparkling magic gleamed at him out of the darkness. There were small glints of enchanted objects in all directions, down there, spread out below them.

Dozens of them?

Hundreds?

CHAPTER TWENTY-SIX
ANCIENTS

P emana sighed deeply as she steered her small sailboat
into Port Omen's familiar harbor.

She *should* be on a ship, precisely turning the wheel to
port, veering the grand vessel toward the Port Omen Guard's
docks.

It had been her dream since childhood, when her father
would bring her to watch the ships arriving and departing
here, and tell her tales of her grandfather's adventures as
captain of the *Prestige*. Her whole life, she had dreamed of
being the one to stand at that wheel, to shout those orders,
to watch the impressive choreography of a practiced crew
bringing one of these majestic machines back into its berth.

And she had done it. She had worked impossibly hard to
attain it, and had been the youngest to ever rise to the rank
of captain, at least in the history of the Port Omen Guard.

But it was all gone. She had no crew, nor ship, nor rights
to access the Guard's docks.

Her grandfather's beautiful bronze sword, the sword she
had regularly stared at in its glass case in her parents' parlor,
until her father shocked her by bringing it out and presenting

it to her in congratulations for her historic achievement…it was gone too.

Cursing quietly, she forced herself to focus on her task and steered her small boat to starboard instead. She kept her head low, desperately hoping none of her former colleagues would see her pulling up to the public marina in her ugly little sailboat.

She docked and paid for an afternoon's use of the slip, then, head still down, made the familiar walk through the streets toward Omen Castle.

She hadn't been gone that long. There was a good chance the guards on duty would know her. She might even be able to get one of the naval officers whose respect she had once earned to help get her into the castle, if it came to that.

Even if she did get inside, this trip was likely a waste of time. She had no capacity to demand that Lord Moredon speak to her. Perhaps he would refuse, and she would have to sail back to Freehome, having failed once again.

But she remembered the look on his face the day she'd resigned her commission. Who really knew how he would respond? It was worth the trip and the try, as they say.

One of the guards at the gate, an older man, knew her. He greeted her warmly. When she explained that she had come to try to speak to Lord Moredon, the guard stared at her for a moment, thoughtful, then nodded. He told the others he'd return, then motioned for her to follow him.

He led her, to her relief, directly into the castle's great hall, where Lord Moredon was seated on his dais, attending to some business. She waited quietly with the guard while the castle's smokehouse master wrapped up something involving supplies of salt and firewood.

Lord Moredon noticed her as he listened, and his eyes locked onto her.

The smokehouse master finished speaking, and silence fell for a moment. Then Lord Moredon cleared his throat and looked away from her.

"Very well," he said. "We'll make sure it gets to you."

He looked down at one of his servants, who nodded that he had everything down. The smokehouse master bowed and withdrew.

Pemana saw Lord Moredon's eyes slide around the room to various people who stood within the crowded court, then he looked back at her, thoughtful.

"We'll take a break," he finally announced. "I could use some fresh air."

The chief servant bowed and began organizing parchments. The guard turned to grin at Pemana, and bowed to his lord as Moredon rose and came down the dais steps.

"Thank you," Moredon said to the guard. "You may return to the gate."

"My lord," the guard said, saluting and withdrawing.

"It's good to see you, Pemana," Lord Moredon said. "Come, walk with me."

"My lord," she said, nearly saluting out of habit, but remembering at the last moment to bow instead.

A pair of guards in blue and silver tabards came forward. She didn't recognize them, and they eyed her suspiciously.

Moredon met her eyes, then turned and walked toward the far corridor that led to a door out into the castle's gardens.

He didn't speak until they had emerged out into the warm courtyard filled with flagstones and vibrant green.

"Wait here," he said quietly to the bemused guards. Then he led Pemana to the small, splashing fountain at the center of that section of the colorful gardens.

"Thank you for seeing me, my lord," she said quietly as he slowed and turned to her.

"Of course, Ca...uh..."

She managed not to wince, but he did it for her.

"Sorry," he said, shaking his head. "Why have you come?"

She bowed slightly again, which was more an excuse to check and make sure that no one was too close behind her. When she stood upright again, she met his eyes.

"My lord," she whispered, grateful for the sound of the splashing fountain. "I came here to discuss a very great threat to the people of the Lastlands with you."

He grunted, and she saw his eyes flash around at all the guards and servants present, before he whispered back.

"I wondered if you would, at some point. Your name has come up in a few...interesting ways, in recent weeks."

"I'm not surprised," she said evenly. "So you know something about what we're trying to do? What we're up against?"

"Actually, I have no idea what you're trying to do," he said, not meeting her eyes. "But what you're up against? I have been developing...suspicions."

"So you heard about Everblue? About the missing people?"

He nodded, a muscle in his jaw tensing.

She whispered even more quietly, causing him to lean a little closer to hear her. "Did you know that Lord Eglamon and Lady Fehndala emptied their dungeons and delivered all the prisoners to...him?"

His eyes widened, then he frowned.

"And there have been a number of other kidnappings as well, including someone...people...personally important to me."

A tide of emotion rose in her, thinking about Kayd and his missing father, and she couldn't help wondering at herself.

Lord Moredon stared past her, his face unreadable.

"I..." she said, then took a deep breath. "My lord, forgive me, but...can I trust you?"

He didn't look at her, but his face softened some, and he quietly sighed.

"Yes Pemana, you can," he whispered. "In fact, I owe you an apology."

"My lord, I..." she began but he interrupted her.

"No, hear me." He met her eyes. "Given what you just told me, I can no longer deny what I'd already begun to...fear. I'm sorry that I didn't stand up for your career, Captain. I should have stopped it. You didn't deserve what happened to you."

She stared at him, surprised. "You honor me, my lord."

"That event, and many other things that have been happening recently are starting to make more sense to me, although I still don't...well." He broke off, and sighed. "I suppose it doesn't matter at this point."

He looked down, then back up into her eyes. "I don't know what I can do to make this right, Pemana. I've been...maneuvered into a position where my direct power to intervene and bring you back is limited."

"Oh, forgive me, my lord, for being unclear," she whispered quickly. "I can't come back to your service."

"Oh," he said, looking surprised and almost embarrassed, though he quickly recovered. "Very well," he said. "Then how many I assist you?"

"My lord," she whispered, and this time she just openly looked all around to make sure no one else could hear. "My...colleagues and I...are making arrangements to bring this ugly matter to its conclusion. Once and for all."

Moredon's eyes widened.

"May we call upon you to do what is within your power to assist us?"

He stared at her for a moment, eyes first wide, then narrow. For a long several seconds, she watched the struggle play out in his eyes as he considered the full scope of what she was asking of him to personally risk.

Then, to her relief, she saw resolve settle over him, and he swallowed hard, but spoke clearly and firmly.

"Yes. On the honor of my house."

"Thank you my lord," she breathed. "I..."

"But there's something you need to know," he interrupted her and stepped closer, his voice even quieter. "The...uh...the other players, shall we say, have already maneuvered their pieces in this game of yours."

She saw his eyes continuing to dart around the others closest to them.

"It won't have been made public yet, but decrees have been issued. Ostensibly, they're anti-piracy measures. But it's you and the Lady Lyrrek that they're looking for, and some others whose names escape me."

She nodded, unsurprised.

"Eglamon spearheaded the effort, with Fehndala's backing. They're setting up a blockade that stretches across the northern waters of the Lastlands. They've manipulated the Council into having each holding put up ships, dozens of them all told. They'll probably be positioning them already."

He cleared his throat grimly. "It was controversial. Lord Kandrum asked what was so important about Fool's Gold that justified the expense, and never got an answer in the ensuing arguments, now that I think about it. And Lady Ilda was upset about the accusations against Lyrrek, but got shouted down when she tried to ask questions."

He looked away at the sky. "I'd begun to wonder just what else is up there that they're trying to protect."

"He has a palace, it seems. That's where the missing people are disappearing to, we've been led to believe."

Moredon looked back, eyes widening.

"The orders," he said and paused, then sighed. "The writ includes orders to seek out Lady Lyrrek's ship, this *Horizon,* and…to attack it with fire arrows."

"Just like Everblue," Pemana said.

He winced and nodded. "Your name was mentioned as a target as well," he went on. "In fact, I might have endangered myself, just by speaking with you today."

He drew himself up to his full height, nodding slowly. "But in for the silver, in for the gold. Tell me how I can help."

"Well my lord," she said, "I'm not on the Council, and I have limited knowledge of its intricacies, of course. But it seems to me that *someone* must have the responsibility of holding these errant lords and ladies accountable for their misdeeds, and whoever that is should probably get ready to…let's say, undertake some deeds themselves."

He stared at her for another long moment, then grinned. "It's been a real shame, Captain, not having you as part of the Guard. We're lesser for it." He nodded sharply. "But you're right. It's long past time some things were remedied. And one of those things, I hope, will be the mistake I made in letting one of my most promising and valuable people resign her commission."

Her eyes burned at his words, but she held herself steady.

"There are aspects to my new…role…that I can't really discuss, my lord…at least not yet," she whispered. "We haven't really figured out how to tell the world it's about to change."

He looked at her strangely.

"All of that means that I can't really return to your service, at least not in that way." She smiled. "But I do believe that soon, there are going to be a lot of opportunities for all of us to do some good work together, for Origin and her people."

She looked over her shoulder, meeting the eyes of one of the sour-faced guards, the one watching them the most intently.

"I'll find a way to speak with you again when we know more," she said. "Until then, Sky watch over you. Because I have a feeling someone else is as well."

Aether leaned quickly away from the table they'd just inspected, and felt Lyrrek's grip around his arm tighten. They hurried away together and let the darkness reclaim yet another chamber filled with horrible things.

The evidence of atrocities was everywhere. He had decided not to put too much mental focus into trying to figure out just what these people had been doing. Because it was far from obvious whether they had been undertaking some sort of experiments, or just outright torturing and maiming people.

There were desiccated corpses everywhere.

The preservation spells laced throughout the construction of this place had kept decay and rot at bay. So the flesh of the dead was dried and shrunken, their hollow eyes wide, their mouths open in empty, long-silenced screams.

"I don't want to be here anymore," Lyrrek said quietly as they hurried into the hallway. "I don't understand what was happening here, and I don't want to."

He gripped her fingers in his as they made their way back out into the main space.

He focused quickly, once more, with his magical senses. Nothing they had found so far had been of any utility. All of it had been simple modifications of preservation spells applied to small boxes, or bottles, or old cabinets that despite their spell protections and pristine condition, stood ajar and empty, as if someone had fled in a great rush with everything they once held.

This was true all over the place. All that was left here was the evidence of a lot of people moving out in a big damn hurry. And, of course, there remained plenty of evidence that whoever had been living and working here must have been insane monsters.

"I want to leave too," he said, stopping. "Do you mind if we find out what the big circle is before we go?"

"I don't mind," she said quietly. "But after that, let's get out of here. Whatever these people might have known, it's not knowledge I want."

"Nor I," he said as they started toward the far doorway, barely visible at the edges of the staff's light at the end of the wide hall.

Ahead of them, both could sense a strange, large circle of what seemed to be stones that were giving off a faint, unfamiliar magical signature. The circle was quite wide, a couple dozen paces across probably. So somewhere ahead of them, there must be a large chamber.

The corridors branched and diverted them a time or two as they tried to find their way back to the circle. But at last, a long corridor ran straight toward it, ending on another set of carved double doors, the grandest they'd seen.

Aether focused again and tried to check for anything unusual on the doors, but he could only sense the great circle ahead. So he opened his eyes, and pushed a door open with his staff.

As they stepped through, the staff's light illuminated a wide, impressive, vaulted hall. It was obviously a throne room or something similar, bigger than any chamber he'd ever seen in the Lastlands. A grand dais that spanned the width of the far end held at least a couple dozen impressive throne-like chairs.

And on the floor in front of the dais, almost as wide as the chamber itself, someone had placed a great circle of stones, stones that looked like fresh rubble from the fallen castle above.

"Not magic I recognize," Lyrrek said, frowning down at the stones.

"No," he said. "It's…weird. For some reason I feel like it's almost more an echo of a spell, you know? Like whatever it was has mostly faded away."

"Maybe," she said. "But I still wouldn't touch it."

"Or go in the circle," he agreed.

"We should leave," she said quietly.

He nodded, and started to turn. As he did, he raised his staff a bit, gazing across to the far end, just to see if it looked like they were walking away from anything especially interesting down there.

And he froze, pulling her to a stop.

"Lyrrek, look," he said. "In the biggest chair, the one highest up."

There was something in it. The slumped form of a person?

One more corpse was hardly noteworthy at this point, but something gave him pause.

He looked over at Lyrrek. She nodded.

"Then we leave."

"I promise."

There was a space the width of a corridor between the outer wall and the circle of stones, so they carefully went single file along the wall, staying as far away from the unknown magic as they could.

As they approached the dais and its couple dozen thrones, Aether heard Lyrrek gasp.

There *was* someone slumped in the greatest of the thrones. It was, indeed, another desiccated corpse, but this one's light gray robe was shredded across the midsection, and the bottom half was stained dark brown with ancient dried blood.

On the flagstone at the foot of the throne lay a roll of paper and an old, well-trimmed quill, where the slumped form's skeletal hand had dropped them.

Aether felt Lyrrek release him so he could bend and pick up the paper. He looked at it in the light of the staff for a moment, then his eyes widened.

He knew that handwriting, though it was jagged and uneven.

"Lyrrek," he said quietly. "It's him."

"I had a feeling, somehow," she said. "Read it."

He nodded and took a breath, then began to read aloud.

Kohlia, my beloved, I fear you are dead.

If you are, be not saddened, for it's quite possible I will be joining you soon.

Those last dragons got one through my defenses. Admittedly, there were three of them squabbling over me at the time. I still won and destroyed them. But I do fear that I didn't emerge unscathed.

Tragically, by the time I made it here to the Underhall, I discovered that the Pantheon had put their plan into motion more quickly than I anticipated. They are gone from this poor, forsaken world. Origin will be without magic, now, once we are no more. Except for the dragons, of course.

The real inconvenience in that for me is that there are, unfortunately, no aspirants here to drain. So I am reduced to trying to heal the mess the dragon made of me with only pathetic natural magic. Perhaps it will be enough to save me, in the end. I am uncertain I will have the strength, as it is slowly fading from me.

If I fall and you do, by some fate, find me, I want you to understand and have the best chance to survive. Our masters have taken everything, including the surrounding villages, and have fled this world. This is the secret of my work for the last few years, that which I longed to share with you, and dared not. But as our masters have abandoned us, I suppose there is no longer any need to keep the secret. The work is already completed.

I may finally tell you about the labors of the dark prophets of the Pantheon, the ones you asked about all those years ago. They were working at the behest of the Shining One to resolve a strange resonance in their timelines. Supposedly, the Shining One himself first identified the threat, hundreds of years ago, and commissioned the dark prophets to delve into the magic of identifying the nature of the threat and how it could be avoided.

This was the greatest secret of our order. Eventually, the dark prophets determined an approximate timeframe, and though they only ever produced conflicting confusion as to the nature of the threat, they were certain it would be enormous, a global catastrophe.

Over a century ago, the Shining One quietly commissioned a new council within the Pantheon, to begin considering the possibility of fleeing the planet itself, as the prophets were so clear that the threat would consume the whole world.

You've been involved in Council of Twenty-Seven work a few times. But you didn't get to experience some of the strangest work we did. With our combined powers, the Shining One reached above the skies of Origin, into the unfathomable stars above, and we saw much that remains of confusing fascination to me. But we found that our sun is but one of many floating out there in the great, dark void. That's what the stars are, enormously distant suns. And we found that those other suns had worlds accompanying them, too. The Pantheon have maintained this as one of the most secret teachings of our order.

With the combined magic of the Council, we detected two places in the void that gave off signatures of magic.

We toiled hard for a hundred years, and discovered a way to rend the very fabric of being itself, to slip through from a here to a there. It was fascinating magic. We never managed to actually transit the gaps ourselves, working only in councils of nine. But the Shining One was confident that with the right group of twenty-seven of us, we would be able to open a doorway between Origin and the other worlds out there whose magic seemed to promise another hope for life, away from the danger surging toward us.

Eventually, the dark prophets became frantic. Time was running out, they were certain.

Plans were made for the grand attempt to connect Origin with the more promising of the two worlds we could sense.

I and a few others were dispatched to the distant underhalls to gather the rest of the Pantheon. We were told we had eight weeks to return before the first attempt.

Judging by what happened next, I surmise that some of the prophets must have convinced the Shining One that the threat was imminent, and they made the attempt early, before the most powerful wizards among us had returned to assist in the twenty-seven-fold spell.

Something went wrong.

Can you sense it? If you focus on the area north of us, there was once a hidden fortress of the Pantheon there. The Shining One sent them to make the attempt there, I think.

They must have failed. There is a magical instability dancing around out there. It connected to the world with the brighter magical signature, but not in a stable way, preventing the Pantheon from fleeing through.

They would have been destroyed had they succeeded, I think. Because it is now obvious to me that the incredibly strong magical signature of the chosen world was simply its powerfully magical native life. We sensed the dragons that are now terrorizing us. That unstable portal began randomly bringing nightmares through into our waking world.

Yes my love. I am afraid that, under the wise guidance of the Shining One and our masters, *we* are the ones who caused this dragon calamity. And they will now destroy everything, just as the prophets promised.

For as you can see here on the ground before you, the Pantheon made one more attempt. I expect they learned from their initial failure, and connected safely to the second world we detected. And now they have fled and abandoned us here.

I think our only hope is to stay here and defend what remains of this fortress, to have faith that at some point our masters will open the portal again from the other side, to check if anyone else made it through. It has probably been several weeks since this all began, though I have lost track of the days. Perhaps it is too late already.

I grow weak, my love, but even if I have succumbed by the time you arrive, I would still remain here and hope they open the portal once more. I'm not sure where else in this world will ever be safe again, otherwise.

Kohlia, I will…

The last word failed and scrawled away in an uneven line.

Aether followed Lyrrek as she climbed up through the hole into the late afternoon sunlight, drawing in great breaths of the clear mountain air.

He laid his staff down and stepped up to her. She turned and leaned forward into his chest, sighing, and they held each other for a while.

Finally he took her haversack from her and opened it, withdrawing a waterskin, pulling the stopper and handing it to her.

"Wait here," he said, and she nodded and sat down on the rocks.

Then he turned and focused, settling himself magically into the dragon's mind.

Quickly, the big indigo female stood, and with a determined expression on her face, she ran up onto the pile of broken castle and buried the hole she had made earlier in rubble, even deeper than it had been before.

Aether had the dragon approach them, then released her with a mental nudge to stay there for a moment while they prepared to leave.

"I think we should fly south for a bit, if you're up for it," he said down to Lyrrek. "Think you could clear another dragon if one found us?"

She nodded, standing. "Yes. I'm fine. I'm just really ready to be anywhere but here."

"Me too," he said quietly, and after checking over the dragon's saddle, he helped Lyrrek climb up onto her back.

As he worked on her straps, Lyrrek closed her eyes, concentrating.

"I feel it out there," she said, her face turned northward. "The…disruption, or whatever, that the dragons came through. It's still out there."

"After two hundred years," he said, shaking his head.

"I can't believe these monstrous fools caused all of this. They wrecked the world."

Aether nodded, tightening the last strap. Then he looked up at her.

The dragon turned her head back to look at them, leaning her long neck down to peer closely at them with her beautiful, sparkling eye. Aether patted her on a scaly shoulder, thoughtful.

"It's true," he said. "They did all of this, but on the other hand, look." He gestured up to the dragon's haltered head, her indigo scales shining golden sparks of late sunlight at them as she waited. "Maybe we can take this calamity of theirs and turn it into something else, something…good."

"Maybe," she said, looking down at him with a small smile. "But not today, and far away from here, all right?"

He managed a weak grin himself. "As you wish, my lady," he said, and he jumped up to take his seat with her astride the dragon's strong back.

Chapter Twenty-Seven

On Deck

P emana sat, stunned, as Lyrrek and Aether told them the tale of how their world had come to be destroyed by dragons.

Veytra, Orenna, Kayd, and Pemana all sat, wide-eyed, for a long few moments after Lyrrek finished the last details of their silent flight home.

Pemana understood the silence. What was there to be said?

But she frowned, thoughtful. Something was tugging at the back of her mind.

And then she saw it.

"He thought I was one of them," she said in quiet wonder.

They all turned to look at her.

"What?" Kayd asked.

"The Swordfish." She looked up into his eyes. "The strange things he asked me. He thought I was a scout they sent back through."

"Woah," Aether whispered under his breath.

"Wait…" Orenna began, eyes widening as she took in the implications.

Pemana finished for her. "Yeah. That will mean that the Swordfish is one of them too. Sent back by this order of evil wizards that refers to itself in divine terms. And he found us, and he's been working to conquer us ever since."

"Shit," Orenna said.

They all turned to look at her.

A knock at the door to the alley made them all jump. Kayd got to his feet and opened the door, then nodded and stepped aside.

Emrek stepped in. He looked even more disheveled than before, and Pemana saw signs of new, rather sloppy mends on his dark leather robes.

He froze as he entered the room and turned, seeing Pemana and the others sitting in the kitchen there, staring at him with strange expressions on their faces. Emrek stared back at them for a moment, then cleared his throat. "Are you all well?" He looked over his shoulder at Kayd and back. "Were you expecting me or something?"

"No," Aether said, sighing. "Sorry. It's a long story, I'll fill you in later." He got to his feet. "Come in, make yourself comfortable. Did you run into any trouble up there?"

"Quite a bit, yes," Emrek said flatly, but he did take a nearby chair. Lyrrek rose and poured a cup of tea and brought it to him. He took it and nodded solemnly at her.

Aether joined Lyrrek and they resumed their seats.

Pemana watched Emrek take a sip and a deep breath. "There are ships on station, anchored out between the main islands and the far northeast. A lot of the ones I saw were New Brightwall colors, but there were a couple others."

"We heard about it," Pemana said, nodding. "The Swordfish got himself a Council-ordered blockade to keep us out. They're supposed to burn us with flaming arrows if they find *Horizon* trying to get through."

Emrek's eyes widened. "That's a bit much, even for him," he said thoughtfully. He shook his head and went on. "I did manage to infiltrate his palace though."

"You did?" Aether asked, sitting up straighter. All of them perked up.

"Yes," he sighed. "Not for very long, but I snuck through in the middle of the night, when they had minimal patrols going. I couldn't see much, but I did at least locate the general area of the dungeons. They were where you'd expect them to be."

"What did you find?" Lyrrek asked.

He looked down into his cup. "I was almost discovered. So I didn't get to stay long and take a head count or anything." He looked up toward Aether. "But just from what I did manage to see? I'd say there might be as many as a hundred people there to rescue."

Pemana whistled. "That's more than we can fit in *Horizon*. A lot more."

And then Pemana noticed that Aether was smiling, his eyes sparkling. He looked at her and realized she was watching him.

"What?" she asked him, and he stopped smiling and swallowed, then grinned again.

"Oh, nothing," he said. "I just have a couple ideas about that problem, if only that one. But I should have more information about it soon. Let's just say we don't need to worry about it today."

Deldrum stared, mouth open, as he stood in the open doorway, keys in hand.

His lantern's light shone back at him from hundreds of glints of bronze, reflecting off the blades and guards of weapons, gleaming from all directions.

But all he really saw in that moment were two bright gleams of gold, the candle lantern's flame reflecting purely back to him off the polished steel blades of the sword and dagger, where they sat on stands in the most prominent place in the Swordfish's armory.

He'd done it.

Deldrum let himself stare for another moment, then quickly went back to the door, drawing it silently closed behind him and locking it. He darted his eyes up and down the corridor, making sure he was still alone, that no one else had seen him.

His plan had succeeded.

He'd been volunteering for night watches, especially the longer corridor patrols. He'd been worried his willingness would get him noticed, since most of the guards avoided the night shifts.

He didn't get that many patrols, so each time he did and they handed over the set of guard keys, he checked every door he could that seemed likely to hide an armory.

It was a very difficult thing to get away with. There were some fifty keys bound into three conjoined rings. It took him multiple passes of checking keys at a particular door to find the right one, sometimes, as he could only spend so long at any one spot. And for weeks he had been finding nothing but storerooms.

He'd begun to doubt and was starting to think about just leaving at the next opportunity whether he'd found the weapons or not. But then he had found this door, and for some reason, a thrill of excitement ran through him.

It wasn't one of the one's he'd checked already.

And then, he'd gotten pretty lucky with the key. It was only the sixth one he tried, and the lock had clicked open.

So now he knew that the armory was on a lower level, on the way down toward the deep corner of the island palace where the supply ships docked, above the storerooms and the long corridors leading to the dungeons. If he were to escape during unloading a shipment or something, then that would put the armory practically right on his way out.

He went about his patrol, his mind entirely focused on memorizing the key's shape and location relative to the marked ones he was supposed to care about on the fifty-key chain.

Timing would be everything. Hopefully he'd get lucky and manage to catch a night patrol when there was a supply ship docked. If he got the sword and dagger concealed on his person and managed to slip out to the ship, then perhaps he could steal one of the vessel's sail tenders and disappear into the night without having to murder too many sailors or fellow guards along the way.

It would do for a start. He'd have to look for other opportunities, too. Sometimes the crew of a supply ship all came in for dinner, for example. Or perhaps some other unexpected distraction would arise.

If it did, he knew how to get his sword and dagger now, and then he would be long gone from this Deep-cursed place…at least until he was ready to return someday, once he was a pirate king himself, and claim the whole palace for his own.

Pemana yawned and stepped out from the kitchen into the common area, tipping her cup of tea up to her lips and blowing a bit before sipping some of the fragrant liquid.

She lifted her eyes from the cup and looked out the window to the sea yard. The morning was already bright. She'd slept in later than was her usual habit that morning.

At first she didn't notice anything amiss, as she blinked out at the bright gravel of the sea yard. But finally, it hit her.

The dragon wasn't there.

She opened her eyes wide. The sun was already up. If Aether had taken her out flying the night before or something, he hadn't made it back.

It had been two mornings since he and Lyrrek had returned from Bastion. Could the dragon have broken its magical bonds and departed? Nothing in the yard looked destroyed, and she was pretty sure the noise of a dragon attack would have woken her up. They weren't exactly subtle creatures when left to their own devices.

And then, out the window, she spotted Aether coming off the deck of *Horizon* and crossing the gangplank to the stone pier.

Mouth open in alarm, she jogged out the door.

"Where's...she?" Pemana hissed, pointing at the dragon's empty place.

Aether jumped, gasping, and stopped.

"Oh," he said, breathing. "Sorry, Pemana, you startled me."

"Sorry," she replied quickly.

"Everything's fine," he said, continuing toward her. "Lyrrek wanted to try dragon-riding on her own. She left before dawn and took her hunting. They won't be back until tonight."

Pemana could see the pride in his eyes, and relaxed, exhaling.

"Oh, well that's a relief," she said.

"It was a necessity," he replied, and she saw that he had that smile on his face again.

"Oh?" she asked, curious.

"Well, the dragon couldn't be here this morning, you see," he began.

"Why is that?"

The pure *clang* of a bronze ship's bell rang three times from behind him, out on the waters of the harbor beyond the sea gate, and his face lit up.

"I think that might be the answer to your question, actually," he said, grinning widely and looking up at the far wall to judge the shadows. "It's probably about the right time."

He turned, then paused and looked back over his shoulder. "Help me with the sea gates?"

She frowned, confused, but nodded, and jogged around *Horizon's* stern to the mechanism on the right, while Aether ran around the long berth and across the catwalk to the left door's mechanism.

He called the signal, and they both started cranking on their handles, and the sea gates began to separate.

"All the way!" he called as they passed the point where you'd usually stop to let in a sailboat.

What was this? Had he found them a ship to hire or something?

She kept cranking with him until the mechanism creaked up against its limits, and the doors were fully withdrawn. She threw the locking rope over the handles and jogged back around *Horizon* to the middle of the yard, where she'd be able to see out, and finally figure out what Aether was up to.

As she cleared Horizon's dragon-carved bow and looked out into the harbor, her mind stumbled over its own confusion for a moment.

There was another, larger *Horizon* outside their sea yard.

Her eyes bulged from her head, her mouth dropping open, as she finally realized what she was seeing.

A hot rush of feeling thrust up from her stomach all the way into her head, and she had to blink hard.

This is what he had done?

Aether had apparently commissioned them a new ship.

Whoever had built her, they had matched all of *Horizon's* dragon-carved charm, and unique sleekness. Only this vessel was half again as long, and taller, and somehow even more dangerous-looking, with three full masts and polished bronze fittings shining everywhere in the morning sunlight.

Her wood was fresh-polished, gleaming wet from her passage here. The dragon's head stared at her, not exactly identical to *Horizon*, but of a family, a new younger sister, with her own even larger personality, beauty, and deadly charm.

Pemana gasped, and turned as Aether walked back up to join her, an enormous smile on his face.

"Wow, she turned out perfect," he said, coming up to stand next to her. "They really *are* the best."

Veytra appeared at the ship's railing and waved, and he waved back.

Pemana stared out at the gorgeous vessel with him for a long moment, as unfamiliar sailors aboard began lowering tenders full of more sailors clutching long lines, heading into the sea yard to help winch the ship backwards into the long slip.

"I've known for a long time the Guild would need another ship, well before we learned about our current immediate need," he said, turning toward her. "So I ordered us one."

She looked at him, eyes still wide, overwhelmed.

"I hope you'll forgive me, Pemana," he said, speaking quietly. "But I already named her."

He looked back out at the ship, smiling again with gentle fondness.

"I called her *Champion*. And if you happen to be available, she needs a captain."

Aether nodded sympathetically at Emrek, who sat in a chair in Veytra's lab, his eyes wide as he tried to process everything he'd just heard.

"I admit, I did not expect *that*," he finally said. He looked up at the wall. "But maybe it does explain some things."

Emrek turned back to Aether. "Did you find anything up there about their magic?"

"Nothing beyond the traces of the portal spell. Everything else was just variations of protection spells or the preservation magic I showed you."

Emrek nodded, thoughtful. "I thought about that one, but I haven't been able to come up with any ways to use it against lightning magic, or anything else he might know how to do."

"Yeah," Aether sighed and got to his feet, pacing as he pondered the problem. "It seems like we need something to enchant into our swords, since that's what we'd have in front of us anyway in a fight."

Emrek reached below his robe and drew a bronze shortsword, flipping it onto his palms and staring down at it. "Hmm," he said.

"Wait," Aether said suddenly, stopping. "I wonder…"

He turned to look at Emrek. "Why wouldn't a variation of the preservation magic work? It would have to function a bit differently, to give us some control over the incoming spell, to keep it from just blasting through the sword and into the wielder." He stared down at Emrek's sword for a moment, then turned and stepped quickly to the corner, where Veytra kept a brazier. It hadn't been used for a while, since it was the warm season, but it was full of charcoal and ready to light.

He got the bag of tinder and stones and before long, he'd sparked a small blaze and tipped it into the brazier, which began to light.

Emrek watched him silently as he blew on the fire to get it going more quickly. Then Aether chuckled, shook his head, and stepped over to pick up a small, round stone from one of the cups of them on the workbench, and pointed it at the flame. He focused for a moment, and gentle wind began to pour around his hand and onto the fire, causing it to flicker and dance and grow rapidly.

In but a moment, the brazier was well lit, bright flame spreading across the charcoal. Aether turned back toward Emrek.

"Do you mind if I borrow your shortsword?"

Emrek stared at him. "You working on depriving me of another blade?"

Aether chuckled awkwardly. "Uh, hopefully not, no. Just trying to figure out some magic that will protect the blades and us."

Emrek picked it up and handed it over toward him, hilt first. "If you melt it, you're buying me a new one."

"If I melt it, I'll buy you two," Aether said.

He laid the shortsword down on the table in front of him and concentrated on it.

He felt the magic flow over and through him as he focused on the preservation spell and its unique feel. It wasn't exactly the familiar effect he was seeking, but a variant. He carefully imagined the outcome he was looking for, and felt the magical flow modulate.

He took careful note of the subtleties, and then, holding it fast, he directed the flow into the blade.

Once the enchantment was thoroughly planted, he opened his eyes, gasping quietly, and shook his head.

He could see Emrek concentrating as well, studying the magic with his own senses, a curious expression on his face.

Aether picked up the shortsword and turned toward the brazier. "Let's see if we got anything here," he said, and bending down toward the brazier until he felt the heat on his face, he held the blade out into the flames.

It wasn't much to see and didn't seem to be doing anything at first. He tilted the blade flatter, and held it directly above some of the biggest tongues of flame.

He would have expected black smoke to burst out around the edge of the shortsword's blade, as soot was deposited. Instead, there was a slight orange glow at the edges, but nothing more.

Frowning curiously, he withdrew the blade and held it up.

Was it glowing? Not the metal itself, glowing as if just from the forge, but around the blade, a kind of halo of barely visible orange light?

He didn't feel anything different at the hilt, but he held his other hand near the pointed end of the blade, and it was very hot.

He jerked his hand back, and suddenly concerned about damaging Emrek's sword, he pointed it away from them toward an empty corner and concentrated on the magic.

The spell was still in place, and as he studied it, he realized that it was, indeed, charged with a new power, something he didn't recognize. Wondering, he thought carefully, concentrating. Then he opened his eyes to stare closely at the blade and tried to release this new power from the enchantment.

There was a quiet *whoosh* sound, and he saw the orange light vanish!

He brought the blade back near his empty hand, and to his shock, it was cold.

"Well!" he said. "Were you watching that? Magically, I mean."

Emrek nodded. "I think I understood what you were doing."

Aether held the sword out to him, and stepped aside, gesturing toward the brazier. "Want to give it a try? See if you can charge up the enchantment with a lot of the flame's...power, I guess."

Emrek stood and gave him a somewhat annoyed look, but he took the shortsword and plunged it into the flames, concentrating.

Aether stepped back further out of the way and watched with his magical senses as Emrek allowed the fire to feed into the blade. But then he saw all of the flames flicking up from the brazier begin to bend toward the sword, and as they bent further, the flame became noisy, crackling as it raged brighter, feeding even more into the sword.

Emrek finally pulled it away, and now it noticeably glowed.

He bent closer to examine it, then quickly pointed the blade away from him, recoiling from the heat. He pointed it up into the same empty corner and concentrated, and a louder *whoosh* sounded, a bright burst of actual flame appearing from the sword to briefly light the stone walls and ceiling. Then it was gone, as was the blade's glow.

"Hmm," Emrek said, regarding it, touching the now-cool blade and shaking his head slowly. "Interesting, if not an especially powerful effect."

"From a brazier's fire, perhaps not," Aether said. "But imagine if the Swordfish fires that lightning spell at you, and the sword manages to catch *that*? What happens when you point that back at him and release it?"

Emrek's eyes narrowed for a moment, but he nodded. "Still, I wish we could figure out how to test the lightning magic itself," Emrek finally said.

"Agreed," Aether said, sighing. "We've been working on it, but with little success so far, I'm afraid." He stood up from where he leaned and nodded. "Still, I have a good feeling about this spell. Want to get it permanently placed on your blade? That way you won't accidentally remove the spell and have to redo it."

"Permanently?" Emrek asked, staring at him.

"Yeah, there's a permanence spell, and a triplication effect we discovered," Aether said. "Combined, they make your enchantments...stickier, a lot harder to remove. We'll have to get one of the others, but I'll show you. It would be good to know how to do anyway. And I need to put this new spell on...well...you know..."

"My father's sword," Emrek finished for him.

Aether nodded uncomfortably, then cleared his throat. "I can probably get to that one another time."

Chapter Twenty-Eight

DISCOVERIES

Lyrrek dodged around Adept Mahlda, who grinned apologetically at her as she ducked past, her arms loaded with bundles of supplies. Lyrrek returned her smile and cleared around her to continue on into the bustling common room. Their guild hall had been transformed over the last few days, as adepts and apprentices from their field teams had begun to arrive.

At first it had been a trickle of people. But then Beras had appeared with the first of *Horizon's* crew members that he'd been able to round up. Those apprentices had, in many cases, brought in new friends or family for whom they vouched, and Aether had decreed that with those referrals they could receive at least a first bracer and join the crews. Beras had dropped them off and left to go get more sailors. And ever since, it seemed, there had been a steady stream of people coming and going…the vast majority of them studiously avoiding the sea yard and the indigo dragon napping in the center of it.

Lyrrek gently dropped her crate of the lightweight wooden dishes Orenna had found for *Champion's* galley near

the door out into the sea yard, and turned back toward Veytra's laboratory, where the masters were currently engaged
in doing their part to help the guild ready itself.

As Lyrrek started away, Amrelyn came in the door that
led out to the docks outside the wall, and called her name in
greeting.

Amrelyn entered, followed by Jyhnda and an excited
looking Neres, all loaded with assortments of packages and
bundles. Lyrrek greeted them warmly, helped get both the
others settled in their chambers, then she and Amrelyn headed further in to join the other masters.

Champion still needed a lot of work, including having
her windstones fitted, and sourcing all her supplies and kits
and getting them organized and stowed. It was a lot for her
new captain to manage. So Pemana wasn't present in the
chamber when Lyrrek and Amrelyn arrived, but the rest of
their friends were.

"I mean, setting all that aside, what are we going to
do about fire?" Veytra was demanding of Aether as Lyrrek
entered. "The whole thing's over pretty quick if they burn
our ships. Unless we're planning on rescuing the prisoners
on a hundred dragons or something."

"No, I…" Aether began, then stopped, jerking his head
up to stare at the wall, eyes widening. "I mean, we…"

But then he shook his head. "No, it'd be impractical."
He sighed, and looked up to smile at Lyrrek as she walked in
to sit down at the table next to him. He turned back toward
Veytra and chuckled. "That would make quite an impression
though, arriving on a hundred dragons."

Veytra shook her head, but grinned. "Focus. Anyone have any ideas about fire?"

"Any progress on rain stones?" Kayd asked.

"No," Veytra sighed. "I don't think we understand the process well enough. I mean, what is a cloud? Why does non-magical rain fall?" She stared at him.

Kayd looked up and thought about it for a moment, then shrugged, conceding the point.

Lyrrek had a thought. "What about some new use of the windstones? Maybe to blow water up from the waves or something? That happens in storms, right?"

Amrelyn met her eyes, and both of them chuckled and made a show of shuddering dramatically. The others nodded along, eyes wide at their unfortunate firsthand knowledge of that particular reality.

"Sort of a deluge on command? We might be able to come up with something along those lines," Aether said. "Although I can't imagine it would be very fun if they got some fire arrows through and we had to deluge ourselves."

Lyrrek shrugged. "Better to be drenched in sea water than have your ship burn."

"A fair point," Aether said, nodding. "We'll put that on the 'to-be-investigated' list for sure." He bent forward to a piece of parchment on the table and did so.

"What about concealment?" Amrelyn asked. "Has anyone tried variations on the concealment magic, maybe we could hide the ships or something?"

"I've never had any luck getting it to do anything other than conceal things from magical sensing," Veytra said. She looked around at the others. "Any of you?"

A few of them shook their heads.

"Well, Emrek said the blockade ships were still moving around some when he passed through there," Aether said, "so we don't have an exact idea of how far apart they'll be. But I suppose we could look into passing between them in the dark."

"It's a pretty huge risk," Kayd said quietly. "We'd need a backup protection if we were going to try that. Even a darkened ship is going to block out the lights of the next blockade vessel over when you pass between."

Aether nodded, but still made a note of the idea.

"It's too bad the ships don't fly," Orenna said. "Then we could just go over the blockade in the dark."

Silence fell, and everyone's eyes widened.

"Oh yeah," Veytra breathed. "That's the one."

Aether bent forward immediately and wrote on the parchment, nodding enthusiastically. "We already have the windstones, and I assume with enough of them we could have some reasonably good control," he said. "I can't imagine the keel would do as much in the air, so you'd only be taking direct wind from behind to move forward. So it might be slower," he said, tapping the quill on his palm thoughtfully.

"But you wouldn't have the resistance of the water against the hull, would you?" Lyrrek said, tilting her head thoughtfully. "What would stop you from letting the wind push a flying ship faster and faster forever?"

Aether's eyes became very wide. "Just the resistance of the wind you're flying into," he said, thoughtful. "But a flying dragon is a *lot* faster than a ship on the sea."

He grinned and nodded to Lyrrek and Orenna in turn. "Well! Excellent idea."

He turned to Veytra. "Let's get started on the…flight-stones, I guess we'd call them, then," he said brightly. "That one might solve all the problems, if we can figure it out."

Aether reached forward and grabbed another piece of stalker jerky from the pouch on the table and put it in his mouth. Kayd and Orenna had gotten the recipe pretty consistent, but this was a really good batch, nonetheless.

He and Lyrrek were listening to Kayd speak at that moment, as he, Veytra, and Amrelyn argued an approach to the flightstones problem.

"I still think it might be a viable path forward, though," Kayd said.

"Really?" Veytra asked. She grabbed a pea-sized stone and held it on her palm.

"We don't…" Kayd started, holding up his hand, but before he could say more, the stone zipped off Veytra's palm, flashed across the room and smacked into Aether's forehead.

He gasped and recoiled, though thankfully he had ward-stones in his beltpouch and the stone just ricocheted away to clatter out of sight under a bench.

"Sorry!" Veytra cried, eyes wide, but also laughing. "You all right?"

"I'm fine," Aether said, rubbing his forehead out of reflex, but chuckling. "No harm done."

"Well, that did make my point rather well," Veytra said, shaking her head. "Whatever that spell is doing, it's too unpredictable."

"I still think if we could control it, we might make it work," Kayd said. "But I admit that a ship doing that would probably fly apart, rather than just…you know…fly."

"We need something that gives us slower control," Veytra said, thoughtfully, staring at the wall again. "I'll keep thinking about it."

Orenna came in the door and they all greeted her.

Kayd started proposing another idea to Veytra as Orenna sat down next to Lyrrek.

"I talked to Beras," Orenna said. "He thinks that Pemana's going to need him for first mate."

"I wondered if she would," Aether said. "We're probably not going to get much more than a quick shakedown cruise or two."

Orenna nodded. "We're going to be a couple hands light on *Horizon* I think, and probably more like like six or seven short on *Champion*."

"Well, we better figure out someone for first mate on *Horizon*, then," he said. He met Orenna's eyes. "You have anyone in mind?"

"Well, I did have a thought," Orenna said and smiling, she looked over at Lyrrek. "Would you be interested in standing as first mate for this mission?"

Lyrrek's eyes widened. "Me?" She looked back and forth between him and Orenna. "I don't…" Her eyes darted to Amrelyn. "Shouldn't it be Amrelyn? She's a much more experienced sailor than I am."

Amrelyn leaned their way, still half-listening to Veytra and Kayd. "I already told Pemana that I'd be aboard *Champion* with Jyhnda and Neres, to help out with any of the rescued that need healing or anything. I think it should be Lyrrek, for my part."

Lyrrek met his eyes.

"Of course I agree," Aether said, before she opened her mouth. "You've certainly proven yourself to me. And anyway, it's up to Orenna. She's the captain for this one."

Lyrrek looked back at Orenna. "I tried...well, leading, I guess you'd say. I got Jyhnda captured by the Swordfish, nearly drowned Amrelyn and myself, and got Kayd and Pemana struck by magical lightning and almost killed." She looked back at Aether, and he saw genuine concern in her eyes. "I'm not so sure I'm cut out for leading."

Orenna was shaking her head. "Lyrrek, that's not the right way to look at it," she said, and Aether was already nodding along with her as she continued. "You know what I saw? Jyhnda wanted to take a risk, and you made a difficult decision to trust her judgment and let her do it. And we learned some crucial things as a result. You faced great danger, many times, and you still got her, Amrelyn, and yourself all out of there unharmed. And when things went horribly wrong during the rescue, you know what I saw?"

Orenna leaned closer to her until Lyrrek met her eyes. "I saw that it was *you* that ran out there, *toward* the danger, and saved Kayd. *You* knew where to send Aether to rescue Pemana. All of us, we followed *your* lead, Lyrrek, and in the end, we *all* came home. I couldn't imagine undertaking this dangerous thing we're planning without you at my side."

Aether, who'd been ready to add his two coppers if needed, stayed silent, only smiling widely.

Lyrrek's eyes became shiny, but she kept her composure. "All right," she said, nodding slowly. Then she straightened a bit in her chair and saluted Orenna. "Well, you can count on me, Captain."

Pemana stood staring down at the map-strewn table in *Champion's* galley, surrounded by her fellow masters. A moment of silence had fallen while they all considered the large parchment map she'd drawn from Emrek's descriptions of the Swordfish's palace.

She looked again over the marks and arrows, the additions they'd made over the last hour, sketching in the details of a plan of attack.

On the west end of the rocky island, there was a small sandy beach with a short pier that could accommodate a ship, if only barely. Standing on that beach, Emrek said, you wouldn't know the island was inhabited at all, and would be left wondering why this small, finely crafted pier was here in the middle of nowhere.

But if you followed a barely visible trail up the slope for a bit and around a bend, you'd find yourself facing a cleft with a heavily reinforced set of doors built into it.

Aether and his dragon would meet Emrek on the beach, and would employ the dragon's cries to draw everyone's attention to this door, and would assault the palace very noisily from there, hoping to keep the guards thoroughly distracted.

In the meantime, *Champion* and *Horizon* would have worked their way around to the far north side of the island, where Emrek had identified a larger pier, big enough for two ships at once to tie up for supply deliveries or guard patrols, that sort of thing. This back loading dock had an entrance that led directly into the lower levels of the palace's dungeons, if you followed the corridors far enough.

Emrek's memory of the exact layout of corridors on the dungeon level was imprecise, and he'd really only been able to say that the prisoners' cells were "that way," represented on the map as an arrow pointing roughly southwest. The plan had the ships coming in shortly after hearing the dragon's distraction, deploying most of both crews to help stop any guards that didn't run to the front door from raising the alarm over what was really happening at the back.

It was a good plan, she had to admit it. But there was one glaring problem.

The idea was to distract as many of the guards as possible to the dragon and wizards attacking the front entrance…while the ships were able to slip quietly in and out, mostly unnoticed, if they could manage it.

That meant that her new role as *Champion's* captain would put her at the wrong end of the battle.

That wouldn't do at all. She had to be there for the fight against the Swordfish. It was her responsibility. It was her right of revenge. She didn't owe him one. She owed him several.

Pemana met Aether's eyes. "I have to be with you to face him," she said.

They all looked at her.

Aether, in particular, looked surprised. "Oh," he said, hesitantly, then looked back down at the map, frowning. "Well…"

"Why don't we just all go in together at the back docks? Then we can take them all out on the way to the prisoners."

Her friends looked uncomfortable, except Kayd, who was still just staring down at the map.

"I don't think we can do that," Veytra said quietly. "It's too much risk. We want the Swordfish distracted and not noticing that he has to worry about the prisoners. If we all come in the back and he realizes that's what we're after, he might just go straight toward them, either to harm them or hold them hostage."

Pemana nodded. Veytra was right of course. The risk of exactly that happening was far too large to be acceptable. She knew better.

"Well," she said, "Beras could command *Champion* for the first part of the mission, then."

Orenna met her eyes. "Beras is a good sailor, and I think he'll be a really good captain at some point. But is it wise to take our most experienced officer off the deck of the large, new, complex vessel that none of us have any familiarity with operating yet?"

She fell silent, staring back at Orenna.

Orenna had been nearly retired as a sailor by the time Pemana was born. She knew more than any of them, and she was also right, of course.

Pemana hid a sigh. This was starting to feel the same as the way her parents always treated her, questioning her abilities, forever finding problems in her approach to anything she undertook. She hated that her friends treated her like that too.

But something was wrong about that, and it lit up in her mind with the suddenness of a lightstone.

Orenna simply wasn't like that. Not really. None of her friends were. Sure, they debated a course of action. But they did that with each others' ideas too, and even their own. It was just about trying to make sure they did the best possible thing for everyone involved. That was a noble goal.

Her parents, on the other hand, seemed to only ever be worried about how people viewed them, and, especially, with the way Pemana's actions affected those perceptions. It had been that way for as long as she could remember.

Why did she care about that? Why should Pemana care what her parents thought about what other people thought about *them*? The whole thing was so…twisted up on itself. What was the point?

Kayd was the only one not awkwardly staring at her. He still gazed down at the parchment map. His eyes seemed to be focused on the mark she'd made to show where they thought the prisoners' cells were located.

A thought slipped quietly into her mind, for the first time in her conscious memory.

What really mattered, here?

Why did she need to face the Swordfish? What had he really taken from her?

He'd taken the thing she'd wanted as a child, true…or, more to the point, he'd taken the thing her parents had taught her to want. But why did she want it? Because her parents did?

She loved her parents, yes, but what exactly made it necessary that she live her life the way *they* chose?

In truth, her childhood dreams had seemed important. She'd always felt pride in her family's legacy. Her mother had reminded her often that she was part of something ancient and important, something significant that had been before her, and that would outlive her. Her mother had told her often that she would make her own mark on it one day, her own contribution.

She had done so, too. In fact, she'd wielded the very sword.

But what had all of that really gotten her? In the end, the biggest benefit of her busy naval career had proven to be the abundance of excellent excuses it offered for her to fail to meet the hapless men her mother kept discovering that might be "worthy" of the family. After actually meeting the first several, she had learned a painful lesson about her mother's judgment, and had quickly become "just too busy at the moment" for such things.

In the end, she admitted, it had meant running from her family, to some extent. She'd done it for a number of years. Those years had flown by, rather empty, frankly.

But then she'd met these crazy fools.

At first, they had just been the local kids at the tavern, a weird, overly friendly bunch. Then, she'd been drawn into their unexpectedly complex lives as they attracted several other amazing souls into their group. They filled their days with good food and music, and trying to make the world a better place. They looked after one another, and they invited her in and looked after her too.

They took risks, and they navigated the waters of life as they came upon them. Sometimes those risks meant failure, true. But other times, those risks meant that Pemana found herself becoming a wizard, of all things, found herself being handed an opportunity to *actually* change the world.

Her mother had taught her to be entirely wrapped up in her family's legacy, like somehow nothing else in the world mattered…not even when other people were suffering.

She had tried to live that way. She had been successful at living that way, for a time. But she had to admit, it had brought her nothing that she cared to take away, beyond a love for ships and the sea.

She felt tears at the corners of her eyes, then, looking around at the polished wood of the enormous, beautiful vessel that they had *bought for her* with their hard work and cleverness. Yes, it was technically their ship, and she was just captaining it for them. But they'd chosen her as the new *Champion's* captain because she was part of them. They had made her one of them, not because of what she could do for them, but because they cared about her. And this vessel existed because they had need of it, but also because in their eyes, one of those needs was the fact that she herself had been deprived of her place in the world. And they wanted to give it back to her.

And so they had.

She stared at Kayd, still staring sadly down at the map.

All her friends were amazing of course.

But then there was him.

The weight of it descended on her like a mountain falling from the sky.

What had she done?

Why had it taken her so long to let herself see it? She had known what kind of man he was. Why had she let her *mother* of all people convince her, without even a word spoken, that Kayd wasn't what she wanted?

She let herself feel it now, finally. She'd been feeling it for a long time, and had just been refusing to accept it, fighting to hide it…fighting to obey.

But he *was* what she wanted.

And she had spent the last two years doing her duty, diligently shoving him away.

Had she succeeded? Lately he seemed to have given up on her.

Had she finally let herself feel the truth, only for it to be too late?

She stared at him, there in front of her, waiting still, and something told her that maybe it wasn't. But she had to act immediately.

"I'm sorry," she said quietly. She spoke the apology to all of them. But really, she meant it for him.

Pemana looked up at Aether. "You're all absolutely right, of course. The Swordfish is your responsibility Aether." She looked back at Kayd. "I'll be on *Champion*, helping rescue the prisoners."

She took a deep breath, hoping, then stepped over to him and took hold of his arm.

He turned to look at her, a shocked look on his face.

"I told you," she said quietly. "We're bringing your father home."

She smiled at him, feeling a tear break free and roll down her cheek, and no longer caring.

"I think I'm going to need to meet him."

CHAPTER TWENTY-NINE

MOMENTUM

A ether grinned as he and Emrek watched another apprentice skirt nervously around the edge of the guild hall's sea yard, the young man's eyes carefully focused on the sleeping dragon in the center.

"It is...something...to be able to just watch one, up close like this," Emrek said quietly, staring at the heaving mass of indigo scales.

"Did you encounter any dragons while you were up on...well, you know..." Aether said.

"Only from a distance, thankfully," Emrek said.

"I wasn't so..." Aether started, then broke off and cleared his throat. "Well, anyway. This one's pretty friendly once you turn off the part of her mind that thinks she should eat us."

Emrek shook his shaggy head.

Pemana emerged onto *Champion's* deck from her quarters and headed their direction, a parchment clutched in her hand.

She came down the gangplank and walked over, handing Emrek the parchment as she reached them.

"Thank you for your help with these," Pemana said to Emrek, pointing to his copy of the map and plans they had drawn up. "I'm confident this will work."

Emrek rolled the parchment and nodded. "I'll be heading out to finish my own preparations. You sure you'll be able to get these ships up there? All of this will be a waste of time if you show up with a dozen house navy vessels chasing you."

Aether nodded. "We're making good progress. There's more to be worked out, but it's coming together. We'll be there. First light, seven days hence."

"First Light. Seven days," Emrek repeated gruffly, nodding. "Don't be late."

"I promise," Aether replied.

Emrek nodded and turned, leaving the sea yard for the exit out to the public docks outside.

"This remains very strange," Pemana said quietly once the door had closed.

"You are not wrong," Aether said, chuckling.

"Do you think we can trust him?"

Aether was quiet for a moment. "I think so," he said finally. "He does have every reason to hate the Swordfish. I think we can probably trust that, if nothing else."

She nodded slowly. "Do you think we'll pull it off?" she asked him, gesturing at the dragon-headed ships.

Aether grinned. "There have been some developments," he said quietly. "I'll fill you in."

Lyrrek followed Kayd and Veytra out into the sea yard, which was finally peaceful for a moment, and dimly lit, with only a single lantern keeping the darkness at bay.

The dragon was gone for the night, Aether having taken her out for another long flight up to the Amber Coast to hunt roamers. It was a couple hours past sunset, and well dark, a starry night with a rising moon. It ought to be perfect, she thought.

"You're sure I need this?" Veytra said, carrying her jacket. "It's a pretty warm night."

"Trust me," Lyrrek said, smiling. She already wore hers. "You'll be glad you have it."

Veytra shrugged and she and Kayd donned their jackets.

They all made their way over to the piers, near where the two joined to form the angle in their perpendicular arrangement.

At the corner, in front of *Horizon*, a smaller mast rose from the other ten-pacer sailboat of the three Orenna had found. It was the only one left, Lyrrek having given one to Amrelyn to replace hers, and the longer twelve-pacer still stranded up in the dragon's territory at Headwaters.

Kayd bent and loosed the line at the stern from its cleat and hopped lightly aboard the sailboat, which plunged a bit under his weight, bobbing in the dark water.

Veytra beat Lyrrek to the other cleat and so she just followed Kayd aboard.

Once Veytra had the bow line loose, she clambered over onto the sailboat's deck and climbed back to them where they sat at the helm, stopping at the mast to haul on the rope and raise the sail. She tied it off, then climbed down to join them.

She started to take the middle seat on the sailboat's short stern bench, but Lyrrek stopped her.

"Trust me," she repeated, grinning. "You'll be wanting the other corner seat, so you can look out. I've seen it."

Veytra shrugged and took the seat indicated.

"Just don't forget to hold on," Lyrrek said, and took her own advice, gripping her seat.

"Here we go," Kayd breathed, and taking a firm hold of the sailboat's wheel, he closed his eyes for a moment in concentration.

At first, nothing happened.

Did it not work after all? Veytra had said they had this figured out.

But then Lyrrek felt a gentle lurch, and realized Kayd was being cautious with the magical effect until he figured out what the little sailboat could do.

She sucked in a breath excitedly as the boat rose slowly from the water, and heard a splashing of drops falling back down from the hull. Kayd opened his eyes, and with a big grin on his face, concentrated again. Lyrrek felt the gentlest wind coming from their side, as the rising boat began to drift out further from the pier a bit, carefully steering clear of the carved dragon heads of the boat's big sisters as they passed and fell below.

And then they were rising above the sea gate itself, and the lights of ships anchored out in the nearby harbor appeared. Kayd pushed more wind into the sail, and used the windstones to turn the boat's bow out and away from the hall.

Lyrrek grinned at Veytra's gasp as they cleared the top of the building, then the ships' masts, and began to rise up into the night sky above Freehome. The lantern-lit corridors of the alleys and lanes between buildings formed a unique, organic grid-like structure that looked almost like some variety of strange, glowing coral.

"It works," Lyrrek said quietly as they began to pick up speed.

Neither one of them answered, and she saw that both were staring away from her, out into the darkness, taking in their first view of the city at night from the sky above.

She understood. She'd made quite a noise herself, the first time she saw it. But this serene, smooth flight was so different from the intense thrill of riding a dragon. A quiet, reverent awe did, indeed, feel appropriate.

There was a sound of wind, as the windstones generated it to flow them along through the sky. But without the sound of the sea battering the hull as they plowed through it, the experience of riding in the flying sailboat was exquisitely peaceful.

"Well," Veytra said finally, breathless, looking back at Lyrrek. "This is pretty much the most amazing thing I've ever done."

"You'll have to try dragonriding sometime," Lyrrek said, chuckling. "It's intense. But I do have a feeling this just became my new favorite way to travel."

"Agreed," Kayd said quietly. He had a rather solemn smile on his face too.

The boat began a slow turn to the starboard, and the vista of the city's lights spread out before them as they came about.

Veytra whistled.

"The steering windstones at the bow are making all the difference," Kayd said. "Feels like the rudder does still do a little bit once you're moving, but the windstones are much more effective."

"How did you get the flightstones to finally work?" Lyrrek asked.

"It was weird," Veytra said. "Originally we were trying to make stones fly through the air, you know? It sort of worked, but we never could get a handle on controlling it. Finally, I tried something different. I had to get Origin to let go of the stones a little."

"What?" Lyrrek asked. "That is strange."

"Whatever makes you fall back to Origin, I had to…sort of negate it, I guess."

"Well, it works great, whatever you did," Lyrrek said. "This is amazing."

"Ooh," Veytra said, drawing her jacket up around her. They were gaining altitude now, the city falling away, hundreds of paces below. "You were right, it is chilly up here."

"Weird, right?" Lyrrek said. "At least it's not violently windy, like on a dragon. It's a lot more comfortable, traveling this way. Though maybe a bit less fun."

"Should I head back?" Kayd asked as their slow turn over the city brought their course around in the general direction of the Wizards' Guild Hall, now in the distance and far below them.

"No!" Lyrrek and Veytra both exclaimed at once.

They all laughed, and Kayd flew them on, ever faster.

Aether sat on the familiar curved bench that circled *Horizon's* quarterdeck, smiling widely and watching Orenna steer by moonlight. It had been a long time since he'd had the opportunity to just sit here and watch others run the ship. But his role in the upcoming mission was elsewhere, so his only job on this cruise was to observe, in the form of just sitting back and enjoying the performance.

The weather had held again, to his relief, and it was another brightly moonlit night, perfect for what they were attempting.

Horizon soared through the spangled black sky, her lanterns extinguished, moonlight their only illumination. It was just enough light for him to make out the silhouette of *Champion*, racing ahead of them, fifty paces distant. Two tiny glimmers of white light shone at her stern, matching the pair he couldn't currently see on her bow, and the ones on *Horizon's* bow and stern as well. Pemana had insisted that despite the risk of someone on the ground spotting what looked like pairs of tiny stars moving through the sky, it was still too dangerous for the ships to be flying at these speeds near one another in the darkness without at least some small lightstones to let them judge the other ship's location somewhat accurately.

They had covered a lot of distance that night, sailing through the sky far enough north from Freehome that they had been able to spot the lights of New Brightwall. It had felt like a surprisingly short journey.

The ships weren't as fast as the dragon could go, which Aether supposed made sense. They weren't as streamlined as the dragon could be, of course. Dragons were built for the sky, and the ships definitely hadn't been. But while sailing in the sky, they certainly could get going a great deal faster than a ship on the water.

This ought to work perfectly.

They had made a long, wide turn, and headed back toward Freehome, unhurried, as they planned to bring the vessels back down to the sea for a more normal return into the harbor as dawn broke.

Still, it would probably be another twenty or thirty minutes before they reached the point where they planned to return to the sea below. He might as well get a little useful work done. He'd seen all he needed to know this would work.

"Think I'll head below and finish up, you need anything before I go?" he asked Orenna.

"I should be fine," she said. "I expect I'll hear from Pemana about the descent soon."

"Well, yell down if you need anything," he said, and rose.

It was a disconcerting thing, going down those stairs, knowing there was nothing on the other side of the outer railing but several hundred paces of empty air between him and the moonlit glimmer of the black sea below. He stayed well to the inside of the staircase until he reached the main deck and could step quickly toward their cabin door.

He looked forward up the deck, then, waving at Lyrrek where she and a few of the others tended the sail lines, similarly avoiding the edges of the deck.

He opened the door and went inside, and started to light his staff. But he decided that its bright stone was more than he needed and would thoroughly ruin his night vision if he had to go back out on deck. So after closing the door, he took a pea-sized pebble from a pouch and sat down at the map table.

He placed the stone there and cast the spell, and it gleamed, a tiny spot of light illuminating the parchment and quill where he'd left them.

He lifted the parchment and turned aside so the light-stone shone on it, reading over what he'd written earlier. It all made sense, so he added a few final sentences, nodded, and signed it.

The door opened, and he looked up as Lyrrek came in, blinking at the light and tucking her braids behind her ears.

She was smiling widely, and he chuckled. "Everything all right?"

She nodded and sat down across from him. "We ought to be down in a few more minutes, I expect."

"Having fun?"

"Definitely," she said. "The dragon's exciting, but this is just lovely."

"I know what you mean," he said, and grinned. "Though if we're going to do this a lot, we might need to figure out some more substantial railings or something." He reached the parchment across to her.

She returned his grin, took the page and turned away to read by the light of the stone.

"I think that will work," she said, turning back. "Or I hope so anyway. I think mentioning my father and suggesting that she should enlist his aid will help mollify her some."

"I guess we'll find out. I can't really think of anywhere else to take the prisoners."

"She'll help," Lyrrek said. "I'm sure of it. People say she's intimidating, but she was always really sweet to me when I was little. I think she's more soft-hearted than people realize."

Aether nodded slowly. "I hope so. I hope we don't wind up delivering a bunch of poor souls we just rescued straight into another fight."

Aether looked up, and saw that the moon had begun to cross the gate from his perspective, where he stood in the center of the sea yard.

It was time.

He glanced around once more. The crews were set, a few dozen pairs of eyes watching him from the decks of both ships. "Be safe and fight well!" he cried. "Let's bring these people home."

He heard the soft thudding of a few dozen salutes, and the crews moved swiftly across the decks of their ships. Immediately, the zipping sound of ropes whistling through pulleys filled the sea yard as sails were hoisted on both vessels.

"Ready!" he heard Pemana cry, and he stepped over to the lantern and closed its vents. Its light flickered out, and he blinked in the darkness, waiting for his eyes to adjust. By the time he could see again in the dim moonlight, *Champion* was beginning to rise from her berth, drifting forward ever so slightly as she lifted up, raining a shower back into the water below. After a moment, she cleared the walls, and began to pick up speed, upward and out. It was a bizarre, disconcerting sight, something the size of a building silently flying away into the night.

Aether shook his head, grinning.

Once *Champion* was clear, *Horizon* began to rise, and she too cleared the walls, turning outward to follow *Champion* into the night sky.

His smile vanished along with his guildmates. Now that they couldn't see him, he relaxed the vigilant expression of confidence he'd been maintaining for the last several days and sighed.

He'd done a good job, so far, of refusing to allow himself to dwell on the danger into which he was leading them. It had to be done, of course. They couldn't allow the Swordfish to continue to plunder them.

He was glad that it was himself he had placed into the most dangerous spot. He didn't want to think about something happening to one of these people that he cared so much about.

But he also didn't want to think about the fear for his own safety that was trying to gnaw at his guts.

He drew the Silversea sword from his waist and held it aloft, the first moonlight glistening along its edge.

He was confident in the new magical protections they had developed. They had triplicated them permanently into all their blades. But he had no answer for Veytra's ongoing concern, that they had never managed to recreate the lightning spell itself in their testing. Technically speaking, she was correct. They didn't definitively know whether this would work.

He desperately hoped it would. If it didn't, some of them might not be coming back. And he fully intended to place this very sword directly into the path of that lightning. He took a deep breath and swallowed.

He sheathed the sword and lashed the leather strip around its guard so there was no chance it could come loose in flight. Then he stepped over to the indigo dragon where she lay, a great dark shape, comfortably watching him.

"Well, my scaly lady," he said, "I guess we better go join them. It's time we finished this."

She cooed her fanfare of tiny trumpets and stood, stretching her great wings in the moonlight, ready.

Chapter Thirty
First Light

A ether tried to stare out through the wind in his eyes as the dragon glided northward toward the dark mass of the island. It stood out as a large, pure-black shape against the blue-black of the sea as first light began to paint the thinnest slice of the eastern sky.

From what he could tell so far, the map of the island they'd made seemed pretty good, now that he could compare the real thing to his memory of the drawing. He sent the thought to the dragon that she should head for the corner of the island where Emrek would be meeting him.

She slowed her flight gradually as they descended, and he peered ahead, trying to make out the beach and whether it was occupied.

As she began to flap her wings, he could just make out a small boat, dragged up into an out-of-the way corner of the beach behind some rocks.

They came in low and he closed his eyes tight against any grit that got kicked up from the wind of their landing. He felt the gentle shock of the dragon's legs taking the force of meeting the ground once more, and opened his eyes as she flipped her wings to her back, breath heaving slightly as she walked up the beach a few paces.

He saw a shadow detach from the other shadows near the boat and begin slowly approaching them. It was Emrek, of course, tingling with enchantments in Aether's magical senses, from wardstones to the protected shortsword under his robes.

Aether quickly unstrapped himself, the dragon more than happy to drop to her belly for some rest in the sand. Once he had loosed himself, he slipped down her side to join Emrek.

"Anything?" Aether whispered.

Emrek shook his head.

"Well, what do you think, are we ready? It's probably about time."

Emrek shrugged, but drew his shortsword from under his robes.

Aether sent an apologetic thought to the dragon for interrupting her rest, but had her accompany them. She rose readily to her feet, and the two wizards and the dragon paced up the beach toward the track that Emrek indicated as the one that led to the palace's front doors.

There wasn't much flat, rocky ground outside the doors as they rounded the bend. The dragon had to step carefully to avoid slipping off down the slope. But they came around and faced impressive wooden doors set into the stone face itself.

They took their positions, the two wizards standing back a few paces behind the dragon as she faced toward the doors.

Silence fell again as the quiet crunching of their footsteps ceased. Aether drew in a deep, calming breath and smelled the waves behind them, and the spicy vegetal notes of the short, scrubby grasses and succulents that were the island's only vegetation, clinging here and there in sheltered places above them.

The light was growing from the east. It was time.

He pulled his amulet from under his tunic and gripped it, sending a quick thought to Pemana and Orenna simultaneously.

He felt their acknowledgement, and tucked the amulet back below his tunic.

One more quick thought, and it would begin.

They were ready. He concentrated.

The dragon took a deep breath, then leaned forward, and a blasting scream of a dragon roar shattered the silence.

Aether shook his head, his ears ringing. He and Emrek both reached up and covered their ears as the dragon took another deep breath, and roared once more, directly at the door only a few paces away from her.

This time, they heard the opening of a few doors they couldn't see from further up the hillside. A few bowstrings *twanged*, and arrows flicked near to clatter off onto the rocks.

Aether stepped forward and raised his hand. The egg-sized stone he clutched in his fingertips burst into brilliant, unnaturally white magical light.

"We are here for the one who calls himself the Swordfish!" he shouted. "Send him forth to face justice!"

No more arrows were forthcoming, despite him offering such a hard-to-miss target. He heard a few small scuffles of bootsteps from vantages they couldn't see up the still-dark hillside.

"How'd I do?" Aether whispered to Emrek as they waited for a response.

"Eh," Emrek said quietly, with a half-shrug.

Aether grinned.

The dragon's roar echoed from the far side of the island, and Pemana turned to Kayd. "Give the word," she said quietly, and concentrating, surged *Champion's* windstones to push the ship forward toward the pier ahead of them.

Kayd nodded and stepped forward to the rail at the front of the quarterdeck, where all on the main deck below would be able to see him. He remained silent, but lit a small lightstone in his hand and waved it above his head.

She was glad they'd found a place two days before to practice this maneuver a few times. It had to happen fast, and *Champion* was a bigger ship than any of them were really used to, excepting a few of the newer hands.

Her new crew handled themselves well, though, and in but a moment, Pemana was spinning the wheel to turn her to port, until she was parallel to the long stone pier, the sails being yanked down as she used the windstones to push the ship's hull sideways through the waves toward the berth.

As soon as they were close enough, a dozen of the Wizards' Guild's apprentices leapt across to the pier, two with stout lines, the rest with spears.

A yelp of surprise sounded as a guard wearing a black tabard stepped out of a doorway in the cliff face and saw three strangers with spears and determined looks on their faces charging at him.

He didn't get the opportunity to raise any further alarm.

Pemana nodded grimly, and looked over her shoulder to see *Horizon* racing toward the pier behind them, Orenna skillfully making the smaller vessel's more nimble turn and barely needing the windstones at all to push the vessel into the pier, stern-to-stern with *Champion*, where both ships would be ready to make a quick departure as soon as they had completed their objectives.

Horizon's crew of apprentices leapt to the pier as well, and Pemana released *Champion's* wheel and dashed after Kayd to join the rest of their guildmates.

So far so good, she thought, and followed them across toward the double doors carved into the island. There would be a lot more fighting than this, she was certain, and soon. But quick and quiet was the goal for this end of the operation.

Aether stretched. "Well," he said after a moment. "I guess he's not coming out. Ready?"

"Do it," Emrek said impatiently.

Aether nodded, took a deep breath, and closed his eyes, casting the spell.

He opened his eyes as the dragon, blinking at the new perspective. Flaring protection magic in the dragon's long form, he stepped quickly forward on her feet toward the beautiful carved doors and their carefully mortared stone lintel and jambs. Then he rose up on the dragon's haunches and raked her mighty front claws across the whole doorway, tearing everything immediately free from the rock face.

Wood splintered and exploded, and the stonework crumbled apart and fell with a violent crash as he hurled the remnants of the door aside.

As he dropped back down onto her four feet, he peered in through the resulting cloud of dust to see several black-tabarded guards and a few black-robed servants staring out at him, astonished, frozen in shock.

He roared in at them, the satisfying dragon scream finally terrorizing them into panicked motion away from the antechamber inside the ruined doorway.

Then he stepped back, and with a final thought to the dragon, told her that she really felt like waiting outside, nearby, and should defend herself if any of the black-clad humans emerged. He felt her comprehension, her willingness to undertake the simple ideas he planted there. Then he released her mind.

Shaking his head, he swayed a bit, and opened his eyes to see Emrek studying him intently, eyes narrowed.

"I need you to teach me how you do that," Emrek said quietly.

Aether stared at him for a moment, considering, then nodded. "We survive this, you'll have earned it, as far as I'm concerned."

Emrek didn't stop staring into his eyes, but did return his nod.

"Well," Aether said, glancing into the ruined doorway. He drew the Silversea sword. "After you." He bowed graciously and gestured toward the now empty antechamber inside.

"You're the one with the fancy sword," Emrek hissed. "You go first."

"Fair enough," Aether said grimly, and holding the blade up in front of him, he charged in.

Chapter Thirty-One

Steel

D eldrum fumbled through the keys, his fingers still slick with the blood of the fool guard who had refused to relinquish them, frantically trying to find the one that opened the armory door.

He twisted back to let the light of the nearest lantern illuminate the keys again. It looked like someone might have taken one of the three rings off and re-positioned it. Nothing was exactly where he remembered it being.

But if he took into account that this ring had been over there, then that meant…

He counted over and looked at the key and relief flooded him. It looked right.

He spun back, the assortment of copper and bronze keys jingling as he rattled the key into the lock. It clicked and he opened the door.

"Lyrrek!"

The call echoed around the corner into the corridor, and Deldrum froze, shocked.

Running booted footsteps suddenly converged into scraping, and a beautiful young woman dressed like a well-geared sailor slid into the corridor, turning back the way she had just come to return the yell. "I'm here!"

Deldrum's eyes bulged.

She didn't match his imaginary picture of her, of course. Over the last months, the version of her that lived in his head had morphed into a tall, dark-haired and dark-eyed beauty, with a bit of a wicked glint in her eye.

The real Lyrrek had longer hair than in his imagination, wavy, with a pair of braids at each of her temples, and was shorter. She looked more like a princess from a storybook than a pirate queen. But as he considered her, a grin split his face.

She'd do.

"You're not what I expected," he said in his most charming voice. He began to saunter toward her, heat racing in him at the unexpected opportunity to finally meet her.

She started, momentarily frozen, and stared at him as he emerged from the shadows by the door.

He saw her wide eyes flick around the surroundings, clearly alarmed that she hadn't spotted him there.

For some time now, he'd been working on what he'd say when he finally tracked her down. He'd always imagined that occurring in some distant future, him on his amazing pirate ship with his crew of rogues, all daunting and intimidating, her grateful for his generosity in victory when he captured her, and impressed by his mercy as he invited her to dine with the captain, instead of locking her in the hold with the rest.

This circumstance, on the other hand, was most definitely *not* what he'd imagined. But what fool would ignore such an obvious opportunity? Clearly this was meant to be.

Everything was going his way, today.

Her attack had provided him the opportunity to get away clean. She had basically come for him. And thanks to her, he now knew, he was about to claim his sword and dagger and embark from this place to begin his own plunder of the world.

Why not go ahead and claim his woman right away and have the whole of it now? She was standing right there, after all, staring at him, wary…ready.

He didn't stop to consider whether the speech from his imagination would come across exactly the way he desired, under these very different circumstances.

He put all the silky charm he'd ever practiced on a barmaid into his voice and spoke.

"I've been looking forward to…"

She launched into motion toward him so quickly that he almost stumbled over his next step.

The look on her face was not that of his mischievous, daring pirate queen, ready to parry blades and words. She was nothing but cold fury as she raged toward him.

This wasn't right.

He hadn't retrieved his sword and dagger yet. He'd been holding his spear upright on the floor in a non-threatening manner, just wanting to talk to her, and was entirely unprepared to defend himself as she flew at him, drawing a bronze shortsword with terrifying speed, eyes wide, gray, and deadly.

He barely managed to shift the spear over between them before she hit him, from what felt like several angles at once.

Bludgeoning, stabbing pain blasted into his mind from all across the form of him.

And then he broke loose, slipping away into the muttering darkness, quite confused.

Aether kicked out at the mace-wielding guard who was lunging at Emrek's head from behind, disrupting the man's aim enough to give Emrek time to finish off the guard in front of him, before he spun around to help Aether finish the mace-wielder.

Breathing hard, they both pulled back up, swords ready, looking around the waiting chamber in which they'd been fighting.

Fallen forms in black tabards littered the path they'd taken into the palace. But it seemed that for the moment, they had exhausted the immediately available supply of guards.

Aether appreciated the chance to catch his breath, and was impressed to see that Emrek was even a bit less winded than him.

"No sign of him yet," Emrek said softly, readying himself to fight again, and stepping toward the doorway from which the guards had been emerging.

Aether nodded. He heard indistinct shouts echoing back up the corridors at them. What they portended wasn't immediately evident. But so far, the expected sound of more booted feet running their direction hadn't materialized.

He concentrated with his magical senses, and still, was surprised that he didn't see anything that looked like the

Swordfish coming their way. He could sense the mass of the Wizards' Guild and their bracers and wardstones, spreading throughout the palace, ahead and below them, in the direction of the back entrance.

There was another tiny concentration of magic, back a different way, and more directly below him, deep under the palace. Perhaps that was him? It wasn't moving at all, which made him think it probably wasn't the Swordfish. Surely the dragon's roars had awakened anything within an hour's sail of the island.

Unless perhaps the Swordfish was dead?

It seemed unlikely. Maybe he knew some more sophisticated concealment magic than they had seen yet. He hadn't gotten a chance to study the Swordfish during their first encounter before he'd hurled Pemana into the sea, and Aether had been forced to ignore him while he focused on rescuing her.

A new pounding of boots echoed from the corridor, and he and Emrek looked at one another and nodded, separating out to either side of the doorway to give themselves room to fight.

Four new enemies burst through the door, three men and a woman, and the battle was joined again. These four weren't wearing black tabards, the first time that had occurred. Aether wondered what it portended. Had they exhausted the guards already on duty, or something? They had defeated a few dozen, maybe, but that was a lot fewer than the complement of guards that were supposed to be protecting the palace.

Emrek and Aether fought hard against two opponents each, and Aether quickly realized that these four were much more skilled than what they'd seen so far. Aether took several blows that slipped through the protection of his defensive swordsmanship, though his wardstones kept him from harm.

Still, despite their skill, he felt like he was up to the task of defeating these, given some time, and was maneuvering around for a finishing stroke on the first, when suddenly the other man whistled loudly.

He lunged after his target, but all four of them broke away for different entrances to the chamber, scattering. Aether backed closer to Emrek, wondering...

The thought struck his mind just in time, and he spun, whipping the blade of the Silversea sword up in front of him, as the dimly lantern-lit chamber suddenly vanished in a tremendously loud *crack* of blinding blue-white light.

It took him a second, blinking hard, to be able to see again.

He stared up at the blade of the Silversea sword where he held it up before him, and his mouth fell open in awe.

Brilliant blue-white fire gleamed from the blade, forks of tiny lightning sparking off into the surrounding air.

He felt no pain, so apparently the spell was working. The only thing he felt was a strange sensation that every hair on his body was standing on end.

He lowered the bright blade down ahead of him, and blinked down the corridor beyond, through which the last four fighters had emerged.

And he saw the Swordfish, at last.

He was at the end of the corridor, where it branched aside, some dozen paces distant. He wore black trousers and jerkin, black hair pulled back into a tail for the battle, and was lowering a gloved hand, from which smoke trailed, back to his side.

And he also wore a wide-eyed expression of confusion, as he registered the continued survival of his targets, behind the glowing blade of the sword in which Aether had captured his lightning blast.

Aether smiled and met the Swordfish's eyes.

Then he raised the sword and pointed it directly at him.

The Swordfish leapt aside, diving for the safety of the branching corridor's nearest wall, as Aether released the lightning stored in the blade.

The bolt exploded forth and instantaneously connected to the far wall behind the Swordfish with a sizzling *smash* and another thunderous *boom*, kicking a burst of dust and stone fragments from the carefully carved wall.

He heard the Swordfish's curse echoing around the corner, heard him scrambling back to his feet as he fled away from them with a slapping of booted feet on stone.

"Guess it works," Emrek said behind him. Aether felt him grab his shoulder and shove him forward.

He took the hint and broke into pursuit down the corridor, carefully holding the sword up ahead of him as he rounded the corner, then continued racing deeper into the palace after their quarry.

Pemana followed Kayd around a corner, slowing as Lyrrek came jogging into the corridor they'd just entered from further in.

"You all right?" Kayd asked Lyrrek.

She nodded, grinning. "Jyhnda and Amrelyn, and several others, have the guards pretty well blocked off up ahead. I don't think they'll be able to push through to the lower level from here," she said quickly. "I'm heading back down to help with the prisoners." She jogged around the corner and continued off.

Kayd nodded, taking one last glance where Lyrrek had come from, and started to turn with her, when Pemana, turning to follow him, noticed something out of the corner of her eye.

Beyond the fallen form of a black-tabarded guard, a door stood open into a dark chamber, a multitude of keys dangling from its lock.

But something had glinted inside, reflecting lantern light back out at her as she turned.

She wasn't sure why, but something about that glint made her freeze, and she called for Kayd to wait.

She heard his footsteps pause and turn back as she stepped toward the doorway and pushed it the rest of the way open, reaching into a pouch and withdrawing a stone.

Light gleamed from her hand and flashed back at her from dozens and dozens of places, sparkling on bronze and copper spear tips, sword blades, mace points, and scabbards.

She gasped.

Kayd came up beside her in the doorway.

"What is it?" he asked, and she heard the impatient concern in his voice.

"It's an armory," she breathed, staring around, awed.

She turned her head sharply to look at him and met his eyes. "My grandfather's sword…" she began.

He nodded immediately, and pointed for her to proceed left along the wall, while he reached into a pouch for another stone.

She moved quickly, eyes darting, as she stared at the swords, spears, daggers, and more, looking frantically for anything that sparked that recognition, that excitement at seeing her grandfather's sword that had been so familiar since her childhood.

Kayd's light gleamed into being behind her, throwing strange new shadows around as he searched the other direction around the chamber.

She rounded her end, looking over, behind, and under everything she could.

And then she heard him gasp.

"Pemana!" he said, breathless.

"Did you find it?" she demanded, spinning and starting toward him.

"No, but get over here!" he said.

She jogged around the corner and toward him, still scanning through the bronze and copper weapons along the way, until she came up beside him and froze.

There, on two stands, situated on a dais at the prominent centerpiece of the chamber, sat two gleaming weapons, the only two things in this room that reflected back the pure white light of their lightstones without coloring it.

"Sky above," she whispered, stunned.

One stand held an arming sword, and a smaller second one held a matching dagger, both blades shining of highly polished steel.

"Did you find your sword?" Kayd asked, turning to continue on where he had been looking.

"No," she said quietly, unable to take her eyes from the weapons before her.

She heard him shuffle around, peering behind things, checking the corners.

"I don't see anything that looks familiar in here," he said softly, coming back to stand by her.

She still hadn't moved.

"I don't think it's here," she said quietly.

He was there next to her, and stared down at the sword and dagger with her.

"Well," he said, "maybe you're supposed to get these instead."

She jerked her head up to stare at him, eyes wide. "What? You found them, they're yours."

He looked down at them a moment, then shrugged. "Eh, they look small for me. I like my spear," he said. And then he spun once more, as if registering something he'd seen. "Although…now that you mention it…"

He walked swiftly over to a bronze greatsword that lay on a different table and bent closer to it. "This might be worth thinking about," he said, leaning his spear aside to lift the long bronze weapon and examine its heft.

"New swords for everybody," he said, smiling grimly.

Pemana turned back to face the unfathomably rare weapons displayed so beautifully in front of her, mouth open.

For her?

She laid aside her replacement sword, which was a serviceable weapon, but far from special, and reached out for the black leather hilt, lifting the steel sword from its stand.

The balance was perfect.

Her grandfather's sword had, indeed, always been too long for her. She had always known it, but she'd never realized what a hindrance it had been until now, as she lifted this steel blade and swung it.

This sword felt as if it had been made just for her. It felt like a part of her already.

Kayd came back to stand next to her, holding the long bronze greatsword in one hand and his spear in the other, and looked down at the steel blade in her hand.

"How is it?" he asked quietly.

"It's perfect," she mouthed.

She reached out and picked up the dagger, holding it up to compare to the sword.

"Do you want the dagger?" she asked, holding it over to him. "You should get something."

"I like this big one," he said smiling at her. "I think those were meant for you, and you should keep them together."

She stared at him, then back down at the gleaming steel blades, trying to comprehend.

He reached forward and grabbed the black scabbards from where they rested behind the stands.

"C'mon Captain," he said. "Let's catch up to Lyrrek and enchant these, quickly, and then we need to...you know...find my father."

Pemana snapped herself free from her awed reverie and nodded sharply, following him.

Chapter Thirty-Two
Capsized

The Swordfish's fleeing bootsteps, echoing from around the corner of the corridor ahead, suddenly slid to a halt.

Aether slowed as he approached the corner, and quickly glanced out, but didn't see anyone. He stepped around the corner, alert, sword up and ready. He entered into the largest chamber he and Emrek had yet encountered in the Swordfish's palace. A vaulted ceiling rose above them, and ahead of them the chamber stretched across, dimly lit by a few candle lanterns at small tables along the length of the center.

Along both sides and down the length of the chamber away from him, long rows of tall shelves ran all the way to the far end. And as his eyes darted about, watching for motion or any other sign of the Swordfish, he suddenly realized what the shelves were for.

"Books?" he gasped aloud, and then sucked in a breath in awe.

There must be hundreds of them. Thousands?

"Well!" he said over his shoulder to Emrek, who entered the room behind him, his shortsword raised. "I think I underestimated this Swordfish fellow. He must not be all bad."

"You're very strange," Emrek said quietly, eyes darting around the library. "It's all just wealth to him, anyway. Is he still in here?"

"I heard him stop running, and he never started again," Aether replied. "I'll take the left." He nodded and headed for the first aisle on his side.

Emrek grunted and went the other way.

"You in here, Fish?" Aether called. "Do you mind if I call you Fish?"

There was no answer. He kept his eyes moving as he crept down the row.

Then he heard a grunting shout from his right, and a strange thudding *crash*, and started to turn. But the first crash immediately became an impossibly fast sequence of loud, splintering crashes heading his way.

He leapt forward, but he was right in the middle of the row, and didn't make it back to the end.

The long bookshelf to his left pitched over and disgorged a landslide of books onto him, pummeling him under their fall.

He felt the sword fly from his fingers as he was pounded, face down, onto the cold stone floor.

The shuddering weight of the bookcase slammed onto the pile of books on top of him, pummeling him more and knocking his head into the ground again.

His wardstones protected him to a certain extent, but he was dazed from the blows, and it took him an instant to confirm he was all right.

He tried to move, but it felt like he was trying to lift the weight of every bookcase on his side of the room at once, and horrified, he realized that he must be, if they had all pitched over onto one another.

He could breathe, but he was thoroughly pinned down. He strained once more, grunting, but it was no use. It felt like he might as well be trying to move a mountain.

Emrek sprinted back down the row of books on his side, and mouth open, watched the tall book shelves crash across the width of the broad room, burying Aether, books thrown free and sliding across the smooth stone floor nearly to where he stood.

At the end of the splintering cacophony, there was a *clang*, and a flash of reflected candlelight among the books sliding toward him.

He stepped quickly forward from the row of books on his side, not wanting to risk the Swordfish trying to do the same thing to him, and as he stepped out into the open space down the center of the library, he saw the hilt of his father's sword lying on the floor under the books at his feet.

He froze, staring down at it, eyes wide. Then he quickly bent and grabbed it up, lifting it ahead of him in awe, just in time to catch a blinding blast of lightning from across the room.

He recoiled away from the instant boom, and cursed, blinded.

"Stop doing that!" he roared, blinking against the glare of his father's sword and his shortsword, both of which now glittered with bright, blue-white fire. He was unprepared for the magic, and as he tried to blink his eyesight back into function, starting to direct the blades down and away, he prematurely released the lightning from them to surge with another *crack* into the ceiling halfway down the chamber.

A shower of dust and stone splinters fell, and he heard the Swordfish curse at the far end of the chamber and stumble away, as he did the same on his end.

As his eyes started to adjust to the dim candlelight once more, he saw motion at the far end of the chamber and a dark shape lurched back his direction. The flashing light and song of flipping bronze gave him just enough warning to duck away from the dagger the Swordfish hurled at him, and it *clanged* off the stone wall behind him.

He heard the Swordfish's boots scuffle as he raced away toward the far wall to Emrek's left, beyond the pile of fallen bookcases. Cursing, Emrek started to give chase. But his eyes were beginning to adjust again and he saw the Swordfish leap to something on the wall.

With a ringing *ping*, the Swordfish yanked a sword off a display on the wall, and turned back toward him.

Emrek slid to a halt.

The Swordfish sauntered back across the room toward him, throwing a long, steel greatsword up to his shoulder as he came back into the light, a very familiar expression of poisonous pleasure on his face as he came toward him.

"This is long overdue, you asshole," Emrek hissed at him. He sheathed his bronze shortsword and lifted the Silversea blade of his ancestors in a two-handed grip. "And it's fitting I'll kill you with my father's sword."

The Swordfish stopped, his smooth face going slack with amazement, and then he laughed, delighted.

"Emrek!" he cried, his voice full of the old, familiar charm and contempt. "You look terrible! I didn't recognize you. You've thrown in with these? Did they find you up on the mainland on their way in?"

"What?" Emrek demanded, easing out into a ready crouch, sliding around to give himself more space for footwork as the Swordfish continued maneuvering slowly toward him. "No, they didn't rescue me. I rescued myself, so I could come find you. We have unfinished business."

He lowered his father's blade to point at the Swordfish's chest, and roaring, leapt at him.

Pemana heard the relief in Kayd's voice as he breathed the words.

"It's him."

"Kayd?"

She heard the astonished voice inside the cell, and relief washed over her too. They'd found him, and he was alive.

"I'm here," Kayd said quietly. "Step back from the door."

Kayd also stepped away from the door, and with a fearsome look of determination on his face, he half-crouched and hauled back, throwing one of the most impressive dragonskin punches Pemana had ever seen straight into the lock.

The whole of the thick wooden door shook violently, and the copper lock itself broke into several parts under the force of his blow. He grabbed the door at the barred window and shook it hard, jostling the pieces of lock loose until he could yank the door open.

Slowly, exhausted-looking people began to emerge from the cell. Six of them came out, followed by a tall man who bore enough of a resemblance to Kayd to identify him.

Kayd's father stared at him, eyes wide. "Are you…hurt? How did you do that?"

"I'm fine," Kayd said, raising his unmarked hand for his father to see. "It's a long story, and we need to get you out of here."

"How did you find me?" he asked. And then he noticed Pemana standing there, grinning.

He raised his eyebrows appraisingly, and shot a look back at Kayd.

"Father, this is Pemana," he said quietly, pulling him forward to her. "Pemana, my father, Ehkud."

She stepped up to them and took Kayd's arm in hers, and grinned again at the surprise she saw in his eyes. She placed her palm on Ehkud's arm.

"I'm glad to finally meet you," she said quietly, smiling at him.

Kayd's father looked back and forth between them, and then nodded a slight bow to her. "Thank you both for coming to rescue me," he said.

They heard footsteps jogging toward them, and Lyrrek appeared around the corner.

"You found him!" she said, relief in her voice. "I have to go back to the ship, and can take him with me. But…will you two…um…"

She looked a bit sheepish. "Now that we have everyone else…will you two go see if Aether needs rescuing please?"

Kayd straightened up, and nodded immediately. He turned to his father. "This is Lyrrek," he began.

Ehkud's eyes widened. "*Lady* Lyrrek?" he interrupted, confused.

"Just Lyrrek is fine," she said, grinning, and took Ehkud's arm. "Delighted to meet you, Kayd's father."

He chuckled, staring around at all of them. "Name's Ehkud," he said politely, a somewhat dazed look on his face as he allowed her to lead him away.

"We'll find him, Lyrrek," Kayd said after them, and met Pemana's eyes.

The possibility suddenly registered. Aether might still need her help.

She nodded immediately and tightened her grip on the hilt of her new sword.

"Let's finish this," she said grimly.

Chapter Thirty-Three

Maelstrom

E mrek gasped for breath, beating back four more vicious swings of the Swordfish's greatsword, no longer trying to get his own attacks in.

He just didn't have the strength left.

He knew he would be all right if he could just get a minute to catch his breath again, rest his screaming arms. But the Swordfish seemed tireless.

Emrek had been backing away from him for what felt like hours at this point, trying to deflect and absorb an endless onslaught of blows from the Swordfish's mighty blade. But he just kept laughing, and swinging, and laughing, and swinging.

Emrek saw he was running out of space behind him, and desperately wondered how he would turn the tide.

His mind, beginning to descend into surreality in its exhaustion and panic, laughed at him. It was pointless, trying to turn back a tide. One just drowned.

He deflected another blow, and this time managed to use some of his remaining strength to pivot the Swordfish's attack into the wall next to them. The jarring strike threw the Swordfish back, his hold on the greatsword awkward for a moment, a pained expression on his face.

Emrek let his defense fall and stepped back, gasping for breath, taking the seconds of rest he could get.

It helped. But it was a mistake.

The Swordfish recovered almost immediately, and smoothly turned the sword back toward him in a fast strike.

Emrek barely got his blade up. The blow threw him off balance, and when he scrambled backward to try and keep his footing, he stumbled.

He went down onto his back, the sword bouncing off his chest.

The Swordfish stabbed down at him, and he managed to jerk aside, the blade narrowly missing him. But the stab had been pretty slow. Maybe the Swordfish had been hesitant to mar his blade.

He rolled onto his hands and knees and scrambled forward, away from the Swordfish, trying to use that hesitation as a chance to get back up.

Unfortunately, though, he felt the Swordfish's boot on his ass, then, and was shoved forward to slam face-first into the wooden door ahead of him.

It flew open and he slid out onto his stomach, grunting, then rolled again, finally coming back up into a crouch, and raising the blade just in time to deflect another blow as the Swordfish caught up to him.

He lunged back to his feet with a grunt and they faced off again, circling one another in the large open space they'd entered. As they rotated, Emrek finally realized where he was.

It was the Swordfish's throne room.

He had been here before. Emrek thought he'd probably been one of the first people to see it that wasn't involved in its construction. At the time, the Swordfish had seemed very excited to receive Emrek while looking down on him from an ornately carved stone throne, like something out of a storybook about kings that his mother had read to him when he was small.

But none of that offered him any advantage that he could see now.

And then there were suddenly booted feet running at him from behind, and he cursed, the Swordfish's laughter saying he was going to take a breather himself and let his guards handle him for a minute.

Emrek didn't have the strength for niceties. He barely bothered to defend the spear thrusts aimed his way.

Thankfully, none of them had maces. So he just quickly dispatched them, one at a time, while they ineffectually stabbed at him.

As he spun back to face the Swordfish, though, he realized he had stopped laughing.

The blade of the long steel greatsword caught him in the side of the face.

The Swordfish had struck him with the flat of the blade, employing it as a blunt instrument, and Emrek spun away from the hard blow, his father's sword slinging free from his nerveless fingers.

The room spun as he fell, and he clattered onto the floor, rolling over onto his back to stare at the carved vaults of the stone ceiling, stunned.

"You always were a fool," the Swordfish said warmly, laughter still dripping from his voice.

Emrek turned his head slightly and could see him strolling away, back toward the doorway. Once he had put some distance between them, he turned back to face him and lowered his sword.

"Goodbye Emrek," he said.

The Swordfish raised his gloved fist and pointed it at him. Emrek could see the hole burned through the glove's index finger.

He saw a flash of something there, like a faceted black stone.

The Swordfish's voice was suddenly cold. "Say hello to your father for me, when you see him."

Pemana heard the Swordfish say "Goodbye Emrek," and gasped.

They weren't going to make it.

They'd crept forward, wondering at the sudden lack of the sword-fighting sounds they'd been chasing through the palace. Then they had heard a voice down the corridor.

They had sneak-jogged as quietly down the corridor as they could toward the open door at the far end, not wanting to rush into something they weren't prepared for.

But then the Swordfish stepped into view, and raised his fist to point at something out of their sight.

"Say hello to your father for me, when you see him."

Kayd burst into motion and threw himself forward into the chamber, leaping straight at the Swordfish, who only managed to half-turn toward him, eyes wide in alarm, before Kayd crashed into his shoulder with all of himself.

Pemana saw the lightning blast away into the chamber beyond her sight as she leapt after Kayd, desperately hoping none of the lightning had gotten him again.

But it hadn't. He and the Swordfish both went down, bouncing off one another from the violence of Kayd's assault. The Swordfish nearly lost his sword as he rolled away, but he scrambled for it, and caught hold of the pommel.

Kayd slammed down to the floor with a grunt, but also managed to keep a firm grip on his new bronze greatsword as he lunged back up onto his feet.

Pemana slid into the room, sword raised, taking in a quick, amazed glance across the huge chamber, with its carved dais and throne. She saw Emrek slowly getting to his hands and knees, dragging himself toward Aether's sword where it lay nearby. Aether himself was nowhere to be seen.

A dreadful feeling flashed through the pit of her stomach.

But before she could do anything about it, the Swordfish shouted and, back on his feet, swung his sword…a large, steel greatsword, her amazed mind registered…hard at Kayd, who was closest to him.

Kayd managed to get his own sword in position, and with a clang of sparks, parried the blow over his head, then cut hard back down to smack his own blade into the Swordfish's forward thigh.

Pemana didn't see any penetration or blood, but the Swordfish roared in pain and scrambled backward from him.

Hmm. Maybe his protection magic wasn't as effective as the dragonskin spell? Interesting. Her mind filed it as she used the Swordfish's reflexive withdrawal to run forward and stand with Kayd.

Kayd met her eyes, and he nodded solemnly at her, then turned to face the Swordfish, his big bronze greatsword at the ready. Pemana took her position, her new steel blade raised.

The Swordfish rubbed his thigh, an expression of cold fury on his face as he turned back to them.

But then he saw the weapons they were holding, and his eyes widened. His expression became unhinged.

"Those are mine!" he screamed, spittle flying from his mouth, standing up from his ready stance to point at them.

"I doubt that, thief!" Pemana roared right back at him.

He lunged wildly forward at them.

Kayd caught and redirected the Swordfish's blow away from her, and immediately pushed him back. Now that he was fully engaged, she realized that Kayd had picked up a lot of skill over the last couple years.

He parried the Swordfish's rage-fueled blows again and again, using his own momentum against him, throwing him off balance more than once after an over-reach.

She circled around them, still ready, but leaving Kayd free to work.

Emrek came up next to her, breathing heavily, the Silversea sword in his hand once again.

"Where's Aether," she demanded quickly.

"Buried in books," he said, breathing heavily. He pointed at the Swordfish. "Must be…magic. He has…impossible stamina."

Pemana cursed and turned her attention back to the fight.

Kayd had maneuvered him around a bit, and Pemana saw the opening to step forward and complicate the Swordfish's defense for him.

He roared and spat as she and Kayd took it in turns to parry, deflect, and counter his strikes.

The Swordfish was an excellent swordsman, unfortunately. He seemed well able to handle their combined assault. And she quickly realized that Emrek was right. Sword fighting was an enormously muscular activity, and tended to exhaust its participants rather quickly. But the Swordfish had been battling for an unknown amount of time, and just kept coming at them.

She felt her own arms beginning to burn. If hers were already getting tired…

"Kayd, rest your arms," she said. "I've got him."

The Swordfish spat again, roaring as he lunged for Kayd, and this time, Pemana caught his strike and parried it up.

She yanked the long steel dagger from the sheath at her belt, and, grinning, remembered her training against greatswords. One didn't get a lot of opportunities to practice those ancient skills, here in the Lastlands, where there had never actually been a war.

Well, the ways of war had returned, it seemed.

She put the dagger to good use, deflecting the Swordfish's raging attacks well enough to poke him twice with the tip of her sword blade. Again, nothing drew blood, but the Swordfish screamed curses at her and seemed to grow even more outraged.

She tired more quickly now that she was carrying steel in both hands, and though she held her own, she was relieved when Kayd roared "my turn!" and dove back between them with his sword.

She fell back next to Emrek again, breathing hard.

"You want to take…a turn?" she asked him.

"Maybe when my arms work again," he said, tiredly. He nodded at Kayd. "Looks like he's got him handled."

She watched Kayd fight.

They did seem pretty evenly matched, and she was impressed. Kayd's technique was definitely less…refined. But he used his strength well, and was clever in the way he used his greatsword against the Swordfish's finer steel one. He kept letting the Swordfish over-extend himself.

In fact, there was something strange about the pattern of the Swordfish's attacks. As she rested, she watched him, and it had her frowning after a moment.

He was obviously enraged, but there was something else…

She had it. It was frustration.

His blows at Kayd demonstrated it. He kept exerting more force than necessary, swinging angrily…but not at Kayd.

He was swinging angrily at Kayd's sword.

That was a strange strategy, and she frowned.

Then it hit her. He was using a steel sword. Kayd's was just bronze.

He must be trying to break Kayd's blade. And he was frustrated because it wasn't working.

Indeed, Kayd's sword bore no signs whatsoever of damage. Of course this was true, they had enchanted the blades with a complex spell that incorporated both the new capturing magic and a form of the dragonskin spell that protected themselves. It meant that Kayd's bronze sword was probably indestructible to most normal damage.

Pemana could tell. She could almost feel the fuzzy, glittering strength of their enchanted weapons *without* focusing on them with her magical senses. Hadn't the Swordfish noticed? Of course he couldn't break Kayd's sword. Especially not with an unenchanted blade like his, steel or no steel.

And why *was* he using an unenchanted sword? The only magic on him…was the barely detectable magic coming from his hands…the magic coming from the rings…rings that he always seemed to keep concealed under gloves.

Stunned, she suddenly realized what it must all mean. It burst from her lips.

"He's not a wizard!"

The flow of the battle paused, and Kayd stepped back, tilting his head to regard the Swordfish, and taking the chance to breathe.

"What?" Emrek demanded.

The Swordfish, face flushed and contorted into a feral scowl, roared wordlessly and launched himself toward her.

Kayd caught his blade and redirected it once again, putting himself between Pemana and the Swordfish.

She knew what to do, almost immediately. She closed her eyes, and opened herself to the magic, letting its powerful flow deluge her, like a waterfall through her form.

"Help me, both of you!" she cried.

Kayd understood her immediately, and though it must have been a tricky thing to do while keeping up his defense against the Swordfish's attacks, she felt Kayd's mind join hers in the cast, fluctuating and unsteady as he fought of course, but solidly there...a truly masterful demonstration of magic and martial skill.

He just kept impressing her, more and more, all the time.

It took Emrek a bit longer to realize what she meant, but then she felt him clumsily join, and the power surged exponentially through her.

She reached out with the triplicate power and her magical intent honed to a fine point, and wiped the spell from the first ring she could find on the Swordfish's hand.

Immediately, he flared into sparkling magical signatures in her senses.

She had gotten one of his protections, including, apparently, the concealment spell. And now she could see the other three rings, split between his two hands.

She didn't really know if the Swordfish was a wizard or not, because he reacted like he realized what she'd done. Perhaps it was just chance. Either way, he roared again and kicked out at Kayd, managing to drive him back a pace, and raised his fist to point it at them.

She saw the sparkling magic of the lightning ring, directed at them. She saw the rage bursting in the Swordfish's eyes, as he told the ring to kill them all.

She shoved with all her magical potency, and the lightning ring's spell *smeared* under the combined strength of their triplicated magical assault.

Lightning exploded from the ring, but it seemed to smear along with the now-indistinct spell. Instead of blasting forward at them, it siphoned directly across into the great steel blade that the Swordfish was currently holding up next to his head.

They all fell back from the blinding ball of screaming blue-white fire and arcing lightning the Swordfish became.

Pemana released the triplicate cast, and they all gasped and held up their hands against the blinding light, stumbling hastily away.

At last, with a loud *pop*, the great ball of lightning that had been the Swordfish blasted away to fly backwards half a dozen paces, and the lightning vanished, leaving them momentarily blinded.

The steel greatsword flew clear to clang to the floor, and the Swordfish landed with a weighty *splat* and slid to a halt, motionless and covered in drifting ashes that had once been his clothing.

Pemana, Kayd, and Emrek stepped gently forward and stood there for a long moment, shocked, viewing the smoking form.

"Hmm," Kayd said, breathing hard as he walked over to the steel greatsword. He nudged it carefully with his booted toe, then bent and picked it up. "Nice sword, actually, despite the dings." His battle with the Swordfish had left quite a mark on the steel blade. But it gave it a certain character, these marks of the heroic battle in which Kayd had just won it.

Pemana looked over at Emrek, who still held the Silversea sword, clutched tightly in his hand.

She sheathed her own sword and dagger. "All right. Now where's Aether?" she demanded.

CHAPTER THIRTY-FOUR
PREPARE FOR...FLYING

The bookcase above Aether creaked as Kayd strained to lift at least some of its weight off of him. With all the books they'd dug loose around him, and with Pemana, and even Emrek, helping pull on his arms, they managed to help him worm himself free at last.

He crawled forward, stiff and gasping from the ordeal of being buried for so long, and flopped onto his back on the stone floor, happy to just be able to breathe freely.

"So...did we...win?" he managed to wheeze up at them.

Pemana nodded and grinned, pointing at the steel greatsword in Kayd's hand.

Aether let Kayd pull him, a little unsteadily, to his feet. Then he noticed Kayd's eyes, and followed his gaze to Emrek.

Ah. Aether sighed, nodding. Emrek held the Silversea sword, tightly clutched in his hand.

Perhaps he had earned it? Aether didn't know how the Swordfish had been defeated, but he did know that he hadn't been the one to do it.

But no, he decided. The Silversea sword was Lyrrek's, now. *She* had earned it, paid very dearly for its return, in fact, and he only wielded it on her behalf, and at her command as his lady.

"Thank you," he said calmly, and pointed toward the sword in Emrek's hand.

Emrek looked up and met his eyes, and Aether saw the annoyance there.

"So everyone gets a fancy steel sword but me, then?" he demanded gruffly.

Aether nodded again, but with understanding. "When we're done here, and it seems we may be, you are more than welcome to loot this entire palace for anything you want. You've earned it. But that sword, I'm afraid, isn't mine to give away," he said, and held out his hand.

Emrek stared at him for a long moment, then sighed.

"I still can't believe she gave him that crown," he said. But he handed the sword to Aether, hilt first.

Aether thanked him, and returned the sword to its scabbard. He started to turn and follow Kayd and Pemana, but something occurred to him, and he stopped and turned back.

"I meant what I said, of course, help yourself to anything you find here," Aether said. "But…if you'd be interested in something more, I do have something that I *can* give you. Sort of a personal thank you, from me to you."

"Oh?" Emrek said, a degree of disinterest in his voice.

Aether nodded. "Take all the time you want, looting this place. I suspect once we've gone, the blockade will break up, and you shouldn't have any trouble leaving here if you wait a bit. Then, if you can, you should come back by the guild hall in Freehome, a couple hours before dawn. Let's say, two days hence."

Emrek eyed him, raising an eyebrow.

"I'll make it worth the trip, I promise," Aether said.

Emrek finally sighed, shrugged, and nodded, and Aether grinned.

"Two hours before dawn. And don't be late!"

Aether took in the strange sight before him and shook his head. The brand-new dragon-carved ship that now honorably carried the name *Champion,* her polished wood still shiny and fresh, sat low in the water under the weight of fifty-seven additional grateful souls, who had packed themselves into whatever bit of spare deck they could find in her hold. It was cramped, but thankfully they wouldn't have to endure the conditions for long.

Aether's harnessed dragon lay comfortably on the sandy beach a few dozen paces beyond the pier, occasionally flicking her great wings and raising up little puffs of dusty wind, watching Kayd haul the gangplank up and aboard for stowing without a great deal of curiosity.

Out to sea a short distance, *Horizon* already hung in the air, a dozen paces above the waves, water dripping from her hull. Orenna waved at him from the helm, and he waved back, watching as the ship's sails filled, and she began to drift up and away from them, slowly and with great inertia under the weight of the few dozen extra people crowded in below her decks.

"Prepare for...flying, or whatever," Pemana shouted from *Champion's* helm, and Aether chuckled. This new world they were inventing was probably going to need some updated terminology.

He saw Pemana concentrate for a moment, and then the long, sleek, dragon-carved hull of *Champion* began to rise out of the sea. He was close enough, there on the shore, to feel the wind as Pemana activated the ship's windstones, and her sails began to fill as well. Kayd and Veytra saluted him from the rail, excited grins splitting both their faces, and he laughed and returned their salute. Then he let the stiff breeze carry him along the beach to the waiting dragon.

She turned to face him as he approached, eyeing him calmly. It really was amazing, he thought, admiring her gleaming indigo scales and noble countenance, how much less threatening the dragons seemed when they weren't trying to eat you. Thoughtful, he walked carefully forward and reached slowly up to check the bindings of the dragon's halter. She watched him with a large eye, and lowered her head for him so he could reach the crucial area above her forehead where the halter's mind control stones were sewed in. Everything seemed to be holding up well against the wind of their flights.

He checked all the straps and bindings of the saddle as well, and everything looked good and firm, so he patted the dragon on the shoulder and leapt up to pull himself into position astride her back.

The dragon shifted under him as she felt his weight, and stood, flipping her wings out with a shake. He gulped at the exhilarating feeling of the powerful body moving underneath him. Then she stretched her neck, tail and wings all at once, extending herself to her maximum dimensions with a great yawn. Aether chuckled as he worked to strap himself securely to the saddle.

Once he had lashed himself firmly in, he bent low and hugged the dragon's neck, wrapping the straps around his wrists and gripping the thick handles on the neck strap. He felt his heart begin to beat at the thought of flying again.

Aether considered taking full control of the dragon's mind for takeoff, but as fun as that would be, it would probably be wiser to save his mental strength just in case they encountered something unexpected. So he chose the less taxing option, and simply sent the dragon the thought that it would be really rewarding to soar alongside the two flying ships that were now moving off at greater speed into the sky, and how satisfying and fun it would be to protect those two ships from any threats they encountered along the way.

Immediately, the dragon leapt down the beach and bounded into the sky. Aether opened his eyes and then had to mostly close them again as the wind became a roar, and then he and the dragon were racing up alongside *Horizon* and *Champion* to circle them in a wide, lazy glide as the ships continued to pick up speed, sailing through the sky west toward freedom.

As the dragon circled around, he saw Veytra waving at him from *Champion's* quarterdeck. Aether brought the dragon in close enough that they encountered some of the magical wind the ship was generating, and the dragon had to beat its wings to keep from losing altitude.

"I see the blockade!" Veytra shouted and pointed as they drifted near enough to hear her.

Aether squinted out to the west and realized she was right. He could just make out the tiny specks of ships, and realized there were a few of them visible, stretching in a line over the horizon.

"Make for the biggest ship you see!" Aether yelled, and he saw Veytra laugh, though he couldn't hear it over the wind. She saluted and left the rail to relay the order to Pemana and then across to Orenna.

Aether urged the dragon on, and she slipped sideways out of *Champion's* windwake and began gliding forward once again in the direction of the blockade ships.

He saw the largest one, and turned to look at Veytra to see that she was pointing what looked to be generally in that direction. He nodded his head in exaggerated fashion as confirmation, and the dragon and both ships adjusted their headings.

As they flew nearer, Aether squinted into the wind, staring down at the deck of the large patrol ship, its dark-orange banners hanging limp as the ship sat at anchor in its blockade station. They were just high enough to be out of arrow range, and as they flew overhead, close enough that Aether could make out the crew on the deck fifty paces below, he saw the flabbergasted looks on the faces there. Aether could even see archers, but none of them lifted their bows to fire, simply staring up in shock at the dragon and rider flying overhead, escorting two beautiful sailing ships flying in formation just behind. He saw Lyrrek appear at *Horizon's* railing and lean out, waving down at the crew of the patrol ship below. Aether saw one crewwoman, a dumbfounded look on her face, numbly wave back, and had to laugh.

He squinted into the wind ahead of them at the western horizon. They'd have to fly a good way further before they risked putting back down to sea and docking somewhere. But they were making much better speed than their pursuers would be, down there, confined to the sea and its waves. And frankly, it didn't look much like anyone on the ship, now slipping away behind them, had the presence of mind to try to pursue them just then.

Aether looked over at *Horizon* and *Champion*, sailing serenely through the sky, and smiled. He let the dragon relax and comfortably soar along, gliding in and out amongst the ships of the Wizards' Guild's tiny flying fleet, protecting them all as they carried their rescued charges safely home.

Lyrrek leaned on *Horizon's* rail, watching the waves of Vigil's harbor as the ship drifted forward toward the familiar spot against the long stone pier. *Champion* was already at her berth there, sailors jumping across with mooring lines.

She couldn't hide a big smile as she watched *Horizon's* crew carry out her orders swiftly and efficiently, the sails coming down, hands scrambling to prepare to dock.

Well, they were Orenna's orders, technically, of course. But Lyrrek didn't mind taking some of the credit at this point. It was her tired voice that had done all the shouting over the last very, very long day, after all.

And they had done it.

The Swordfish was gone. The two ships were filled with exhausted, rejoicing people, all of them more than ready for their ordeal to end.

She had every reason to be proud, of herself, and of her dear friends.

"Oh, good," Lyrrek heard Orenna say. She turned to follow her look up the road toward Silversea Castle, and saw that the gate had opened, emitting a large stream of people in dark-gray tabards and servants' robes.

The group started making its way down toward the harbor, and she recognized the pair leading it. Her father was there, with Lady Ilda, who held his arm as they slowly made their way toward the harbor.

She jogged down from the quarterdeck and helped the crew finish docking. In moments, the ship was secure, and the first of the rescued were beginning to come up from below, blinking in the sunlight and smiling at their freedom.

With a grinning salute up to Orenna, Lyrrek stepped across the newly laid gangplank and started for her father and the Lady of Vigil.

"My lady," she called solemnly. She walked up to them. "The Swordfish is dead."

Ilda's face went slack with shock, staring back at her.

"There will be a lot more work to do to clean up the mess," Lyrrek said, then gestured over her shoulder to the first of the grateful rescued, a few of whom were already falling on their hands and knees on the stone pier, kissing the ground. "But we made a good start today."

Already, a desperate looking woman, followed by three small children, was racing forward, eyes wide, to dive onto a tired-looking man, as he fell to sit with his family in the road, reunited and weeping.

Lyrrek looked back and her father was smiling widely, watching the spectacle. Ilda, though was staring at her, mouth still open, speechless, for the first time that Lyrrek could remember.

And then, in another first, her great aunt reached for her, and caught her up into a surprisingly strong hug.

"I'm so proud of you, dear," she whispered into Lyrrek's ear.

She looked up over Ilda's shoulder, surprised, and patted her a little awkwardly on the back. Her father was there, wearing the same warm, happy expression as everyone else at this joyous reunion.

But then she saw his eyes widen, staring past her, up and out to sea. A look of absolute horror fell across his features.

Lyrrek released Ilda and spun quickly to look, but then breathed in relief, and laughed.

"Oh, it's all right," she said quickly. She turned and raised her voice, raspy from all the shouting of the last day, and yelled above the buzz of conversation around them.

"It's all right, everyone!" she called. "The dragon is with us!"

Darkness still lay over the Wizards' Guild Hall in Freehome when Aether was startled awake.

He had dozed off in the kitchen, sitting with a cup of tea, trying to wake up...

A knock at the alley door startled him again, and he jumped to his feet to open it.

Emrek stood there, looking a bit less unkempt than he had recently. He even wore some new, less noticeably outlandish clothing, though they were in the hunters' style and were quite practical. His cloak looked new as well, and was almost Silversea dark gray.

His hair and beard were still long, but even they had a bit more of a groomed appearance.

"Morning," Aether said, yawning as he stood aside to let Emrek enter. "Sorry, I dozed off, waiting for you."

Emrek grunted, but didn't say anything, just staring at Aether expectantly.

"Cup of tea?"

Emrek shook his head. "I ate before I came here, since you had me up so early."

"There was a reason for it," Aether said, grinning. "I wanted us to be able to speak quietly, without causing a scene."

One of Emrek's eyebrows shot up as he continued staring at him.

Aether chuckled. "Don't worry," he said. "You'll see."

Emrek narrowed his eyes at him for an instant, then he seemed to sigh, as he bent his head and reached for the satchel at his waist.

He withdrew a clinking pouch and held it up, meeting Aether's eyes.

Aether tilted his head quizzically as he felt...something...from the bag.

He focused on it with his magical senses, and immediately understood.

It was full of enchanted rings! Fifteen of them, probably, maybe more.

Emrek handed Aether the bag, and Aether opened it to look in, eyes wide.

"I figured he'd have some interesting things stashed away somewhere in that palace," Emrek said gruffly as Aether peered into the bag. "I was right."

Inside the bag was the pile of magical rings, as he had sensed. There was also a folded piece of paper.

"Deep under the palace, probably almost all the way back down to sea level, I found a locked chamber. Looked like he spent a lot of time in there." He pointed toward the bag. "I found these under a flagstone. Messed up a dagger pretty good figuring out how to pry it up."

Aether magically examined the rings again. It looked like only a few enchantments, most of them duplicated many times, with a few exceptions.

It reminded him of what you'd find if all their apprentices piled up their Wizards' Guild bracers on a table.

"I've decided he must have been part of an expedition or team of some kind, and he kept all their rings," Emrek said. "Probably murdered the rest, knowing him."

"Interesting," Aether said, looking forward to the chance to study the rings' magic later when he had more time.

"Be careful with the paper," Emrek said. "It's a bit fragile."

Aether nodded, and gently withdrew it, setting the jingling bag of rings down on the table next to his tea.

He carefully unfolded the paper, and breathed in amazement.

It was a map.

Most of it had been drawn by a skilled hand, dark confident lines of mountains and coasts, the names of ancient lost cities written in even lettering.

The map centered on an unnamed glyph in the mountains just north of Bastion. Not far south of the city, small notes in a different hand began to appear, sketching in additional details in places, noting progress in certain others...all leading down toward the Amber Coast, where the notations ended.

Emrek pointed to the glyph at the center. "Whatever this is, it wasn't labeled, but its the dead center of the map."

Aether nodded, a grim expression on his face. "I've been there, believe it or not," he said quietly. "I don't recommend visiting, really. It was...unpleasant."

Emrek stared at him again, then shook his head.

"Well, thank you for this," Aether said, indicating the bag. "We'll examine everything with the rings carefully. It'll be useful to know all we can, if..." He met Emrek's eyes. "Well, I guess I should probably say *when* more of them show up."

He smiled at Emrek. "Thank you. That's just one more reason for me to repay you."

Emrek stared at him expectantly again, and Aether chuckled. "Come with me," he said.

He led Emrek out into the lantern-lit sea yard, and made sure to leave a little space between them and the slumbering dragon as they passed, though Emrek didn't seem concerned by her presence at this point.

They walked across the long stretch of sea yard toward the corner of the two piers, where, to the right of *Champion's* dragon-carved bow, and in front of *Horizon's*, a much smaller sailboat-sized mast was visible against the black water inside the sea gate.

Aether turned back to face Emrek as they reached the edge of the pier, and gestured down toward the sailboat.

Emrek looked down at the boat for a moment, studying it, then back up at him.

"I already have a boat," he said quietly. Then he looked back down at it. "Though, I suppose it does look nicer, and a bit bigger than mine." He looked back up, and Aether saw him stare at *Champion's* newly carved bow for a long moment.

"Thank you," Emrek finally said, though without much enthusiasm in his voice.

"Ah," Aether said, grinning. "Don't judge this book by its cover." He turned and began freeing a mooring line. "This is a special boat. Step aboard, I'll show you."

Emrek watched him for a moment, then shrugged and climbed down next to the sailboat's helm.

Aether stepped across with the forward mooring line, pushing them away from the pier with his foot, then coiled and secured the line. Then he climbed back across the boat's upper hull, begging Emrek's pardon as he reached around him for the stern mooring line, then coiled and stowed that as well.

"You planning for a storm or something?" Emrek asked, watching him make more preparations for their departure than was usual for a short sail.

"Oh, no," Aether said, grinning. "But it will probably be windy. You'll see. I'm glad you wore a cloak."

He finished and sat down at the helm.

"Windy?" Emrek asked, a confused expression on his face. "You didn't even open the sea gate, how is it..."

He swallowed the rest of his words with a gulp, as Aether smiled, closed his eyes and concentrated. The sailboat lurched upward, trailing a shower of seawater to splash below them.

Emrek gasped, grabbing at the top of the cabin door in front of him and staring about, eyes wide, as the sea yard walls fell away, and they sailed out into the pre-dawn darkness above Freehome's harbor.

A quiet song of wind built up around them as Aether brought them quickly up to speed, coming about to the west so that Emrek could have the best possible view of the lantern-lit streets of Freehome.

Emrek stared out and away across the city, his head jerking around as he took in the sights below, even leaning out a bit to stare almost directly below them, though he did keep a tight grip on his seat as he did so.

Aether just smiled and flew, navigating them above the slumbering city in silence.

Finally, Emrek turned to face him, a hungry look in his eyes.

"You want to give me this flying boat?" he said.

"If you'll take it," Aether said.

"This thing is priceless," he said grimly. "What's the catch?"

"No catch," Aether said, shrugging. "Why would there be a catch? And actually, it's not priceless, Orenna found a pretty good deal on a few boats if she bought all three at once. It was pretty reasonable."

"But it *flies*," Emrek said, turning again to stare out at the glittering city passing below them.

"Oh, well, that part we did ourselves," Aether said, grinning. "And it's not that hard. You could probably figure it out on your own, studying the flightstones long enough. But I'll certainly show you how we did it, if you want to know how to make more."

He concentrated for a moment, making sure the boat was on a level course ahead, and gestured for Emrek to swap him places.

Eyes wide the entire time, Emrek listened as Aether explained the nuances of the flying boat, how to use the flightstones to get Origin to let the boat rise up away from her, and how to use the windstones in flight for both propulsion and steering.

They sailed the sky over Freehome for at least an hour, until the first deep blue appeared at the eastern horizon, and Emrek headed them back toward the harbor and the Wizards' Guild Hall, landing them gently in the waters outside the sea yard, as Aether indicated.

As Emrek floated them toward the small dock outside the sea gate, the door next to it opened and Lyrrek emerged, looking a bit sleepy, but smiling and waving to them.

"I saw you approaching," she called quietly, walking down the gravel alleyway toward the dock.

Emrek parked them next to his old boat, which Aether had agreed to dispose of for him.

Aether climbed up onto the dock to join Lyrrek, who took his arm, and turned back to face down to Emrek at the helm of the boat.

"Listen," he said. "I suspect I know what you'll say, but I'll offer anyway."

Emrek raised the eyebrow again.

"This is the Wizards' Guild," Aether said quietly, glancing around to make sure no one else was near. "And you are, after all, one of Origin's very few wizards. Just so you know, if you ever wanted to be a part of this, what we're doing, you'd be welcome."

Emrek stared at him for a moment. "And who's the leader of this 'guild,' yourself?"

Aether grinned and nodded. "For now at least." He put an arm around Lyrrek.

"Thank you for your help, cousin," Lyrrek said.

Emrek looked at her and nodded slightly, then met Aether's eyes.

"You know," he said quietly, "I hated being a lord. It never brought me anything but misery, even as a child, all the rules and requirements and…" He shuddered. "At the time, I thought when I was finally in charge, things would be different. And they were. They were vastly worse."

He looked down at the boat, then back up at them. "This life, though?"

He didn't finish the thought, just left it hanging in the air between them, sort of a parting gift. Then he closed his eyes, concentrating for a moment, as the sailboat rose from the sea and turned away into the first light of dawn.

Aether and Lyrrek watched him rise to a sufficient height to begin drifting away as the windstones inflated the boat's sail. He turned to face them, and they both saluted him.

He didn't say anything. But he did return their salute, before turning and racing his new flying sailboat away toward the light at the horizon.

Aether and Lyrrek watched him go for a while, then sighed, hugged each other, and went back inside.

Chapter Thirty-Five

COMEUPPANCE

L ord Moredon took a deep breath, then slowly let it out, steadying himself as he marched through the grand corridor in the Ruling Council's complex in Freehome. He nodded to the Council guards in their pale gray tabards that guarded the last doorway, and proceeded past them, leading a large procession of his own Port Omen guards in their blue and silver along behind him.

He turned to his guard commander as they approached the Council Chamber itself, and he grinned back.

"I'm sorry I won't be able to watch this, my lord," the gruff commander said. "It sounds like it ought to be quite a show."

"Well, I expect you'll get to see the good part," Moredon said.

"We're at your service, my lord," the commander said, and broke off their escort, indicating where he, and the dozens of guards he led, would wait just outside the Council Chamber doors.

Moredon nodded at him, breathed deeply once more, and pushed open the great double doors that led to the deliberation chamber from which the Ruling Council of the Lastlands officially governed all people on Origin.

Save for the great semi-circular table and the chairs everywhere, the chamber was empty. But the far doors, which opened onto a large elevated plaza outside the chamber, were standing open.

Lord Moredon sighed, relieved. If his gathered colleagues were already outside, taking advantage of an unseasonably comfortable late-summer afternoon, then half the difficulty of this challenging encounter had already handled itself.

Now he just had to keep them out there long enough for events to play out. It would still probably be a challenge. They didn't know why he had summoned them. And the Ruling Council were, unsurprisingly, a rather ungovernable lot in and of themselves. Council meetings were always a clash of strong personalities. To some extent, they always had been, in the eight years since he had ascended to govern Port Omen.

But over the last year, two of the Council's members, Lady Fehndala of Eagle's End, and Lord Eglamon of New Brightwall, had both regularly made Council business a difficult, uncomfortable affair.

He understood the reasons, finally. Pemana and her…colleagues…had exposed it, had helped him see what he didn't want to see.

And as Pemana herself had said, it was now time for Moredon to do his part.

He stepped out the open doors into the salty breeze and approached the gathering of *his* colleagues, these heads of the noble families that collectively, ruled the world.

He spotted Eglamon and Fehndala immediately, off to one side alone, their heads together, whispering to one another. The rest were broken into a few groups.

Fehndala spotted him coming, and he saw the unpleasant look on her face.

She looked like she'd been under a lot of stress lately, did the Lady Fehndala. Eglamon too, as the old man turned to follow Fehndala's gaze.

Moredon hid his grin.

The buildings of the Council's grand complex, on the edge of the grounds of Castle Redwall itself, were one of the architectural gems of the Lastlands. They had been built more than a century before, but subsequent Councils had made additions and modifications to meet the requirements of both their own comfort and the need to remind the common people of the grandeur of the work taking place here.

One of the Councils had added on this sturdy, elevated plaza, which spread out in a large semi-circle, jutting off the upper floors of the Council building. The plaza itself was the edge of the walled complex on this northern side, and allowed the Council members to walk out and look over the sprawl of the city of Freehome below them.

All of it would provide a perfect setting for the historic events that were about to play out here.

"Well Moredon," Fehndala called in her nasally voice, "what is this all about? I hate it when you waste our time."

Moredon met her eyes calmly, determined to play his part well. "Oh I assure you, this will be of great personal interest to you, my lady," he said.

Lord Kandrum saw him approaching the group and nodded, stepping over. "So what *is* going on then?" he asked quietly as most of the other lords and ladies turned to listen as well, curious.

"Someone needs to address the Council," Moredon said, making no effort to quiet his own words. "I believe that you will be familiar with them, Lord Kandrum."

Lady Ilda leaned around from one of the groups and gave him a smile, and a wink of greeting.

Moredon chuckled and returned her smile.

And then he heard the first hissing intake of breath from among his colleagues, and immediately after, the first of the distant clanging bells from down by the harbor. And then, the first of the screams tore across the streets of the city, as people looked up and saw the worst nightmare of every Lastlander coming true before their eyes.

He finally spotted it himself, the dark shape above the horizon, heading their direction.

"It's all right," Lord Moredon called, his voice ringing out and silencing the scramble among his colleagues as some of them began to frantically point out the dragon in the sky.

"These are the people I called you to hear today," he shouted. "The dragon is under their control, and will not harm anyone."

"The *what*?" Eglamon wheezed loudly, spinning to face him.

Fehndala was the first to start toward him, panic in her eyes.

"You're not leaving yet, my lady," Moredon said firmly, and put himself directly in her path.

"Move!" she hissed and tried to shove past him.

He had never taken his martial training that seriously, really. His people hadn't fought wars with one another since the dragons came, and the training of the nobility for war was really just ceremonial at this point. But nonetheless, he did keep himself in shape. And Fehndala was elderly and unfit.

He grabbed her shoulders, and simply held her firm, watching carefully to make sure she didn't reach for a weapon.

She looked stunned, then outraged, then fearful, all combining to contort her already pinched face. She seemed so surprised that she didn't really struggle.

"You're not going anywhere until this is finished," he said firmly, his voice cold, and pushed her gently back.

Some of the others started to back away toward the door as the screaming and cacophony of bells became louder, and it became obvious the dragon was flying directly toward them.

"My friends," he said loudly, "you have my word, you are in no danger here. Please, I assure you, you most definitely want to be here to witness this historic moment."

Fehndala looked like she was about to make another break for the door, and Moredon stepped toward her, again placing himself in her path, and met her eyes, staring.

"Don't be rude, Fehndala," he said, as she turned back, her gaze drawn inexorably to the approaching dragon. "You have guests."

He placed a firm hand on Eglamon and Fehndala's backs as they tried to retreat again, and held them both in place.

The dragon swooped toward them, afternoon sunlight gleaming from its shining indigo scales. Two figures were visible now on its back, crouched low over its shoulders.

The dragon's wings began to beat harder and faster, and it loomed out of the sky before them, rising up to its fullest size as it slowed to land delicately in the center of the plaza, little more than a dozen paces away from them.

The wind of its beating wings blasted their robes around them, and the younger among the group helped keep some of their elders from falling from the force of it.

Even knowing what to expect, Moredon had to admit that it was an awesome and primally terrifying thing, a dragon landing right in front you.

But Ilda was patting her fellow ladies and lords, a big smile on her face, once she recovered herself from the blast of wind.

"It's all right," she said, speaking loudly in a cordial tone. "I've met the dragon. They even let me pet it! It's quite friendly, apparently, as long as you don't remove its hat."

She continued encouraging her frightened colleagues as Moredon chuckled, holding the shoulders of Eglamon and Fehndala firmly as the indigo dragon flipped its huge wings to its back and lowered itself slowly onto its gray belly.

The two people riding on the dragon's back sat up and began freeing themselves from the saddle.

"Ahh," he heard Kandrum say quietly.

"She does know how to make an entrance, doesn't she?" Ilda said, looking at Kandrum.

"They are rather memorable," he agreed.

The rider in front, a handsome young man wearing a dark-gray short robe, swung a leg over the dragon's shoulder and slipped off to drop lightly to the ground. The second rider, a beautiful young woman wearing a dark gray robe lined with silver, waved to the assembled nobility.

"My lords and ladies!" the woman called from the dragon's back in a clear, strong voice. "Thank you for letting us come speak with you today." She followed the young man's lead and swung her leg over, settling her lower robe over the practical-looking trousers and boots she wore underneath, and accepting the hand he raised to her as she slid down to the flagstones.

The two of them paused there, in front of the dragon, an impressive sight, and bowed to them all, before proceeding toward them.

"My name is Lady Lyrrek of House Silversea, for those of you I haven't had the pleasure to meet yet." Her clear voice rang in the silence that had descended.

Moredon grinned. Ilda was right. Her great niece *did* make an entrance.

"And this is my colleague, Master Aether of the Wizards' Guild," she said.

They were already pretty quiet, standing there, collectively stunned at the surreal events occurring right in front of them. But at that statement, eyes went wide across the group, and you could hear a drop of water fall.

"The what?" Kandrum finally said.

"Didn't you wonder how they got that crown of yours?" Ilda said, a touch of glee in her voice.

"Wizards?" Kandrum repeated.

Moredon found it notable that neither Fehndala nor Eglamon had anything to say about this revelation. But perhaps they already knew magic was real. If recent revelations were accurate, then it was possible the Swordfish himself had demonstrated that to them at some point.

He felt Eglamon give up then, the tension in his shoulder, his muscles on the verge of flight, finally relaxing. He even began to tremble slightly.

Moredon thought he understood. It was probably a relief on some level for this to all be coming to an end at last.

"There is no such thing as a Wizards' Guild," Fehndala spat.

"It's true, we're unofficial yet," Master Aether said, stepping forward to stand next to Lady Lyrrek. He glanced around the group, smiling pleasantly. "The rest of you will receive our charter application in due course."

He turned to look at Fehndala and Eglamon, and his smile faded. "But today, I'm afraid, we have some unpleasant business to attend to first."

"The Swordfish is dead," Lady Lyrrek said.

Several gasps echoed from the gathered dozen nobles. Moredon was surprised at the number. More of his colleagues seemed to know that name than he might have expected.

"His kingdom of criminality will be dismantled over the coming weeks, with your help," she went on. "But unfortunately, that must begin here, with two of the Swordfish's principal backers and collaborators." She gestured toward Fehndala and Eglamon, staring at them with cold eyes. "Lord Eglamon and Lady Fehndala," she finished.

"You have no proof!" Fehndala spat, and tried unsuccessfully to shake off Moredon's hand.

"Don't be ridiculous," Master Aether said, his voice firm with an authority that belied his apparent youth. "Of course we have proof. It's already been distributed to the Council Magistrates, and copies have been entered into the official Council Record by Lord Moredon."

Aether nodded solemnly to him, meeting his eyes, and Moredon smiled and bowed his head in acknowledgement and greeting.

"Fehndala and Eglamon," Lyrrek went on, her voice sharp, "have been in collusion with the Swordfish's operation for some time, and both participated in and personally profited from his criminality. You may review the evidence at your leisure."

Lady Lyrrek stepped toward them, her hands behind her back, staring at Fehndala, as Eglamon's gaze had fallen to the ground at his feet. "You had the power to take action against the Swordfish."

Her eyes traveled the length of the group. "You will *all* have had your reasons for why you allowed him to do what he did to our people, when you collectively had the power and responsibility to stop it. And frankly, we might even understand and sympathize with many of those reasons."

She turned and walked back toward the dragon, before turning to face them all again.

"But those decisions are in the past. Today, the time has come for the Council to finally stand up for what is right, and to deal with the criminality of its own members."

That was his cue. Moredon took a deep breath, and spoke forcefully.

"Motion to initiate proceedings to eject Fehndala and Eglamon from the Ruling Council, to depose them of governance of New Brightwall and Eagle's End, and to strip them of all noble titles and claims!"

"Aye!"

The collective shout was just as forceful.

"Opposed?" Lady Lyrrek demanded.

Silence fell, except for a gasping whimper from Fehndala, which under Council bylaws, did not count as an opposition vote.

Moredon finally released them, then stepped back toward the doorway into the Council chambers.

"Guards!" he shouted. He heard the sound of booted feet immediately.

Moredon's guards rushed in, slowing rapidly as they spotted the dragon lounging beyond the Council members. Eyes wide and darting back and forth, they took hold of Fehndala and Eglamon, as Moredon indicated.

"Eglamon and Fehndala are to be imprisoned in the dungeons of Redwall Castle pending decisions about their trials," Moredon said to his guard commander. "See to their comfort, if you would."

"Very good, my lord," the commander replied, doing an admirable job of hiding his grin, and led them all hastily away. As they withdrew, Fehndala finally found her voice again, this time in a pitiful wail that trailed off as the guards pulled her away after them.

Moredon turned back again to the remaining nine of his colleagues.

"I want to apologize," Master Aether said, coming to stand next to Lady Lyrrek. "I suspect you will have some trepidation about how this all just occurred, and I know this is all very disruptive."

He turned and looked toward the dragon, a smile on his face. "In fact," he went on, "I strongly suspect that things are about to get a lot more disruptive in our world in the near future."

He turned back to look at them again, and his smile seemed genuine. "But we want you to know, from the outset, that we in the Wizards' Guild regret the necessity for any disruptions, and are here to work with the Council to minimize and mitigate any problems, and indeed, to be of service where we are needed."

"With all due respect," Lord Kandrum said, "Master…Aether was it?"

Aether nodded pleasantly at him.

"Forgive me," Kandrum said, "I remember meeting you of course, I'm just not very good with names. But what is this 'wizard' business? I admit I am very impressed that you seem to have tamed a dragon, but what do you mean by a 'wizards' guild?'"

Aether smiled widely. "Of course, my lord. One moment." He reached into a pouch and withdrew something.

He opened his hand flat, and on his palm lay a smooth, light-colored, rounded stone.

"I beg your indulgence for a moment," he said. "This is a surprisingly tricky bit of magic, actually, pairing both of these effects. I've only just figured out how to do it."

He closed his eyes, obviously concentrating hard.

Suddenly, to a chorus of gasps from around the gathered nobility, including Moredon himself, the stone burst into gleaming white light, and rose a couple paces up into the air to float there, still and bright, a tiny moon hanging in the air above Aether's head.

They all took a step back, awed.

Moredon saw the look of pride on Lyrrek's face.

Aether opened his eyes with a sigh, looking up and blinking at the light that glowed so brightly, even in daylight.

"Magic is real, you see," Master Aether said, calmly. "And with great effort, we've learned how to wield it."

He turned and looked at the dragon once again. "We learned it from them. They use it instinctively, as part of their very nature."

He turned back. "But though it can be tricky to master, magic is simply a skill that, in our experience, *anyone* can learn and use, at least to some extent."

Moredon felt a surge of excitement and hunger within himself at that pronouncement, and nearly gasped again.

"And we are willing to teach anyone who is willing to subject themselves to our tests of character and prove themselves worthy of the power," he finished, holding out a hand and catching the stone as it dimmed and fell.

Lyrrek stepped forward again and looked sternly down the length of them. "Honestly, I was conflicted about the idea of offering to let Council Lords and Ladies apply to be Wizards' Guild apprentices," she said. "You haven't always proved that responsible with the power you already have."

There was a bit of muttering at this, and Master Aether spoke again.

"Trust is earned, my lords and ladies of the Council, and our apprenticeships are designed to let one earn that trust. You won't receive special treatment from us just because of your bloodlines, but do know that we have decided you will be allowed to apply...just like anyone else."

Moredon immediately understood the implications of that last bit. He doubted he was the only one.

Indeed, it seemed their world *was* about to dramatically change.

He swallowed.

"You take a great deal upon yourself, young Master Aether," Kandrum said quietly.

Aether only smiled at him. "I understand your meaning, Lord Kandrum," he said. "But know that in fact, we did *not* take this upon ourselves. We were content to live our lives, trying to mind our own business. I only discovered the use of magic because of the corruption of one of your own former members, who exiled me to the mainland to hide his own crimes. And now, here we are again, driven to intervention because of the corruption of two more."

He looked down the length of them, his smile fading. "And sadly, few of you seem to be blameless here. Your people are struggling in ways that you could have alleviated. True, in recent years, the Swordfish caused much of this. But regardless, you have, to date, chosen to do nothing, content to continue your comfortable lives at their expense. You have failed to live up to your obligations to care for your suffering people. That will not continue."

He was losing them. Moredon could feel it, and found that he wasn't entirely free from discomfort himself.

Master Aether, though, seemed to sense the mood shift as well, and smiled again. "But fear not," he said. "I can well imagine your concerns. It's difficult to conceive of making do with less, even if you are in a much better position than everyone around you. That's only human, I suppose."

He nodded slowly. "And perhaps you see us as just another potential parasite, something new in the Swordfish's place that you will have to feed to survive."

There was a telling silence after he spoke those words.

"But there is something that you're not seeing yet. We have no need of anything from you, no desire to take anything that is yours. Quite the contrary."

Lyrrek walked up to him and took his arm, and they both smiled.

"Don't you see?" Lyrrek said. She nodded her head over toward the dragon.

"We…have tamed…the mainland," Aether said.

Now the silence turned thunderstruck, and Moredon did gasp, finally seeing it himself.

"There is an entire continent up there," Aether continued, "a land of history, and resources, and ideas we've lost. And yes, there are monsters. He pointed to the dragon. "But those monsters, we have learned, may be safely harnessed to some rather amazing purposes."

"We have figured out how to ride dragons, my lords and ladies," Lyrrek said. "We have figured out how to make ships *fly*."

"The Lastlands need no longer be our refuge, need no longer be our prison," Aether said. "What will our world become, do you suppose, if we *all* become wizards, and we *all* work together to reclaim our birthright, and rebuild our homeland?"

Moredon looked down the line of his colleagues, fascinated. They were all staring back at the two wizards, open-mouthed. Even Ilda looked astonished, and she must have had some idea of all of this already.

Master Aether gave them all a small bow then, and turned, taking Lady Lyrrek's arm and starting back toward the dragon.

"So!" Kandrum said, as Aether helped Lyrrek up onto the dragon's back. "How will we 'apply' to learn this magic of yours, then?"

Lyrrek grinned as Aether helped her strap herself in. "There will be an announcement soon on that front," she said, and there was a mischievous note in her voice.

"What kind of announcement?" Kandrum asked.

"Fear not, my ladies and lords," Lyrrek said as Aether jumped up and worked on his own straps. "You'll know it when you see it, I assure you."

Master Aether saluted them as the dragon rose to its feet, and Lyrrek waved at them.

Then, the dragon turned, raised its wings high, and with a single great leap, surged into the sky, the wind blasting their robes around them one last time.

They all watched in silence for several long moments as the dragon flapped away toward the horizon and was gone.

And then chaos erupted, as the other lords and ladies rounded on Moredon and Ilda with loud questions.

Chapter Thirty-Six
PEACE

A ether stood waiting at the pier in Vigil Harbor, next to *Horizon's* gangplank, his hands behind his back.

He could go wait in the cabin, but he was being kept well entertained, watching the workshop across from Quehlo's store, where a new shipwright operation had opened up recently.

He watched a few apprentices working in the once-familiar yard, enjoying the afternoon sun, laughing and teasing each other as they scrubbed on new oars with stones and sand.

He resisted the temptation to go over and talk to them, deciding to leave them to their work.

But he couldn't keep from smiling.

Motion up the road caught his eye, and he turned to watch, as Lyrrek and Lady Ilda strolled down the road from Castle Silversea, arm-in-arm, a quartet of guards in dark gray tabards trailing behind.

Ilda was keeping up with her much younger great niece quite well now, with no trace of a limp at all in her gait.

Ilda gave him a nod and smile as they approached the pier at last, and he bowed deeply to them both.

"Well, we'll tell your father he missed you, my dear," Lady Ilda said, giving Lyrrek a quick hug and a pat on her back. "And thank you once again, for...well..."

"Of course, my lady," Lyrrek said solemnly. "And if you have any recurrences, or just need us for anything, have one of the apprentices send word to us."

"I will," Ilda said, smiling widely. "At least until I can get one of those amulets for myself."

"And I have no doubt that you will, my lady," Lyrrek said, laughing.

Ilda waved at them and turned, walking quickly away back up the road, obviously intent on enjoying her restored freedom of movement, her guards falling in and jogging to catch up.

Aether returned Lyrrek's quick kiss of greeting and then stepped aside, bowing graciously and gesturing to her to precede him across the gangplank.

"She's feeling better then?" he asked as they nodded to their crew of apprentices to begin the preparations for departure.

"Much," she said. "I had a fascinating conversation with one of the local Healers' Guild masters, too, while I was up there."

"Oh?" he asked, following her up the stairs to *Horizon's* quarterdeck.

"She was...well, they're in a bit of an existential panic, I think," she said, chuckling a little. "They're quite worried we're going to render their entire purpose obsolete, now that we can heal just about anything with enough spellwork."

"Well, that's ridiculous," Aether said, astonished. "We don't want to end the Healers' Guild. There's so much they do that we can't. What did you tell her?"

"I improvised a little," she said. "I hope you don't mind. But I told her that I thought she was looking at it the wrong way. I said that in my view, anyone who showed sufficient devotion to becoming a healer to have gained their guild certification had already demonstrated the proper character to learn magic from us. I said that rather than fear that the Wizards' Guild was going to make the Healers' Guild unnecessary, they should think about all the ways that learning magic could transform and improve the things they've always done."

She sat down on the bench next to him while they waited for the crew to finish a few departure preparations.

"And I told her we'd invite healers from everywhere to come to our guild hall for training, or whatever we needed to work out. And…" She paused and looked a little sheepish as she met his eyes. "This is the part where I was…flying without straps, let's say. I told them if they wanted to allow dual memberships for Healers' Guild members, we'd be happy to work that out too."

"Brilliant," he said immediately. "I think that's an excellent idea. Exactly what I would have done."

She smiled widely. "How's Sedren doing?" she asked.

"Very well, Quehlo says," he replied, getting to his feet as he saw that they were about ready to get underway. "School is going well, from the sound of things, and he's made some friends. I promised him he could invite some of them over to the Guild Hall in Freehome for a visit sometime. He seemed *really* excited about that."

She laughed and rose. "That will be fun." She looked out over the deck. "Well, what do you think, should we get going?"

"I will still need to take the dragon out hunting tonight," he said, "we probably should."

"As you wish, Captain," she said, grinning.

She stepped to the railing. "All right, you lot!" she shouted. "Let's get those sails up! Cast off the lines, and prepare for flight!"

Aether grinned at her, and saw Sedren and several other children emerge from Quehlo's shop to join a congregation of excited youngsters that were appearing from several directions, given permission by their parents to go down to the harbor and watch *Horizon* depart. Aether pointed at Sedren and waved, and he and the others near him waved excitedly back, turning to demand of each other if they'd seen how Captain Aether waved at *them*.

He laughed. "All right, let's give 'em a show," he said quietly to Lyrrek. "Ready?"

She nodded, grinning, and took a stable pose, hands behind her back, booted feet spread at shoulder's width, her hair, held in check by the braids at her temples, blowing softly in the breeze.

Aether concentrated, and there was a gentle lurch upward as he activated the magic of the ship's flightstones. *Horizon* began to rise from the sea next to the pier, accompanied

by a chorus of water falling from her hull, and an even louder
chorus of cheers from the watching children.

Pemana sorted once again through the rather impressive
collection of her maps and charts where she had laid them
out on the broad map table in her cabin aboard *Champion*.
The ship was large, and the captain's cabin was one of the
largest she'd encountered. And, thankfully, the map table in
her quarters was also larger than any she'd enjoyed before.

She luxuriated in the extra space, surveying the collection. While it was a great start, there were a few more she
needed.

Actually, the way things were going, she was probably
going to need a *lot* more new maps, especially of areas
of the mainland. She was excited for their upcoming trip
north, as important as it was, to be over and done with. She
couldn't stop thinking of working out a collaboration with
the Cartographers' Guild once it was all finished. But their
mainland adventure would have to happen first.

She did have to admit that she was looking forward to
this upcoming expedition. She had a feeling it would all turn
out to be pretty satisfying.

The preparations had gone quite well, though she was
grateful for the healing magic, lest they all develop permanent cramps in their writing hands. But they had gotten
ahead of Aether's proposed schedule, so she had given the
rest of the crew a couple days leave.

She should probably give herself some time to relax too. But as well as things were going, a lingering worry kept tickling at her mind, that there would be some other thing she was missing, some shortcoming in her planning or decision-making that caused everything she'd achieved to just collapse again.

She caught her thoughts charting that familiar course toward self-doubt, though, and stopped.

Actually, she reminded herself gently, she and the others had done pretty well, in the end. She sighed and nodded, and even managed a small smile.

She glanced out at the shadows outside, and saw that it was probably about time.

She stepped over to the personal lockers that held her clothing and opened them, shuffling through the selection of quite utilitarian garments, trying to pick something…well, something a bit less utilitarian, at least. Finally she settled on a dress-like robe, and pulled it on quickly, checking in the small mirror that her braids were keeping her hair from going too wild.

It would do. She closed everything back up, and went out to *Champion's* deck.

Kayd was already in the sea yard, leaning against the wall of the guild hall in a handsome, new-looking short robe and boots. He smiled broadly at her, and stood tall, waiting patiently for her to join him.

"Well, what do you think, are you hungry?" he asked as she approached.

"Starving," she said cheerfully, returning his smile. "What's this place you have in mind?"

"It's a fancy tavern over near Redwater Castle," he said, turning and walking with her toward the door out into the streets. "The food's supposed to be quite good, from what I hear. Bit of a trek, but it's a nice evening for a walk."

"Sounds perfect," she said.

He opened the door and stepped out into the alley, looking around, then turned back with a smile and a half bow. He gestured for her to join him, then closed the door behind them.

"Didn't get a chance to ask you when you got back this afternoon," he said as they started walking together down the alley. "How are your family doing?"

"They're not too bad," she said, chuckling darkly. "Though we had a bit of a rocky start, because I just blurted out that I lost my grandfather's sword."

Kayd winced.

"It started going downhill fast, but you were right. I drew the new steel sword, and told them I considered it a replacement heirloom, and would wield it in trust for the family. But my mother demanded to know how I would have managed to acquire such a priceless treasure, so I just shrugged, pulled out a stone, and showed them Aether's new flying lightstone spell."

Kayd turned to stare at her, eyes wide.

"Let's just say, they lost their composure when they learned wizards are real, and I'm one of them."

He whistled in amazement, and she returned his gaze, mirth in her eyes. "Next time, I'm taking you with me. It was hilarious. And I...um..." She hesitated, watching him. "I think they want to meet you."

She saw his eyes widen even further, almost comically, and wondered, for a split second, whether she might have been wrong about him.

But then he smiled broadly, a happy, if somewhat disconcerted look on his face, and relieved peace flooded her heart.

"I'm with you, Captain," was all he said.

It really was a beautiful evening, a tiny hint of approaching autumn's coolness an excellent accompaniment to the early pink and orange colors of the sunset.

She reached over and slipped her arm around his as they walked, and saw the delighted surprise in his eyes as he smiled down at her.

It was an odd place for an impromptu meeting of the Masters' Council of the Wizards' Guild, this quiet beach on the jungle-lined Amber Coast, gently lit by the early light of dawn and the small campfire in the center of the group.

Aether, Lyrrek, Pemana, Kayd, Veytra, Orenna, and Amrelyn all sat around the fire, finishing their quick breakfast of stalker jerky, cheese, and shipbread soaked in one of Orenna's delicious herbal teas.

"Well, I think we've gone over everything," Aether said. "Any questions?"

Pemana leaned back against Kayd and smiled, shaking her head.

"I don't think so," Veytra said, grinning where she sat next to Pemana. "This is going to be fun."

"It's going to be a really long day," Lyrrek said, chuckling. "But yes, probably pretty fun."

They had already packed up their camping gear, so when Aether finished his breakfast, he poured the last of the tea over the small, hissing fire to put it out, then walked down to the sea to cool and rinse the pot so it could be packed away with the rest in Kayd's kit.

They all stood and checked over each other's gear, tugging at straps, helping one another sling the bulging leather bags over their shoulders and securing them where they couldn't come loose or open prematurely.

Finally, they all seemed ready, and Aether looked over the group of them. There were more than a couple nervous grins, but all nodded.

"All right. Let's go change the world," he said, grinning at them.

They all turned and began walking down the beach, each making their way toward one of the seven dragons that lay comfortably down the length of the sand, watching them expectantly, the dawn light gleaming off scales of gray, indigo, and greenish-brown.

Aether walked up to the large indigo female that had been his companion for these many weeks.

He checked over the straps of her saddle, harness, and halter, then patted her on the smooth, scaly shoulder.

"Almost done, my lady," he said quietly. "I've really appreciated all your help. One last big flight today, and once you're rested up, we'll head back up here and get you back to your territory, I promise."

She cooed her rumbling trumpets at him, and he grinned, climbing up onto her back and strapping himself in.

He settled the large satchel at his side, checked over the saddlebags one last time, and nodded.

"All right, it's time," he said. "Let's fly."

He sent her the thought and she leapt excitedly skyward, flapping her wings mightily and turning to glide down the beach along the length where his guildmates were arrayed on their dragons.

He saw six fists raise in readiness, and raised his own in return, the signal given.

Six dragons took off and rose up from the sands, flapping southward out over the sea, a couple of them roaring the excitement they could all feel.

Aether and the indigo dragon turned along behind to join them in their loose formation. The pink sunrise blazed light off the shining wings of the seven dragons as they and their riders began the long flight south toward the Lastlands.

Chapter Thirty-Seven
The Day

I n the future, this morning would come to be known as "the Day of Seven Dragons." Masters of the Historians' Guild would write many books about the events surrounding the birth of the Wizards' Guild, and would come to the consensus within only a handful of years that this day had been as consequential to the history of Origin as that of the dragon calamity itself.

Soon after dawn, criers walked the streets of cities throughout the Lastlands, ringing bells and telling the people to expect something amazing to occur throughout the day, and that when it did, there would be no cause for panic. People were very curious, given recent implausible rumors that had been flying about.

But as no more information was immediately forth-coming, most shrugged and went about their work...until mid-morning, that is, when those in the city of Vigil heard their neighbors shouting and screaming, bells ringing once again.

They looked out and saw neighbors staring skyward, stunned expressions on their faces. They rushed out to join them and looked up to see a sight they had all long feared.

Dragons were flying in the sky above the city.

But as panic began to set in, people realized, stunned, that these dragons had riders on their backs. Terror changed quickly into confusion as people reminded each other that they had been told to expect something out of the ordinary today. They stopped running, turning to watch the dragons, seven of them in a great V, flying overhead, their riders waving down at the people below.

Crowds formed throughout the city, and milled about in the streets. A rumor flashed through that their own Lady Lyrrek was one of the riders! And they reminded each other of the strange stories about the dragon visiting Vigil with her not long ago, or of the dragon that supposedly flew over Freehome. No one had believed those stories at the time, as there had been no word of attacks. But now…perhaps…

And then, someone shouted that the dragonriders were throwing something.

Small, folded squares of parchment came raining down from above.

There were a few who were fearful of them at first, but most scrambled to catch them, or found brooms to reach for ones that landed on rooftops.

The dragons made one last low pass over the city, their riders waving below them before they disappeared off to the southeast, and gradually the people gathered in small clusters, unfolded the squares of parchment, and began to read.

"Dearest friends and Lastlanders!" the parchments began.

"We are the Masters of Origin's new Wizards' Guild. We have visited you today to demonstrate to you that magic is real! And keeping us all safe from the dragons is only the beginning of what we can do."

Murmurs of shock and confusion began to fill the streets as the people read.

"We are happy to tell you that from what we have seen so far, we believe anyone can learn to use magic, if they're willing to work at it. And if you prove yourself, we'll be willing to teach you."

Gasps began to punctuate the bubbling noise of conversation.

"Watch for our posted notices, and we'll reveal details about apprenticeships in your city. In the meantime, be good to one another. Your character will be judged to determine if you are responsible enough for the burden of these powers. But let none despair! We look forward to all of you joining us eventually in our great endeavor. Together, we are going to take our world back from the dragons!"

There was a buzz of stunned excitement, of course, but people were mostly left puzzled and reflective after all they had just witnessed.

These events repeated not long after in the city of Shale Island, and then again in Cask, and then Merit.

Eventually, every city in the Lastlands, from Vigil all the way to Dawn's Hope, received their visit from the seven dragons. Every city was showered in small folded parchments. Every city was abuzz with conversation and confusion.

In all cities, the Council lords and ladies (some quite newly ascended) called a day of rest, as it seemed unlikely that much more productive work was going to get done that day anyway.

A few weeks went by, and some people questioned what they had even seen that day, and wondered whether it had all been some sort of strange, inexplicable hoax. People in outlying farms and villages who hadn't seen the dragons were often rather hard to convince that their city-dwelling cousins hadn't all lost their minds.

But then the notices actually appeared, posted first in Freehome, then Vigil, and then all the cities of the Lastlands, as more and more people began to encounter actual members of the Wizards' Guild.

Soon, they were everywhere, and everyone knew someone who was learning magic.

And then, everyone was learning magic themselves.

And before even a year had passed, the Healers' Guild, working closely with their new Wizard allies, ended all illness in the world, and while they were at it, broke the curse of aging itself.

And all across the Lastlands, ships, and the hearts of the people along with them, began to fly.

The End

EPILOGUE

Veytra gripped hard to the worn wood of the dragon saddle's handles as her mount came out of his glide and began beating his great gray-brown wings. He leveled them off and began to slow as the wide expanse of forest flashing below gave way to the farm fields and more rustic wooden structures that were the outskirts of the settlement at Redwater.

It was still a fairly small village, only a fraction of the city it had been two-and-a-half centuries before, when the dragons destroyed it. Even after more than forty years of work, there were only a few dozen sturdy stone buildings clustered around the village square, and from there outward, a couple hundred more homes, shopfronts, and warehouses, all constructed of wood, many still roughly hewn.

Here on the mainland, people were rebuilding the Old World. But it was slow work that took a lot of careful co-ordination, considering that the wild dragon frontiers were never more than an hour's flight away.

Veytra hadn't visited Redwater more than a few times. But she remembered where the stables were, near the harbor, and veered the dragon off toward them with a thought.

The stables were crowded, she saw, as they glided in from above. At least a couple dozen dragons were sprawled in their great stalls in the wide yard, mostly napping in the late afternoon sun. A few raised their always-haltered heads to watch a newcomer approach, as Veytra's mount beat its wings hard and slowed them to drop out of the sky, landing gracefully on the wide expanse of gravel in front of the sturdily-built wooden main building.

The big dragon flipped his wings to his back and settled down onto his gray belly while Veytra removed her flying cap and shook out her long, black braid, then unclipped her belted jacket from the saddle.

The door at the front of the main stablehouse opened and a man stepped out, wiping his hands on a small cloth that he tossed back in through the door before walking toward her and her dragon.

Veytra slid down the dragon's smooth, scaly shoulder and stepped toward him, opening her flying jacket.

"My lady," the stablemaster said, bowing. "Someone new to stay with us for a bit then, or are we keeping him?"

"Just for an hour at most, and no, I'm definitely not staying."

"Ah," he said, his eyes on her. "Pity. Any special handling? Does he need fed or anything?"

"Not that I was told," she said curtly. "Thank you."

The stablemaster bowed again and a look of concentration came over his face as he turned to stare at the dragon.

Veytra strode quickly away before the beast started moving around again.

She slung her jacket over her arm and paused to wait for a cart pulled by a large, haltered roamer to rumble by, nodding politely at the driver's tip of her brimmed hat, then started up the rutted dirt road that led along past a few other wooden structures toward Redwater's harbor.

Several sets of masts rose from the docks there, but as had ever been the case, *Horizon* tended to draw the eye. That was especially true these days, in her gleaming Wizards' Guild banners of white trimmed with silver.

"I wondered if that was you," Aether called as she approached the ship. Veytra craned her neck to see him where he sat up on the quarterdeck.

"That was an impressive dragon," he said.

He rose, shaking out his intricate master's robes, and started down the quarterdeck stairs.

She realized it had been a while since she'd seen him last. His hair was longer, draping to his shoulders, the top and sides bound at the back of his head. The beard he'd been growing for the last several years was attaining truly wizard-like dimensions.

She knew the people loved the fact that these days, Master Aether and Lady Lyrrek really looked like they'd walked straight out of some storybook.

"You know I hate being summoned," Veytra said as she took a long stride across from the pier to *Horizon's* deck, and saw him falter at the bottom of the stairs.

He sighed and continued toward her, grinning ruefully. "I know," he said. "It couldn't be helped. And thank you for meeting me here. I would have come all the way to Dragonhearth to talk to you, but I'm due in Bastion in a few hours."

"So what was so important that you couldn't tell me over amulet?" she asked, reaching him and grabbing him for a quick hug.

He looked out past her at the sprawl of Redwater, at the people wandering among the small warehouses and shops of its waterfront, and drew back. "Come below. We can talk there."

She nodded and followed him.

"How's your wife, she still down in Port Silversea?" Veytra asked as they reached the table next to the galley.

"For the moment," Aether said with a grin. "Though she threatens to leave on a daily basis. If I'm not back in a couple days, she says she's going to just leave Ilda to it and fly out of there."

"How are the spinners holding up?" Veytra asked.

"They're great. This ship feels a bit weird at times, though, rattling around inside it by myself."

He sat down on one of the benches at the galley table. "Not that I've had time to feel lonely," he said with a chuckle. "Still, it's good to see you. Been too long this time."

"So what was so important?" she asked.

"There's been an incident."

She cocked her head. "There's always an incident."

He looked up at her again. "Well, this one was different. We detected new portal spells a few weeks ago."

She was in the process of adjusting her robes, but froze at his words, staring at him.

"Three years ago, the last time it happened, something strange happened in Bastion immediately after, you recall?"

She nodded. "Unknown men at the tavern wasn't it?"

"Yes, strangers that arrived without dragons or flying boats or anything and caused a bit of a scene before vanishing."

She nodded again.

"Well, this time, after they detected the portal spells, the watchtowers sent out dragonrider patrols right away, of course, but they still didn't find anything. The Guild kept a good watch around Bastion, including even more extra patrols, but still never saw anything unusual."

He got to his feet and went to the galley counter to grab a couple mugs. "Ale?"

She thought about it for a moment, hesitating, but then shrugged and nodded.

"A few days ago, though, something strange happened here."

"In Redwater?" she asked.

He nodded. "Nearby. A rider was patrolling up north, near the frontier, and thought he saw a campsite or something in the forest below. He turned his dragon to come around to take another look, but never got the chance."

She stared at him as he handed her a mug. "What happened?"

"He lost control of his dragon."

Her eyes widened, and he nodded and continued.

"Suddenly, it turned to look at him, and the rider was pretty sure he saw confusion there, and only had a split second to catch it with the mind control spell, when he realized it was about to rip him out of the saddle with its teeth."

Now Veytra's mouth fell open as well.

"He managed to control it long enough to get it to the ground, but he couldn't release the spell cast, because he could feel that the dragon's halter had ceased functioning, and every time he tried, the dragon started to wake up and want to kill him again."

"What did he do?"

"He could feel himself getting tired, so he had the dragon claw off its own halter and saddle, then flew it north toward the frontier as far as he could before releasing it back into the wild."

She was silent a long moment, amazed. "Do we know why it happened?"

Aether met her eyes, and shrugged. "The saddle was too much to carry, since he was facing a several-hour hike back, and it seemed there might be danger in the forest nearby. But he did bring the halter with him, thankfully."

"What happened to it?"

"What you'd expect. Someone wiped the magic from it."

Veytra was thoughtful for a moment. "Would have taken at least three wizards, presumably. The spells were properly triplicated?"

He nodded. "As far as I could tell, yes. There were residual elements of the magic lingering, but they had clearly been wiped into dysfunction."

"So it wasn't a rival, or someone he pissed off at the tavern, then?"

"It doesn't seem so. The rider's friendly enough, and isn't aware of any issues with anyone. Nothing that would warrant a murderous conspiracy, anyway."

Veytra fell silent, thoughtful.

"You said 'new portal spells' earlier," she finally said. "The towers detected more than one?"

"Yes. A flurry of four across several minutes."

She was silent for a long moment, thinking hard, a sense of excitement suddenly born in her.

"So what are you going to do about it?" she finally asked.

"Well," he began, and she sensed him grow a bit uncomfortable. "Orenna held a master's council meeting, and it was decided that we needed to do something."

She watched him.

"And?" she said finally.

"The idea was to approach a skilled and experienced wizard with maybe a bit less on her plate at the moment, and to ask her if she was available to lead a guild effort to investigate."

She stared at him, careful to hide her suddenly roiling emotions.

Was this it? Was this the Opportunity?

Veytra felt the old hunger again. It had been a long time. Lately, she'd been doing a pretty good job at distracting herself from it altogether.

She continued to stare at him. "You refer to me, I...presume?" she asked coldly.

She felt his discomfiture grow. "Um...yes," he said, with a slight nervous chuckle. "I'm sorry, I know you're busy too, of course. It's just…everyone is kind of overextended at the moment."

Well, he was correct. She did keep herself very busy. She had an extensive network of connections to be maintained among the regulars of at least five different taverns, two in the city of Dragonhearth, near her frontier estate, and a full three back in Freehome, within a short hike of the grand house she owned there. She was the famous heart of those extended bar families, and they depended on her, their lives seeming to circle around her own at times.

It was quite a contrast to other parts of her life.

But here was Aether, proclaiming her essential to her Wizards' Guild family. Or, at least, proclaiming her available.

Even something like that had been…a while. She supposed maybe it counted for something.

She stared at him for a moment, then sighed. "I can make it work." She downed her ale, then set the mug down on the table and rose. "What kind of time do I have? I'll need a few days to…settle some affairs…make some preparations."

"Of course," he said, standing and placing their mugs in the basin. "Take all the time you need. Take a week."

She could practically feel his relief.

"I can reach you by amulet if anything changes suddenly," he said, gesturing for her to precede him back up the stairs. "I just didn't want to risk talking in detail with you about all of this when we don't know who might be trying to listen. At least now that we've spoken about it, if I need to update you further, I can speak in vague terms."

"Right," she said quietly as they emerged back out onto *Horizon's* deck. "Give Lyrrek a hug for me."

"I will," he said, smiling widely at her, hands clasped over his robes.

She turned to go, nodding, and hopped lightly across to the pier. She didn't look back as she heard *Horizon's* spinners, yet another of Veytra's magical inventions that everyone seemed to take for granted these days, whir up into motion as Aether raised the ship's sails with a spell.

She didn't look back, hearing the splashing of water from *Horizon's* hull back into the sea as Aether headed skyward in his pretty flying ship, alone.

As she neared the stable, several dragon heads lifted up to watch her curiously as she crunched across the gravel. She watched them back, uncomfortable, struggling to stop herself from imagining the chaos if one of those dragons broke its mental bonds and found itself standing free within a bustling village filled with slow-moving human-shaped food. Even if everyone here but the youngest children were wizards, it could be a mess until they got it sorted out.

And she definitely did not permit herself to imagine what would happen if *all* of those dragons broke free.

The stablemaster came back around, followed by the big gray-brown dragon, and she pulled her jacket and flying cap on as he counted her payment. Once he'd nodded, she quickly checked over the dragon's harness, then ignored the stablemaster's offer of assistance, leaping backwards up into the saddle in a practiced move and clipping herself in as the man hastily headed back inside.

Within seconds, the great burst of wind from the dragon's wings nearly blew the door back open on him as they launched skyward.

Veytra grinned to herself as she turned back to let the wind of flight sear into her face again, enjoying the bracing cold of it as she turned the dragon back in the direction of the city of Dragonhearth.

She would have a great deal to do, given the open-ended nature of what Aether had asked of her. She would have to make sure both of her houses were ready for prolonged vacancy, just in case.

She sighed, letting the wind yank it from her lips. Several decades earlier, someone with her means would have simply given instructions to the servants about how things would be cared for until her return. These days, no one really worked as servants anymore. That was a good thing for them, Veytra supposed. But it did always seem to mean a lot of extra work for everyone.

Then again, Veytra's "means" weren't as abundant as they once had been, anyway. It had, indeed, been a long time since she'd done much work for the Wizards' Guild…or the Smiths' Guild…or anyone else for that matter. That was part of the enthusiasm she'd had to hide from Aether when he asked for her help. She'd be getting paid handsomely for the work he'd just asked her to undertake, she'd see to that. But her need for some fresh gold to replenish her hoards was only part of it.

She didn't want to think about it, but the thought was there in her mind anyway.

Maybe this work would finally lead to the Opportunity.

It was hard to say whether it would. Nothing lately had seemed likely to deliver on that promise. She had even tried to forget about it completely for several years. But sadly, the effort only ever served to remind her of the way the world always forgot about her when it came time to hand out accolades and acknowledgement for the accomplishments of the Wizards' Guild. Who was she, next to the great Master Aether, discoverer of the dragon magic? Next to the universally beloved Lady Lyrrek of House Silversea? Next to the famous heroes, Captain Pemana and her brave husband Master Kayd, who had faced down the terrible danger of the Swordfish together with swords and magic and freed the world? These were the well-known founders of the Wizards' Guild, recognized everywhere they went, praised and elevated at every turn.

People even talked about Orenna, as she had succeeded Aether as Guild Master several years ago. It was a position that *should* have been Veytra's by rights, although Veytra bore Orenna no ill will about it. The Wizards' Guild, tens of thousands of them together, had decided that one. And everyone loved Orenna, including her, of course.

But it seemed that no one ever even remembered Veytra. No one ever used the word "hero" to describe the one who had invented half the magic they used in their daily lives. No one ever remembered to praise Veytra for her enormous contributions to their society and the way it functioned these days, ways that would have been unimaginable to people half a century ago.

It had all grown quite tiresome over the years.

In fairness, they didn't talk much about Amrelyn either. But Amrelyn had hidden away with her family on Vigil Isle and was mostly helping raise grandchildren these days. She had made her choices and gotten what seemed to matter most to her.

But it was deeply unfair, the way the rest of the world ignored Veytra.

She sighed again, realizing her thoughts had gotten away from her, and in her distraction, they had flown a bit off course. She focused for an instant and had the dragon correct their route.

For a long time she had dreamed of it all changing, dreamed that someday she would get her Opportunity. Someday, something she did would make *her* the one that everyone recognized when the Seven were gathered together. It was only right. She'd been there, in the heart of it all, from the beginning.

And maybe this was finally it. This group that called themselves the Pantheon, the ones who had escaped Origin, were back apparently, once again sending scouts to the world they had abandoned. And it seemed that this time, perhaps, they weren't making the mistake of sending non-wizards to do a dark wizard's job.

But what was that job, exactly? What were their intentions? What were they hoping to accomplish?

Someone would have to answer those questions. Someone would have to find the intruders and discover the true nature of their dark plots and schemes.

Someone would have to hold them to account for sending the Swordfish. Someone would have to judge them for wrecking the world for two hundred years when they abandoned it to the dragons.

Orenna, Aether, and the rest had just decided that someone should be her.

Perhaps, at long last, her time had come.

Veytra grinned into the wind, her narrowed eyes ahead on the towers of the city of Dragonhearth, just then beginning to appear over the horizon.

Afterword

Thank you so much for reading *The Dragon Calamity*. I really appreciate your time, and I hope it was as fun to read as it was to write.

I want to especially thank those heroes among you who review and rate books you've read. You probably already know this, but it's a huge part of helping a book find its readers today. I, of course, would be forever grateful if you felt this book was worthy of a bit more of your time in that way.

Thanks again, and I look forward to sharing more of the Wizards' Guild's adventures with you in the conclusion to the Origin Cycle, *The Dragon Machination*, coming soon.

- James Wheeler

James Wheeler is a musician and author from Kansas City, where he and his wife Bree split their time between working on music for their band, The Rogue Planets, writing and editing James's novels, and providing daily entertainment to their family of porch rescue cats.

For more information, visit therogueplanets.com.